THE WORLD OF THE GATEWAY

The Gateway Trilogy (Series 1)
Spirit Legacy
Spirit Prophecy
Spirit Ascendancy
The Gateway Trackers (Series 2)
Whispers of the Walker
Plague of the Shattered
Awakening of the Seer
Portraits of the Forsaken
Heart of the Rebellion
Soul of the Sentinel
Gift of the Darkness
Tales from the Gateway

THE RIFTMAGIC SAGA
What the Lady's Maid Knew
The Rebel Beneath the Stairs

PLAGUE OF THE SHATTERED

PLAGUE OF THE SHATTERED

The Gateway Trackers Book 2

E.E. HOLMES

Lily Faire Publishing

Lily Faire Publishing
Townsend, MA

www.lilyfairepublishing.com

ISBN 978-0-9984762-1-6 (Print edition)

ISBN 978-0-9984762-2-3 (Digital edition)

Cover design by James T. Egan of Bookfly Design LLC
Author photography by Cydney Scott Photography

To my sister Courtney, the brightest, most unbreakable diamond of them all.

Lost in the forest, I broke off a dark twig
and lifted its whisper to my thirsty lips:
maybe it was the voice of the rain crying,
a cracked bell, or a torn heart.

Something from far off it seemed
deep and secret to me, hidden by the earth,
a shout muffled by huge autumns,
by the moist half-open darkness of the leaves.

Wakening from the dreaming forest there, the hazel-sprig
sang under my tongue, its drifting fragrance
climbed up through my conscious mind

as if suddenly the roots I had left behind
cried out to me, the land I had lost with my childhood—
and I stopped, wounded by the wandering scent.

-Pablo Neruda, Sonnet VI

CONTENTS

PROLOGUE

SOMETHING HAD SHIFTED.

Lifted.

She was no longer pinioned to the empty air, but free and floating.

The Caller had done it. She had promised she would, if she could find a way, and she had actually kept her word. She would never have believed another Durupinen capable of keeping her word, not after all she'd been through, but the Caller had proven her wrong. Despite this knowledge, she did not move, at first. The profound shock of freedom prevented her, briefly, from exploring the boundaries of it. After so many years of captivity, she'd almost forgotten what it was to exist without the weight and restrictions of the Castings that had acted as her chains.

What followed was a flexing and testing of energy, a relearning of what it was to form, to move, to be. As she worked her spectral muscles, tested her strength, she felt her incredulity fade away, to be replaced by a growing, leaping excitement. At last. At last she could escape this infernal place and answer the call of the Aether. The insatiable pull of it had been her deepest torture these many years.

She kept low to the ground, slinking along in the shadows, trusting, perhaps foolishly, to physical obscuration to mask her phantasmal form. She would not linger, that was certain. She would not risk being discovered and imprisoned once more. She would follow the pull, stronger than the tides, to the nearest Gateway home.

Even as she thought it, her need for it expanded, a thirst she must quench or else risk shriveling into nothingness. Her incompatibility with this place, with the living world, would surely crush what remained of her if she didn't Cross soon.

Suddenly, she felt the pull of it: the Gateway. It was close, closer than she'd ever dared imagine. Could it truly be so easy to find after so many years of being thwarted in her desire to seek it? Might it merely be a ploy to ensnare her once more?

She must know. She must follow it wherever it led, consequences be damned.

Some chambers she could not enter; they were most likely warded against intrusion. No matter. Whatever miseries lay incarcerated within would not distract her from the lure of her goal. The Gateway tugged her onward, a sensation so strong as to be nearly physical, triggering memories of a form she had not possessed for well over a century.

At last she could see it ahead, like a glowing orb lodged in the chest of the Caller, and she could not turn from it, she could not veer off course.

Come, the Caller was saying, drawing her in. *Come and find your way home.*

Yes. Yes, at long last she would traverse that final swift stanza of the tragic poetry that was her life on earth. The Caller was welcoming her, welcoming her into the arms that would close around her and embrace her through to her ultimate rest.

There was a moment—a twinkling of an instant—when she knew that something was frightfully, desperately wrong. The door toward which she was barreling— utterly unable to stop herself— was not open to deliver her to what lay beyond. The Gateway was singing its song, but it was sealed against her.

I have been deceived.

And this thought, sagging with the weight of her horror, was the very last that she had before she Shattered.

I

———

DREAM PORTRAIT

HER EYES WERE WIDE and dark and well-deep. Her hair was dark also, swept up onto her head in an elegant Victorian style. Her lips were curved into a wry little smile, suggesting humor and also strength of character. An intricate Triskele pendant lay framed in the hollow of her throat. She was the first thing I saw when I opened my eyes.

And I had absolutely no idea who she was.

Unfortunately, I often woke up this way, staring into the face of a stranger. It was an occupational hazard of being a Durupinen who also happened to be a Muse. As a Durupinen, I could see and communicate with spirits as part of my role in Crossing them over from the living world to the spirit world. As a Muse, that communication often came in the form of art; in my case, a sketch or drawing that I sometimes completed involuntarily. This time, for instance, I woke from my sleep to find myself crouched in a squatting position at the end of my bed, a charcoal pencil clutched in my trembling, aching hand, having just created the image of the mysterious woman on a sheet of paper taped to the wall.

"Oh, hell," I muttered as I flopped back into a supine position on the bed, dropping the pencil to the floor and shaking out my hand, which was now cramping up. I *so* did not need this today. I was beyond exhausted.

It had only been a few hours since I'd arrived back at Fairhaven Hall, seat of the Northern Durupinen Clans. Thanks to a red eye flight and a drive from Heathrow to the Cambridgeshire countryside, I was jetlagged and ravenous by the time we'd arrived at the castle. I'd raided the dining hall for pasties and then collapsed, fully clothed, on top of my old bed. It may have been mid-morning, but I'd intended to get a few hours of sleep before facing any of the people I would have to see while I was here.

Instead, only thirty minutes after I'd fallen asleep, here I was, bleary-eyed and shaky from the onset of a ghostly Visitation.

The door creaked open. I half-expected the face I'd drawn to peek around it, demanding to know why I'd failed to do justice to her aquiline profile, but instead, my twin sister Hannah tiptoed into the room.

I smiled watching how carefully she eased the door silently shut behind her, how she made absolutely sure to step over the creaky floorboard just beyond the threshold.

"Jeez, you are so loud!" I said.

Hannah jumped with a squeak of surprise and spun on the spot. "Oh, no! I was being so careful! Did I seriously just wake you up, Jess?"

I laughed. "No, no, I'm just messing with you. You were quiet as a mouse. I was already awake." And I gestured to my new artwork.

Hannah's gaze followed my hand and then her mouth dropped open. "You're kidding! Already? We've barely been here an hour!"

I shrugged. "I know. What can I say? The place is crawling with restless floaters."

Hannah came over to sit on the bed beside me. She reached out and rubbed my arm consolingly. "Do you want me to leave so you can try to get back to sleep?"

"No, don't worry about it. I can't now. She's made sure of that." And I jerked an accusatory thumb over my shoulder at the portrait.

"It's a good thing you thought to hang the blank paper up," Hannah said.

"Yeah, well, I'm more prone to them when I'm exhausted, plus this place is swarming with spirits, so I figured, better safe than sorry."

"She's really pretty," Hannah remarked, leaning in to take a closer look. "Do you know who she is?"

"No, we didn't get that far," I said. "But I'm sure she'll be back soon. They usually are. And when she shows up again, I'll be sure to inform her that if she wants any help from me, she'd better find me when I'm awake, or else plan to bring coffee as a peace offering. So, how is the old place?"

Hannah smiled. "The same, really."

"Did anyone run screaming when they saw you?"

"I wouldn't say 'screaming' exactly. But a couple of people

4

suddenly remembered that they had somewhere else they needed to be as soon as they spotted me," Hannah said with a sigh.

In truth, the resident Durupinen at Fairhaven had good reason to be wary of us. A little over three years ago, Hannah and I had arrived there as new Apprentices, ready to learn how to control and use our gifts. It wasn't long before Hannah was identified as a Caller, a Durupinen who could summon spirits to her over long distances and even use them to do her bidding. It wasn't just the sheer power of this gift that put the other Durupinen on their guard; Callers were historically met with fear and mistrust because of an ancient Prophecy.

The Prophecy foretold the birth of twins, one of them a Caller, who would be born of the illicit relationship between a Durupinen and a Caomhnóir, the guardians who protect us. According to the prediction, the Caller twin would have the power to reverse the Gateways and unleash an army of the dead back into the world of the living, allowing our ancient enemies, the Necromancers, to seize power. The other twin would have the power, through her own sacrifice, to stop this awful future from coming to pass.

Thousands of years of Durupinen history. One set of twins destined to destroy or save the world. One guess which twins they were talking about.

Jackpot.

I didn't like reliving that traumatic experience, so suffice it to say, we managed to prevent the rise of the Necromancers and the destruction of the Durupinen way of life. However, our role in the Prophecy left many Durupinen extraordinarily wary of us. Our time here at Fairhaven would likely feel more like a return to the scene of the crime than a happy little reunion.

Hannah had certainly handled the news better than I had that we would be returning to Fairhaven again so soon. It was only about two months ago that we had been summoned back by the Council to face an ultimatum: either we cease our systematic dismantling of scam artists masquerading as psychic mediums, or we join the ranks of the Durupinen Trackers, where we would continue to take down the scam artists, but in an official (and supervised) capacity. We had agreed to become Trackers, and our first case had ended a little over six weeks ago, leaving us no reason to believe that we would have to set foot here again so soon. Unfortunately, the

Council, and the intricacies of its political system, had other plans for us.

Two weeks previously, our Aunt Karen had arrived at our apartment, armed with a box of cannolis and a sheepish smile.

"Hi, Karen!" Hannah had cried, flinging her arms around her.

"Karen! What are you doing here?" I'd asked, snatching the box with a whoop of glee.

"Just wanted to see my favorite girls!" she answered, but her smile didn't quite reach her eyes.

"A lawyer really should have a better poker face," I told her. "What's up? Just come out with it already."

"Okay, well, I came over because I have something kind of important that I have to ask you to do," she began, tossing her purse on the coffee table and taking a seat on the sofa. "And I brought the cannolis because I thought they might soften the blow."

"I knew it!" I said, my mouth full of ricotta. "I knew these tasted like guilt!"

"What is it, Karen?" Hannah asked.

"Well, every five years the Northern Clans have a huge meeting. It's called the Airechtas, and every clan sends a representative to speak for them. They have votes on important issues, hold elections for vacant positions, and so forth. It is essential that every clan be accounted for. And I can't go."

I swallowed before I was quite ready and started sputtering. "Why not?" I managed to choke out.

"It's the case I'm working on for the firm. I've been told, in no uncertain terms, that if I can win this case, I'll be made a partner."

"What?! Karen, you never said anything! That's amazing!" Hannah cried.

Karen smiled. "I didn't want to jinx it. And it's by no means in the bag yet. It's going to be a struggle to the bitter end. But the first major hearing has been scheduled for the week of the Airechtas."

I felt a pit of anxiety open up in my stomach, making me instantly regret the cannoli. I knew exactly where this was going. "Can't they just move the hearing?" I asked.

Hannah gave me a very stern look. "You can't just rearrange a trial to fit your schedule, Jess!"

I flushed a little. "I'm just asking."

"I've been able to move things around before, but this judge is particularly inflexible when it comes to court dates," Karen said. "He's got a reputation for it. I can't risk alienating him so early in the process. Too much is riding on this case."

"So, you want us to go to the Airechtas?" Hannah said, asking the question for her.

"I hate to ask you," Karen said, "but I don't know what else to do. It's quite simply not an option for any clan to miss it."

"You're the Clan Elder, though. Are we even allowed to go in your place?" Hannah asked.

"As long as I inform the Council that I am bestowing all of our voting rights upon you, and that you have permission to speak for our clan, there's no problem," Karen answered.

"What will we have to do?" I asked.

"That's the good news!" Karen said eagerly, obviously pleased that I was even entertaining the idea. "All you would be required to do is show up, sit through the meeting sessions, and vote."

"Vote on what?" I asked.

"On whatever issues are brought to the table," Karen said. "Members will make propositions and suggest changes. They'll be discussed—usually ad nauseam—and then the assembly will vote. That's it, really."

"Are we even informed enough to vote? Will we understand the issues that are being voted on?" I asked.

"You know much more about what's going on in the Durupinen world than many of the other clan representatives who will be attending. Some of them haven't had contact with the Council since the last Airechtas," Karen said.

"Lucky them," I muttered.

"Anyway, the Council will explain each issue in great detail. They will provide you with all of the information you'll need to make an informed decision. And I know that you will vote wisely. I have complete confidence in both of you," Karen added with a smile.

"Okay, now you're just buttering us up," I said.

"Who, me? Never!" Karen said, handing me another cannoli and flashing an innocent smile. "So, what do you say, girls?"

I hesitated. On the one hand, it really didn't sound that bad. On the other, nothing in the Durupinen world had ever turned out to be easy or painless, in our experience. Hannah didn't give me a chance to hesitate any longer, though.

7

"Of course we'll go," she told Karen. "You concentrate on winning that case and getting your name on the letterhead."

Karen reached across the coffee table and squeezed Hannah's hand. "Thank you so much. I knew I could count on you girls. And I know it's a big deal, asking you to go back there again. I didn't do it lightly. If there was any way I could have done it myself—"

"It's fine, Karen," I said, trying really hard to mean it. "We'll take care of it."

§

And so here we are. I slid off the bed and walked over to the window. The grounds outside were thickly blanketed with snow, transforming the woods, gardens, and fountains into a vast collection of indistinguishable white mounds. I had never been here in winter before; it felt more isolated and otherworldly than ever.

"Ugh, I just don't understand why we have to be here in person," I grumbled. "It's the 21st century, for heaven's sake! Why couldn't we just have called or Skyped or something?"

"You know the Council," Hannah said. "They've been doing things the same way for centuries. They don't exactly embrace change. Celeste told me the last official change to the voting process was ratified in 1882."

I rolled my eyes. "And I bet they'd been trying to get that change through since the invention of the wheel."

At that moment, Milo sailed clear through the wall, in full strut like a runway model. He reached the fireplace, turned and beveled, and struck a dramatic pose. "The Spirit Guide has arrived," he announced in a low sultry voice.

"Milo, we really need to work on your self-confidence," I said, shaking my head sadly. "Seriously, don't be afraid to get noticed."

Hannah giggled. "Hello, Spirit Guide. What's with the catwalk?"

"Life is a catwalk, sweetness!" Milo said. "Well, in my case, the afterlife is a catwalk, I guess. Anyway, I have an announcement. I've had some time to think about it and I love being back here."

"You've got to be kidding me," I said.

"Nope, not kidding. Totally serious. We can stay forever, as far as I'm concerned," Milo insisted, perching himself on the edge of the fireplace mantel and crossing his arms imperiously.

"And why exactly do we want to stay where we're treated like the social equivalent of lepers?" I asked.

"You two might be lepers," Milo said. "I, however, am queen of the castle around here, and I am loving it!"

"Explain," I ordered.

"It's the other ghosts," Milo said. "They're all in awe of me because I'm Bound to the two of you. It's like I'm some sort of celebrity on the deadside because I was involved with the Prophecy. They're literally following me around everywhere, bombarding me with questions."

"Like the ghost version of the paparazzi?" Hannah asked, smirking a little.

"Exactly!" Milo said. "And basically, it's just confirming what I always knew about myself, which is that I was born to be famous."

"Well, then, I'm so glad you're getting your time in the spotlight. In the meantime, the two of us would like a little less attention," I said. "It's going to be a nightmare, especially when all the other families arrive. Most of them have only ever heard of us until now. We're going to be on display like some kind of sideshow attraction."

Over the next twenty-four hours, the castle would be flooded with Durupinen from all over the world whose families have roots in the Northern Clans. They would all be staying for the duration of the Airechtas. Many of them, like us, had only first seen Fairhaven when they arrived for their training, and many hadn't set foot here since. These were Durupinen who had successfully made their lives far from the shadow of this castle and all of its machinations. They had escaped the vortex; tales of Prophecies and Necromancers were just stories to them.

And now here Hannah and I are, the storybook monsters come to life. Step right up, folks.

"You've just got to learn to use your mystique to your advantage," Milo said. "Let them believe the rumors. Encourage them. If they stare at you, stare right back. No one's going to bother you; they'll be too terrified of what you might do to them."

"That's not really the kind of reputation we want to have, Milo," I said.

"Well, it's the reputation you've got, so you might as well roll with it," Milo said with a shrug. "I certainly am. The new spirits here are so gullible."

"Yeah, and let's not forget why all the spirits here are new spirits," I said, with a bite of impatience in my voice. Milo's face, alight with mischief a moment before, fell into lines of misery.

"Oh, yeah. Right. I... sorry," he said quietly.

"Hey, speaking of new spirits," Hannah said, perking up. "Have you seen this one among your admirers?" and she pointed to the portrait I'd just made.

Milo's eyes widened as he looked at me. "Already? We just got here!"

"I know, I know," I said. "But she was insistent. Have you seen her?"

Milo drifted over, examining it closely. "No, she doesn't look familiar," he said after a moment's consideration. "She didn't give you any information?"

"Just the image. That's all I've got." I dropped my face into my hands and started rubbing my eyes. I was so tired they were beginning to ache from the forcible act of keeping them open.

"Well, it's like you said," Hannah said. "She'll probably be back again. They usually are, if they need something."

"Yeah, I guess we'll see." As if I didn't have enough to be nervous about, being in this castle again. Now this strange girl's face would keep cropping up in my head, tying my life and her death together with a string of vague images until I can discover who she was and what she wants from me. Her eyes bore into me as I stared down into them. There was a plea deep inside of them, but I could not interpret it. With a shiver, I pulled the picture from the wall and shoved it under my bed, knowing that her eyes were upon me still.

2

FRIENDS AND FOES

I MANAGED TO AVOID the main floor of the castle for the rest of that afternoon by claiming I had a headache from my psychic drawing episode. I fell into an uneasy sleep after an hour or two of tossing and turning, trying to ignore the slivers of bright sunlight slipping between the drapes and the sounds of conversation and footsteps reverberating throughout the castle, which, for all its beauty and history, was basically a giant stone echo chamber. Three hours later, when Hannah nudged me awake to see if I wanted to go down to dinner, I felt barely more rested than before I'd fallen asleep.

"I'm not hungry," I grumbled. A cartoonishly loud growl from the region of my stomach immediately called my bluff.

Hannah giggled. "Liar. Come on. It'll be fine. We'll grab some food, find a table, and terrify onlookers from a distance. It'll be great."

"No. I want to stay here and sulk."

Hannah trotted back over to our door with a mischievous smile on her face. "I knew you'd say that, so I brought a couple of people by to help convince you."

She pulled the door open to reveal two grinning faces.

"Get out of bed, you lazy tosser!" roared Savannah Todd, striding across the room, leaping onto my bed, and knocking me flat.

"She can hardly get up if you crush her, Sav," said Mackenzie Miller, choosing instead to just take a couple of steps into the room and wave at me. "Alright, Jess?"

"Mackie! I didn't realize you were going to be here!" I gasped. "Okay, Sav, seriously, get off me!"

"Shhhhh, I'm looking into your eyes," Savvy whispered, stroking my hair.

With a laugh and an almighty grunt, I heaved her off me. She fell to the floor with a thud and a cry of "Bloody hell!" I slid off the bed and crossed the room to throw my arms around Mackie.

"It's so good to see you!" I told her. I hadn't seen her in almost two years, not since my last visit to London to visit Savvy, when the three of us had met for a drink in a pub. She looked exactly the same. She was still tall and lanky, her hair still cropped short into a pixie cut, her smile broad and her eyes warm. She had been the first year Head Girl when we'd started at Fairhaven, and had also been one of the only Apprentices not to treat us like total outcasts. She'd been one of the many driven out of Fairhaven by a fire Hannah accidentally caused while enabling our escape, and then she had been imprisoned along with the rest of the Apprentices when the Necromancers invaded the castle. We'd kept in touch by email and social media over the last few years, but seeing her in person made me feel like she had transcended the theoretical to the actual.

"So, how are you? What have you been up to?" I asked Mackie.

"I got accepted into that graduate program. I'm going for my teaching license. Women's Studies," she said, smiling broadly. "I guess I enjoyed my days of bossing you all around as Head Girl so much that I'm looking to make a career of it."

"That's so exciting, Mack! You'll be a great teacher," Hannah said, beaming at her.

Mackie shrugged. "I think I'd rather be a perpetual student, but I'll give it a go."

"Why are you here, then?" I asked. "You don't have to vote, do you? Isn't Celeste going to handle all that?"

"Yeah, I've managed to steer clear of the voting. But I got guilted into coming back to help with wrangling all the guests. Celeste has me running around giving tours and helping clans to mingle. I've only just managed to slip away; I've been at it since seven o'clock this morning!"

"That's because you're a prat, aren't you? Should have said no, shouldn't you?" Savvy said. She was still lying on the floor, as though she had decided, having found herself there, that she was quite comfortable.

"That's enough out of you! Aren't you the one who said you'd never set foot here again? And here you are, a mentor," Mackie said, laughing. "Whose brilliant idea was that, then?"

Savvy shrugged. "I'm a natural, what can I say?" She rolled over and jumped to her feet. "Shall we go down, then? I'm starving!"

Seeing a pair of friendly faces was exactly the boost of confidence I needed—a reminder that I'd had a few real friends at Fairhaven, despite the disastrous end to my time here. "Yeah, alright. Let's get this over with."

§

If the sight of two old friends hadn't tempted me out of my room, the mouthwatering smells wafting out into the lobby would certainly have done the trick. The castle may have masqueraded as a college, but the food was anything but campus dining hall fare. Several dozen women were milling around the room when we entered. All of them were wearing name tags, like we had just walked into the weirdest high school reunion ever.

"Oh yeah, Celeste gave me some of those name tags. I think I've got them here in my..." Hannah's voice trailed away when she saw the look on my face. The last thing we needed was labels.

Sure enough, as we crossed the room to the buffet line, several people were nudging each other and nodding in our direction. By the time we had filled our plates, the outright pointing and staring had begun. I felt the eyes on us all the way over to our favorite isolated table in the corner.

"Wow, they're really not subtle about it, are they?" I muttered, tucking into a dinner roll.

"Ah, don't pay them any mind," Savvy said. "They're just a load of nosy old cows. Ignore them, and they'll soon find something else to gossip about."

I stared at her. "Really? That's your response? To be mature?"

Savvy swallowed a mouthful of steak and ale pie. "Sure. Why not?"

I laughed. "I just thought, seeing as it's you, you'd have some different advice for us. Something involving profanity, or crude hand gestures, or mooning."

"Well, that's jolly good fun too, if you like," Savvy replied. And without warning she dropped her fork onto her plate with a clatter and pushed her chair back from the table as she stood up. She had her belt half-undone and one foot up on the seat of her chair before any of us realized what she was doing.

"No!" we all shouted in unison. All three of us reached up and grabbed her by the sweater, pulling her back down into her seat.

"Oi! Why all the fuss? You're the one who suggested it!" she cried.

"I know, I know!" I said, choking with laughter now. "I should have known better. For the love of God, please keep your pants on!"

"If you like," Sav said with a wink. "You know where my arse is if you need it."

"I'll let you know," I said.

"Glad to see being a mentor hasn't changed you, Savvy," Mackie said, with a pat on Savvy's back. "Good on ya."

"How's that going, by the way?" Hannah asked.

Savvy's smile faltered. "Eh, it's a bit rough to be honest. Frankie—that's my mentee—she's... well, she's a tough nut to crack."

"Really? Even for you?" I asked. "I thought you said she'd taken a shine to you? You must be the most laid back mentor ever."

Savvy grimaced. "That don't matter much when your mentee don't believe in ghosts."

Hannah choked a little on her mouthful of soup. "I'm sorry, what? She doesn't believe in ghosts?"

"Nope," Savvy replied baldly. "It's... well, it's a sad story, actually."

"Go on, let's hear it," Mackie said, leaning in.

"Well, she had a pretty strict upbringing," Savvy said. "Parents are a real pair of twats, if I'm honest. Filthy rich, you know? And they never had much time for her, what with traveling all over the world on yachts and all that tosh. So, she's been banging around fancy boarding schools all her life. And she is smart, let me tell you," Savvy shook her head and let out a low whistle. "We're talking straight A's at Cheltenham here. Charmed life. But then, one day out of nowhere, her Visitations start."

"But she must have known they were going to," Hannah said. "Her mother must have told her, right? Or another relative?"

"Nah, she's the first in her line, just like me," Savvy said.

"Oh, that's right!" I said. "That's why they asked you to mentor her, isn't it? Because you both had that in common?"

"That's about the only thing we have in common, but yeah," Savvy said.

"So, another Gateway somewhere must have closed for good, right? Isn't that why a new one opens up in a new line, to keep things balanced?" Hannah asked.

"That's right," Mackie said. "The old one closes, and a new one opens. It can pop up anywhere in the world. It just appears on the Léarscáil, and that's how the Durupinen know where to find it."

"What the hell is a Léarscáil?" I asked, stumbling over the unusual word.

"Aw, come off it, you've never seen it? Oh, that's right, you never made it that far in your training here," Mackie said with a sheepish smile. "We usually get to take a trip up to the South Tower in our second year of Apprenticeship, just to have a look at it. It's a giant map of the world that marks geographic shifts in the concentration of spirit energy, using this massive pendulum. I'll have to take you up there; it's fascinating, how it works."

"I would love to see that!" Hannah said, eyes alight with curiosity. "It's right here in the castle?"

Mackie nodded. "Yeah, every High Priestess's residence has one, and there's a Durupinen in charge of monitoring each one, recording and analyzing the shifts in spirit energy. It can be used to predict all sorts of things, not just the opening of a new Gateway."

"Will you really take us to see it? That's fascinating!" Hannah said. "Jess, wouldn't you like to see that?"

I shrugged. "Sure, I guess. Sounds better than sitting through this stupid Airechtas." I turned back to Savvy. "Sorry, Sav, keep going with your story."

"So anyway, Frankie's away at school, and she sees her first ghost right in the middle of an end of term test, but she thinks it's a hallucination brought on by stress. Thinks she's going mad."

I laughed, although it wasn't really funny. "I know that feeling."

"Me too," Hannah said grimly.

"Yeah, but you both tried to hide it, didn't you? That's a normal reaction. Frankie went straight to her headmistress and told her what was happening, and then from there to a shrink for medication. She didn't even stop to consider that what was happening to her might actually be real. She took a leave from school, booked herself into one of those retreats for the wealthy and doped herself up on every pill her doctor would prescribe her."

"Lot of good that did her, I'm sure," Mackie said, shaking her head sadly.

"Actually, anti-psychotic meds can block out spirit activity pretty effectively," Hannah said, a faint pink flush creeping up her face.

"The right combination of medications, along with a determination not to notice things, can work wonders."

Mackie gaped. "You can block out spirits with meds? Really?"

Hannah nodded. "Some of those drugs are really strong. It's like walking around in a haze. And you can usually explain away any activity that does manage to penetrate the shield. Your mind is relieved to continue the oblivion. It's willful ignorance, but it never lasts long. No matter what you take, the spirits break through eventually."

There was a moment of awkward silence as we all processed the awfulness of Hannah's words, and then Savvy jumped in. "By the time Celeste and Siobhán found her, Frankie was well and truly hyped up on those meds. They tried to tell her what was really happening to her, but she wouldn't hear a word of it. Celeste told me that, at one point, Frankie screamed at her that she and Siobhán weren't real and threw a chair at them."

"Holy shit," I said breathlessly. "I mean, I didn't want to believe it either, but it was better than thinking I was going crazy."

"You'd think, but Frankie would rather be mad as a hatter than a Durupinen, and that's the truth," Savvy said.

"So, what did Celeste and Siobhán do? How did they get her here?" Hannah asked.

"They couldn't bloody well leave her where she was. They needed that Gateway to be open and functioning properly, just like the rest of them, but Frankie wouldn't go willingly. In the end, they met with her parents and orchestrated a 'transfer' to another, more prestigious mental facility."

"What mental facility?" I asked.

Savvy gestured grandly around the dining room. "You're looking at it, mate."

Hannah gasped. "So, they lied to her?"

"Yeah," Savvy said. "Only way to get her here. We've been trying for a few months now to get her to participate in her training, but she absolutely refuses to believe that any of it is really happening. She says we're just 'encouraging her illness.' It's a bloody nightmare."

"Wow," I said. I tried to imagine sticking to a spirit-free version of reality while at a place like Fairhaven, which was quite literally swarming with spirits. It was hard to believe that anyone could be that stubborn. "Sounds like you have your work cut out for you."

16

"You've got that right," Savvy said, shaking her head. "I was excited about it when I first started. You know me, I love a good challenge. But now I've got to admit, I'm discouraged. I just keep telling her it's no good denying reality, that she'll have to accept it sooner or later, because it ain't going away. No joy so far."

"What about the other half of her Gateway? Doesn't she have someone else to help her through it? It can't just be her!" Hannah said.

"She's got a second cousin here with her. Her name's Penny. They'd never met before arriving here. Penny's Visitations started out of the blue as well, but she's just accepted it, and she's ready and willing to learn. Problem is she won't be able to put any of her skills to use if Frankie doesn't cooperate," Savvy said.

"Maybe I could talk to her?" Hannah suggested timidly.

Savvy perked up at once. "Would you?"

Hannah shrugged. "Sure. I'm not sure if it will help, but I could try."

"That would be brilliant, Hannah! Cheers!" Savvy said, raising her glass to Hannah and swigging it down in one gulp. "I wasn't too keen on being a mentor at first, but now that I'm in it, I don't want to get the sack because I'm cocking it up."

"Funny, that's basically how I feel about this entire trip," I said. "I really didn't want to come, but now that I'm here, I'm afraid I'm going to vote wrong."

Mackie gave a little snort of a laugh. "How can you vote wrong? It's voting. I think the only way you can do it wrong is by... well, *not* doing it!"

"I spend most of my time trying to steer clear of Durupinen drama, and now I have to make informed decisions about how it should all be run! It feels sort of—I don't know—hypocritical," I said.

"Hey, you've got to police a Gateway, so you get a vote. It's only fair. They're letting me vote, after all, and who's less informed than yours truly?" Savvy said. "I'm the first in my clan, and I slept through most of my training, remember? I'm basically a vacuum of Durupinen information."

I laughed. "Okay, I'm starting to feel slightly more qualified." I should have realized Savvy would be voting, but I hadn't thought of it. At least having her here would liven things up, although I could also imagine a scenario where we got in a lot of trouble, like the kids who won't stop goofing around in the back of the classroom. I'd have to seriously consider how close we sat to each other, and if the hilarity would be worth the dirty looks.

"You're not voting, right Mackie?" Hannah asked.

Mackie shook her head. "No boring meeting sessions for me! Celeste is representing our clan in the Airechtas. She's got an important role this year, as Deputy Priestess. Hey, speak of the devil!"

Mackie looked over our heads and waved. We all turned to see Celeste hurrying across the room toward us. Her face was full of concern.

"Oh lord, she doesn't look very happy, does she? Wonder what I've forgotten to do now?" Mackie muttered, rolling her eyes.

Celeste arrived behind Mackie's chair and gave her niece's shoulder an affectionate squeeze. "Hello, girls! Jess, I haven't seen you since you got in! How are you, dear?"

"Jet-lagged, but I'll survive," I said with a smile.

"Mm-hmm," Celeste said distractedly. She seemed to not even have really listened to my answer. Her eyes kept darting over her shoulder.

"Everything alright, Celeste?" I asked.

"Yes, of course," she said, and then sighed. "No, I'm afraid not, actually. I detest having to be the one to tell you this. You should have had more warning, but I only just found out myself, or I would have—"

I felt my heart speed up. "Celeste, what is it? Just tell us!"

"I didn't want to take the chance that you'd just turn the corner and there she'd be," Celeste said. "I still can't quite believe they've allowed it, but—"

Hannah's fork clattered to the table and she gasped. Her complexion had gone the color of milk as she stared at what must surely have been a terrifying apparition in the doorway.

"What is *she* doing here?" Hannah asked in a strangled whisper.

We all turned. Marion Clark was striding into the dining room with her head held haughtily high, as though she were surveying her kingdom rather than simply arriving for a meal. The first time I'd ever seen her had been in this room, on my first morning at Fairhaven. She had introduced herself as a member of the Council and proceeded to explain to Hannah and me that we were outcasts who didn't belong amongst the Apprentices, and that we would never live down the shame and dishonor with which our mother had tainted us. As if that wasn't enough, she then tried to have us thrown in prison for the crime of our parentage, and capped it all off by engineering a coup to replace Finvarra as High Priestess. The last time I'd seen Marion was the day before I left Fairhaven in the aftermath of the Isherwood Prophecy. She had been entering the Grand Council Room escorted by two Caomhnóir, where she would face the consequences of her disastrous decisions. Her face had not looked quite so smug then.

"What the hell?" I hissed. "What the actual hell is she doing here? Fiona told me she was banished from the castle after everything that happened with the Prophecy!"

"She was," Celeste said. "She's here on special dispensation from the Council for the Airechtas. She made the request at the last minute, and it was only just approved last night. Siobhán handed me an updated list a few minutes ago, and I happened to see her name on it. Of course, I hastened to find you right away, because... well, I didn't want her to surprise you like that." She gestured helplessly toward the doorway, where Marion was now shaking hands with a small knot of chattering women.

"Who approved her request?" I asked, incredulous. "Shouldn't the whole Council vote on something like that?"

"Typically, yes, a decision like that would require a vote from the entire Council. But she appealed directly to Finvarra, and Finvarra granted her request," Celeste said.

"Finvarra?" I cried, struggling to keep my volume under control. "But... Marion tried to unseat her! She actually ordered that Finvarra be locked up! What in the world would make Finvarra grant her request?"

Celeste shook her head. "I can't say for sure. It seems that Finvarra made the decision without consulting any other Council members."

"Karen's going to flip out when she hears about this," I said. "She never would have sent us if she thought Marion was coming."

Celeste nodded. "I would hardly blame her."

Over Celeste's shoulder, I watched as Marion broke free from her circle of greeters. She took a few steps across the room and then froze as her eyes found mine. Once upon a time her haughty face would have curved into a malicious smirk. She would have strolled across the room and humiliated us with an entitled tirade about the importance of duty and tradition. But not today. Today, still tainted by her recent disgrace, she stopped in her tracks, eyes widening, complexion whitening. She then changed course abruptly, bypassing the buffet line and heading straight to a table as far from us as she could get without leaving the room.

Hannah and I turned to look at each other, eyebrows raised.

"Wow," I said. "I guess she wasn't expecting to see us again, either."

"I guess not," Hannah said. Her mouth twitched.

"Are you smiling?" I asked her, breaking into one myself.

"Maybe. I don't know. That was… kind of awesome," Hannah said with a shrug.

Savvy roared with laughter. "The old cow goes scurrying for cover at the very sight of you? That's brilliant!"

"Yeah, well, she recovers herself quickly, that one," Mackie said. "I wouldn't count on her being all meek and contrite this week."

My smile faded. I turned to Celeste. "And you have no idea why she wanted to be here?"

Celeste grimaced. "I said I had no idea she was coming. I actually have a pretty good idea why she wants to be here, though."

"Why?" Hannah, Savvy, Mackie and I all said at once.

Celeste leaned over the table, and we all huddled around her so as not to miss a word. "You know Marion was stripped of her seat on the Council three years ago. That seat has remained vacant since then, because a Council seat can only be filled once every five years at the Airechtas. Every single clan must participate in the selection process and vote in the election; it is compulsory. That seat is now up for reelection this week, and I'm quite sure that's why she's here."

"She's not actually going to try to get it back?" I hissed.

Celeste shook her head. "She can't. Even if everyone in that room were to stand up and vote for her to regain that seat, she is ineligible to retake it. In fact, her entire clan is forbidden from running for it. But she will undoubtedly try to influence who does get the seat. It will be important to her that the space is filled with a like-minded clan, someone who could put forward the same kinds of policies and votes that she herself would have contributed."

"So, she's here to campaign for someone?" I asked.

"That's a succinct way of putting it, yes," Celeste said.

"Well, at least we know what we're going to do with one of

our votes this week," I muttered. "Voting against whoever Marion suggests for the Council."

"That goes for me as well," Savvy said. "I don't even need to know who it is, if I'm honest."

Celeste gave us a stern look. "Now, girls. It's part of your duty to listen to all of the arguments, all of the speeches, and then make an informed decision about that open seat. You mustn't let biases rule your better judgment."

I cocked an eyebrow at her. Her mouth curved into the merest suggestion of a smile before she could get it under control.

At that moment, Finn marched into the dining room. He scanned the room until he found us, and made a beeline for our table. Celeste saw the purpose with which he approached and stepped swiftly to the side to make room for him. Finn gave her a respectful nod as he passed her and strode right up between Hannah and me.

"Marion is here," he said without preamble.

"We know. She's sitting right over there," I said, pointing.

Finn looked up and seemed to shrink a little. "Oh. Right. Well, I'd hoped you hadn't seen her yet."

"It was good of you to try to warn us, Finn," Hannah said.

"Yeah, everyone is just a little bit behind the ball on that one today," I told him. "Celeste tried to head her off, too, but it sounds like she surprised everyone by showing up."

"Are you both... that is to say... are you quite... alright?" He avoided my face so completely that he might have been asking the question to his boots.

"We're fine," I said.

"Right. Well, then. I'm due out in the courtyard for a Caomhnóir roll call and meeting," he said and, giving a stiff little bow, he turned on his heel and marched out.

I immediately dropped my eyes to my plate again, and began shoveling food into my mouth, trying to appear completely unaffected by the arrival of Finn Carey, but the truth was that my heart and mind were racing with more emotions than I could conceivably keep track of.

I heard Hannah ask Celeste a question about the structure of the Airechtas sessions, leaving me free to recover from the encounter.

I was starting to feel like I had cornered the market on complicated relationships, and my relationship with Finn was no different. Finn had been assigned to Hannah and me as our

Caomhnóir during our first month at Fairhaven, and by all appearances at the time, he absolutely loathed me. He barely spoke to me or looked at me, if he could help it. I had chalked it up to his strict Caomhnóir upbringing; all Caomhnóir were taught that Durupinen were basically evil temptresses who would stop at nothing to distract them from their all-important duty of protecting our Gateways. This attitude sprang from the ancient and strictly kept rule that relationships between Durupinen and Caomhnóir were forbidden. So, imagine my surprise when I learned that it was only his deep feelings for me that kept Finn at such a distance. And imagine my further surprise when, once I dug through all my resentment about the archaic system of burly men protecting helpless women, I realized I had feelings for him, too.

When we had all survived the Isherwood Prophecy unscathed, it seemed for a short time like Finn and I would be together. But Seamus and the other Caomhnóir caught wind of our budding romance, and he threatened to reassign Finn if he didn't keep our relationship strictly professional. And so, it was another three long years until, barely two months ago, we finally gave in to our feelings for each other while on assignment for the Trackers. We had been secretly together ever since. I hadn't told anyone, not even Hannah, though I was quite sure she and Milo had a shrewd idea of what was going on. And now that we were back at Fairhaven, under the stern gaze of the Council and the Caomhnóir Brotherhood, we had to pretend that we loathed each other on principle, just like when we first met. If our relationship was discovered, the consequences were almost too terrible to consider. Finn would surely be reassigned to another Gateway, as far from me as they could conceivably send him. I would have to live my life under the watchful eye of a new and likely hostile Caomhnóir, who would make it his life's mission to ensure that Finn and I never crossed each other's paths again.

All of this was rocketing around inside me every time I saw Finn—the love, the fear, the paranoia, the resentment—all roaring in me at once like a many headed monster. And the worst part was that I could see no solution. There was no happy ending here.

The one upside to this absolute train wreck of a relationship was that I had developed a remarkable poker face. I swallowed my food and looked up once more, to find the conversation about the Airechtas in full swing around me.

"...will start with the opening ceremony and then the daily

22

sessions will begin. Each day there will be a morning session, during which all proposals for the day will be brought forth on the agenda, and arguments heard. Then in the afternoon, after everyone has had time to consider what they have heard that morning, there will be a vote on each measure one by one. Then the decisions will be recorded in the official register and the Airechtas will be dismissed for the day."

"That sounds straightforward," Hannah said, with more interest than I would have thought she had in the subject. Then I saw her catch my eye, and I knew she had brought it up to distract from the Finn incident. God bless my sister and her timely bursts of intuition.

"Oh, it is. We've got it down to a science, several centuries later," Celeste said with a smile. "You'll be bored out of your mind with the efficiency of it all. Well, if you're sure you're both alright, I'm going to dash. Lots to do still, before the Airechtas officially kicks off."

"We're fine," I assured her, and Hannah nodded in agreement. "Go organize boring meeting stuff."

Celeste gave my shoulder an affectionate squeeze and then hurried away across the dining room, pausing here and there to shake a hand or share a greeting with someone. Finally, with a last look at us over her shoulder, she swept out into the entrance hall.

§

Hannah, Mackie, Savvy, and I sat up for a long time chatting in a common area off of the dining room. Milo finished his victory tour of the castle and grounds and decided to grace us with his presence. It was a welcome distraction to be around such good friends—it almost made me forget where I was and the fact that I didn't want to be here. We talked and laughed until a maid came around to douse the fire and lock up the lower rooms for the night, effectively kicking us out. When we arrived back at our room, I was surprised to see Finn standing there outside our door like a bouncer at the world's lamest dance club. Hannah and Milo said hello to him, but slipped quickly inside, closing the door behind them and leaving us alone in the deserted hallway.

"Hey," I said.

"Hey, yourself."

"I wasn't sure if I'd see you again today," I said, and was instantly annoyed at how forlorn my voice sounded. I reached for his hand but drew back at once. "Whoa! You're freezing!"

"Braxton held an official roll call, and it took a bloody lifetime to get through all the clans. The barracks couldn't hold us all; we had to move out to the courtyard. We were freezing our arses off," Finn said with a chuckle. "I just hope we don't all wind up with pneumonia. Enough about that, though." He reached out for both of my hands and held them tightly, ignoring my gasp at the chill. His eyes didn't just look at me; they searched me, as though they would find any hurt or pain hidden there and smite it. "Of course, we couldn't really speak freely in the dining room. How are you really, with Marion here?"

"I'm fine. Really!" I added, when he narrowed his eyes in suspicion. "It was definitely a shock to see her walk in, but once we got over that, it was pretty anticlimactic. Honestly, I think she was as unhappy to see us as we were to see her."

Finn still had a suspicious gleam in his eye, but he let it slide, which was refreshing for him.

"I was proud that you showed some restraint and didn't karate chop her in the face," I said to him.

He actually threw back his head and laughed. It was such a wonderful sound, when he let himself make it. "When have you ever seen me karate chop anyone? I don't even know any karate!"

"You don't know karate?" I cried, throwing his hands off of mine. "What kind of bullshit Caomhnóir are you? I demand a replacement!"

"Could a new Caomhnóir do this?" he asked, and planted a kiss on me that nearly knocked me flat. I reeled from it, for the brief moment it lasted, and then I felt a sinking sadness as the tingling pressure of the kiss receded from my lips. The kisses would be so few and far between while we were here. It only deepened my resentment of the place. Seriously, I wanted to kick the nearest bit of stone I could reach just to vent my frustrations.

Finn could see the aggravation in my face. "I know," he said. "I hate this, too."

"Did anyone... did you get the sense that anyone suspected anything?" I asked, dropping my voice to a faint whisper despite the fact that we'd already made sure of our absolute solitude.

"No. I can't imagine that anyone here would tiptoe around the suspicion that a Durupinen and a Caomhnóir were involved with

24

each other. They would leap on it at once, like Seamus did when he first discovered us."

I shivered, maybe from the cold still radiating from Finn's hands, but also from the awful chill of that memory. That interference on Seamus's part had led to three heartbreaking years of distance between Finn and me, distance that we'd only managed to bridge a few short weeks ago. "This was the biggest reason I didn't want to come here. I hate having to stay away from you."

"As do I, love. As do I," Finn whispered. He brought one of those achingly cold hands up to my face and ran a finger along the line of my jaw before leaning in and kissing me again. "But I would have had to come here anyway, for the Caomhnóir's role in the Airechtas, so this time apart would have been inevitable. At least we have stolen moments like these to see us through. Have patience. A few more days and we'll be home again."

"Yes, but even there we have to be so secretive," I said, reaching for Finn's hand and bringing it back to my cheek. "I hate that we can't be open about this."

"I do, too," Finn said. "It's a terrible way to have to live. But what choice do we have?"

A sudden sound at the end of the hallway caused us to leap apart. We stood, hearts thundering for a few moments, but no one appeared.

"Coast is clear," Finn said. He was back at his careful distance, his professionally indifferent expression back on his face. "I think it was just a door shutting."

I laughed sadly as I tugged at my own door. "A perfect metaphor," I said.

ELEANORA: 6 APRIL 1864

6 April 1864

Well, Little Book, I sit here by the fire in the drawing room, writing feverishly, much to the delight and satisfaction of my mother, who has insisted that keeping a diary will be beneficial to me. She does not mean beneficial to my health, or my happiness, or any other tangible part of my person. Rather, she means beneficial to our social and economic status. Puzzling, you say? Allow me to explain to you.

I know many a fine young lady of substance who write in a diary almost nightly, but it is their custom to share their musings and compositions with their families. They sit in their drawing rooms on quiet evenings such as this one, reading aloud from their books so that their parents and siblings may remark upon their observations. It is meant, I suppose, to encourage intelligent conversation and to improve a young lady's proclivity toward articulate self-expression. However, the reflections I record in you, Little Book, will most likely remain a cozy little confidence between the two of us.

As she handed you to me this morning, my mother remarked, "You are entirely too free with your speech, Eleanora. You simply let fly with whatever thought resides in your head at the moment. It is terribly improper, and I fear that you will disgrace yourself publicly before you are safely married off. A loose tongue in the presence of the aristocracy is a social peril we cannot afford, my darling. And so, I thought this diary would serve a useful purpose in helping you to express these thoughts... silently." And with that, she dropped you into my waiting hands.

I had several thoughts in that moment that I had no desire to keep silent. But, as arguments with my mother are rarely, if ever, productive, I decided to swallow back my thoughts and thank her as politely as I could. I even managed a smile. Aren't you proud of me, Little Book?

My mother is watching me most carefully now, and the expression on her face is the absolute epitome of smugness. She does so love to be right that I did not have the heart to tell her that I had no interest in you at all, Little Book. I certainly don't mean to insult you. You really are a lovely book. Your silk cover is quite pretty, and your pages are creamy and smooth. As books go, I'm sure you are delightful. But I harbour no desire whatsoever to record my thoughts within you. I do so merely to satisfy my audience, who is now sniffing loudly and trying to catch my eye, so that she may celebrate her victory over my free spirit. I am carefully avoiding her gaze. We cannot let her have all of the gratification. It sets a dangerous precedent for our future mother-daughter battles.

The truth of the matter is, I have never felt compelled to write a thought when I was perfectly capable of speaking it aloud. This rendered me a less than satisfactory pupil in the eyes of my governess. But how else is one to become a part of the conversation, if one does not speak up? How is one to gain insight into one's friends and acquaintances? How is one to find the answers to vexing questions if one does not ask them?

There is another reason I feel so compelled to speak freely in company, and I must confess to you that this reason is rather shocking. The truth is, Little Book, that I must keep a large and terrifying secret every hour of every day. I often feel that the weight of it will crush me into nothingness. There is a crucial part of my very self that I am forbidden to ever reveal to anyone, not even my dearest friend or the man I wed.

I am a Durupinen, my dear Little Book. I can converse with the dead, observe their clandestine rovings about the world, and someday I will aid them in their journey to the realm beyond our own.

I have never seen these words written down before. I have been staring at them now for several long minutes, and I am fighting a strong impulse to rip them to shreds and throw them into the fire. Do you suppose that they are truer, that they hold even more power over me now that I have recorded them in this form? Or have I instead expelled them from me, drawn like poison from a wound?

And now I must confess something else to you, and this confession comes as rather a surprise to me. Most unexpectedly, I find that I feel lighter after giving these words to you to hold, Little Book. You have lifted them from my shoulders, if even for a moment, and for that I must thank you. And, I suppose, thank my mother. It seems she was right, in a sense. You are most helpful, though not in the way that she intended you to be.

And so, as much as it grieves me to bolster my mother's sense of *superiority, I believe I shall be writing in you regularly after all. How vexing.*

Eleanora

3

THE PROPOSITION

"**M**ILO, FOR THE LAST TIME, I am not giving you credit for the hair."

"This is utter betrayal. This is treason, I will have you know!" Milo cried.

I dropped my newly dyed head into my hands. "Milo, you are not a monarch, therefore no one can actually commit treason against you. You do know this, right?"

"Treason!" he hissed. "I've been saying for years—*years*—that you should lose the black and warm up your tones. In fact, every time I say, 'Good morning,' or 'Hello,' or 'See you later,' the subtext I'm screaming at you is 'DYE YOUR DAMN HAIR!'"

I shook my head. Every Durupinen in the castle had probably sensed the earsplitting shriek of delight that met me when I opened the bathroom door a few moments before to reveal to Hannah and Milo that I had dyed my hair. After six years of jet black tresses, and more than a few life-altering experiences, I'd decided that I was ready for a change—only this time, it was a change that I actually had full control over, which was new and different for me, now that we were Durupinen. And, also a departure from recent tradition, I had made the decision without giving a good goddamn what anyone else might think about it. It had been liberating to see the rich brown color replace the signature black, and even more so to layer in the bright red highlights. It felt like I was stripping away some of the vestiges of the events that had so altered the course of my life. I watched them swirl down the drain in dark cloudy rivulets. Much like my recent tattoo, it was a symbolic way of reclaiming another part of my life.

And apparently, of ruining Milo's.

"Milo, I'm not going to tell every person who compliments my hair that it was your idea. I'm just not going to do that," I said wearily.

Milo huffed. "Well then, I am just going to have to do it myself. And I can't believe you went with that shade of red, it's got way too much violet in it. I can't believe you didn't go to a colorist to do this!"

"We're in the middle of the countryside in a castle full of ghosts, Milo. My professional stylist options were limited. I needed a change. It was either this or a new tattoo, and I've heard it's generally frowned upon to attempt those on yourself."

"Hair color is not a DIY project either, sweetness!" Milo cried. "I mean, consult me on the shade, at least! You've gone way too cool for your skin tone, especially with all the black you insist on wearing!"

"Wait, so you're saying I chose the wrong color and you *still* want credit?" I asked.

"I'm saying that when someone—as in, *me*—has an inspired idea to raise your fashion game, you have to let him execute it properly, and then give him credit! It's like at awards shows! What's the first thing every interviewer asks a woman on the red carpet?"

"Something sexist that makes her want to claw her own eyes out?" I suggested. Hannah snorted.

Milo ignored my joke and plowed on as though I hadn't answered. "They ask her who she's wearing! Because it's all about making a statement, and the maker of the statement matters!"

I stared at Milo. He was getting weirdly upset about this, more than just his usual display of sass. His energy was pulsing with something deeper, something that was seeping through our connection and pricking at the corners of my eyes, as though I was about to cry. Hannah had noticed it, too. Her smile had vanished from her face.

"Okay, I give!" I said, raising my hands in surrender. "Full credit to you, to anyone who notices."

Milo took a deep breath and folded his arms, looking satisfied. "Well, good. Because absolutely everyone, living and dead, will notice. Now if you'll excuse me, I'm off to tell the floaters to be on the lookout for your new locks. Creating a healthy buzz beforehand will boost the wow factor when they finally see you. And for God's sake, try to wear something blue today. It will make your highlights pop." He vanished on the spot.

"What the hell was that all about?" I asked Hannah.

"I don't know!" Hannah replied, looking mystified. "He gives fashion advice all the time. I never saw him get upset about it before, not really. I'll ask him about it later."

"Yeah, better you than me," I said.

"I really like your hair though, Jess. It looks nice on you."

I turned to face the mirror on the wall. "Yeah, I like it, too, I think. It was time for a change. Plus, we look more like sisters now, don't you think."

Hannah rolled her eyes. "Ugh, I didn't think of that. It's going to be a lot harder now, denying that we're related when you embarrass me in public."

I spun around and gasped. "Hannah Ballard, that was sassy! You just sassed me!"

She grinned mischievously. "I spend entirely too much time with you and Milo. The sass was bound to wear off on me eventually." She turned and pointed to the wall by my bed. "Another one, huh?"

I looked where she was pointing. "Yeah." Another psychic drawing hung taped to my wall. It had happened again in the middle of the night. I'd woken already sitting up straight, hand aching, head pounding, with a strange, overheated feeling, like I had a fever.

"Isn't that the same girl as the last sketch?" Hannah asked.

"The very same. She's very persistent, but she's not giving me much to work with," I said.

"How do you mean?"

"She's not giving me any sense of what it is she wants—no clues, no context. She just sort of... stares at me. It's like I'm seeing her, but there's no message she's trying to send."

"Hmmm," Hannah said thoughtfully, looking at the girl again. "Maybe she doesn't know what she wants yet?"

"Well, I wish she would make up her mind before interrupting my sleep again," I grumbled. I crossed the room, pulled the picture off of my wall, and shoved it under the bed with the other one.

One spirit's face was replaced with another as Milo sailed clean back through the wall.

"Have you finished announcing my new coiffure from the top of the highest towers?" I asked him, tempering the sarcasm with a smile, just in case he was still upset.

Milo attempted half a smile in return, but then his face settled back into an uncharacteristically serious expression. "I came back to give you a message. From Carrick."

Hannah looked up sharply. "From Carrick?"

Milo shrugged apologetically. "Yeah. He cornered me out on the grounds. He wants you to meet him in the entrance hall as soon as you can. He's waiting for you there."

Hannah and I stared at each other. Everything inside my body seemed to have twisted into a tight, painful knot. Carrick. Our father. Well, the ghost of our father, but that was the only way we'd ever known him.

"Why?" I asked sharply. "Why does he want to see us, did he say?"

Milo shook his head, and his expression was knowingly sympathetic. I could feel waves of empathy rolling in through our connection, washing over me, trying to soothe me. "He didn't say. He just said he needed to see you, and could I please go find you to deliver the message."

"Well," Hannah said, and I could hear the struggle raging behind her voice. "I guess we should get going, then. I'm sure he wouldn't have sent for us if it wasn't important."

"Right. Yeah, obviously," I said. I looked down at the bathrobe I was still wearing. "Just give me a minute to get changed and we can go."

Milo nodded. "I'll let him know you're on your way," he said. "Just give my energy a little tug if you need me, okay, sweetness?" he added, winking at Hannah.

She smiled weakly at him. "Yeah, okay."

Milo turned back to me and pointed imperiously to my suitcase. "Don't forget. Blue."

§

Carrick was waiting for us in the entrance hall, just as Milo had promised. He hovered by the fireplace, staring into the fire as though each leaping flame held a sentence he longed to read. He wasn't easy to see at first; the glow of the fire outshone him, so that he seemed to fade into the wall behind him.

We walked over to him—Hannah just behind me—and stood for a moment, waiting for him to notice us. When he didn't, I cleared my throat.

34

"Uh, Carrick? Hi," I said, ever a masterclass of awkwardness.

He looked up, almost startled, and straightened up like we had announced a military inspection. "Jess. Hannah. Milo found you then, did he? Excellent," he replied. I could hear him struggling against the formality in his voice. "I... that is... it's nice to see you both."

"You, too," I said, because that's what you were supposed to say. The truth was that I didn't know if it was nice to see him or not. Mostly what I felt whenever I was around him was an unsettling mixture of discomfort, curiosity, and anger. I forgave myself this confusion, though, because perhaps never in the history of the world was there a father-daughter relationship so fraught with strange and unfortunate circumstances as ours, starting with the fact that I'd only ever known him as a ghost.

All of this rose up between us like a wall in the few moments of silence that had followed my reply, a wall that Carrick valiantly attempted to scale as he said, "I... well, I've come because Finvarra sent me, but... that is to say, I was glad of the excuse. I would have sought you out myself before long."

"Yeah, we would have come to find you, too," Hannah said. Maybe it was her loss of direct emotional connection with our mother, but speaking to him seemed to come much more easily to her than it did to me.

There was a long awkward pause, made more awkward by the fact that Carrick had a habit of bouncing on the balls of his heels when he was nervous. I decided to take pity on him and speak before he turned into a ghostly pogo stick.

"So, you said that Finvarra sent you to find us?" I prompted.

"Yes!" Carrick seized on the question like a drowning man to a lifeboat. "Yes, she has expressed a wish to see the two of you in her office. I volunteered to track you down and escort you there."

Hannah and I looked at each other in surprise. "She wants to see us? Why?" I asked, trying to sound less nervous than I felt.

"I must admit, she did not confide her motives to me, merely the request to see you. Would you be so kind as to follow me to her office, please?" Carrick asked. He was certainly endeavoring to keep his tone friendlier than any other Caomhnóir in this place was bothering to do. I'd rarely heard the word "please" from any other member of our overprotective brotherhood, but then again, I didn't get the impression that we had much of a choice but to follow him.

"Uh, sure. We don't have to be anywhere right now," I said.

"Very good, then," Carrick said, and he started marching down the hallway.

Assuming this meant we were to follow him, Hannah and I set off. I reached out and gave her hand a quick squeeze. It was clammy and trembling, as I had expected it would be.

"Why don't you track down Milo?" I nudged her. "See if he wants to come along?"

Hannah smiled, looking slightly calmer just at the thought. "Good idea," she said. I felt our connection to Milo expand with light and warmth as she sent the request humming through it. Almost instantly, his reply came singing back.

"You need me, I'm there. That's the deal, sweetness."

"I don't know if Finvarra will let you into the office during... whatever it is she's asking us there for," I warned him. "But even just having your moral support would be helpful."

"I'll be right there," he assured us.

Carrick, who had heard none of this, seemed to realize that he had left us far behind him. He halted his steps long enough for us to catch up to him.

"I do apologize. I'm not used to keeping step with anyone," he said.

"That's okay," Hannah said.

"Yeah, it's good to keep moving in this castle. These hallways are freezing in the winter!" I said. "At least we're keeping our heart rates up!"

"I heard all about your first assignment for the Trackers," Carrick said, in an attempt to make conversation. "I was pleased to hear that you handled it so well."

"You heard that we handled it well?" Hannah asked, surprised.

"Oh yes," Carrick said. "Catriona isn't one to hand out compliments to anyone, but after hearing the details and reading between the lines, it sounds as though you dealt with the challenges admirably, whether she wants to admit it or not."

"Oh," I said, feeling profoundly relieved. "Thank you." I'd been worried that word of our attempted Crossing would have reached the Council, or maybe even Finvarra, and that there would be fallout from it. So far though, it seemed, Catriona had either not divulged this detail to others, or those she had shared it with had not thought it worthy of note. Either way, it was just fine by me.

We couldn't say anything more to Carrick at that point, because we had begun the long climb up the staircase of the North Tower, and it was all we could do not to collapse in a breathless heap, let alone carry on a conversation. Carrick did not knock to announce our presence, and yet we heard Finvarra's voice from the other side of the door the moment we arrived at the threshold.

"Enter, please."

It took me a moment to realize that Carrick would have a connection to Finvarra just as Hannah and I had to Milo, and that must have been how Carrick had alerted her that we had arrived. It was strange to think of anyone else having the same kind of bond we had with Milo.

"Wait for me, sweetness!"

"Think of the devil, and the devil will appear," I said as Milo zoomed into being beside us.

"And just who are you calling a devil?" Milo asked, a single eyebrow perfectly arched in his outrage.

Before I could answer, Carrick cleared his throat and gestured toward the door, which was now open.

"Hello again, Carrick," Milo said.

"Spirit Guide Chang," Carrick said, nodding respectfully.

"Did you notice Jess' hair? Doesn't it warm up her skin tone?" Milo asked.

Carrick looked flustered. "I... I'm afraid I did..."

"You don't need to answer that," I said to Carrick. "Seriously."

"Do you think it would be alright for Milo to come with us?" Hannah asked quickly.

Carrick did not even hesitate, glad of a question he could safely answer. "Of course. The three of you are Bound, and Finvarra understands the closeness of that bond better than anyone. You needn't even ask. Please, enter."

Prepared for a "no," it took me a few moments to absorb the readiness of the answer, and to shuffle myself forward through the door. What I saw when I walked through it froze my steps again.

Finvarra sat in a wheelchair in the back of the circular room, gazing out over the grounds which were visible from the enormous windows behind her desk. She was attached to an IV; a plastic bag full of fluid hung from a metal stand beside her chair. It was shocking to see how much she had deteriorated since we had last seen her less than two months ago. Her sunken cheek rested on a shriveled, wasted hand. Her neck looked abnormally long, and her once lustrous hair was so thin that I could see her mottled scalp through it.

Hannah had been unable to stifle a gasp, and Finvarra smiled slightly at the sound of it before she turned her head to face us.

"Am I that stunning?" she asked in a quavering voice that nevertheless maintained its regal tone.

"I... I just... sorry, I didn't mean..." Hannah stammered, but Finvarra silenced her with a wave of her skeletal hand.

"A poorly delivered joke, my dear. Believe me, I know what I look like, though I've decided that looking in mirrors is bad for my morale, to say nothing of my vanity." Her eyes were kind, and I felt Hannah's body relax beside me.

"No one told us how ill you are," I said. "It's just a little bit of a shock, that's all."

"I don't doubt that," Finvarra said. "Please, do sit down."

She gestured over to a small sitting area where two wing chairs and a settee were all grouped around a coffee table. We sat in the wing chairs and then watched nervously as Carrick used his energy like a poltergeist, sliding Finvarra's wheelchair and IV stand slowly across the floor just as if he were physically pushing it. Every tiny movement seemed to jostle and pain Finvarra, and she sat tensed with her eyes screwed up against the discomfort until the chair rolled to a gentle stop beside the settee. It was gut-wrenching to watch.

"There now, what a production," Finvarra said when she had gathered the strength to speak again. "Imagine so much fuss just to cross a room."

We had no idea what to say about this, so we just smiled politely. With the exception of visits to my grandfather at the Winchester Home for the Aged, I'd never spent any time around anyone who was so sick, and I could feel my palms starting to sweat. I had an unrelenting urge to run from the room so that I didn't have to look at Finvarra and face the awful truth about the bleakness of her future.

"Now, then. How are you both?" Finvarra asked, endeavoring to keep the tone light and cordial.

Hannah looked at me as though she were stumped and wanted me to answer. "We're fine, thank you," I said. Courtesy dictated that

I next ask how she was, but the answer to that question was so obvious that I didn't bother.

"I was pleased to hear," Finvarra went on, "that you did so well with your first assignment with the Trackers. I had a full report of the situation when Catriona returned."

I smirked a bit. "I didn't get the impression Catriona was all that impressed with the job we did," I said.

Finvarra made a sound that was half-chuckle, half-cough. "Catriona is never impressed with anything. She fancies it makes her seem more mysterious, but I must admit I find it rather dull."

I caught Hannah's and Milo's eyes and we all grinned. It was strange to hear Finvarra criticizing another member of the Council, but kind of awesome at the same time.

"So, is it your intention to remain with the Trackers, as least for the immediate future?" Finvarra asked.

"Yes," I answered. "For now, at least."

Finvarra nodded. "I am glad to hear it."

We sat in silence for a few moments. Surely this couldn't have been the only reason Finvarra wanted to see us? I mean, she could have asked us this in passing at any point during the upcoming Airechtas. It was little more than small talk, really. Why the urgent meeting? Why the privacy?

As though my silent questions had floated across the coffee table, Finvarra shifted slightly in her wheelchair, wincing, and folded her hands in her lap. "You are probably wondering why it is I have asked you here today. I deliberated for a long time about whether I would. I nearly did so when you were here in October, but talked myself out of it. However, the Airechtas is upon us now, and I have run out of time."

I squirmed a little. What did she mean, run out of time? She was obviously very ill, but surely wasn't days from death. Or was she? Carrick was certainly watching her intently, as though assessing the toll that each movement, each word, was taking on her meager store of energy.

"As you may already have deduced, there is an empty seat on our Council to be filled at this year's Airechtas. Marion has been stripped of her position as part of the punishment for her actions of three years ago. I assume you know that Marion's Council seat once belonged to your family?"

Hannah and I nodded. Karen had told us as much when we had

first arrived at Fairhaven Hall. Apparently our clan, the Clan Sassanaigh, had been one of the most powerful for centuries, until our mother's disappearance and attendant dishonor had caused our fall from grace.

"I must now confess something to you both. I was primarily responsible for your clan's loss of that seat. I had just become High Priestess, and I was determined to establish my authority in the midst of a messy and divisive situation. You never knew your grandmother."

It wasn't a question. She knew that our grandmother had died before we were born. The stress of our mother's disappearance and our grandfather's accident with the Gateway took a fatal toll on her heart.

"She was a... difficult woman. She did not have many friends on the Council by the time your mother ran off. She had played the system too many times, become entangled in too many underhanded bargains and betrayed too many alliances. When the opportunity came to strip her of her Council seat, I leapt at it. I knew it would be a popular decision, ensuring that many would be loyal to me going forward."

She stared at us as though waiting for us to comment on this political chess gambit, but we knew better. When we didn't offer words of support or condemnation, she went on.

"Your grandmother ought to have borne the weight of her own mistakes, but not those of your mother. Still, I raked her over the coals for a situation she could not possibly control. When word reached me shortly thereafter of her death, I was quite relieved. She could not cause trouble, could not bring her political prowess to bear on me for what I had done to your family. I could not have hoped for a cleaner ending to the scandal. The guilt for my part in it would not come until many years later."

She looked down at her hands and then quickly away again, as though she had forgotten how skeletal they had become and couldn't bear to be reminded. "I did not see my motives then as selfish, but I recognize them as such now. Your family gave centuries of devoted service to the Council, but all I could think about was elevating my own power and status. I told myself that I was doing it for the good of the Northern Clans, but that was merely an excuse, a paper-thin shroud that tore away at the slightest touch, exposing what I really was."

"Why are you telling us this?" I asked suddenly. It was like listening to someone in confession, and I couldn't stand the guilt of it all. "It doesn't matter to us what happened back then, honestly. We don't care about that Council seat. I mean, sure, it would have been nice for someone other than Marion to have had it, but—"

"I am telling you," Finvarra interrupted, "because it matters to me. I am reaching a point where the mistakes of the past are hanging like stones around my neck. I cannot escape the weight of many of them, and shall have to drag them through the Gateway with me."

I squirmed. She was talking about her own death so matter-of-factly. We dealt with death every day, but to be able to face it yourself with such detached composure? I couldn't help but admire her strength.

"But this mistake," she went on, pointing a quaking finger at the two of us, "I have the opportunity to fix, and I will take it."

Hannah and I looked at each other, mystified. "Fix it how?" Hannah asked.

"The seat that once belonged to your family is now open. Your family is part of the Durupinen once more. I think you should run for the open seat and reclaim your family's legacy."

4

PROS AND CONS

I BLINKED. Beside me, Hannah may as well have been made of stone. Only a tiny exclamation of "Oh, shit!" from Milo intruded on the surreal quality of the moment.

"Come again?" I whispered.

"Tomorrow at the opening of the Airechtas, the Council will hear nominations for the open seat. It will be one of the first orders of business. I intend to nominate the Clan Sassanaigh. I am hoping you will accept the nomination."

"I... I don't... what?" I stuttered helplessly. I looked at Hannah for support, but she was staring at Finvarra as though she had just suggested that we jump out of the window behind her.

"You want one of us to be on the Council?" I asked.

"I know that your aunt will have nothing to do with it. She has made it very clear over the past few years that she has no intention whatsoever of jeopardizing the life and career she has built to take up the mantle. But you girls are young. You have not yet carved out a path. The options lay before you, as numerous as the stars in the sky. I am merely presenting one of them for you to consider, a constellation that may not have caught your eye."

I swallowed, but it did not help me find more of my voice; my throat suddenly felt like it was full of sand. "I still don't understand. You all hate us... don't you?"

Finvarra shook her head impatiently. "That is a juvenile interpretation, and I think you know it."

"Well, if we're so juvenile, I can't imagine why you'd be offering us this opportunity," I said, a spark of anger cutting through my shock. "Have a good long look at how we've been treated here from day one and then you tell me how we're supposed to interpret the Council's feelings!"

Finvarra closed her eyes and pressed her fingers over them, as though her head was beginning to ache. Carrick slid forward a few feet, hovering like a concerned shadow, but Finvarra merely sighed and looked up at us again. "Forgive me. I do not wish to argue with you. I merely meant that there are many complicated emotions surrounding the Prophecy and your role in it, but hatred is not one of them. I will not deny that some Council members fear you and your abilities. Others simply mistrust you because you grew up away from our ways and traditions. But there are those among us who believe you would be an excellent addition to the Council."

"And are these individuals on drugs, or just crazy?" I asked politely. Milo burst into nervous, maniacal laughter, which he quickly stifled. Hannah elbowed me hard in the ribs.

"What Jess means is, it seems unlikely that anyone would want us on the Council," Hannah said. "We haven't exactly had a warm reception since we've been back here."

Finvarra nodded. "I do not deny that there are those who will not understand my decision to nominate your clan. However, there will be many more who will see your history, your abilities, and your perspective as an asset to our Council."

"Did Karen know about this?" I asked. So help me, if she knew this was coming and didn't warn us...

"Not in the slightest. I imagine her shock would mirror your own," Finvarra said. "I am preparing myself for what will surely be a devil of a phone call, in fact."

It was a joke, but I didn't laugh. I couldn't even smile. I could not seem to form a complete thought; my brain was sputtering inside my skull, like an engine that wouldn't turn over. What Hannah said next further incapacitated my ability for coherent speech.

"What do you think, Carrick?" she asked.

Carrick looked positively alarmed at being addressed, but he recovered quickly. Throwing a quick glance at Finvarra, he said, "I do not pretend to understand all of the inner workings of Council politics," he began carefully, "but I am sure that your experiences with the Council, especially your negative ones, will have endowed you with some strong opinions about how things should be done differently. Joining the Council would ensure that those opinions would be heard and respected."

Finvarra smiled indulgently at Carrick, and I was seized by a sudden suspicion that she had fed him the answer through their connection. Could he really give us his honest opinion while in her presence?

Carrick did not stop there though, and I was quite sure that his next words were his own. "In her time here, your mother saw much she would have liked to change. I believe Elizabeth would have leapt at the chance to enact some of those changes."

I could not tell how these words affected Hannah. Her face, though thoughtful, remained inscrutable. For me, they were like a sucker punch to the stomach. There was no way that dragging my mother into this conversation was going to help me make up my mind. The mention of her name merely added another log to the fire of confusion burning inside me.

Perhaps some of this confusion was showing on my face, because Finvarra cut in, her voice calm. "I do not expect you to make a decision here and now. I only wished to warn you that the nomination is coming. You are free to accept or decline as you see fit. I have no expectations about your decision, and I make no guarantees about the outcome of the vote, should you decide to run for the seat. It is simply my wish to give you the opportunity to reclaim what should have been yours. Please consider it."

It felt like a dismissal. Hannah and I looked at each other and then stood up, turning for the door. But a question bubbled up from deep inside me and I had to ask it, no matter how rude it sounded.

"Finvarra, you and I have never gotten along. From the beginning, I resented being here, and you resented having me here. We've had more than our fair share of arguments. I harbor no illusions that you actually like me."

"I don't have to like you to nominate your clan for the Council," Finvarra pointed out.

"No, but you do have to respect us, and I'm not convinced that you do," I said. "So, I have to ask: how much of this nomination is because you think we really would do well on the Council, and how much is because you're trying to ease your own burden of guilt?"

If Finvarra was offended, she did not let on. Perhaps she had no energy left for such taxing shows of emotion. She merely looked thoughtful for a moment, weighing the question carefully before answering it.

"I am not sure. It is certainly some of both. But I will say this. I do respect you. You have faced great hardships, and you have overcome them. You have persevered against incredible odds and shown great bravery and resourcefulness. Either one of you would be a credit to the Council of the Northern Clans, whether it eases my guilt to see you there or not."

§

"So, that was bizarre, huh?" I said across the space between our beds. Hannah and I hadn't slept in the same room since college. There was something warm and comforting about it, a biological something that felt soothing and complete when I could hear my twin breathing in the same room. How strange that I had never realized I was missing it for so many years.

"Very bizarre," Hannah agreed. "That was not what I was expecting Finvarra to say, that's for sure."

"No kidding."

"So, what are we going to do?" Hannah asked, after a moment of silence.

"About what?" I asked.

"About the nomination. When she calls for us to run for the seat, what are we going to say?" Hannah asked.

I rolled over and looked at her, incredulous. "What are we going to say? Are you really asking that?"

She frowned at me. "Yes, of course I am."

"We're going to politely decline. Thanks, but no thanks," I said.

Hannah didn't answer. She looked back up at the ceiling, her face thoughtful.

"Aren't we?" I asked. "What possible other response could we have?"

"You don't think we should at least consider running for the Council seat?" Hannah asked quietly. Her shoulders were tensed, anticipating the intensity of my reaction.

"Us. On the Council. Here. At Fairhaven." I said blankly.

"Yes."

"You think we should consider it."

"I think it's worth discussing, yes," Hannah said.

I sat up, tucking my legs under me and staring at Hannah. "Say that again with a straight face."

She too sat up, tucking her knees up to her chin and wrapping her arms around them. "I think we should discuss the option of taking the Council seat."

We sat staring at each other in absolute silence for a solid ten seconds.

"Say something, Jess," Hannah finally said.

"I can't," I said. "My brain just exploded."

"Oh, come on!" Hannah cried. "Is it so absurd that we just talk about it? It's a big opportunity to just blow off without a second thought."

I took a deep breath and blew it out slowly in an attempt to remain composed. "Hannah, where do we live?"

Hannah hesitated, as though this was a trick question. "Salem."

"That's right. And where is Salem?"

"In Massachusetts."

"And is Massachusetts located in the English countryside?"

Hannah rolled her eyes. "No."

"No! And how about our jobs? Your graduate program? Our apartment? Our friends? Every plan we've ever made for our future? Are any of those things located in the vicinity of this godforsaken castle?"

"No," she said dully.

"Exactly! So, what is there to consider? When the Prophecy came to pass and we actually managed to survive it, we made a pact never to come back here if we could possibly help it. We've been forced to break that promise a couple of times, but by and large, we've stuck to it pretty damn well. What in the world would possess you to go back on it now?"

"I... I don't know. When we made that decision, there was no prospect of a Council seat," Hannah said.

"You're right, and if there had been, I would have run away even further and considerably faster!" I cried. "Are you telling me you actually want to take this seat?"

Hannah shrugged. "I don't want to dismiss it out of hand."

"So, you would consider quitting school, giving up on all your future plans, and moving here?" I asked.

"Well, it sounds ridiculous when you say it like that," Hannah said.

"That's because it is ridiculous! It is one hundred and fifty percent insane!" I cried. "What about becoming a social worker? What about helping kids like you get out of the system? What about all of the good you wanted to do?"

"Jess, I haven't decided anything yet. You are getting way ahead of me here, and it's starting to feel like an attack. Will you please just stop talking and listen to me?"

"But Hannah, this doesn't make any—"

"Jess, seriously, shut up!"

And I did. I shut up, mostly because I was shocked that my sweet and mild-mannered sister had just told me to shut up. She had never done that before, no matter how often I might have deserved it. She took advantage of my momentary silence and plowed on.

"I do want to do good," she said. "I'm not going back on any of that. But doesn't this Council thing seem like it might be an opportunity to do good? Just think about it, Jess. Just think of all the Durupinen rules and regulations and policies we have complained about since we got sucked into this system. Now imagine if we were actually in a position to change them!"

I had no desire to be in that position, but I humored her and let her keep talking.

"Just think about how long some of those Council members have been here. The same families. The same representatives. The same ideas and traditions, just recycled over and over again. What if someone could come in and shake things up? What if some new blood is exactly what this Council needs to force it out of the Dark Ages and into the 21st century!"

"And you think we should be that new blood?"

Hannah bit her lip. "I don't think we should completely rule out the possibility. I... I think we might actually be able to do a lot of good here, too. Imagine, somewhere in the world, two girls just like we were: lost, confused, terrified about what was happening to them. Now what if we could enact policies and safeguards so that no one was ever left in the dark like that again?"

This brought me up short. "I... that would be good, I guess."

"Exactly. And who's to say anyone else on that Council would ever even consider addressing that issue? They're all generations deep, steeped in Durupinen culture from the time they can speak. Wouldn't it be nice for the outsiders and the reluctant ones to have a voice in that room?"

"Well, sure, but..."

"Just imagine if someone on that Council had been looking out for us instead of for themselves—if someone had had our backs when we got here. Things might have gone very differently," Hannah said.

48

"That's not really fair," I said, starting to feel defensive because she was making so much sense. "Celeste was there for us. And Fiona is a great mentor."

Hannah raised one eyebrow. "Jess, the first time you met her, she threw a chair at your head, didn't she?"

"Well, yeah, but once she resigned herself to the fact that I wasn't going anywhere, she got over it," I said. I wasn't quite sure how, but all of a sudden I was practically yelling at her.

"My point is that it all could have been so much easier," Hannah said. "And I'm not just talking about us! Think about how many times you've complained about something the Council said or did!"

"Exactly! And they're not going to change just because we're around! I don't want to subject myself to them on a regular basis!"

"Neither do I, particularly, but I might be willing to, if it meant we could enact a decision based on common sense instead of tradition! There could be a voice for the way things should be done instead of the way things have always been done!"

I shook my head. She was making too much sense, and I was determined not to be influenced in the slightest. "I get it. I just don't see why that voice has to be us."

Hannah laid back down. "It doesn't have to be us. I just think we should consider it, that's all. Just consider it. You honestly couldn't think of a single Durupinen policy you'd like to change? Any mandates you'd like to help overthrow? This could be our chance."

She was staring at me, eyebrows raised and a knowing look in her wide brown eyes. I felt the heat rise to my face and I looked away. She didn't need to say anything else. I knew exactly what she was talking about, and it was probably the only thing in the world that could convince me to consider Finvarra's offer.

I wasn't sure how much Hannah knew about Finn and me, but I didn't underestimate her intelligence. She was one of the most quietly observant people I'd ever met. I knew she had her suspicions. She hadn't asked me outright if Finn and I were together, but I knew that that was out of respect for me. We were close, but we didn't force each other to confide in one another. Maybe it was because we had spent so long apart that we could allow each other this space without resentment. If one of us said that we didn't want to talk about something, that was the end of it. Still, though I had never told her that Finn and I were together, she found little ways to hint at her suspicions. When Finn came over to our apartment, she would always find a reason to excuse herself, so we could be alone. When he called, she always handed me the phone. And she smiled at me in these moments, just a little. Because of course, she knew.

She knew that Finn and I were in love. She knew that we were secretly seeing each other. She also knew that there was a very good reason my relationship with Finn was completely under wraps. If the Durupinen or the Caomhnóir ever found out we were together, we would likely never see each other again.

I was not being dramatic. For centuries, relationships between Caomhnóir and Durupinen had been forbidden because of the very Prophecy Hannah and I had been the subject of. The Prophecy had spoken of twins, born of the relationship between a Durupinen and a Caomhnóir, who would have the power to save or to destroy the entire Gateway system. Trying to prevent the Prophecy from coming true—and because none of them had ever read even a single Greek tragedy, apparently—the Durupinen had instituted the ban on these relationships and brutally punished those who broke the law. Of course, their attempt to avoid the Prophecy only served as the vehicle to bring it about. But we had survived it. Hannah and I had saved the Gateway system, not destroyed it, and a centuries old fear was laid to rest. But in its wake, the law against Durupinen-Caomhnóir relationships remained, and Finn and I were forced to live a life in the shadows, unless someone fought to overturn it.

Someone like me. Damn it.

I had absolutely no desire to voice any of this, so after several minutes of loaded silence, I muttered, "I didn't realize you were so political."

"I don't think I am, really. But when something like this falls in your lap, you can't just ignore it. Not even you, Jess."

The stubborn childish part of me longed to shout, "I can, too!" I grudgingly told it to shut up. Instead I said, "Okay, okay, I will think about it."

Hannah's expression cleared. She gave me a small smile. "That's all I'm asking. Thank you."

"Whatever. Now can we talk about something else? Like, anything else?"

"Sure."

In the silence that followed we both cast around for something to say. Then, in a very different voice than before, Hannah said, "So, Finvarra is really sick, huh?"

I sighed. This wasn't really what I had in mind when I suggested a topic change, but I couldn't exactly ignore it. "Yeah. It's awful, isn't it?"

"Well, I was just thinking... what does that mean for Carrick?"

"Obviously it must suck for him. I mean, he's devoted first his life and then his afterlife to her protection, and now this terrible thing is happening to her and he can't protect her from it. I bet he's feeling pretty helpless right now," I said.

Hannah nodded. "Yes, that's true, I'm sure, but that's not what I meant."

"Oh," I said, frowning. "What did you mean, then?"

Hannah hesitated, as though she wasn't even sure she wanted to continue. "Well, he's Bound to her. Their souls are connected. He can't Cross as long as she's alive."

"Yes, that's right."

"But she's dying. So..."

She didn't need to finish the thought. The realization hit me and then dropped like an anchor into the pit of my stomach, making me feel instantly sick. It hadn't even occurred to me what Finvarra's death might mean for Carrick. Carrick's soul and Finvarra's soul were linked. When she died, and her soul Crossed over, Carrick would be able to Cross as well, no longer tied to the living world. Would he choose to go? I would never presume for a second that he should choose to stay because of us, and yet a startling array of emotions flew through my head, leaving me dizzy and confused.

On the night I had discovered that Carrick was our father, he told me he had Bound himself to Finvarra so that he could continue his search for our mother and, by extension, for us. He stayed behind for us, though we were not the ones he was Bound to. Was it so presumptuous to think he might choose to stay behind for us again? At the same time, it felt completely insane that he would make such a decision. He barely knew us. Our relationship was a mere product of circumstance, not any sort of deep or evolving state. We'd spoken only a handful of times since we'd discovered who he was. And now that our mother was gone, and the Prophecy had blown over at last, was the paper-thin bond between us enough to keep him here? I could not even begin to articulate any of this. It churned and roiled inside me.

"He'll have a choice to make, I guess," I said.

"No, Jess, I don't think he will. I think he has to Cross with her," Hannah said very quietly.

My pulse quickened with a touch of something that smacked of panic. "He does?"

"I think so," Hannah said again. "I researched everything I could about being Bound, after Finvarra told us that Milo had Bound himself to me. I wanted to know every detail about what Milo had done, because I felt so guilty about it. Anyway, I read that the Bound spirit can stay in the living world as long as half of the Gateway he is Bound to is still alive, but when both the Key and the Passage have Crossed over, he must follow them. His soul must follow where they lead, even in death. The bond can only be broken in the Aether."

My mind was refusing to absorb this information. "What are you telling me?" I asked.

"Finvarra's sister died several years ago. When Finvarra dies, and it looks as though that day isn't far away, Carrick will have no choice but to go with her," Hannah said, her voice now a tremulous whisper.

Wow, the sucker punches to the face just kept on coming today, didn't they? First, we had to see Finvarra, whose deterioration was a direct result of our actions. If we hadn't exposed the rampant Leeching process in the Northern Clans, she could still be using it to keep herself healthy. And now, before we'd even considered whether we would try to get to know him, our father would likely be gone from this world, too.

"Jess?"

"Yeah."

"Are you okay?"

"Yeah."

"I'm sorry. I didn't want to just tell you like that. I thought you realized..."

"I probably should have, but I didn't."

"I'm sorry," Hannah whispered. "In retrospect, that was a lot to drop on you in one conversation."

"It's fine. I'm fine."

I'd used the magic code word for "I don't want to talk about this anymore", and Hannah took it as such. She murmured "Good night," and rolled over. I listened to the sounds of her breathing ease gradually into the steady patterns of sleep, which refused to rescue me from my own churning thoughts until nearly dawn.

ELEANORA: 1 MAY 1864

1 May 1864

I open you tonight, Little Book, for the first time in nearly a month, but it is with great need of your solace. If I do not put these words down right now by the light of this sputtering candle, I fear I may drown in a tumultuous sea of their terrible and immutable truths. Forgive me if I sound quite melodramatic, but the events of this night have left me in a state of despair.

I have been seeing ghosts nearly all of my life. You might think, knowing what you do of my mother, that this would shock and distress her, but you would be mistaken in your suppositions. The truth of that matter is, my ability to see ghosts has been inherited directly from her. Her lineage has been a part of the Durupinen for centuries, and her own skill at communication with the dead is outmatched only by her ability to camouflage it from others. Indeed, I have never once, in all my nearly eighteen years, seen her flustered by the presence of a spirit. In this regard, there is much to be learned from her.

The Durupinen always emerge in pairs. When I was a small girl, my mother told me that, someday, I would have a companion in my Visitations, someone with whom to share the burden, and that would make it lighter and easier to bear. That day arrived today, or rather, in the dead of this night.

My heart is still racing from the screams that echoed through the house mere minutes ago, and tore everyone from their slumber. The screams were issuing from my sister Hattie's room. As my own bedroom is closest to hers, I arrived first and I found her cowering under her bedclothes as the spirit of a housemaid apologized over and over for waking Hattie whilst she attended to her housekeeping duties.

We always knew there was a chance that Hattie would one day experience the Visitations. Even Hattie knew, though that knowledge could hardly prepare her for the ghastly reality of it. As a child, I longed for Hattie's gift to awaken, wishing, quite selfishly, to no longer be alone in my abilities. But there in Hattie's darkened room tonight, cradling her in my arms and wiping the tears from her cheeks, I felt nothing but sadness, and a fervent desire to save her from the frightening place her world has now become.

What comfort can I offer her? What words of consolation? That she will grow accustomed to the unannounced guests? That there will come a day when the unexpected hiss of their voices in her ear will not curdle the blood in her veins? I cannot promise these things; the words are hollow and meaningless in the midst of this waking nightmare.

Our mother came at last to Hattie's room, and after much effort, managed to calm Hattie's fear enough so that she could fall asleep. But when she wakes again at last, it will be to stare into the unforgiving face of the same, immutable truth about herself and the dark and winding path along which we now must journey together.

The collar of my nightdress is damp and salty with Hattie's tears, and I cannot help but add my own, drenching the lace which is now more handkerchief than nightdress. Even as I write, our mother is making arrangements for us to travel to Fairhaven Hall, the ancient castle seat of our clan, where Hattie and I will begin our formal training as Durupinen. We could leave as soon as a fortnight from now. I am at once filled with excitement and trepidation. I long to learn the secrets of our gift, and yet I feel as though I am turning the page on a terrifying new chapter in my life and, once turned, I cannot go back. From this day forward, the spirits who have always hovered on the outskirts of my life will become the center of my existence. It is both humbling and daunting to know what has been entrusted to us. I must swallow my fear, however; I must be strong for Hattie, who has so little strength herself.

Eleanora

5

HOST

HANNAH WAS ALREADY AWAKE when I peeled myself out of bed the next morning. Milo was there too, perched on the edge of the fireplace like he was trying to warm himself. The firelight shimmered dully through him.

"Good morning, sleeping beauty!" he crowed at me.

I grunted acknowledgment of his existence, and noted that he was being much too nice to me, which meant that Hannah had already told him all about our conversation from the previous night. This didn't exactly bother me; it was an unspoken rule that we had no real secrets from Milo. He was too deeply connected to our emotions and our thought patterns for much to get by him, so there was really no point in trying to exclude him. I suppose I should have been grateful that she'd already filled him in; that way I wouldn't have to sit through the conversation all over again.

"Shouldn't you get going?" Milo asked me.

"Get going where? Are you saying real words? Why are you even attempting to speak to me before coffee?" I groaned, rolling back over.

"You've got that meeting, don't you?" he pressed.

"It sounds like English, and yet I cannot comprehend anything you are saying. Please leave a message at the beep," I said from beneath the muffling weight of my pillow.

"You can sass me all you want, but I don't think Catriona is going to accept 'lack of caffeine' as an excuse," Milo said.

I shook some of the cobwebs of sleep from the corners of my brain. "Catriona?"

"Yes, sweetness. Your Tracker mentor. With whom you are supposed to meet in half an hour," Milo said slowly.

I sat straight up. "Half an hour?" I repeated, mild panic zinging through me, rousing me.

"Yes, indeed," Milo said. "You can always take the chance that being late won't piss her off, but I don't think you're that delusional, even before coffee."

I leapt from my bed. "Why didn't anyone wake me up?" I cried.

"I forgot," Hannah said.

"I didn't," Milo said. "I just like to watch you freak out."

I tested the boundaries of my curse word vocabulary as I stumbled around the room, tossing off my pajamas and throwing on my jeans and a sweater, then attempting to brush my teeth and pull my boots on simultaneously. Fifteen minutes later I was jogging down the hallway, desperately hoping that, if I ran fast enough, I would have time to stop for sustenance in the dining room before I had to face Catriona.

One large, black, mouth-scalding cup of coffee later, I found Finn waiting in the entrance hall for me, standing at attention with his chest thrown out like he was patrolling the gates of Buckingham Palace. Several other Caomhnóir stood talking nearby, and so I dug into my memory, trying to remember how we used to speak when we both thought we loathed each other. This was not easy, since what I really wanted to do was throw my arms around him.

"Hey," I said, trying to sound indifferent at the sight of him.

He stopped short, his eyes wide. "Your hair."

I pulled at a lock self-consciously. "What about it?"

"It's... different."

"I dyed it," I said with a shrug. He just continued to stare so I said pointedly, "What are you doing here?"

"Waiting for you, of course," he said curtly.

"For me? Why?" I asked.

"You have your meeting in the Tracker office this morning with Catriona," he replied.

I laughed. "Yeah, I know I do. That's where I'm headed. That still doesn't explain why you're here, though."

"Well, I would think that was fairly obvious. I'm coming with you," he said.

I glanced at the other Caomhnóir in the corner. Was this an act for their benefit, or was he actually serious? "And why, exactly, would I need you to come with me?"

"For confirmation. No doubt she will be asking further questions regarding Whispering Seraph. I was also present, and can corroborate any answers that you provide to her," Finn said swiftly, as though he had prepared the answer verbatim, and was merely waiting for the appropriate moment to give it.

I shrugged. "Suit yourself. But you're wasting your time, Finn. I don't need you there."

He inclined his head, still unsmiling. "I would prefer to be present, and unneeded, than needed and not present," he said.

I snorted with laughter and set off down the hallway. His heavy clunking steps fell in behind mine. We walked along several long hallways, not speaking to each other. The further we got from the entrance hall, the fewer people we passed, until we reached a narrow staircase and found ourselves completely alone.

I sighed as though I'd been holding my breath since the moment I'd seen him. "I really hate this," I said.

"Hate what?" he asked.

"This!" I said, and I gestured to what felt like the gaping space between us, standing two steps apart from each other. "And I hate talking to you like that."

"That's how all Durupinen talk to their Caomhnóir," Finn pointed out.

"I know, and it just reminds me how royally screwed up the entire dynamic is. Two people who have to work so closely together for so many years should not be interacting with each other like that. I mean, how can they possibly function with such ingrained disrespect in every interaction?"

Finn shrugged. "It's just the way it's always been done. I, for one, never questioned it for a moment, until I met you."

"It just doesn't feel right, especially now."

"Just keep reminding yourself that it's vital for our cover. Honestly, you do it very well. If I didn't know better, I'd almost swear you despise and resent me," Finn said, and he smirked at me.

"I know! That's why I hate it!" I said. "I don't even like to pretend those things! It makes me feel terrible."

"I know something that will make you feel better about it," he said.

"Oh really? And what's that?" I grumbled, crossing my arms.

"This." And he reached out and grasped my arms, pulling me down onto his step and kissing me fiercely. I gasped in surprise but recovered, throwing myself into the kiss gratefully. My heart beat hard and fast against the inside of my chest, as though it were trying to break free of my ribs and shoot straight between his, nestling in there next to the heart whose call it longed to answer. When we broke apart a few moments later, we were both short of breath.

"What's gotten into you?" I panted.

"What do you mean?" he asked.

"You're breaking our rules. You know, the ones that *you* insisted we abide by to make sure our relationship stays a secret," I said. "Not that I'm complaining, believe me."

"You started it," he shot back.

"Excuse me? You kissed me! How did I start it?" I said with a hint of a laugh.

"Look at you. A stunning new hairstyle and you just sprung it on me with no warning! You have no business looking that beautiful on a Monday morning. How is a man supposed to control himself?"

I laughed outright. "You're delusional. I've only been awake for twenty minutes. I haven't even unpacked my makeup. I look like absolute hell."

He reached down, took my hand, and lifted it to his mouth, planting a kiss on the smooth underside of my wrist. "Hell," he said softly, "is utterly lovely."

I smiled, but it faded as quickly as it had come. It was hard to revel in a moment that I knew we had stolen, like criminals, from the hours of feigned indifference and disdain we would have to endure while we were here. It was starting to wear me down, and Finn knew it.

"As much as I love hiding in a darkened stairwell with you, we should probably get going," I said. "It wouldn't be smart to keep Catriona waiting."

Finn squeezed my hand once, and then dropped it. "You're right, of course. Onward and upward, then."

The Tracker office was located on the fifth floor. I had been there twice before, once when it belonged to Marion, for a disciplinary meeting with Savvy, and the other to meet with Catriona to learn the details of our first ever Tracker case. I was no less nervous on this occasion than I was on the other two, and so I felt a distinct sense of resentment the moment I turned the corner and spotted the door.

Catriona had asked to meet with Hannah and me separately. It was an intimidation tactic and we both knew it. She wanted to make sure that both our accounts of the events at Whispering Seraph matched up. Finn said that it was standard operating procedure among the Trackers, and the Caomhnóir, too, but it still felt like Catriona was taking a bit more pleasure in it than was strictly necessary. Hannah's meeting would take place immediately following mine, so that there would be no chance to confer with each other in between. This made me feel like a criminal rather than one of Catriona's own mentees, not least because there were a few details of our mission we had decided to keep to ourselves. First, we agreed there would be no mention of my allowing Talia and Grayson to share their goodbye. The Durupinen were obsessive about secrecy, and so I was pretty sure I'd be raked over the coals for using a Melding casting to help the two of them.

The second secret was my own; well, mine and Milo's, as he was the only one present at the time. When Catriona had refused to allow Irina to Cross, and instead had Caged her so that she could await official Durupinen justice, I had made a promise to Irina that I would find a way to set her free. Milo and I had both seen the utter horror her life had been in the Traveler camp, chained and guarded like a dangerous beast, all for the crime of wishing to Walk rather than remain trapped in her body. Whatever crimes she had committed at Whispering Seraph, the Durupinen had driven her to it, and I would not stand by and watch her punished for it. I had no idea yet how I would make good on that promise, of course, but I at least knew I needed to keep my mouth shut about it.

Finn took his position outside the door, at attention, his eyes scanning the surrounding hallway for signs of... I'm not really sure what. Danger, I guess? I snorted.

"If I get too rowdy in there, are you going to bounce me?" I asked in a murmur.

The corners of his mouth twitched, but otherwise he gave no indication that he had heard me.

The door to the Tracker office was cracked, but I knocked anyway.

"Enter, if you must," came Catriona's bored voice.

I pushed the door open to reveal Catriona sitting behind a desk, head bent over a comically large book; it was the kind of tome that you expected to see in the hands of venerable wizards or evil sorcerers in fantasy movies. As I crossed the room to the chair in front of the desk, she turned one of the thick, yellowed pages. I caught a glimpse of an illustration of what seemed to be a

Geatgrima, surrounded by dozens of runes. Then she dropped her head into her hands and began massaging her temples.

"Are you okay?" I asked her.

"My head is aching and fit to burst, and no wonder, trying to read through this bloody monstrosity," Catriona said. With a groan, she flopped forward, thumping her forehead against the book three times.

"Don't!" I cried instinctively.

"Why not?" came Catriona's muffled voice from under a curtain of glossy golden curls. "I can't possibly make it any worse, so I may as well knock myself unconscious."

"I... do you want me to come back later?" I asked, half-standing up.

"No, don't bother," Catriona replied, lifting her head so that her nose was an inch from the page beneath her. She had bags under her eyes and looked exhausted. "Ugh, I am too attractive to be stuck behind this monstrous thing doing bloody research." She slammed the book shut with a disgusted grunt; the pages expelled a musty cloud of dust into the air. "If the Council doesn't hire another Scribe soon, I'm going on strike."

"Do we have Scribes here?" I asked, surprised. I'd never met one at Fairhaven, though I had befriended one in the Traveler camp during my time there. In fact, if it hadn't been for Flavia and her general brilliance, I probably wouldn't have made it out of the Necromancer attack alive.

"Of course we do. They work in the library," Catriona said, swiping at the dust motes so that they wouldn't settle in her lustrous blonde hair. "You probably assumed they were librarians. But our most senior Scribe recently retired, and they've yet to find a suitable replacement. No one wants to be a Scribe anymore, and frankly I can see why. What a mind-numbing slog." She pushed the book aside and settled back in her chair. "Well, enough of that. On to something else tedious. I've got a fair amount of paperwork to go through with you."

"Really?" I asked. "That sounds... boring."

Catriona smirked. "Oh, it is, I assure you. Lest you thought Tracker work was all danger and glamour, let me set you straight." She reached into her bottom drawer to extricate a large, overstuffed folder full of papers, and slammed it onto the table in front of us.

"What exactly do I need to fill all of this out for?" I asked. "I gave a statement to you right after we left Whispering Seraph. What's left to do?"

"Everything you said, along with everything your sister, Caomhnóir, and Spirit Guide said, has been compiled into a testimony file that will be turned over as evidence to the Traveler Clan. They'll use it in the Walker's trial."

"Irina," I said, more sharply than I intended. I had to make a conscious effort to keep my voice as casual as I could as I went on, "Her name is Irina. So, have they set a date for the trial yet?"

Catriona shrugged unconcernedly. "Not that I'm aware of, no. Although when they do, you'll likely get called to testify, so I daresay you'll know before I will."

My heart leapt into my throat, where it nearly choked off my next words. "Testify? In front of the Traveler Council?"

"Yes, of course," Catriona said, as though this were a longstanding arrangement instead of entirely new information. "Do forgive me, but I assumed you had the most basic of understandings of how trials work. They will undoubtedly want to question you about what you witnessed. You will all need to testify, I expect."

I nodded, but my brain was whirring. When last I'd seen Irina, trapped and despairing in the basement of Whispering Seraph, I'd had no idea how I would make good on the promise I'd made to her. Now, it seemed the Travelers themselves might present me with an opportunity.

"Do you know where she is now? I asked.

Catriona looked up at me squinting, one hand pressed to her forehead. "Who?"

"Irina," I said, looking at Catriona with some concern now. "Are you sure you're okay?"

"I'm fine, I'm fine. Leave off me," Catriona snapped. "Irina was taken to the Traveler camp and returned to her body. She's not been transferred to a *príosún*. The High Priestess Ileana informed us that they have adequate means to keep her locked up until her trial can commence."

"Yeah, they certainly do," I muttered bitterly.

"Look, I know you were worried about that Walker, but believe me, you're wasting your time," Catriona said. "The best thing you can do for her is to finish this bloody paperwork, so they can proceed with the trial. First off, we've got to go through your statement that you gave when we debriefed at Lafayette Boarding House," She pulled a thick packet off the top of the pile and slid it across the desk to me. "It's been transcribed from the audio recording I made of your interview, so I need you to read through and make sure that everything looks accurate. Sign the bottom of each page as you finish it."

"Okay," I said.

"Be thorough, now. By signing, you're swearing that everything in your statement is true," Catriona said sharply.

"Mm-hmm," I said, keeping my eyes on the pages in front of me. I didn't want my face to give away the twinges of nervousness I felt at her words, knowing what I'd intentionally left out of my statement.

For a few moments, there was no sound in the room except for the gentle crackling of the fireplace in the corner, and the occasional rustle of a paper as Catriona occupied herself with some work. It felt strange, reading my own words on a page, full of "ums" and "wells" and other things I never realized I said so often. It was like having an out of body experience, so I felt startled, and even a little disoriented, when Catriona suddenly spoke a few minutes later.

"Where am I?"

I looked up sharply. "What did you say?"

She looked up from her papers, brow furrowed. "Sorry?"

"What did you just say?" I repeated.

She looked at me like I'd lost my mind. "What are you talking about?"

We stared at each other for a moment. Had I imagined it? "Didn't you just say something to me?"

"No, but I will ask you this: how are we meant to get through all of this if you can't focus on one simple task?" Catriona snapped.

"I... okay. Never mind," I said, too confused even to retort. I looked back down at my paper, trying to find where I'd left off. I groped around on the desktop for the pen and had just set it to the bottom of the first page to sign when it happened again.

"What is this place?"

There was no mistaking it this time. Catriona had definitely spoken. That was unmistakably her voice. I looked up at her again and saw her just as before, poring over the book in front of her, seemingly oblivious to what I had just heard.

"Catriona?" I said tentatively.

She did not answer. Was this supposed to be some kind of a joke? I leaned in, taking a closer look at Catriona's face. At first glance, her eyes had seemed focused on the page in front of her, but now that I was looking more closely, I could see that her eyes had glazed over and slid out of focus.

"Catriona?" I said, louder this time. "Can you hear me?"

No response. No acknowledgement of my presence. A creeping feeling began to steal across my skin, plucking at the hairs and raising gooseflesh. Only one thing could cause that feeling, and yet, how was it possible? This office, like many of the rooms in this castle, was Warded.

"Finn?" I called out. My voice cut through the silence, higher and sharper than I'd intended, and the door flew open so fast it was as though he had already had his hand on the knob, anticipating trouble.

He barely managed to cling on to his detached demeanor. "Jess? Catriona? Everything alright in here?"

"No, there's something wrong with Catriona!" I said, not taking my eyes off of her.

"What do you mean, wrong?" Finn asked, taking a cautious step forward.

"She was complaining of a bad headache when I came in, and then we were just sitting here, going through these papers and she started... talking."

Finn frowned at me. "Talking? And that's strange?"

I shook my head impatiently. "She was just sort of blurting things out, but she didn't seem to know she was doing it!"

"What sorts of things?" Finn asked.

"I think the first time she said, 'Where am I?' and the second time it sounded like, 'What is this place?' She didn't even hear herself do it!"

Finn's expression turned wary. He threw a cursory glance toward the doorway to confirm what we both already knew: the room was properly Warded. Then he took several cautious steps toward Catriona, who continued to stare blankly down at the book in front of her as though she were in a trance.

"Catriona?" Finn asked, his voice light and friendly. "Catriona, can you hear me?"

A shudder ran through Catriona's face, making her mane of hair tremble, but otherwise giving no indication that she had heard him.

"Catriona, can you answer me? Can you tell me if you are alright?" Finn said as he slowly rounded the corner of the desk. He kept his hands up and visible in front of him, to show he was not a threat to her.

Several long seconds of silence, and then, "Where am I?"

Catriona's voice was completely devoid of its signature lazy drawling tone. Her words were quick, light, and higher pitched than any I'd ever heard her utter. They also sounded scared.

Finn glanced quickly at me, then back at Catriona.

"You're in your office at Fairhaven Hall, Catriona," I said.

Catriona raised her head and looked directly at me, and it felt as though all the air had left my lungs. Her eyes, usually a bright blue, had been swallowed into wells of darkness. In that moment, there was one thing of which I was absolutely certain: the face may have been Catriona's, but the person staring out of those eyes was a complete stranger.

Catriona—or whoever she was—cocked her head to the side. "Who is Catriona?"

6

POSSESSED

F INN AND I LOOKED at each other again. I saw my own fear and confusion reflected in his eyes. He had no more idea what was happening than I did. I took a breath and tried not to panic. We were Durupinen. We spent our lives surrounded by the dead. It wasn't so strange to think that one might be using Catriona to communicate. After all, they used me all the time; they just tended to use my artistic skill rather than my voice and my body. It didn't necessarily mean that anything was wrong.

"You're Catriona," I said to her, trying to sound as reasonable and matter-of-fact as I possibly could. "That's your name."

Catriona shook her head so hard that her hair whipped around her like a tornado. "No, I do not know that name."

"Oh no. No, this isn't right," Catriona whispered, as sudden animal panic distorted her features. "No, this isn't right."

"What isn't right? I asked her.

"Closed! Closed! Locked up tight! She promised! She promised me!"

"Who promised you?" I asked. I kept it all conversational, like two friends chatting over a cup of tea.

Catriona's face, already porcelain, drained to a milky pallor. Her eyes widened. Then, with no warning at all, her arms began to flail. Her entire torso started shaking. She knocked the lamp and papers from her desk as the tremors became convulsions, and slid out of her seat onto the floor.

"She's having a seizure!" I cried, jumping up from my chair and darting to the other side of the desk. Finn ran over to join me, and we both knelt beside her, watching helplessly as she writhed.

"What should we do?" Finn asked, knocking the chair away from Catriona before she could concuss herself on one of the legs.

"I don't know!" I cried. "Fiona had a seizure kind of like this once, but it was a psychic drawing. This seems more like a Habitation, doesn't it?"

"There's a spirit in there, certainly," Finn said. "But I don't dare try to expel it, not without knowing more about how it got in there in the first place."

A loud, popping sound made both of us jump. A log on the fire had broken as it burned, and tumbled in two smoldering pieces onto the bed of ashes in the grate.

At the sound of it, Catriona opened her mouth and let forth a scream unlike anything I had ever heard. It seemed to contain several voices at once, each in terrible agony. Her back arched right off the floor, as though she were being lifted to her feet by an invisible hook attached to her sternum. Impossibly, she rose to her feet. Finn and I scrambled back from her in alarm as she continued to scream, but she was not looking at us. Her eyes were fixed, with breathtaking terror, on the fireplace at the far side of the room.

For a long, breathless moment, we both just sat there, immobile, watching her. Then she launched herself toward the fire.

"No!" Finn and I both shouted together, scrambling after her, but she didn't fling herself onto the flames. Instead she wrenched an enormous tapestry off of the wall and began using it to beat and smother the fire into submission. Choking smoke and ash filled the room as we dashed toward her. Finn reached her first. He threw his arms around her waist and heaved her away from the hearth. I tugged the heavy tapestry out of the embers and stomped on it where I could see the dry old fibers had begun to smolder. Catriona continued to kick and scream, flailing with unnatural strength to return to the fire, to dash it out at all costs.

"Jess, go for help!" Finn grunted as he struggled to keep a hold on Catriona.

"Finn, I can't leave you here! What if she—"

"Jess, go! Now! I can't hold her like this for much longer. We need help!" he growled. "Just listen to me for once and go!"

I was too scared to deliver my usual withering retort. I turned on my heel and fled the room. I tore down the hallway, skidding around the first corner and then nearly crying with relief at the sight of Seamus and two other Caomhnóir striding up the hallway. They froze when they saw my panic-stricken face, and without my even having to say a word, started running toward me.

68

"What is it, what's wrong?" Seamus called. One hand had flown to the Casting bag tied at his belt.

"It's Catriona," I said, turning and jogging with them back toward the Tracker office. "We were in a meeting together. One minute she's talking about paperwork, and the next she's possessed!"

"Possessed?" Seamus repeated, sharply. "What do you mean? Clarify yourself."

How much clearer did I need to be? "I mean that there is a spirit inside of her, and it took over her body!" I panted. "At least, I think that's what happened. Then she tried to attack the fireplace. Finn is in there with her right now. He's restraining her, but he needs help!"

We were heading straight for the doorway to the office. The Caomhnóir pulled ahead of me with their powerful strides. Braxton reached the office first, and had just put a foot over the threshold when it happened.

Catriona let loose a gut-wrenching scream, and an explosion of spirit energy burst from the room. All three Caomhnóir were blasted off their feet and slammed into the walls. I dove around the corner that led to the stairwell, tumbling down four stone steps before I could catch myself. I felt the blast of energy blow past the top of the staircase, and heard the stained-glass windows on both sides of the hallway above me explode. The rainbow shards hit the wall over my head and showered down on top of me like little daggered raindrops.

Catriona's scream went on, but no longer from the direction of the office. It was a part of the energy that had erupted outward, and I could hear it traveling through the halls above me, echoing off the stones, so that more and more screams seemed to join the first. Then all the screams died away, leaving a hollow silence in their wake.

For a long moment, nothing happened. I stayed frozen where I was, huddled on the stairs with my hands thrown over my head, braced for another explosion, but nothing happened. Gingerly, I pulled my arms away from my head, examining them as I did so. They were peppered with tiny cuts and gashes, a few of which were bleeding. I shook the bits of glass out of my hair and carefully clambered to my feet. As the shock wore off, my legs began to shake under me.

I peeked cautiously around the wall into the corridor above. All three Caomhnóir lay in heaps on the floor. Seamus and the young Caomhnóir were stirring, trying to pull themselves into seated positions. Braxton, who had taken the brunt of the blast through the open doorway, lay motionless against the wall at the base of one of the shattered windows.

I stumbled toward the office, terrified of what I might find on the other side of the door.

"Finn?" I called, my voice high and cracked with fear.

"Jess?"

I let out a cry of relief at the sound of his voice as I entered the room. Finn was still clutching on to Catriona, who now lay as limp and senseless as a ragdoll in his arms. The room had been utterly destroyed by the force of the blast. The massive desk had been flipped upside down, papers strewn everywhere. The chairs were little more than splintered piles of wood, and the windows here, too, had been blown out.

"Are you okay?" I asked him in a shaking voice, mastering the impulse to throw myself at him. "And Catriona... oh, God, is she..." I swallowed the word, unable to utter it.

"She's alive. Her pulse is racing, but she's breathing alright," Finn assured me. I noticed he had his fingers already pressed against Catriona's wrist.

"What happened in here?" I asked. "What caused the explosion?"

Finn lowered Catriona carefully to the floor, gently placing her head to rest against his leg. "She did it. Or the spirit did it, I suppose. I was struggling with her to keep her away from the fireplace, and then she just... lost it. She went still for a moment, and I thought she was giving up. And then suddenly she... well..." he gestured weakly around the room to indicate the destruction. "As soon as the explosion happened, it was like whatever was inside her was gone, and she went limp."

"So, you think the spirit is gone?" I asked.

Finn nodded. "I do. If that wasn't the spirit leaving her, I'm not sure what it could have been."

Seamus stumbled into the room, squinting dazedly around. "Everyone alright in here? What the bloody hell is going on?"

Finn launched into an explanation of what had happened. I was barely listening. I was staring at Catriona, whom I had never seen have a vulnerable moment since I'd met her. She was unfailingly in control, often bordering on apathetic, in every single interaction I'd ever had with her. Dramatic and emotional situations did not faze her. Devastation sometimes downright amused her. I had never even thought her capable of vulnerability, and so to see her there, huddled against Finn like a sleeping baby, was unnerving.

"I'll check the integrity of all the Wards here," Seamus said. "They must have been compromised, though how, I could not say."

"Not necessarily," I said, tearing my eyes from Catriona.

"Pardon?" Seamus asked. If he was trying to keep his disdain for me out of his voice, he was failing spectacularly.

"I just mean that, whatever spirit that was, it might have attached itself to her before she got to the office," I said, trying to sound reasonable instead of snarky. "Isn't it feasible that she and that spirit came into contact somewhere other than in this room?"

Seamus seemed too distracted to consider this properly. He acknowledged my words with a vague, "Mm-hmm," while he began an investigation of the office, examining all of the markings that adorned the doorframes and windowsills.

The young Caomhnóir poked his head in the door, clearing his throat to announce his presence. "Begging your pardon, Seamus," he said, and there was a tremor barely detectable beneath the forced toughness of his voice. "Braxton is still unconscious, sir. He's taken quite a knock to the head. I think he may need medical attention, sir."

Seamus did not pull his eyes from his work, but waved a hand over his shoulder. "Catriona should go to the hospital ward as well. Arrange it, Charles, and swiftly. Alert the Council. This matter will not go uninvestigated. Hostile spirits are not meant to enter this castle, and so if one has managed to breach the defenses, it must be addressed at once."

Charles clicked his heels together in a smart salute and bowed himself out. I stood awkwardly, unsure what I could do to help anyone in the room.

"Should I go and get help, too?" I asked.

Seamus shook his head. "Charles will take care of it. Stay here. The Council will no doubt have questions for you, and they cannot ask them if you are off traipsing about the castle."

I opened my mouth to argue that I had never traipsed in my life, thank you very much, but Finn shot me a warning look and I changed my mind. It was no good stirring the pot with Seamus, especially given his previous knowledge of my relationship with

Finn. For something to do, I pulled the tapestry further away from the still leaping flames in the fireplace and used the golden fire irons to sweep the scattered ashes back into the hearth.

It did not take long, though, for Celeste, Siobhán, Fiona, and several other Council members to arrive, along with Mrs. Mistlemoore, who ran the hospital ward. Behind them followed their assigned Caomhnóir, all on high alert like attack dogs that had scented something threatening in the air.

"What's happened here?" Celeste asked, wringing her hands. "Charles said Catriona has been attacked?"

As Mrs. Mistlemoore hurried over to examine Catriona, Finn and I tried, as best we could, to explain what had happened. With each word, the Council members' faces grew grimmer and grimmer. Meanwhile, Mrs. Mistlemoore was assessing Catriona. She pulled out all the things I would have expected to see in a medical bag; a blood pressure cuff, a stethoscope, and thermometer. But she also examined Catriona with a wide variety of Castings, encircling her head with a glossy black feather, then pressing an amethyst to various points on her body, and finally using a waxy pastel to mark her chest with a rune of protection.

"She'll need to be taken to the ward," Mrs. Mistlemoore announced, getting to her feet with some difficulty. "Something is Habitating inside her, that's certain. I'll need to perform further Castings to learn more, however."

"It's still in there?" I asked, surprised.

"That's what I said," Mrs. Mistlemoore said brusquely. "Why do you ask?"

"Well, it's just... we thought the explosion was something leaving her," I said. "What could that have been if it wasn't a huge burst of spirit energy?"

Mrs. Mistlemoore sighed. "There's no telling until I examine her further. But I will say that something still resides within her, and whatever it is has taken a very firm hold." She nodded to the Caomhnóir by the door, and then slipped past them to examine Braxton, who still lay motionless where he had fallen.

The rest of us watched in silent horror as Catriona was carried out on a canvas stretcher by two of the Caomhnóir.

Celeste turned to me. "Jess, we will undoubtedly need to speak to you and Mr. Carey further, but I can't say for sure when that will be. We will need to wait for Mrs. Mistlemoore to finish her examination, and for Seamus to finish his investigation here."

"Yeah, of course," I said, a tremor in my voice. "Whatever you need. I'll be back in my room."

Celeste nodded, then looked expectantly at Finn.

"I'll report back to the barracks now. You can reach me there," he said promptly.

"Very well," Celeste said. "I'll send for you both soon."

Interpreting Celeste's words as a dismissal, Finn and I exited the room. When we had put two floors safely between us and the chaos in the Tracker office, Finn reached out and gave my hand a quick squeeze.

"You're alright, are you?" he asked in a low voice as he strode along.

"I guess so, yeah," I said. "Kind of freaked out, but otherwise I'm okay."

We turned a corner and saw Hannah running toward us with Milo floating along behind her.

"Jess! Jess, are you okay? What's going on?" she gasped as she approached us.

"We're fine!" I said. Then I braced myself as she barreled into me, nearly knocking me over in a violent hug. For a little thing, she sure could pack a punch. "How did you even know something happened?"

"I was on my way up to my meeting with Catriona, and we saw the Caomhnóir carrying her down to the hospital ward on a stretcher!" Her eyes were full of tears.

"We asked them what happened to her, and if anyone else was hurt, but they basically ignored us," Milo said, rolling his eyes. "Sweet and accommodating, as usual."

Finn and I relayed the story to our second horror-struck audience in less than ten minutes.

"Catriona looked awful!" Hannah said with a shiver. "And there was something... strange."

"You think?" I muttered. "We've all seen a lot of spirit stuff, but I've never seen anything like that."

"Yes, you have!" Hannah said.

I turned to her. "What are you talking about? Did you listen to any of that story just now? When have we ever seen anything like that?"

Hannah was already shaking her head before I had stopped speaking. "No, no, no, I'm not talking about something we've seen, but something we've felt."

I looked at Finn, and then at Milo. Their faces were just as blank as my memory. "Nope, nothing springs to mind here. Enlighten me."

"Do you remember when we found Annabelle trapped in her flat by the Necromancers?" Hannah asked.

I nodded. Of course I remembered. I would never forget it. We had broken into the apparently empty apartment only to find Annabelle hidden in plain sight under a depraved Casting. The Necromancers had created a cage out of spirits they had ripped apart and woven back together like some ghostly Frankenstein's monster. I still felt sick to my stomach just thinking about it.

"Well, I didn't sense those spirits at first, because they weren't whole spirits. They were just... pieces, and so it took me longer to figure out what I was feeling," Hannah said.

"Yeah? And?" I prompted. I was still missing something.

"I just felt it again."

Finn and Milo and I gaped at her.

I swallowed back a hard lump of panic. "You..."

"I just felt it. The same sort of feeling. Again," Hannah whispered.

"Are you saying that Catriona is the victim of a Necromancer Casting?" Finn asked, his voice crisp and cutting with his own barely contained fear.

Hannah's eyes were beginning to fill with tears. "I don't know. I don't know for sure, but I do know what I felt—what I *sensed*—when Catriona was carried past me. It felt very similar to what I felt when we discovered Annabelle."

For a moment, we all just froze, horror-struck. Milo was the first to come to his senses.

"Well, let's go then!" he shouted suddenly. "What are we waiting for?"

"Go where?' Hannah asked.

"To the hospital wing! To the Council! To Finvarra's office! To the top of the North Tower with a freaking megaphone, if we have to!" Milo cried. "We are not going to ignore a single hint that the Necromancers might be involved, and neither is anyone else."

Hannah twisted the hem of her shirt nervously in her hands. "But what if I'm wrong?" she asked.

"What if you're not?" Milo shot back. "We were right last time, and it nearly meant the end of the world. We're not letting them ignore anything this time. I don't care how far-fetched it sounds."

"I agree," Finn said. "We cannot afford to take any chances in situations such as this. If you're wrong, Hannah, no harm done. But if you're right, we may just avoid another catastrophe."

Hannah looked at me for guidance and I nodded seriously at her. "I know you don't want to draw attention to yourself, or to anything that drags up the Prophecy again, but we can't keep this quiet."

Hannah closed her eyes for a moment, like she was saying a short prayer. Then she opened them and took a deep, steadying breath. "Okay. Who should we tell?"

Finn considered this for a moment. "Let's head to the hospital ward," he said at last. "This information might be of the most use to Mrs. Mistlemoore in treating Catriona. From there, we can determine what to do next."

We all agreed, and set off at once. We jogged along in the wake of Finn's enormous strides, no one speaking, each of us focused on fending off the fear.

ELEANORA: 18 JUNE 1864

18 June 1864

Dearest Little Book,

Did you think I had forgotten all about you? I have been at Fairhaven Hall for nearly a month, and I have been so busy that I've had not a moment to write about it! Between the classes and the mountains of work I must complete, my most fervent desire in the evening is to topple onto my bed and let sweet sleep wash over me.

I have always dearly loved learning, and never has the topic of my learning been so utterly fascinating! Most fortunately, Mother has been instructing us in Gaelic and Old Britannic since we were very small, or I expect the Castings would be quite daunting to learn. The library here is magnificent, and the grounds are beautiful. But I must say, the best part of being here is the lack of secrecy. For all my life, I have had to hide what I am and what I can do. It has, at times, been draining and isolating. I have often felt that my gift has stood as an invisible barrier between myself and other people. But here, I never need to hide the appearance of a Visitation. I never have to wear that mask of normalcy that was such a crucial part of my life back in London. I feel free—liberated for the first time since I was a very small girl. I have made several dear friends and have already found more enjoyment in my time here than I ever thought possible when setting out.

Hattie has had more difficulty in adjusting to our new lives, but she is managing, and I am doing all I can to assist her. The Visitations are still a new experience for her, and so she is often frightened and caught off-guard. She has not yet learned to recognize the subtle signs and changes that will warn her of the appearance of a spirit. Hattie has never been strong of will or of constitution—prone to illness and fainting. She has had several such fainting spells since we have been here, and I confess I sometimes fear that the strain of our gift is taking a toll on her health. However, there is no help for it: the Gateway resides inside us, and tame it we must, for it is our calling.

Mother, while pleased we are excelling in our training, has been insufferable on the subject of social obligations. She is unwilling to allow our responsibilities here at Fairhaven to interfere in any way with our participation in the season back in London. A long parade of balls, socials, galas, and events awaits us in the all-important aristocratic circles, and Mother will not hear of missing a single one. As a result, Hattie and I have already made three trips back to London just in the month we've been here. We've both begged her to allow us a respite from the social whirlwind, but she would not hear a word of our pleas. Our absence would be remarked upon, she insists, and only so many excuses can be made before rumors begin to fly.

I've stopped arguing with her. It isn't worth the energy that might better be spent elsewhere, such as mastering the many new aspects of our gifts. There are many here at Fairhaven who have been identified as having additional classifications beyond that of Durupinen. Our teachers have identified that there are those among us who have unusual ways of relating to and communicating with the spirits around us, and so therefore, some of the Apprentices receive additional training. For example, it has been determined that Hattie is an Empath. This means that she experiences Visitations in a heightened emotional state—that is to say, she experiences the emotions of spirits in a much more visceral way than the rest of us do. She has a mentor now who is working with her to help her exercise some measure of control over how these emotions affect her. I do not seem to have any special aspects of my gift, much to my relief. Some may consider their additional titles of Empath or Muse or Visionary a badge of honor, but I think the responsibility of being a Durupinen is more than enough to cope with.

And, as I might have predicted, I am nodding off over your pages, Little Book. Thank you as always for listening. You are the only place where all of the aspects of my life can converge without worry or consequence, and I am ever so grateful for you.

Eleanora

7

DIAGNOSIS

W HEN WE ARRIVED OUTSIDE of the hospital wing, Finn quickly grabbed the arm of a passing nurse, to ask if we could speak to Mrs. Mistlemoore.

The woman pursed her lips at us as though Finn were asking some enormous feat of her. "She's quite busy right now. I'll let her know, but I wouldn't expect her right away. Perhaps you should sit and wait."

"It's about Catriona," Finn said. "Hannah thinks she might—"

"Yes, yes, you can tell her when you see her," the woman said with a dismissive wave of her hand. "Now, if you'll excuse me, I'm needed inside." And with one last, harried look, she pushed the door open with her hip, backed through it, and disappeared.

"Whatever happened to bedside manner?" Milo asked with an offended snort. "That woman had entirely too much attitude!"

"She was busy, Milo," Hannah said quietly.

"And that gives her the right to be rude to people? Sweetness, I am an expert in the art of strategic sass, and I can guarantee you, her attitude had nothing to do with how busy she was. That woman is rude twenty-four seven, three sixty-five," Milo said, crossing his arms.

"Well, we'll just have to hope she's rude *and* efficient," Finn grumbled, peering through the windows at the top of the door.

"Can you see anything?" I asked him.

"Not as such, no. They've got Catriona at the other end of the ward, and there are screens up all around the bed. I can see people coming in and out."

"It's too bad we couldn't just flag down—"

A horrific scream cut off my words. I leapt up just in time to watch through the window as several people dove out from behind the screen around Catriona's bed, throwing their hands over their heads. Several lit candles flew through the air, smashed into the opposite wall, and extinguished.

"Tie her up, then," came a frantic woman's voice. "We've got to restrain her or we'll never get these Castings done! And for God's sake, move those candelabras back from the bedside before she kills us all!"

"What the bloody hell was that about?" Finn muttered.

"The fire again," I said softly. "Remember how badly she flipped out when she saw the fire burning in the fireplace in her office? She must have done the same thing when she saw the flames on the candles."

"We told them what happened with the fireplace," Finn said through gritted teeth. "Why in blazes are they putting open flames by her bed? Did they listen to a bloody word we said?"

"Evidently not," I said. "I don't think we should hold our breath that Mrs. Mistlemoore is coming out anytime soon, not if Catriona is throwing flaming objects all over the place."

"So, does this mean that the spirit that's possessing her has a fear of fire?" Milo asked. "That's got to be a clue, right?"

"We can't say for sure yet that it is a spirit," Finn said. "But that's a fair guess, Milo. Certainly, whatever it is does not want to be anywhere near an open flame. Whether that is out of fear or some other motivation remains to be seen." He peered back through the window, but all was quiet again. With a sigh of frustration, he shuffled back over to the bench and sat down. After another minute or so of fruitless spying through the window, I joined him.

We sat outside the hospital ward for at least an hour, alternating between long stretches of anxious silence and bouts of increasingly wild speculation. Periodically, commotion would break out on the other side of the doors, and we would all jump up to catch a glimpse of nurses or Caomhnóir rushing in and out of the bed space. At one point, Hannah spotted smoke wafting out from behind the screen, but it turned out to be a bunch of sage that one of the nurses was using for a Casting. Finally, Celeste, Siobhán, and Fiona came scurrying down the hallway, along with three other Durupinen I had never seen before. They did not stop to chat, however, sparing not even a glance for us as they pushed their way through the ward doors.

Another hour passed without a glimpse of Mrs. Mistlemoore. Finn was just suggesting that perhaps we should all go get something to eat and then come back, when Mrs. Mistlemoore finally emerged. She looked exhausted. She held a damp cloth in her hand, which she was using to wipe chalk dust and sage soot from her arms and face. We all stood up automatically at the sight of her, but she waved us back onto the bench.

"How is she?" Hannah and I asked in unison.

"Resting. Comfortably, I hope," Mrs. Mistlemoore said, with an edge to her voice that suggested she wasn't entirely confident in the "comfortable" part. "I'm sorry you've been waiting so long, but I couldn't leave her in that state."

"We understand," I said at once. "Do you know what's wrong with her?"

"Something is forcefully Habitating in her," Mrs. Mistlemoore replied, her expression grim.

"You mean she's possessed?" Milo asked, his mouth gaping in horror. "Like, Exorcist-style?"

"Durupinen do not employ the term 'possession.' That is a religious construct. But for all intents and purposes, yes, she is possessed," Mrs. Mistlemoore said wearily.

"But how could that have happened?" Finn asked. "The Wards on the castle ought to have prevented anything hostile from entering, shouldn't they?"

"Not if it was already inside her when she returned," Mrs. Mistlemoore said. "This is most likely something that attached itself to her while she was outside of the castle. It's the only way to explain how it slipped in past the Wards."

"How could something like that happen?" Hannah asked, her voice fluttery with panic. "Wouldn't she know if a spirit had Habitated?"

"That's not the kind of thing that escapes your notice," I added, an involuntary shiver running its icy finger up my spine. I had once barely survived a forced Habitation during my first paranormal investigation with Pierce, before I even knew I was a Durupinen. A Necromancer spirit named William had entered my body and tried to force his way through the Gateway, which was closed at the time. It was the most excruciating pain of my life; if Annabelle had not been able to expel him, the trauma of it could have killed me. And ever since then, when I'd allowed Milo to Habitate with my consent, there was still no ignoring the utterly bizarre sensation of sharing your physical and mental space with another soul.

81

"I agree, it would certainly be very difficult for a spirit to Habitate without the knowledge of the Host. Only non-sensitives, with no understanding of the spirit world, could possibly be an unwitting victim of a Habitation by a spirit. But the fact is... we are not entirely sure if it is a spirit," Mrs. Mistlemoore said. "We cannot establish contact with it, and we can't draw it out, which is worrisome. We ought to be able to expel it fairly easily, but the Castings are not working."

"That's why we're waiting here," Finn said. "Hannah sensed something when she was near Catriona, and she wants to tell you about it."

Finn looked pointedly at Hannah, who swallowed hard and cleared her throat. "Um, yes, that's right." With many nervous pauses, Hannah told Mrs. Mistlemoore about our experience with the spirit cage that the Necromancers had used to imprison Annabelle. She explained how the spirits had been somehow torn into pieces and then reassembled into a mass, and how she had felt a similar, fragmented spirit energy when Catriona was carried past her.

Mrs. Mistlemoore looked pale and nauseous at the very thought. "On that first occasion when you encountered these partial spirits, you couldn't sense them the way you could normal spirits? None of you?"

Hannah shook her head. "Not at first. It was very difficult to detect them, because they weren't whole souls. I couldn't Call them either. It was just this... muddled mass of confused energy. They camouflaged themselves."

"I could expel them, though," Finn said. "It took a massive effort, but I was able to shift them away from Annabelle so that we could rescue her. Whatever is Habitating in Catriona cannot be expelled."

No one spoke for a moment, trying to make sense of Finn's words. I'd forgotten that Finn had indeed been able to use his regular expulsion Casting to blast the spirits away. If he hadn't, we would never have even seen that Annabelle was lying right there on the bed in front of us.

"Well, we could still be dealing with the same thing," Milo said thoughtfully. "Those messed up spirits weren't inside Annabelle's body. They were just surrounding her, sort of hovering around her like a cage, weren't they? It might have been easier to expel them because they weren't actually attached to her?"

Mrs. Mistlemoore's thick gray eyebrows drew together as she mulled this over. "That is possible, of course. So very many things are possible when dealing with the spirit world. Just when I think I've seen it all, something new comes along to prove me wrong."

The door behind Mrs. Mistlemoore swung open and Celeste emerged, looking troubled.

"I've got to give an update to Finvarra," she said to Mrs. Mistlemoore, before noticing—for the first time, it seemed—that we were all standing there. "Jessica, what are you still doing here? You've given your statements about what happened, haven't you? You needn't feel obligated to stay. We can send someone to find you if we have any more questions."

"They've got more information for us, and it might be important," Mrs. Mistlemoore said, and she briefly recounted what we had just discussed.

§

Celeste turned to Hannah with wide eyes. "You are sure of this, Hannah?"

Hannah shook her head. "I'm not sure of anything. I just know I felt something very similar to the torn up spirits the Necromancers used."

"Do you know where Catriona was before returning to Fairhaven for the Airechtas?" Finn asked. "Is there a chance she might have come across a Necromancer Casting in her most recent work for the Trackers?"

"The other Trackers are retracing her steps as we speak, reviewing her case notes and work logs. Her Tracking partner, Katrina, has been summoned back from the field to help as well. The last place we know for sure that Catriona traveled on official Durupinen business was the Traveler Clan encampment in the north country."

My heart skipped a beat. "Ileana's clan?" I asked sharply. "The encampment I stayed in three years ago?"

Celeste nodded. "The very same. She has been following up on your Tracker case from October, I believe. The Walker you captured has been taken back there pending her trial."

"We didn't capture her," I said. Realizing my voice sounded

sharp, I tried to calm my tone as I went on. "We just Unmasked her. Catriona was the one who captured her."

"Well, as you say," Celeste said, clearly with little interest in this distinction. "She's been back and forth to the encampment several times over the past few weeks. That's where we're starting our investigation. The Trackers will try to discover if something could have happened there that might explain this Habitation."

"The Necromancers were there," Finn said. "Three years ago they attacked the encampment. They used those same fragmented spirits as part of their assault on the Travelers. Is it possible some of their Castings linger there, or perhaps that some of those spirits were left behind?"

"I couldn't say, but it is certainly possible," Celeste said, chewing anxiously on a fingernail. Please, excuse me. I must relay this information to the Trackers at once. They need to be aware of this possibility, as much to protect themselves as to inform their investigation. Hannah, thank you for providing us with this insight. It may just be the key to helping Catriona."

Hannah gave the smallest of smiles as she nodded. "Of course, Celeste. I hope it helps, truly."

"Is there anything else we can do?" I asked.

"Not for the moment, no," Celeste said with a sigh. "Just be sure to be present for the first session of the Airechtas this afternoon. I can't believe we still have to hold these meetings today, on top of everything else! Excuse me, please."

She hurried off, pulling a cell phone out of her pocket as she went.

"Well, if there's nothing else, I'll be getting on," Mrs. Mistlemoore said. "I'll be sending regular updates on Catriona's condition to the Council."

She trudged back through the hospital ward door. The rest of us stood around in silence for a moment before we all seemed to collectively realize that there was no reason to stay there anymore, and started walking back toward the entrance hall. Finn excused himself at the doors, saying he needed to return to the barracks to prepare for the opening processional of the Airechtas. I followed Hannah and Milo into the dining room. It was packed with people, all getting something to eat before the long afternoon of sessions began. I knew I should eat something, too, but as I walked past the trays of delicious food that had been laid out for the luncheon, I felt no hunger—only a vague and unsettling nausea. I grabbed a cup of coffee and a pair of dinner rolls, and made my way over to our traditional corner of solitude.

§

I sat staring into my coffee, thinking. I'd never cared for Catriona, but that didn't mean I wasn't profoundly disturbed by what I'd just witnessed. I had never seen Catriona display even the faintest sign of weakness—or indeed, much emotion at all. She was always so aloof, so impressively unconcerned with even serious situations, that watching her victimized like that was deeply disturbing. It was as though I had watched, helpless, as an impregnable fortress had been breached. And of course, watching the complete bafflement of Mrs. Mistlemoore and the others had only deepened my disquiet. I generally expected not to know what the hell was going on in the Durupinen world—it was basically my default setting these days. But if the Council and the entire hospital ward staff, with all of their collective experience in the spirit world, couldn't understand what was happening to Catriona... that was truly unsettling.

I was not so naïve as to believe that the Necromancers would never resurface; after watching the Council's hubris drive the entire Durupinen world to the brink of decimation, I was not about to repeat their mistake. Still, I had hoped that we would not face such a dangerous threat again so soon. An open assault was frightening, but at least you could see it coming. An attack like this—if that's actually what it was—was a different kind of terrifying. It was insidious and undetectable. Whatever was Habitating in Catriona had done so without her realization. She had carried it unwittingly into the castle, a poisonous seed taking root inside her. Even as I tried to convince myself that Mrs. Mistlemoore and her staff would heal Catriona, I could not silence the nagging fear that she might be beyond their help.

"Jess?"

"Huh?"

Hannah's inquisitive gaze pulled me up out of the rabbit hole my fears had sent me down. I met her eyes, and knew she understood exactly what I'd been brooding about.

"You really should try to eat those," she said, pointing to the dinner rolls. "And something else, if you can manage it. That session is going to be long this afternoon, and somehow I don't think the Council gives snack breaks."

I tried to smile. "Really? You don't think they have ancient tables set up for donuts and coffee in there?"

"I don't think pastries are part of the ages-old traditions of Durupinen lawmaking," Hannah replied.

"Well, that's a crime. We should definitely suggest a policy change," I said, before biting unenthusiastically into a roll.

"Speaking of making policy changes, we haven't really had a lot of time to think about what Finvarra told us yesterday," Hannah said quietly. She had dropped her eyes to her lunch; she'd eaten barely a bite, either.

"No, we haven't," I said with a sigh. "And it sounds like she's going to nominate us whether we want her to or not."

"So, what should we do?" Hannah asked. "I mean, what do you want to do?"

I finished chewing my roll, which had suddenly taken on the taste and consistency of gravel in my mouth. "I don't know yet. I honestly don't. She's going to nominate us regardless, so I don't think we have to decide anything yet."

Hannah nodded thoughtfully. "That's true."

"I mean, most of the Durupinen either mistrust us or are terrified of us. I can't imagine that anyone is actually going to cast a vote to let us anywhere near a Council seat, can you?"

Hannah shrugged. "I don't know. Maybe not."

"And even if we wake up in some weird alternate universe where we are voted in, we don't have to accept that seat. We could decline it. No one can force us to serve on the Council."

"That is also true," Hannah said.

I looked around the room. Three or four people at the nearest table were staring at us, hastily turning away when I caught their eyes. I laughed. "You know what? I say we just let Finvarra nominate us. It will probably be amusing to watch the panic that ensues. Maybe it will ease the mind-numbing boredom."

"That's the spirit!" Hannah said, actually grinning now, then turning to Milo. "How about you, Milo? Did you decide if you are coming to the meeting?"

"I may make an appearance," Milo said airily. "It's important to exercise the special privileges of the Spirit Guide."

Mackie had explained to us that ghosts were not allowed in the

Airechtas sessions, unless they had been summoned there for a specific purpose, such as to give testimony or to act in some other official capacity. The one exception to this rule was Spirit Guides, who were considered an extension of a clan's Gateway, and therefore invited to attend all sessions. They could not represent the clan in an official capacity—only Durupinen could do that. Otherwise, I would have cheerfully left the meetings to him and found somewhere to hide until this entire process was over.

"Be sure to use the connection to let me know if things get interesting, though," Milo said. "I don't want to miss any Durupinen cat fights or drama."

I rolled my eyes. "Ah, yes. Everyone's favorite reality show, 'Durupinen Policy Decisions'. About as exciting as C-SPAN, I'd imagine."

"Hey, you're going to have Marion in there. I would not underestimate the potential for edge-of-your-seat drama if I were you." Milo said, and though he said it lightly, his eyes were troubled. "Just remember, her brand of drama queen thrives on a steady diet of attention. Don't feed the queen, you got me?"

"I'm not going to say two words to her, if I can help it," I said firmly. "Whatever she's trying to stir up, I'm staying out of it, if I can."

"'If you can' being the operative words, sweetness," Milo said. Ever the mature adult, I stuck my tongue out at him.

A sudden striking of a gong made all three of us scream. I swiveled in my seat to check the grandfather clock in the corner and saw everyone rising from their chairs and proceeding toward the door out to the entrance hall.

"And so, it begins," I muttered.

8

THE AIRECHTAS

S ILENTLY, WE JOINED THE LINE in the entrance hall. Mackie was walking along it, consulting a clipboard and instructing other Durupinen where to stand. We approached her and waited while she made a note on her list.

"Hey there, you two. Want to know your spot in the parade? You're right behind the marching band," she said, gesturing along the line.

"Very funny," I said. "Just tell us where to go."

"Wait, we need to put these on," Hannah said, reaching into her bag, and pulling out our clan sashes and Triskele pendants. She handed them to me with an apologetic look on her face.

I swallowed every snarky, whiney comment I had and flung the sash irritably over my shoulder. As if it wasn't bad enough we had to attend this thing, we also had to endure a freaking costume change.

"You know Fairhaven," Mackie said genially, perhaps in response to the look on my face. "Nothing passes without the appropriate pomp and circumstance."

"We noticed," I said, and then leaned in so that no one would overhear us. "Did you hear about Catriona?"

Mackie's smile slid off her face. "Yeah, I heard about that, alright. I've been trying to dodge questions about her for the last few minutes. Is she going to be okay, do you reckon?"

"I have no idea. She was far from okay when we left the hospital wing," I said. "Did Celeste mention if they have an official diagnosis?"

"Nah, they're just as stymied as they were when they brought her in. Celeste isn't sure how much to tell everyone. She doesn't want to draw attention to it, but at the same time they can hardly hide the fact that one of the Council members is conspicuously absent from today's proceedings," Mackie said.

"Is there even any point to having the meeting today? I thought every clan had to be accounted for, without exception; that's what Karen told us. Can the Airechtas even proceed with a Council member missing?" Hannah asked.

"It could, if Catriona had someone to stand in for her, but the only other Durupinen from her clan is Lucida and... well..." Mackie trailed off, looking sheepish.

"She's not exactly available," I replied.

Mackie grinned. "Precisely. Anyway, I don't think they ever vote on anything in the first day or two. It's all policy proposals and propositions and suggested amendments and the like. I expect they will just keep pushing the voting off, until Mrs. Mistlemoore can get Catriona back into form again. They're bound to figure out what's wrong with her soon."

She said this with a forced note of confidence, though her brow remained furrowed as she went back to her clipboard. A moment later an older Durupinen woman laid a hand on her elbow and leaned in to ask her something about seating arrangements, and so we left Mackie to deal with that and took our places in line.

"Hello, Jessica. Hannah," a voice said from just over my shoulder.

Róisín and Riley Lightfoot were standing directly behind us.

"Hi, Riley. Hi, Róisín. It's... uh... been a long time," I said awkwardly.

I had been so intent on avoiding everyone's gazes that I hadn't even noticed them, and even if I had, I might have pretended not to. Róisín and Riley had both been first year Apprentices with us at Fairhaven three years before, but I couldn't exactly call them friends. Both had belonged, by default and family association, to Peyton Clark's elite clique. Peyton, being the spawn of Marion, was exactly as nasty as you'd expect her to be, and her clique had behaved according to her agenda. Róisín and Riley had participated, if somewhat reluctantly, in the constant campaign of humiliation and alienation that had plagued us during our first few miserable months at the castle. They had even helped Peyton and the other girls kidnap us in the middle of the night and trap us in the old ruins of the *príosún* hidden away in the wooded area of the grounds. Róisín had gotten cold feet when Peyton summoned the Elemental to torment us, and had abandoned the ritual hazing to go find help. If Finn and Carrick hadn't rescued us on Róisín's information, I cringed to think what would have happened to

Hannah and me in that circle. But Róisín had refused to take credit for helping us when I tried to thank her. She was terrified that her interference on our behalf would jeopardize her social position among the other Apprentices, and so had continued to give us the cold shoulder in public. In fact, I don't think she spoke another word to me, friendly or otherwise, until this totally unexpected hello.

It seemed the cold shoulder had melted in the intervening years, however, for Róisín gave us a warm smile and her voice, when she replied to my greeting, was friendly.

"It has been a long time. How have you both been?" she asked, as though we were old chums catching up over a nice latte and a scone.

Hannah shot me a startled look before turning back to Róisín to reply, "Fine, thanks. You?"

"Very well, thank you. We're excited to participate this year. This is the first time both of us have been of age for an Airechtas, so it's our first time sitting in on the sessions," Róisín said. "Our mother will still be casting the vote, as she is on the Council, but we will be able to be a part of the process."

"Yeah, that's... great. I guess," I said. What the hell else could I say? Honestly, I couldn't be less enthused about being a part of the process. In fact, I was pretty sure it was "the process" that had royally screwed up my life over the past four years. The process, as Savvy would say, could well and truly sod off.

Róisín seemed to recognize our confusion, because her smile collapsed into a contrite expression. She sagged, dropping her eyes to her own fidgeting hands. "You probably can't understand why I'm talking to you, particularly in light of how I behaved in the past. I know we haven't... that is to say... I'm sorry for... I'd like to start over, if you would be amenable to that."

Hannah and I looked at each other again. "Start over?" I repeated.

Róisín was blushing now. "Well, yes. A lot has changed since we last saw each other. That is to say, I've changed. Look, I never liked the way the other Apprentices treated you, but I was scared—scared that they would shut me out if I disagreed with them. Status is hard fought and easily lost around here, as you well know." She shook her head briskly. "But that was no excuse for the way that I behaved, and I—we—want you to know how sorry we are."

She looked over at Riley, whose expression was somewhat truculent. She did not meet our eyes, and I could tell from the sour twist of Riley's mouth that this reconciliation had not been her idea.

Normally, I might have nursed a grudge a little longer, or at least let Róisín apologize a few more times before letting it go. But here, in the depths of the vipers' nest, I was ready to clutch at any offer of friendship like a drowning man clutches at a life preserver. And Hannah, it seemed, felt the same way, for she piped up before I could open my mouth.

"It's okay, Róisín," she said. "It was a long time ago, now."

Róisín looked at Hannah skeptically, and opened her mouth again, but I cut her off.

"Seriously. Water under the bridge," I said, even managing a smile.

Róisín's expression cleared at once. Riley was still frowning, fiddling with her clan sash, although it was perfectly draped over her shoulder.

"That's brilliant. I'm so pleased, really. So, you two will be voting, then?" Róisín asked. "Or is your aunt with you?"

"No, Karen couldn't be here," I said. "So, unfortunately, we will be doing the voting."

"Why unfortunately?" Róisín asked.

I started to tell her that I'd cheerfully have a root canal instead of sit through this political garbage, when a familiar voice distracted me.

"I can't even get her out of the room! She's gone and locked it from the inside, and she's not answering me anymore!" Savvy was saying to Siobhán. The two of them were standing on the first landing of the grand staircase, but Savvy's voice, even louder than usual in her aggravation, carried clearly over the entrance hall.

Siobhán was making shushing gestures with her hands, glancing around nervously. When she replied, her voice was low enough that I couldn't make out what she was saying, though whatever it was made Savvy snort derisively.

"Really, Siobhán? You think I haven't tried that? I'm telling you she's not coming down!" she cried. "And if you shush me one more time, I'll show you what loud really sounds like!"

I stepped out of line and started for the staircase, but Hannah caught my arm.

92

"Jess? Where are you going? The procession is about to start!" she whispered.

"I'm just going to talk to Savvy. I'll be right back," I said.

"But what if the line starts without you?" Hannah asked. She fidgeted nervously with her sash.

"Look, do you want to come with me, if you're so anxious about it?" I asked her. "It's just a line of people. I'm pretty sure we can just step right back into it if it leaves without us. It's not a train, Hannah."

Hannah made a face at me and followed me across to the staircase. When we reached the foot of it, we could finally hear what Siobhán was saying.

"Perhaps if Celeste or I were to go up and speak with her—"

"Be my bloody guest," Savvy cried, throwing her hands up in the air. "If you can get her out of that room, I'll take up abstinence."

"From what?" Siobhán asked, smirking sardonically.

"From bloody *everything*!" Savvy hollered. Several people nearest the stairs craned their necks to investigate. "Mind you, she thinks you're part of her hallucination, so if you manage to pull that one off, you're a bleeding miracle worker, you are."

"Sav? Everything okay?" I called softly up the steps.

Savvy spotted me and immediately turned away from Siobhán, who was still talking, and descended the steps.

"This is not what I signed up for, I'll tell you that for free," Savvy said as she arrived at the bottom of the staircase.

"What happened?" Hannah asked.

"It's Frankie! She's still convinced she's concocted this place inside her head. She won't come out of her room, she won't read any of the books we gave her, she ignores every lesson, every assignment. We even took the Wards off her bedroom and told the resident ghosts to have at it. They're floating in and out of there morning, noon, and night, and she still won't admit she can see them."

"Wow, really?" I asked. "You've got to give her credit, she's committed."

Savvy snorted. "Yeah, well if she doesn't un-commit soon, I'm gonna go round the twist. We all thought she'd come around by now, but it's been weeks, and she hasn't budged an inch. Siobhán's acting like this is my fault, but no one's pinning this on me. You can't mentor someone who refuses to believe you exist, for fuck's sake." She pointed to a red mark just below her jawline. "When I went up there just now to try to coax her down, she threw a book right at my bloody head!"

"Yikes," I said. "You okay?"

"I'll live. Might have to kill her, though. Maybe she'll believe in ghosts if she is one," Savvy said, rubbing her jaw.

"Why does she need to come to the Airechtas?" I asked. "She doesn't need to vote, does she?"

Savvy shook her head. "Nah, she and her sister don't become an official clan until they're initiated, and we can't do that while she's... well..."

"Rejecting all attempts to bring her back to reality?" I suggested.

"Yeah," Savvy said ruefully. "I spent the last hour trying to convince Frankie to come downstairs. I gave it a go for as long as I could, but Phoebe and I have to be at the Airechtas as well." She pointed to her own lavender sash and pulled a face. "We're the only ones in our clan, so we can't count on anyone else to sit through it for us. I would have made Phoebe go alone, but she's such a moron, I doubt she'd know when to raise her hand."

Savvy looked over her shoulder. I followed her gaze. Phoebe stood at the very back of the line. She was staring blankly into space, twisting a strand of hair around her finger and chewing on it. Poor Savvy detested being so closely tied to her cousin, whom she'd only met a handful of times during her childhood. At first, I'd thought Savvy was being too hard on Phoebe, just because Phoebe had grown up in a tiny country village, but my subsequent interactions with her had justified Savvy's many complaints: Phoebe was, in all likelihood, the dullest person ever in the history of the world. No wonder Savvy was on a constant quest for her next irresponsible, spontaneous decision—she was just trying to balance things out.

"I can talk to Frankie later tonight, if you want," Hannah offered. "When the Airechtas is over."

Savvy sighed in relief. "Would you? I'd be ever so grateful. I know you mentioned it before, but I wasn't going to pressure you, especially now that Frankie's taken to throwing things."

Hannah laughed lightly. "Sav, I've been her. Seriously, however badly she's dealing with it, I've been worse. Trust me. On the meds, off the meds, in denial, in full-out panic mode, I ran the whole spectrum before Jess and Karen broke me out. I can get through to Frankie, I know I can."

"Better wear protective headgear, then," Savvy groaned, rubbing the mark on her face. It was just starting to bruise.

A second gong resounded through the hall, making my head ring. At the front of the line, the massive double doors of the Grand Council Room creaked slowly open.

"Good luck staying awake," I said to Savvy over my shoulder as we rejoined the line. She grinned at me, then flipped me off. I turned back around, and gasped at the sight before me.

Even in my unenthused state, the sight of the inside of the hall took my breath away. All the candles in the ancient wooden chandeliers had been lit, casting a dancing golden light over the entire space. Long mahogany tables stood end to end across the entire length of the room, draped in gold cloths that were embroidered with a pattern of Triskeles and Celtic knots in glinting silver thread. High-backed chairs stood along the tables. A silver panel of fabric was tied to the back of each one, embroidered with the name of the clan who was to sit there. The bare stone walls were no longer visible. Instead, the many elaborate tapestries from the upper halls of the castle had been brought down and hung, so that we now seemed to be processing into a portrait gallery. Every High Priestess of the last millennium gazed regally down upon us, seeming to exert collective authority over the proceedings from beyond the Aether.

I scanned the tapestries until I found the haughty, imperial gaze of Agnes Isherwood, my own ancestor, bearing down on me. Was it naïve that I thought I could see a family resemblance in her long straight nose, her dark hair, and her wide eyes? Did I perhaps just wish I saw some of myself up there—a desperate attempt to prove to myself that I belonged here in this castle that seemed constantly to be chewing me up and spitting me out?

Agnes Isherwood wasn't just a distant ancestor to whom time had eroded my feeble connection. She was a Seer who made the very Prophecy that had shaped the course of my life, and so many other lives as well. The Isherwood Prophecy had sown the seeds of fear amongst the Northern Clans, and those seeds had flourished and run rampant—a stifling, choking weed that had entangled many Durupinen before us, twisting and knotting them in a snare they could not escape. As I stared up into her face, I could not tell if I wanted to salute Agnes Isherwood's image, or hold a lighter to the damn thing and watch it go up in flames.

Tearing my eyes from Agnes, I followed Hannah down the center aisle between the tables, searching as I did so for our clan name on any of the chairs. Finally, I spotted Clan Sassanaigh in the second row from the front. We slid into the aisle to stand behind the chairs, but did not yet sit, taking our cue from the many other Durupinen already standing in their assigned places.

"Do you think anyone would notice if we just grabbed a spot in the last row?" I asked Hannah, leaning in so that no one would hear me. Róisín and Riley were standing in the row directly behind us.

"This isn't exactly an open seating situation, Jess," Hannah hissed. "We just have to suck it up. Besides, I don't think this meeting is going to be any shorter or any more interesting from the back row."

"It would be if I was asleep," I muttered, so quietly that she either didn't hear me, or pretended not to.

As we stood behind our chairs, waiting for everyone to file into their places, I ran my fingers over the delicate silver embroidery on the chair cover. Now that I could see it up close, the sheen of the fabric was worn down in places, and a few of the seams were slightly frayed. This chair cover, with our clan name on it, was probably the oldest piece of fabric I'd ever touched. It ought to have been in a museum... well, if clandestine matriarchal societies shrouded in centuries of secrecy actually *had* museums.

Finally, a hush settled over the assembled rows of Durupinen as the last of the seats were filled. After a few long moments of anticipatory silence, a lone flute began to play, the sound of it filling the hall so completely that it was impossible to tell where the musician might be hiding. As the melody swelled with quintessentially Celtic tones, the members of the Council started filing in. I turned to watch their procession toward the raised benches at the head of the room, and took immediate note of their attire. I had stood before the Council a number of times, but they had always been dressed in their own street clothes. Now each wore a long gold robe, not unlike something a particularly flashy gospel choir might don, except with unusually high collars and lace-edged sleeves that draped from their wrists and trailed behind them like trains on wedding dresses. As they drew closer, I could also see that upon each head rested a delicate circlet of hammered gold leaves on a twisted vine. I knew they must be hundreds of years old, and yet it did not seem possible that something so fragile could last for so long and still be in such pristine condition. Could objects, like people, be repaired and renewed through Leeching, I found myself wondering?

Fiona stumped by me, looking bad-tempered as usual. Her circlet was slightly askew and the hands peeking out from the sleeves of her robe were splattered with paint, as were the tips of her grubby old work boots. Several Durupinen were staring at her as she stomped past, their expressions disapproving. As she passed our row, Fiona caught my eye and gave me a wink and a grimace that quite clearly said, "Can you believe we have to participate in this arcane bullshit?" I fought against a laugh that threatened to bubble up in my throat.

The Council members filed into their places in the benches and turned to face the assembly. I realized as I listened to the music swelling that it was incomplete. The last time I'd heard music accompanying a Durupinen procession was when Hannah and I were being Initiated as our clan's new Gateway. As we had walked to the central courtyard, nervously clutching our candles, a flute and a violin had serenaded us. That violin had been played hauntingly by none other than Catriona; now, it was the absence of her playing that was haunting. Equally haunting was the gaping hole in the Council formation, where Catriona ought to have been standing at that moment.

A military drum began to pound a steady rhythm and the Caomhnóir trooped into the room in tight marching formation. They were outfitted in their formal uniforms, each draped with the sash of the clan they were sworn to protect. I could just glimpse Finn's stoic face in the fourth row, his chest thrown out as though it could barely contain the deep-seated pride he felt for his duty. I smothered the fluttery feeling he set off in my stomach and the smile that was trying to tug at the corners of my mouth; surrounded by the entirety of the Northern Clans was probably not the best place to betray my forbidden relationship with Finn.

The Caomhnóir split off and filed into two long lines, one on either side of the Grand Council Room, so that they seemed to be standing guard over the tapestries along the walls above their heads. As the last Caomhnóir assumed their posts, the final beat of the drum struck, echoing through the room so that the silence that followed it seemed almost oppressive. Then the doors to the hall opened again and Finvarra entered to renewed melodies from the flute.

Rightfully, she ought to have been sweeping up the aisle on her own two feet with sure, and steady steps. Instead, two Caomhnóir pushed her wheelchair slowly toward the front of the room. Carrick floated along behind them; deep concern for his mistress had carved his face into a craggy landscape of worry. Finvarra looked shrunken and feeble, somehow even frailer than when I'd seen her yesterday. She was wearing robes of shimmering gold fabric. A circlet, much more elaborate than the others, clung precariously to what was left of her hair. Beneath that circlet, though, Finvarra held her chin high and a fierce fire burned bright in her eyes. She seemed determined, through sheer force of will, to lay claim to her dignity and her power before the entire assembly, regardless of the state of her health. I felt a totally unexpected surge of pride that she was our High Priestess. In spite of all of our clashes and disagreements, I felt nothing but respect for her in this moment.

Because that's the thing about women, isn't it? You can push us down, and you can bury us, and you can heap the world on top of us, until we must surely crumble to dust. And instead, we turn into diamonds.

I seemed to be alone in my reaction, however. All around me, gasps and cries of shock rose from the crowd. Evidently, many of the Durupinen had not known Finvarra was ill, or at least did not realize the severity of her condition. Three seats away from me, an older woman had burst into sobs, which she quickly stifled with her hands. She turned and buried her face in the shoulder of the woman beside her, who began to stroke her hair as tears dripped silently down her own face. I stole a glance at Hannah; her bottom lip was trembling.

Finvarra did not deign to notice any of these reactions from her audience. The Caomhnóir wheeled her into her position at the High Priestess' throne, but they did not move her into the seat itself; perhaps they thought she would not be able to tolerate being lifted from her wheelchair. Perhaps she simply did not want to suffer the indignity of everyone watching her struggle.

When Finvarra was in position, she raised her arms and the flute died away on a long, haunting note and went silent. The mutterings and whisperings amongst the assembled Durupinen died away as well.

Finvarra's voice, though shot through with a quiver that she could not master, was full of unbridled fierceness, as though she dared everyone in the room, with every word, to deny that she was at anything less than her most powerful.

"Welcome, my sisters, to the 203rd Airechtas of the Durupinen of the Northern Clans. For over a millennium now, the clans of the Northern Isles have met once every five years in the week leading up to the winter solstice. As we gather together, we look to the future, and recommit ourselves to our sacred duties as the keepers of the Gateways. In many ways, this year is no different; we will make proposals, cast votes, and shape our policies as we have always done. In one important way, however, this Airechtas is, perhaps, the most significant we have ever held."

Though utter silence had fallen at the first sound of her voice, the quiet deepened now. My own pulse sped up, sure I knew what she was referring to, and wishing I could sink through the floor and out of sight as she continued to gaze imperiously over us. I felt like every single pair of eyes behind us was now boring into the back of my head like hundreds of tiny drills.

"For hundreds of years, we have feared the coming of the Isherwood Prophecy. We shaped our policy around its looming threat. Its terrible weight forced our hands again and again as we tried in vain to throw it from us. There has not been a time, in living memory, when we did not live in fear, looking over our shoulders for a whisper, a sign of its approach."

A woman standing diagonally in front of us actually turned around to sneak a glimpse of Hannah and me. I turned and met her eyes so fiercely that she whipped her head back around at once, blushing furiously.

"And now, for the first time, the threat of the Prophecy is gone. We have come face to face with our greatest threat, and we have survived it. Our sisterhood cannot help but be shaped by the absence of the Prophecy now, just as it had always been shaped by its presence," Finvarra said. The mandate in her voice was clear. "In the immediate aftermath, appropriate measures were taken to investigate every detail and to punish those responsible for the near-destruction of our world. Those measures were devised not only by the Council of the Northern Clans, but also by the

International High Council. They were not made lightly, and they will not be questioned further. They will not be made the subject of further debate, or used to drag down the vital work we must do this week."

I shifted my footing so that I could see Marion out of the corner of my eye. Her expression was stony, with no hint of her trademark smugness. Her hands, clutching the back of her chair, were white at the knuckles.

"We will not allow our enemies to divide us even as we try to heal. We will not look back; we will not look to shift blame, to point fingers, to propagate fear and mistrust. That was the way of the past, and it nearly destroyed us. From today, we only look forward. How can we learn and grow from this experience we have had? How can we take the lessons gleaned from it, and apply them to our clans? How do we recommit to our Calling?"

She looked sternly around the room. Several people shifted and looked at each other, as though unsure if Finvarra was actually expecting someone to answer her. No one spoke up, though, and Finvarra continued. "We will explore this question as we move forward this week. It should be the foundation for all that we work toward. Before you propose a policy change, or an amendment, or contribute any suggestion to the week's proceedings, you must first be able to answer that question: how does this move us forward?"

All around the hall, heads were nodding in agreement. Whatever Finvarra lacked in physical strength at the moment, she more than made up for in authority and inspiration as she spoke. Her audience was captive to her, just as it always had been when she was able to stand on her own two feet. In fact, I thought I could sense an even deeper respect now, running like a current through the room.

"As you have all no doubt noticed, I am not long for this world," Finvarra said. A ripple of murmuring rose and fell within the crowd. A few Council Members seemed to be attempting to quietly protest the pronouncement. Finvarra was having none of it.

"Swallow your protests, please. Do not think I seek your reassurance. Who understands the workings of death better than we, with one foot in the living world, and the other planted firmly in the world of the dead. For many years, I denied the inevitable. I delayed my fate, through means I now cannot look upon without sincere regret."

Another outbreak of whispers shivered through the room, and

I understood why. Finvarra had fended off her illness for several years through a common but morally reprehensible process called Leeching. Through Leeching, a Durupinen siphoned energy from a Crossing spirit and used that energy for herself. Finvarra used it to heal herself, which I suppose was better than the majority of the Council, who were using the spirit energy purely for the purpose of maintaining unearthly youth and beauty. But that practice had come to a screeching halt with the investigation in the aftermath of the Prophecy. The International High Council had sanctioned Finvarra and the others for the Leeching. Some had lost their Council seats or other official positions. Karen had confided that it was only under the condition that Finvarra allow her illness to progress naturally that she had been allowed to stay on as High Priestess. It had seemed so harsh at first—a death sentence. But the more I thought about it, the more I realized that all her "sentence" did was put her on equal footing with the rest of us mere mortals.

Finvarra went on, bursting my bubble of thought. "I am prepared for the journey I surely must take, and soon, but not before I ensure that our sisterhood is on solid footing for the future. I feel it incumbent upon me, as the High Priestess, to set the expectations very clearly as we begin. Petty political stunts will not be tolerated. We were very nearly destroyed a few short years ago. I will not stand by and watch us destroy ourselves, not with ill-conceived sniping and juvenile grudges. We have critical work to do. We have a Calling to live up to. It is time to decide if we are worthy of it."

Women all around me were shifting uncomfortably or bristling with silent resentment, but I wanted to stand up and cheer. Facing one's own mortality must be a truly terrifying and eye opening experience, but Finvarra wasn't backing down from it. Hell, she wasn't even blinking. We'd gotten a glimpse of this new resolve when she'd called us into her office, but now, clinging to her dignity before this assembly, she was truly a force of nature.

"Trusting that we will choose to honor my words, let us begin. Council Secretary, if you would officially call us to order, please," Finvarra said, inclining her head graciously toward Siobhán, who was hovering anxiously in the shadows behind the throne. She stepped forward, looking relieved that Finvarra had been able to get through her opening address. She watched as the two Caomhnóir slid Finvarra's wheelchair away from the podium, and then took her place at the microphone. Celeste came and stood beside her, a sheaf of parchment scrolls and folders in her arms.

"The assembled clans being present, and the High Priestess having addressed the assembly, I officially call to order the 203rd Airechtas of the Northern Clans. Let the roll be called and recorded in the register."

With a great ripple of motion, everyone took their seats, and the session began.

ELEANORA: 27 JUNE 1864

27 June 1864

Dearest Little Book,

It is a sorry state of affairs when the worst havoc being wreaked in your life is not by the many spirits that haunt your every step, but by your own mother. This is the state in which I find myself tonight.

Surely you must know by now, from my near constant griping, that my perceived value in life is to land firmly under the thumb of some wealthy gentleman, preferably before the venerable age of twenty and whilst wearing a wedding dress. Some of my earliest memories are of my mother correcting me for showing too much intellectual curiosity in public. I remember one occasion in particular when I was about five years old, and I had asked what stars were made of.

"It is not for a young lady to ask questions," she would admonish me. "But if a question must be asked, a young lady must nod and smile, and defer to the gentleman's opinion or explanation at all times."

I did not think much of this advice, particularly because my pompous and overbearing elder cousin had chosen that moment to inform me that he personally had created the stars by shooting his archery arrows up into the sky and tearing holes in the darkness. I was not about to nod or smile, or defer to such utter nonsense as that. The ensuing argument between my cousin and me about the validity of his claims left my mother quite vexed with me.

I have since learned to temper my opinions with demureness and my inquisitiveness with a healthy dose of charm, although I am still not the delicate wallflower my mother would prefer me to be. But never has my patience been more thoroughly tested than at a dinner party this evening when I was paired with Harry Milford.

I have, of course, known the Milford family for many years. We have hovered around the outskirts of their circles, occasionally brushing elbows in the context of balls or charity work. My mother has lamented, time and again, the fleeting nature of our social connections with the Milfords, as their money and influence would prove incredibly beneficial to our family. I have always praised the infrequency of those same connections, as I have always found Harry Milford to be possessed of both an abundance of confidence and a dearth of intelligence.

But tonight I found myself thrust into his arms not once, but many times throughout the evening at Lord Huddleston's ball. First, Harry's mother made a considerable show of introducing us, though we have been introduced several times before. Then she orchestrated a very long conversation between us, during which I nodded endlessly as Harry regaled me with tales of his hunting exploits. I was expected to attend breathlessly to his description of his new velvet hunting coat, a fully ten minute long endeavor that would have bored a corpse to tears. Then I was alarmed to discover that it was Harry's intention not only to dance with me, but to claim every dance of the evening and demand my undivided attention between them.

I found myself seated beside him at dinner, where he proved to have as little interest in gentlemanly table manners as he did in allowing me to express even a single fact about myself. I was constantly aware of both of our mothers' hawkish attention to our interactions, and had to endure several ill-mannered jokes from Lord Milford about his son's fine taste in companions. In the end, after Harry had consumed entirely too much wine, I was forced to extricate myself from his increasingly bold liberties by insisting I was not feeling well, but that I sincerely looked forward to seeing him again later this week at Lord Kentwood's ball. I then practically sprinted for the door.

It was very clear to me as I rode in the carriage home that some kind of arrangement had been agreed to between the Milford family and my own, or, at the very least, that an arrangement was being discussed. I waited up in the drawing room for my mother to return from the ball, meaning to confront her about it, and was attacked instead.

"Eleanora, what in the world is wrong with you? Couldn't you see that Harry Milford was angling for your attentions?"

"I was not feeling well. I have a headache," I said shortly, not caring to elaborate.

"I don't care if your head was falling off of your shoulders! How dare you jeopardize such a significant social connection! Surely it could not have escaped your notice that Harry would not be parted from you all night! He is to inherit an enormous fortune, and his father's title to boot! What do you mean, fleeing from him as though the building were on fire?"

"I do believe the glint and glimmer of that fortune has blinded you to the nature of those attentions, Mother!" I replied when I had recovered sufficiently from being scolded like a naughty child. "Harry Milford may be noble, but he is no gentleman, I assure you."

My mother scoffed. "No gentleman, indeed. He is a fine young man and an excellent prospect for you."

"A fine young man? He spent half of his time preening and gloating and the other half working his way steadily through a week's supply of wine!"

"A man of his stature is bound to gloat. It is not your place to criticize him, Eleanora. He is not the one who needs to seek approval."

It was at this point that I think I may have shrieked rather indelicately. "Are you suggesting that I should be working to seek his approval?"

"Of course I am!" my mother snapped at me. "If you can secure this match, you will have a title. A title, Eleanora, just think of that! Lady Milford! It will be a crowning achievement for our family."

"A crowning achievement? To chain myself to a preening, insolent braggart for the rest of my life? What possible achievement could I claim besides an astounding disregard for my own happiness?"

"You are being selfish!" my mother insisted. "Do not think of yourself. Think of your family! Think of your cl—"

She stopped herself, but it was too late to cover for her error.

"What does our clan have to do with it?" I asked her. I had to repeat the question several times before she would finally deign to answer it.

"The Council has determined that your marriage into the Milford family is crucial to the Durupinen's ability to wield political influence. The match is being arranged with their assistance."

I felt quite light-headed, unable to comprehend what she was telling me. "Is this what I am to you? Is my happiness to be sacrificed for political influence?"

"Don't be so dramatic, Eleanora," my mother scoffed. "No one is being sacrificed. This is a match to which we would have aspired regardless of the Council's involvement."

"You may have aspired to it, but I would have refused!" I cried. "I am not naïve, Mother. I understand that position and money have weight in matters of matrimony, but they cannot be the sole considerations!

You cannot possibly expect me to sacrifice every hope of happiness for the sake of a Durupinen political agenda!"

"I certainly do expect it," my mother said bluntly, which left me too stunned to reply. She went on, "With your gift comes responsibility, Eleanora. That responsibility takes precedence, in this instance as in all others. The decision has been made. Make your peace with it."

I feel as though the walls of my room are closing in upon me as I write these words. I have always known I would have to choose wisely in matters of love, but I had always taken for granted that love itself would be a factor. What am I to do? Am I honestly to be shackled to a man I despise for the rest of my life? Oh, Little Book, if only there were a Casting I could write upon your pages that would whisk me far away from here, I assure you, I would already be gone.

Eleanora

9

CONTAGIOUS

DESPITE HER POWERFUL, passionate opening to the meeting, Finvarra appeared more than happy to turn over the running of the session to Siobhán and Celeste. The Caomhnóir settled her in a less prominent position in the back corner of the platform, where a nurse tucked a blanket around her legs and felt her pulse. Carrick drifted over beside her chair, leaning down to speak quietly to her. Whatever it was he was saying to her, Finvarra waved it off with an impatient flick of her hand. Then she closed her eyes as though overcome with exhaustion, and lay her head back on her headrest. She did not move again for quite some time. Carrick stood guard over her, looking ready to destroy the first person to disturb her moment of rest.

The taking of the official attendance seemed to last forever. Each clan name had to be called, the participants had to stand and say their names, which then had to be recorded in a massive, gold-gilded book by hand with a quill. It probably didn't help matters that Savvy's Caomhnóir, Bertie, was the Council scribe, and appeared to consider his penmanship a matter of monumental importance. Just behind him, Fiona was looking daggers at him as he recorded each name with painstaking care.

"Someone better hurry Bertie along, or else he is going to get a chair to the back of the skull courtesy of Fiona," I whispered to Hannah, who smothered a giggle with the back of her hand.

Most of the people in the room were using the roll call as an opportunity to turn around and stare at whomever was being introduced, and then whisper conspiratorially to their neighbors. I could only imagine what they were saying; exchanging clan gossip and commenting on appearances, probably. And then it was our turn for the general scrutiny.

"Would the representatives from Clan Sassanaigh please rise and state your names for the official record?" Siobhán called.

As Hannah and I nervously rose to our feet, we were met with an obvious increase in the muttering and whispering, so much so that I actually felt the need to raise my voice when I stated my name. When we sat again, it was with scarlet faces and a serious desire to sink through the floor.

In an effort to distract myself from all the unwanted attention, I dropped my eyes to the table in front of me and picked up a folder that lay there. It was imprinted with a gold Triskele and contained a large stack of papers that had been stapled together into a packet. I started to flip through it, just for something to do, and saw that it was a summary of what would be covered in the session that day. The whole thing was divided into sections and subsections, with addendums and footnotes, like an outline for the most tediously boring research paper of all time. Oh God, this was going to be torture.

"The Council would like to acknowledge Deputy Priestess Celeste Morgan," came Siobhán's voice, cutting into my document-induced horror. I looked up. Everyone around us had begun murmuring again, but the focus was no longer on anyone in the crowd. Every eye seemed to be drawn to the empty seat in the Council benches. They must have reached the point in the roll call when Catriona's clan ought to have acknowledged itself.

"Thank you, Siobhán," Celeste said as she reached the podium. Siobhán stepped aside so that Celeste could stand before the microphone. "I wish to address the absence of one of our Council members, Catriona Worthington."

The assembled Durupinen went silent, clearly eager for an explanation.

"Catriona has fallen very ill and could, under no circumstances, attend the meeting today. Our hospital ward staff is hopeful that she will make a full recovery, though they do not yet understand the exact nature of her illness."

A woman a few rows back stood up. "What do you mean, the exact nature of her illness? Is this a physical ailment or a spirit-induced issue?"

Celeste threw a quick glance at Siobhán, who gave a tiny nod. "I wouldn't like to speculate too much—after all, I am not a medical professional—but the incident does appear to be spirit-induced."

"But what's happened? What's wrong with her?" another voice called from the back of the hall.

Celeste put up a hand. "As I've said, I really can't speculate about—"

"Why are we so concerned?" a third, harsher voice added. "Her clan has disgraced itself beyond recovery. Why have we allowed her to maintain her Council seat, anyway?"

A great number of voices rose in reply to this question, and Siobhán actually had to step back to the podium and use the gavel there to silence them. I glanced at Hannah. Her eyes were wide, though she kept them trained on her clasped hands in her lap.

"It is not up for discussion or debate at this moment," Celeste said in a commanding voice, "whether Catriona should or should not continue as a member of this Council. That matter has already been thoroughly discussed, investigated, and voted upon."

"But not by us," the third voice continued. I turned to look at the speaker. I had never seen her before. "We were never consulted."

"You were consulted when you voted on your Council representatives," Celeste said. "The women sitting up on this platform now are your chosen delegates, and they have been entrusted to make decisions on your behalf. If you do not trust their judgment or fitness, by all means, vote them out at your next opportunity, and I include myself in that. The Trackers and the International High Council investigated this matter and found Catriona to be innocent both of any wrongdoing in this matter, and also of any knowledge of her cousin's wrongdoing. Do you suggest their investigations lack merit?"

The woman mumbled something about, "... never said that..."

Celeste took advantage of the woman's momentary embarrassment and went on, "Unless you have further evidence to provide us, we must rely upon the thorough investigations that have already been conducted. The guilty party, Lucida Worthington, has been tried, convicted, and sentenced to spend her life imprisoned at the *príosún* on the Isle of Skye. We are not in the habit of punishing one of our sisterhood for the crimes of another. We will not begin to do so now. If you take issue with this policy, I suggest you take it up with the International High Council. I'm sure someone there would be delighted to explain it to you."

The dissenting woman flushed pink, but her expression remained defiant as she lowered herself slowly back into her seat. Several other people around her were casting stony looks up at Celeste, but she had already turned away from them.

"As I was saying," she went on, "Catriona is still a voting member of this Council and her absence will impede our proceedings. In the interest of avoiding delays, I move that, though we press forward with discussion and debate of issues, we hold off on any formal voting until we can ascertain if Catriona will be able to join us. It may save us the trouble of having to nominate and vote in a temporary replacement for her."

"Seconded," Fiona called from the stands. Celeste nodded gratefully to her.

"Very well, then," Siobhán said, stepping forward to the podium again. "A simple majority carries. All in favor of the motion proposed by Clan Turascuain that formal voting be postponed pending the health status of our Councilwoman?"

Hands went up all around the room. I was rather alarmed at being asked to vote on something so quickly, but after a moment of surprise, and a silent consultation with Hannah, I raised my own hand tentatively into the air. It seemed silly not to accomplish what we could while waiting for Catriona to recover. Many others seemed to agree; most of them, in fact, although I noticed the woman that had challenged Catriona's continued seat on the council had declined to raise her hand, as had several of the women sitting around her.

Hannah looked at me and raised her eyebrows as though to say, "This might be more interesting than you thought." I conceded with a nod of my head. She might just be right.

"Motion carries," Siobhán called after the votes were counted. She took a moment to be sure that Bertie had recorded the correct tally, and then nodded to Celeste.

"Very well. Let us move then to the first order of business, which can be found on page one of your session agenda," Celeste said with a faint air of relief.

It was tedious for a time. First, each clan had to confirm any deaths and births in the bloodline. Then each clan had to officially record any transference of a Gateway from one generation to the next since the previous Airechtas. I couldn't imagine that they didn't already keep track of these kinds of things; I mean, how else would they know who was coming to Fairhaven for training in any given year? But apparently, it was the formality of it that mattered, so we sat through round after round of clan updates.

Then Celeste stood again and read a sort of proclamation announcing the opening of new Gateways since the last Airechtas. At this point, Savvy and Phoebe were asked to stand and be officially welcomed into the Northern Clans. A few of the Durupinen stood, including Hannah and me, but the reception was lukewarm at best. Savvy, already looking uncomfortable at being made to stand up, looked downright curmudgeonly as she sat back down.

"What is their problem?" I asked Hannah under my breath.

Hannah rolled her eyes. "You know the Durupinen by now. It's all about tradition, and Savvy has none. Is it any surprise they show disdain for new Gateways? They probably resent that the old Gateway had to close."

"Yeah, I bet you're right. It's like the old money versus new money prejudice," I said. "Your status is somehow higher the longer you've had it."

"Exactly. Some of these clans have existed as far back as recorded Durupinen history. You can tell which ones by where they're sitting. The ones toward the front are the oldest clans, and the ones toward the back are the newest."

I glanced around. We were in the second row from the front. That made us one of the oldest families in attendance. Again, I felt Agnes Isherwood's gaze upon me, full of judgment and expectation. It was so tangible that I wondered if her ghost was about to appear beside me whispering heavily weighted words about legacy and duty and tradition. I suddenly felt a little claustrophobic. To dispel the feeling, I took a deep breath and looked up at Celeste who had begun to speak again.

"Next up for discussion is the open seat on the Council," Celeste said. She reached a hand over to Siobhán, who was not paying attention, but instead rubbing distractedly at her temple.

"Madame Secretary? The Council Seat declaration, please?" Celeste prompted her.

Siobhán looked up, confused. "What? Oh, yes. Apologies. Here it is." She extracted a paper from the pile in front of her and handed it to Celeste. Celeste took it from her with a look of mild concern.

"Here we are," Celeste said. "As every clan is aware, having been formally notified of the decision, Clan Gonachd was stripped of its Council seat as punitive action for its involvement in events surrounding the fulfillment of the Isherwood Prophecy."

These words, which she spoke unflinchingly, were met with a ringing silence. The tension in the room, sporadic thus far, was suddenly stifling. Every eye shifted to the middle of the room, where Marion sat, poker-stiff in a seat beside the center aisle. Her expression was supremely unimpressed, as though Celeste's words were barely worth her notice. A woman sitting near Marion gave a snort of disgust. Marion betrayed a tiny smirk and acknowledged the sound with an ironic inclination of her head. It was one of those smug expressions that you just wanted to slap off of someone's face. I clenched my hands together in my lap to suppress the urge. Assault was probably not the smartest choice I could make in this situation, even if it would be the most satisfying one.

I could tell we were hovering on the edge of a confrontation, and perhaps Celeste knew it too, for she plowed on forcefully before anyone else had a chance to speak. "That punitive action has left a seat on the Council open for filling on the event of this Airechtas. Anyone wishing to nominate a clan may do so by submitting a formal written nomination letter to me or Siobhán by the end of sessions tomorrow. On Wednesday, all nominees will have the choice to accept or decline their nomination. A formal debate for remaining nominees will take place on Thursday, and a binding vote will take place on Friday afternoon. All votes will be submitted anonymously, per Airechtas guidelines, and the announcement of the seat will close the final session of the Airechtas on Saturday evening."

My insides in a tight knot, I stole a glance up at Finvarra. She was looking right at Hannah and me, her gaze steely with resolve. I couldn't imagine what kind of unpleasantness was going to be hurled our way when she formally nominated us.

A woman stood up on the Council bench. She was tall and statuesque, with mahogany hair swept back in a twist and lips pulled back in an ingratiating smile. I recognized her at once as Róisín and Riley's mother, and one of Marion's closest cronies; Marion had been speaking with her in the dining hall on the day she had arrived.

"The Council recognizes Patricia Lightfoot," Celeste said, pointing to the woman. Bertie's quill began scratching loudly as he recorded the exchange.

"Thank you for the opportunity to speak. I would like to state, for the record, that many among us are truly disappointed that Clan Gonachd was stripped of its seat without a full vote of the assembled Northern Clans. It seems inherently unequal that Clan Soillseach maintains its seat on the Council while Clan Gonachd is barred from ever serving again. In the first case, the punitive action has been applied solely to the guilty party, leaving the seat unaffected. In the second, the punishment has been extended to the entire clan. I have a hard time seeing the logic in two such disparate decisions."

Several people around her nodded their heads and murmured their agreement. Marion crossed her arms over her chest defiantly, her smirk spreading across her face like poison through veins.

"Your remarks are duly noted. If you take issue with the punishments handed down by the International High Council, I suggest you take it up with them," Celeste said coolly.

"I assure you, I intend to," Patricia said, and she held up a scroll of parchment. "I have prepared a formal complaint, signed by no less than fifteen clans present here. I would like to file a copy as part of the proceedings today."

Celeste looked to Siobhán, who was now massaging her forehead, eyes closed. Celeste cocked her head at Bertie, who leapt to his feet at once and bustled down the aisle to retrieve the scroll, then turned back to Siobhán. I watched as Celeste leaned away from the microphone and whispered quietly into Siobhán's ear. Siobhán shook her head and waved her away.

Patricia plowed on, ignoring the exchange. "Furthermore, I submit this motion for voting, that the Council of the Northern Clans dispute the ruling, and request that the Clan Gonachd be reinstated with its full rights to run for the Council seat again in the future. If Catriona can continue to serve, in the face of Lucida's staggering betrayal, surely future generations of Clan Gonachd cannot be excluded over what was little more than a political squabble."

I laughed incredulously. The sound echoed around the hall, drawing all eyes to me, but my indignation far outweighed my embarrassment. Marion had also looked up at the sound, and I met her eye unflinchingly, hoping that she could feel every ounce of my loathing for her burning through my gaze.

So, this was why she wanted to be here so badly. This was the reason the rest of her family suddenly and mysteriously couldn't represent their clan this week. She wanted to be front and center for this; to orchestrate her family's reinstatement into the hierarchy, or at least, to make them eligible to rise again. And it seemed she had a great deal of support, just as she did three years before when she attempted to orchestrate a coup in this very room.

Celeste was not to be trampled in this exchange, however. "You have every right to file this motion, and the clans here assembled have every right to debate and vote upon it. However, as a Council member, you are well aware how the punitive process works. Matters of this nature must be handled by objective outside votes from a higher court, so as to avoid personal relationships from interfering with due process. Nevertheless, the motion is on the table. Who will second the motion?"

"Seconded," Marion's voice called out over the crowd.

I felt my outrage bubble up toward my lips but Savvy got there first. She jumped to her feet.

"Are you havin' us on? Does she seriously get to do that?" she blurted out.

Celeste turned to face Savvy, her expression stern. "The Council recognizes Savannah Todd of the Clan Lunnainn and urges her to remember that we are in a formal meeting."

"Right, yeah," Savvy said, clearing her throat and standing up straighter in an attempt to appear more dignified. "What I mean to say is, how is it she's allowed to second that motion? It's about her family, yeah? So, shouldn't she be excluded?"

Many of the people sitting around Savvy, who had looked disapproving a moment before, now looked as though they thought she had a fair point.

Celeste sighed. "I see the basis of your objection, but as a voting member here, Marion has every right to—"

"Seconded," another voice called out. It was another of Marion's entourage, seated a row behind her. "Just so there is no contention."

Savvy snorted in disgust and sat down abruptly.

"Very well, seconded. A majority carries. All in favor?" Celeste asked. A slim majority of hands went up; of course, mine and Hannah's were not among them. "The motion carries," Celeste said. "We will hear further discussion on this proposal of a formal complaint, and will vote on it along with the other measures. We move then to the question of—"

A soft whimpering sound drew her attention, and she looked over at Siobhán, who had covered her face with her hands. Celeste dropped her papers and hurried to the other side of the podium.

"Siobhán? My goodness, are you quite well?" Celeste asked. She placed a hand on Siobhán's shoulder, but Siobhán shook it off, stumbling a little as she did so.

"Get it away," she whimpered. "Please, I beg you. Get it away from me." She pointed to the edge of the platform. There was nothing there except for a tall candelabra aglow with tapers and a large Triskele banner on a flagpole.

Celeste looked over at Finvarra, who was leaning forward in her chair. Siobhán's Caomhnóir stepped forward as well, a hand outstretched to help.

"Siobhán?" Celeste repeated, and then called over her shoulder, "Seamus, go and fetch Mrs. Mistlemoore in the hospital ward. Immediately."

Siobhán went suddenly quiet. She pulled her hands from her face and stared at Celeste with wide, terrified eyes. Celeste froze.

"Siobhán?" she asked again.

"Who is Siobhán?" she cried.

I stood up. "Oh, my God."

But even as I stood, in the same moment that I realized what was happening, Siobhán staggered toward the podium. She snatched up the book there and then ran with it to the edge of the platform, shaking off her Caomhnóir's restraining hand. With a wild cry, she swung the book with all her might at the candelabra. I grabbed Hannah by the arm and pulled her under our table as flaming candles and melted wax rained down on the first few rows. We listened as the candelabra fell with a deafening clatter upon the stone floor. I leapt up just in time to see Siobhán taking off across the room, heading straight for a second candelabra. She only made it a few steps, though, before two of the Caomhnóir who had been stationed nearby pulled her to the floor and restrained her.

I darted around my table and sprinted across the room, dropping to my knees beside Siobhán. Her eyes were rolling back in her head, and her body was convulsing.

"She promised, she promised," she was hissing through clenched teeth. "It's closed! Why is it closed? She promised!"

"Celeste!" I cried over the general commotion. "It's just like Catriona!"

Celeste was already hurrying down the platform and over to us. "What do you mean? What's the same?"

"She's saying exactly the same things Catriona was saying back in her office," I said breathlessly. "She's saying, 'She promised!' and something about, 'It's closed.' I don't know what any of it means, but Catriona was saying it, too."

Celeste's eyes widened in horror. "And the fire. Mrs. Mistlemoore told me something happened with the fireplace in the office as well?"

"Catriona lost it when she noticed the fire burning in the fireplace. She tried to smother it with a tapestry from the wall," I confirmed.

Celeste looked down at Siobhán's struggling figure for a moment with an expression of growing horror, then pulled herself up to her feet.

"Everyone please remain in your seats. Stay calm," she called commandingly over the commotion. Desperate for a bit of direction, everyone obeyed. Durupinen crawled out from under tables and climbed down off of chairs, where many had been trying to get a better look at what was happening with Siobhán.

Up on the platform, Council members were flooding down from their benches and Finvarra was struggling to stand up from her wheelchair, while Carrick and the nurse pled loudly with her to stay in her seat. Finvarra was protesting, but it wasn't much of an argument, as she clearly couldn't even support her own weight. Meanwhile Siobhán was writhing on the floor like a frantic animal, blinded from reason by her own—or someone else's—terror.

As Siobhán struggled she turned her head and, for the briefest of moments, two things were clear. First, she was not the person looking out at me from those eyes. And second, I had seen those very eyes somewhere else before, staring out from the wrong face.

"Celeste," I whispered. "I don't know how it's possible, but whatever is possessing Catriona... it's possessing Siobhán, too."

NEMESIS

S IOBHÁN WAS CARRIED, thrashing and screaming, off to the hospital ward, and the Airechtas was placed on recess. Finvarra was whisked away to her tower to recover what little strength she still had. The remainder of the clans were asked to remain in the Grand Council Room until further notice.

With formal proceedings suspended, and nothing to do but wait, people began to cluster into little groups around the room. Savvy shuffled across her row of seats and came over to sit with us, parking herself casually right on top of our table.

"What do you reckon?" she muttered eagerly. "What was that all about, then?"

I filled her in on what I had witnessed with Catriona that morning, and then about our experience outside of the hospital wing. Her eyes widened with every new revelation.

"So, you reckon whatever possessed Catriona is now possessing Siobhán?" Savvy asked. "But how?"

"Well, that's the part I don't understand. I mean, at first I thought Catriona must have been the victim of a forced Habitation. But, like I said, there was no way this could have happened while we were inside the office, because of the Wards. So, that meant she had to be walking around with a spirit inside her for hours—maybe even days—before it took her over like that. I just don't see how that's possible."

"No way, mate," Savvy said. "I've had more than the occasional Habitator, always by choice of course, and there is no bloody way a spirit just strolled into Catriona without her noticing. It's the most invasive experience I've ever had, and that's saying something."

"Don't I know it," I said. "Speaking of spirits who have invaded my body, any word from Milo?" I added to Hannah. She had filled him in through our connection immediately after Siobhán had been taken from the room.

"No, not yet. He said he was going to float up to the hospital ward and see what he could find out. He can't get in there without permission, but he can at least haunt the entrance like we did. Hopefully he'll find out something soon," she replied.

"It's the strangest thing," I said slowly. "I saw those eyes looking at me out of Catriona's face, and I saw them looking out of Siobhán's, but... I feel like I've also seen them somewhere else before."

"What do you mean?" Hannah asked.

"I mean something about those eyes was familiar. Like I'd seen them before."

"And you can't think of where?"

I shook my head, both in reply and in an attempt to shake that tortured stare out of my head. It was a very unsettling feeling—kind of like déjà vu—to realize I knew the person looking out at me from Catriona and Siobhán's faces and yet having not a clue who it might be.

I turned in my seat and looked in Finn's direction. He was standing at military attention beneath the tapestry of Agnes Isherwood. His face, usually impassive when on duty like this, was pulled into a frown of concentration; I could practically hear his gears turning, analyzing this new development and what it might mean. I knew he didn't dare break ranks to come over to talk to me, but he must have felt my gaze, for he let his eyes drop to my face for a moment. There was a flicker of tenderness there, a contraction of the brows that meant to ask, "How are you?" I gave a tiny nod of my head, hoping to let him know that I was fine, and then quickly turned back to Hannah before anyone could notice the exchange. Hannah was already filling Savvy in on what she had sensed, first as Catriona was carried past her, and then when she looked at Siobhán.

All the color drained from Savvy's usually rosy complexion. She had been in Annabelle's flat, and had witnessed the horror of the dismembered spirits used to mask Annabelle from sight. "You reckon the Necromancers are up to something, then? It's got to be them, right?"

Hannah shrugged helplessly. "I don't know. I only know that it felt similar."

Savvy swallowed back something along with her dread. "That casting—whatever it was—was one of the most horrific things I've ever seen, and I've seen some shit. Blimey, I hope that's not what's happened."

"Me too," Hannah said. "I never wanted to see anything like that again as long as I live."

The wait in the Council Room seemed to stretch on for hours. There was no clock on the walls, no way to check to see how long we'd been sitting there. I never wore a watch because I always used my phone as my clock, but no cell phones were permitted in the meetings, and so I'd left it reluctantly upstairs in our room. We alternated between periods of tense silence and waves of agitated whispering. There was no real reason for everyone to keep their voices down, but for some unspoken yet universally accepted reason, we all did, at least at first. But the longer the wait went on, the louder the conversational periods grew and the less cooperative people became with this mandate.

Finally, Marion stood up and marched purposefully over to the Caomhnóir who were guarding the main entrance doors.

"We cannot be kept here indefinitely. Open the doors. I'm going to find out what is happening," Marion said, in the imperious tone she used so well.

Seamus, who was also very masterful in his ability to assert his authority, did not even deign to look down at her as he answered. "We are under strict orders to keep everyone here while the situation is assessed."

"Well then, open this door at once so that I may assess the situation. It has been nearly two hours. We have been given no information. This lack of transparency is utterly unacceptable."

"I understand your frustration. I cannot disobey a direct order from a current member of the Council," Seamus said through gritted teeth. He placed just the slightest emphasis on the word "current." Marion did not miss it. She turned and called back to the room at large.

"Is there a *current* member of the Council who can order this Caomhnóir to stand aside? I will not be kept here like a prisoner," Marion demanded.

Fiona stood up. "The current members of the Council are following protocol that is in everyone's best interest. I don't see any bloody chains on your ankles. Calm down with the theatrics before you get a formal citation for insubordination. That ought to fill your record out nicely. Now why don't you get yourself a cuppa, sit down, and shut up like everyone else. You're embarrassing yourself."

Everyone watched while Marion first formulated, then swallowed her biting reply. Then, with what dignity she could muster, she returned to her seat and sank slowly into it. Her entourage immediately pulled their heads together in a tight, expensively styled huddle.

"Wow, she has a lot of nerve," Hannah whispered to me, but I was completely distracted.

"Cuppa? Did she say cuppa? As in coffee?"

Hannah raised her eyebrows. "Well, no, she probably meant tea, but yes, there's coffee. Right over there." She pointed to a table in the back corner, hidden in the shadows of the balcony, where a row of silver coffee urns, tea pots, and plates of pastries had been set up. A few people from the back rows had already wandered over and were filling cups.

"How long has that been there?" I cried in amazement.

"About fifteen minutes. A couple of Caomhnóir brought it through that side door back there. You didn't notice?"

"No! I was too distracted contemplating the possible rise of our mortal enemies. Why didn't you say anything? You know you have a moral obligation as my twin to alert me to the presence of caffeine!"

"Oh, I'm so sorry," Hannah said sarcastically. "I was a little distracted contemplating the same thing. I didn't really think coffee was a priority."

"Coffee is always a priority!" I hissed, and stalked up the aisle. Okay, so I was being a bit more dramatic than the situation warranted, but my nerves were frayed and my stomach had been snarling angrily at me for the last hour, since I had been too shaken up by my meeting with Catriona to eat much lunch.

I snatched a little white teacup from the stack, lamenting silently to myself how little coffee it would hold, and placed it beneath the nearest spout to fill it.

"Well, well, well, Miss Ballard. We meet again."

I didn't even need to turn around to know who was speaking. In fact, in the interest of avoiding physical violence, I chose not to look. It would be easier to control myself if I didn't have to look Marion in the face.

"Wow, you should really write dialogue for comic book villains," I said. I picked up a muffin and offered it to her over my shoulder. "High-calorie baked good?"

"No, thank you," she said, almost pleasantly.

"Oh, that's right, you can't Leech the extra calories away anymore, can you? I guess you'll just have to work out like the rest of us. I hear Zumba is a good time."

"My, my, insults and sarcasm right out of the gate, then? I take it from your insolent tone that you have no interest in mending fences," Marion said.

I laughed and turned, looking at her for the first time. "Mending fences? You can't mend a fence that the other person has burned to the ground. And I highly doubt that you have any genuine interest in mending anything, except your own reputation."

"I'm sorry to hear you feel that way," Marion said, with a sanctimonious little sigh. "I did approach you in the hope that we might put our past disagreements behind us. You clearly do not feel the same way."

"I'm not a fool," I said bluntly. "How adorable that you think 'disagreement' is the appropriate word choice for your singular vendetta against me and my sister. From the moment we walked in the door here, you made it your mission to kick us right back out of it. I'm not interested in putting anything behind me, and I never will be."

"I'm disappointed in your attitude, Jessica," Marion said. "I had thought that the passage of a few years might have tempered your rashness with a bit of maturity. Evidently I was wrong."

"Sorry to disappoint you, but I'm just as rash and immature as ever," I said, with a huge grin. "So, good luck picking up the shattered remains of your reputation for the rest of the week. It's a big job, but I'm sure you can find your dignity around here somewhere." I indicated the floor of the Council Room with my coffee-free hand.

"The dignity of my clan far outstrips any personal decisions I may have made three years ago. I'm here to remind the Council of that fact," Marion said stonily.

"It's too bad you didn't take that attitude three years ago, when you crucified Hannah and me for my mother's decisions. In fact, correct me if I'm wrong, but I think tearing down an entire clan because of one person's mistakes is how you clawed your way into a Council seat in the first place. I don't know what ulterior motive you have coming over here and trying to make nice with me, but whatever it is, just forget it. I'm not interested."

I watched with satisfaction as the remainder of the smile slipped from Marion's face. She considered me for a moment, her expression shrewd. "I have heard from a very reliable source that Finvarra is going to nominate you for a Council seat."

I tried not to let the shock show on my face, but I don't think I was successful; Marion looked too smug. "I don't know what you're talking about," I said when I'd recovered.

"Don't flatter yourself, Miss Ballard. You aren't that good of an actress," she replied. "How long have you known about Finvarra's intentions?"

I glared at her for a long moment, but couldn't come up with a good reason not to answer the question, other than spite. "Not long. Two days."

Marion looked surprised. "Really? After you arrived? You mean to tell me that her offer had nothing to do with the reason you got on a plane to come here?"

"Not at all," I said coldly. "Not everyone drools at the scent of power, Marion."

"The world is full of fools," Marion replied with a casual shrug. "So, you did not know she was going to nominate you?"

"No."

"Well, then. Now that you know, what are your intentions?" she asked.

"My intentions? For what?" I asked. I knocked back my cup of scalding coffee like a shot and turned for another.

"For the seat. Do you intend to accept the nomination?"

I did not answer right away, choosing instead to fill my teacup all the way to the brim. As I did so, I looked up and saw Finn. He was staring at me, and the question behind his eyes could not have been clearer. *Are you okay? Do you need help?*

I discreetly shook my head and gave him a tiny smile. *I'm fine. Don't worry about me.*

I turned back to Marion, who seemed too intent on my impending answer to have noticed anything. "We haven't decided yet," I said, choosing to tell her the truth, though she did not deserve it.

Marion laughed incredulously. "You expect me to believe that? That you have made no decision in two days as to whether you will run for one of the most powerful positions in the Durupinen leadership?"

"I couldn't care less whether you believe it or not," I said. I took another long sip of coffee to cover my racing thoughts. Where was Marion headed with this? What was her endgame? Why was this any of her business? "You asked me a question and I told you the truth. We haven't decided."

"Well, I have a piece of truth for you as well, my dear. I came over here to offer you a bit of advice," she said, pressing her hands together in a demure little steeple.

I burst out laughing. The sound echoed around the quiet hall, and several people turned to stare.

"What is so funny?" Marion hissed, barely moving her lips. It was clear she did not want any additional attention drawn to our conversation.

"Why do you think I would ever care about or accept your advice? Because it served me so well in the past? Because I value your opinion?" I said, through still more laughter.

Marion took a step toward me and leaned in. It was a power play, but I did not back down. "You may be snarky and impudent, Miss Ballard, but you certainly are not stupid. You've seen how the people here have responded to your presence. They are wary. They are mistrustful. Some are even downright terrified. A grab for power now would only bring more mistrust down upon you. You will be met with a truly unpleasant backlash. People will fight, tooth and nail, to ensure your family does not reclaim that seat."

"And by 'people' I can only assume you are referring to yourself?" I asked coolly.

Marion ignored my question but for a small smile. "I am warning you. Accept that nomination and you will throw these proceedings into chaos. Our clans are still healing. After the Prophecy, we need stability. We need order. It would be in everyone's best interests if you and your sister sank back into obscurity where you belong."

My blood was pounding in my ears. I leaned in so that our faces were only a few inches apart. I could see the particles of her makeup clinging to her skin. "Never dare tell me where we do or do not belong," I hissed at her. Then I stepped back, refilled my coffee and addressed her in a friendly, conversational tone again. "You seem to have gotten a bit off track with your super-villain speech. Please allow me to assist. This is where you launch into the part about how you would have gotten away with it if it weren't for those meddlesome kids. Thanks for the advice, but next time, save it for somebody else, Marion. Or, better yet, keep it to yourself. No one who knows you will swallow a single line of whatever bullshit you're peddling this week. I'll see to that personally."

I walked away from her as confidently as I could, but my hands were shaking with rage. So, this was why she was really here. Sure, she wanted to try to get her family back in the Council's good graces, but this was the real reason for her sudden appearance at the Airechtas: to stop Hannah and me from getting that Council seat.

Hannah watched me approach, her face pale and worried.

"What happened? What did Marion say to you? You look furious," she said as I sat back down in my seat.

Keeping my voice low, so that neighboring Durupinen wouldn't overhear us, I started relaying to her what Marion had said. With every word of it, Hannah's wide eyes narrowed.

"That's why she's here. We are the 'sudden emergency' that meant she had to personally represent her clan this week," she murmured.

"Yup," I said. "Someone else could have presented that request to the High Council. In fact, it probably would have gone over better if Peyton or someone were here instead. No, she wanted to be here to argue against any chance we might have to get that seat."

"Who do you think told her about the nomination?" Hannah asked. She looked around the room as though expecting the culprit to raise her hand. "I can't imagine Finvarra let many people know about it."

"Does it really matter? It was probably one of her friends still on the Council. You know she still has allies here, even if she's been booted out of her seat. Do you remember all the signatures she collected to remove Finvarra as High Priestess? Most of those women are still sitting up there right now."

"She wanted you to say that we weren't going to accept the nomination?"

"Yeah. Then she threatened that things would get ugly if we did accept it."

"And what did you say?" Hannah asked.

"I told her that we hadn't decided yet, but we weren't going to be intimidated into refusing it." I said.

"Really?' Hannah asked, one eyebrow raised. "We haven't decided yet?"

"Well, we haven't," I said, a bit defensively.

"I know I haven't. I was sort of under the impression you had, though."

I shrugged noncommittally. "I told you I would think about it, and I am. Besides, I didn't want to give her the satisfaction of knowing I don't really want it. If it gives her even a minute of disquiet thinking we're going to take that seat back, then it's worth it."

Even as I looked down at my coffee to take another sip, I felt Hannah's eyes on me, probing me with an intensity that felt like an X-ray. Luckily, Savvy chose that moment to jump into the conversation, so I was spared more questions.

"What a hideous old harpy she is," Savvy said, glaring over at Marion, who had returned to her seat with a cup of tea. "Can you believe the nerve of her, even talking to you after what she's done? I've got a mind to walk right over there and offer her a few choice words of my own."

"Don't, Sav," Hannah said quickly. "You'll only make it worse."

"She already got an earful from me," I said. "Trust me, it didn't make a difference."

At that moment, the main doors swung open and Celeste swept up the aisle. Her face, though a mask of calm and poise, was very pale. I felt my pulse starting to race. Savvy jumped down off of the table and scurried back across the aisle to her seat. Around us, many other Durupinen were scrambling back to their own places, looking flustered.

Celeste mounted the platform and planted herself behind the podium. "May I have everyone's attention, please?" she said, although she didn't need to; silence had fallen and every eye had been upon her from the moment she stepped through the door.

"I am sorry to have kept you all waiting for so long, but I wanted to make absolutely sure I had answers for you before returning here. I have some distressing news to report. Before I explain what is happening, however, I need your promise to listen calmly and to follow instructions. Panic and hysteria will only exacerbate the seriousness of the situation. Please remain in your seats and listen to what I must tell you, and I will take questions in an orderly fashion after I have finished."

I looked at Hannah. She looked at me. And through our connection, a single word hovered like a specter of nightmares past.

Necromancers.

II

THE SHATTERING

P ANIC WAS RISING INSIDE ME, threatening to submerge me. It was the Necromancers, it had to be. Why else would Celeste be talking to us like this, using words like "panic" and "hysteria"? Beside me, Hannah was visibly trembling. I slipped my arm through hers and pulled her in close to me. She snatched my hand and threaded her fingers through mine, grasping them tightly. We did not look at each other, but kept our eyes fixed firmly on Celeste, waiting for the bomb to drop.

"Siobhán has been taken to the hospital wing and has been examined by Mrs. Mistlemoore. The hospital staff has concluded that Siobhán and Catriona's afflictions are linked. They are both victims of a Shattered spirit."

A terrified whisper rippled through the room. A few people cried out, but were quickly shushed by their neighbors. I looked over at Hannah, my confusion all over my face, but she shook her head, looking as perplexed as I felt. We returned our gazes to Celeste.

"Please indulge me for a moment as I explain this phenomenon to those among us who have never encountered it," Celeste went on, and the authority in her tone quieted the rest of the whispering. "Sometimes a spirit, in its confusion, will be drawn to a Gateway without realizing that it is closed. It will sense the presence of the Aether, but it will not recognize the barrier standing in its way. Desperate to Cross, it will try to force entry."

Amid a fresh wave of frightened murmurs, a vivid memory flashed through my head. A hooded and malevolent spirit in a darkened library bathroom, trying to force his way through a Gateway—my Gateway—that had not yet been opened. It was the most invasively painful experience of my life, and occasional nightmares about it still left me panting and shaking, drenched in a cold sweat.

Celeste's voice cut cleanly through my thoughts, bringing me back to reality. "Most of the time, the intense pain of the attempt will deter a spirit from trying again. However, once in a great while, a spirit will be desperate enough that it will persist in its attempts until at last, the spirit breaks itself apart."

A hand shot up to my right. "Please, can you clarify? What do you mean, break itself apart?" the woman demanded, shaking back long, dark hair.

Celeste pursed her lips, but answered the question. "It traumatizes itself so that it can no longer hold its energy together into a form. The energy splits off into pieces."

The same woman stood up now, not bothering to raise her hand. "But what do you mean? How can a spirit—"

Fiona stood up from her seat and snatched a glass of water from the table in front of her. "She bloody means like this!" she shouted, and threw the glass as hard as she could against the back wall. We all watched in stunned silence as the glass splintered into a hundred sparkling pieces that dropped to the floor with a musical, tinkling sound, like rain.

Fiona let the silence spiral for a few moments before shouting, "Now let the woman speak and hold your damn questions for the end!"

Celeste closed her eyes as though praying for patience, then said, "Thank you, Fiona. As I said, the spirit will Shatter itself. The severed pieces are called Shards. The Shards scatter on impact. They become confused and frightened. They do not remember who they are, or to which complete soul they once belonged. Each Shard only contains a confused smattering of memories that it cannot make sense of until it is reunited with the other Shards. Their only desperate goal is to seek the comfort of the Aether, and so they wander and Habitate in any Durupinen they can find, hoping to find a way through."

A violent shiver rolled through my body. I didn't want to believe that any of this could be true, that anything so terrible could happen to a person's spirit, and yet it made sense. It explained what Hannah had felt when Catriona had been carried past her. The spirits the Necromancers had used to hide Annabelle had been torn apart as well, though by different means. Countless times now, I had felt the shining purity and completeness of souls Crossing through me, one by one. I had connected with their humanity, and shared in the vividness of their memories. For me, the thought of a soul in Shards was as awful to conceive of as a dismembered body. I felt the urge to be sick, and quickly swallowed it back, fighting instead to focus on Celeste's next words.

"Shards of a Shattered spirit have found their way into this castle. They have nested in Catriona and in Siobhán, whom we now must call Hosts. We are sure now that this is the source of their afflictions," Celeste said.

Another woman stood up, this time in the very first row, thrusting her hand into the air as she did so. "Permission to speak, please?" she called.

"Very well," Celeste said, even as Fiona snorted in disgust behind her.

The woman cleared her throat. "So, this is a case of Habitation, then," she said, in the tone of someone trying to inject sense and reason into the conversation. "Why doesn't Mrs. Mistlemoore use one of the Caomhnóir to expel the Shards? Surely, we can find a way to contain them once they have exited the body, perhaps with a Caging?"

Heads nodded and murmurs of agreement filled the room, but Celeste put up her hand to quell them. "It is not as simple as that. All of our Castings are designed to work on the spirits—whole spirits—that we encounter in our day-to-day dealings. But Shards are not whole spirits, and our magic is not designed to work on them. Wards have no effect on them, because Wards are meant to keep out spirits that are intact. We have no Casting that will expel a Shard, nor any Circle that can contain one."

My mouth went dry. What did this mean?

"What about a Crossing?" another Durupinen shouted all the way from the last row of seats. "The Shards want to cross, don't they? So, give them exactly what they want! Open up the Gateways they are trying to breach and let them through!"

Several of the women around her shouted their approval of this idea, but Celeste was already shaking her head again.

"We cannot do that. It is against everything we stand for, the very reason we are here. To send a single Shard through the Gateway, without reuniting it first with all the others, would be tantamount to abandoning it to wander lost in the Aether forever. No part of that spirit would ever find peace."

"Do you mean to say," the woman in the front row went on, her tone incredulous, "that there is no way to help them? That these Shards will Habitate inside Catriona and Siobhán permanently?"

"Not necessarily, no," Celeste said. "There is one way to facilitate the removal of a Shattered spirit, and that is to get all of the Shards and all of the Hosts together within the boundaries of the same Casting circle. When they have been gathered, there is a casting we can use to put the Shards back together again."

"Well, you've gotten the two of them together into the same room, haven't you?" Marion said, standing up to join the discussion. "Why can't you simply join the Shards now?"

"That is the other difficulty," Celeste said. "We do not know how many Shards there are."

"You mean to say there could be other Shards floating around this castle right now, waiting to infect the rest of us?" Marion asked, and her voice was higher than usual, betraying her fear.

"Yes, I am afraid that is what I am saying," Celeste said. She paused for a moment as a panicked wave of cries and shouts rose and then died. "We are still trying to ascertain if Catriona is the source of the Shattering, or if she is simply the first victim of a Shard Habitation. We are investigating her recent activities with the Trackers, attempting to retrace her steps, and learning what we can of her last few days."

Something clicked in my head as I recalled those terrifying moments in Catriona's office. My legs shaking, I stood up and thrust my hand into the air.

Celeste looked down at me and nodded solemnly. "Yes. The Council recognizes Jessica Ballard of the Clan Sassanaigh."

I ignored, as best I could, the feeling of hundreds of hostile stares boring into me. I cleared my throat. "What you've just explained to us—about what happens to a spirit when it Shatters—well, it helped me make sense of something I witnessed when I was up in Catriona's office."

"What *you* witnessed?" Patricia O'Toole spat. "What do you mean, what *you* witnessed?"

"I was there," I said. "I was there in Catriona's office when the spirit first attacked her."

A fresh round of mutters washed over me, and there was no denying the suspicious tone. I waited, gritting my teeth to bite back a nasty reply to the unwarranted hostility.

"There will be silence, please, so that Jessica can speak," Celeste said sharply. "She has the floor."

"When I realized that something was wrong with Catriona, I left her with my Caomhnóir, Finn Carey," I said, pointing to Finn, who smartly stepped out of line and gave a sharp bow to Celeste. "Then I went to find help, but there were several Caomhnóir right down the hall, including Seamus and Braxton." Again, I pointed out the Caomhnóir, and both acknowledged me with a nod of the head. "As we arrived back at the Tracker office, there was a sort of... explosion. Spirit energy just erupted out of the room, in every direction. It was incredibly violent; it blew us all right off our feet."

Celeste nodded. "Yes, Seamus mentioned the incident when he reported to me."

"Well, that must have been it, right? The Shattering?" I asked. "The spirit that was trying to get through Shattered itself at that moment, and the explosion was caused by the Shards that went flying out in every direction."

Silence hung on the end of my words for a moment, and then Finn took another step forward.

"Permission to speak?" he barked.

"Granted," Celeste said.

"I must agree with Jessica," Finn said. My full name sounded foreign on his tongue, like the name of a stranger. "There was a screaming as well, a screaming that traveled out of Catriona and multiplied into many screams that dissipated through the castle. I did not understand what was happening at the time, but the Shattering would make sense of this phenomenon."

Celeste turned and put her head together with two Council members behind her. A buzzing of discussion broke out in small knots all over the room as this information was discussed. Finally, Celeste turned back to the podium.

"I must conclude that you are correct, Jessica. What you and the Caomhnóir witnessed was the moment of the Shattering. We can come to no other logical conclusion," she conceded.

Fiona stood up, and her face was aghast. "So, this is not a question of an errant Shard or two finding their way into the castle. The Shattering happened here. That means the castle is full of them."

All terrified eyes were now on Celeste, who said, grimly, "Yes."

Several cries and soft screams of panic broke out then, and all around the room, Durupinen jumped up from their seats. A few actually started running for the doors.

"Stop!" Celeste was shouting over the chaos. "Stop! Everyone please! Go back to your seats and try not to panic! Caomhnóir, hold the doors!"

As one, the Caomhnóir around the perimeter of the room stomped their feet, pulling long staffs from their belts and thrusting them out in front of them, creating a sort of human fence. The Durupinen who had run for the exits were all pulled up short, piling up on one another as they stumbled back in their haste not to collide with the staffs.

"You can't do this!" Marion cried, and a dozen shouts echoed her. "You cannot trap us here like sitting ducks, waiting for each of us to fall to these Shards!"

"If everyone could just keep calm, I can explain what we—" Celeste began.

"This is madness!" Patricia shouted over her. "Call off these Caomhnóir at once! We are not obligated to stay here and calmly await our own Habitations!"

"Obligated? Of course you are obligated!" Fiona boomed, her voice like a cannon blast that barreled through the disorder and left it speechless. She stepped up onto her bench, and then up onto the tabletop in front of her, nostrils flaring in her fury. "Two of your sisterhood have fallen! Two of your fellow Gatekeepers are held hostage by forces they cannot fight on their own. And this is what you do? You turn tail and run? Is that what your sisterhood means to you? Is that all it's worth, that you would spit on it, and turn your back to save yourselves?"

No one spoke. No one moved. All was stillness.

"You disgust me," Fiona spat, and the words felt like Shards themselves, cutting into each of us. "Where is your courage? You would walk out those doors knowing that to do so means abandoning two of your own? You leave now, and there is a chance Catriona and Siobhán will never recover. They could lie in that hospital wing for the rest of their lives, mere vessels to a hostile spirit that refuses to let them go."

The shame and embarrassment was palpable in the crowd.

"And if that doesn't move you, because you don't give a flying feck about other living people, think of the Gateways! What about the chaos this will cause, with two Gateways permanently crippled, unable to traffic the very spirits we are bound to protect? There are bigger things at play here than if you get inconvenienced for a few days!"

"Inconvenienced? We could be the next victims of this Shattering!" Marion replied, though her tone was definitely more subdued than before.

"Yes, you might," Fiona said bluntly. "Some of us will surely have to play Host to these things, until all of them have nested and we can reunite and expel them all! There is no other choice! If you consider yourself too good for such a task, do please point out those here present in the hall that you would prefer to do it in your stead."

Though Marion threw a pointed look in my direction, she didn't dare meet Fiona's challenge. Nor did anyone else. It seemed that Fiona took the time to look into every single face in the hall, daring each one to respond before finally saying, "No takers? Very well then. Kindly let your Deputy Priestess continue."

"Thank you, Fiona," Celeste said, nodding graciously to Fiona before continuing. "There is an additional challenge. The Casting used to reassemble the Shattered spirit includes a Naming."

Several people groaned. Others looked even more puzzled than before, including Savvy, who stood up and called out, "Can you explain what that is, for the newcomers, please?" There was a murmur of agreement, which Hannah and I joined.

Celeste obliged. "Some Castings cannot be carried out without knowledge of the Spirit's name. The name must be spoken, as part of the ritual, for the Casting to work. The healing of a Shattered spirit is one of these Castings. Unless we can discover who he or she is, we cannot heal or expel the spirit in question. By using the spirit's name, we can force it to listen, to give us information, and to comply to demands. It cannot refuse us once its name has been spoken."

Keira stood up. "And the Shards themselves are too confused to identify who they are?"

"That's right," Celeste said. "The Shattering leaves them so disoriented and incomplete that they do not have a full understanding of who they are. The more of them we gather, the better the chance that they will collectively remember, but we cannot guarantee it. And so, the Scribes are busy researching and questioning our resident spirits for any information, and the Trackers are retracing Catriona's most recent moves, in the hope that we can identify the spirit on our own. They have already—yes, the Council recognizes Patricia Lightfoot of the Clan Dílseacht."

"You said a few minutes ago, that we need all the Shards in the hospital wing together in order to proceed. Is there no way to find them? They are pieces of spirits, after all, and everyone here is sensitive," Patricia said. She was instantly recognizable as Riley and Róisín's mother. They all had the same jet-black hair and round cheeks. "Surely, with the entire castle on alert, we can track them all down."

"It's not as simple as that," Celeste began, but then, to my utter shock, Hannah stood up and placed her hand in the air. Celeste spotted her at once and pointed to her, "The Council recognizes Hannah Ballard of the Clan Sassanaigh."

If the Durupinen seemed wary at my remarks, it was nothing compared to the tension that met Hannah's turn to speak. She fought to ignore it, though she clenched and unclenched her hands. Suddenly, a soothing voice flowed through the connection, wrapping Hannah in its comfort.

"Don't you let them intimidate you, sweetness. You got something to say and they're going to hear it. We don't play their games," Milo said. He materialized beside her, and I knew the shivery coolness of his presence was as good as a security blanket to her.

"I have some experience in sensing fractured spirits," Hannah said, an audible tremor in her voice. "Three years ago, I came across a Necromancer casting that used fractured spirits to hide someone. The spirit fragments were very, very difficult to sense. We were in the room with them for a long time before we even realized something was there, and I was the only one who noticed, probably because of my Caller abilities."

Celeste nodded. "Go on, please."

"When the Caomhnóir carried Catriona past me earlier today, I sensed it again. It was a similar energy. Again, it was very faint, and very difficult to decipher. If I hadn't felt it before, I don't think I would have picked up on it," Hannah said.

"So, it can be detected," Marion said, pointing at Hannah with a triumphant gesture. "So, we send the Caller around the castle to track down the Shards."

I leapt up from my seat, plowing right over Celeste's attempt to acknowledge me. "First of all, 'the Caller' has a name. Her name is

Hannah Ballard, and you better use it if you are going to address her. Secondly, she is not some canary you are going to shove down this coal mine, to be sacrificed because you're too scared to face the alternative. And lastly, even if Hannah was willing to scour the entire castle for these Shards, what good would it do? You heard Celeste: there is no way to trap them, no way to contain them. In all likelihood, Hannah would immediately become a Host to the first Shard she found, and then we'd be right back where we started."

Marion opened her mouth to retort, but Fiona cut her off. "Jessica is right. We cannot let our fear overrule our good sense, however little good sense some of us may have," she said, and she glared at Marion.

"Thank you, Fiona, but that is not constructive either," Celeste said. "The fact is that there is only one course of action. During your wait in this room, our Scribes have been consulted, and every text about Shattered spirits in our extensive library has been reviewed. Fairhaven must be quarantined. No one is allowed to leave the premises. The Hosts will be gathered in the hospital wing, within the circle that, even now, the hospital staff is creating with the help of the Scribes. When all the Shards have been gathered together, the process to rejoin and expel them can begin."

"Quarantined?" Patricia shouted. "Why must we be quarantined if we have not been infected?"

"Any one of us could be a Host at this moment, and simply be ignorant of the fact," Celeste said. "The Shards do not announce themselves. They take over without warning. We cannot risk that anyone might leave this castle an unwitting Host. The instructions are clear, and we will all abide by them. Anyone who breaks the quarantine will face serious sanctions against her clan. Make no mistake about that."

No one spoke. No one argued. Everyone simply waited for what was next.

Celeste took a long moment to let her threat sink in before she continued. "We cannot continue the Airechtas under these conditions. I move that all sessions be suspended until the Shattering is resolved."

"Seconded," Fiona called from the benches.

"All in favor?" Celeste asked.

Slowly every hand in the room rose into the air, including mine. Hannah's was still shaking.

"Motion carried," Celeste said. "The Caomhnóir stationed outside of this room have secured the entrances to the castle and the borders of the grounds. We will gather here again at eight o'clock tomorrow morning for another update. Any encounters with a Shard must be reported swiftly. Caomhnóir will be stationed with their clans until further notice. The Caomhnóir reserves have been called, and will be assigned to each clan to provide a second shift of protection overnight. We will do all we can to keep everyone as safe as possible."

"Except for those of us being used as sacrificial lambs to this plague of the Shattered," Marion called in a ringing voice.

"No one is being sacrificed," Celeste said with undisguised disgust in her voice. "We are working together to save our sisterhood. If everyone cooperates, this will all be over swiftly. But I will be sure to make note of your dissenting comments, and how unwilling you are to suffer an inconvenience to protect your fellow Durupinen."

"My, oh my, someone give her some aloe for that burn," Milo crowed through our connection, startling me. I had nearly forgotten he was there amidst all the tension.

"Unless anyone else would like to register their lack of cooperation, I hereby dismiss this session of the Airechtas, to be resumed at a later date to be determined," Celeste said. "Dinner is ready to be served in the dining room within the next half hour. Caomhnóir, you may unblock the exits. Stay safe, sisters. Stay vigilant."

ELEANORA: 12 JULY 1864

12 July 1864

Dearest Little Book,

I need not fear prying eyes upon this page. My hands are shaking so badly that the words could surely not be legible to any eyes but my own. My hope is that, by writing about my experience, I can perhaps hold it at a distance and understand it better, for at this moment, Little Book, I am at a loss to comprehend what has happened to me tonight.

Hattie and I attended Lord Kentwood's ball as my mother insisted we should, despite a long and exhausting few days of training at Fairhaven Hall. I had resolved to play my part as the dutiful daughter. I even managed to convince myself, half out of desperation, I suppose, that I was exaggerating Harry Milford's less desirable qualities. I arrived at the ball determined to find some good in him, and therefore some hope for myself.

All I managed to do was to prove that even the most dogged determination cannot grow roses from ashes.

It was apparent from the moment he saw me that Harry Milford has quite made up his mind in regards to our union. He was much more forward than I would ever have expected from a gentleman of his standing. He positively leered at me over dinner; I could hardly swallow my food for blushing. At one point, he actually leaned in and remarked that there was a direct correlation between a woman's appetite and whether her figure was pleasing to a man, and that therefore I should be encouraged to eat up! I could have thrown my glass of wine in his face right then and there, but for the sake of civility, I refrained. I kept hoping my mother would catch on to Harry's behavior, but at this point I think he could have ravished me upon the dining table and she would have found an excuse for it.

After dinner, the men retired to the library for cigars and brandy, and I at last thought I had escaped Harry's clutches, but I was mistaken. I stepped out from the salon where the women had gathered so that I could take in some fresh air outside. Within a few moments I heard footsteps behind me and spun on the spot to find Harry grinning at me, brandy snifter still in hand.

"I saw you through the window," he said to me, still grinning stupidly.

"I was just taking a breath of fresh air," I said, trying not to let hostility creep into my voice. "I was feeling rather overheated. But I am better now. If you'll excuse me."

"Oh, come now," he chided. "You can't honestly think I believe that?"

"Believe what?" I asked him.

"This silly story about being overheated. You are terribly transparent, Miss Larkin. You walked right by the window, where you knew I must be able to glimpse you pass by. Am I to believe that you wanted to be out here alone, when you made such an invitation as that?"

"I hardly think walking past a window constitutes an invitation," I said, and I felt my pulse quicken with something that might have been fear. "However, I am happy for your company back in the house, if you would care to accompany me."

"Back in the house? That rather defeats the purpose, doesn't it?" Harry said with a failed attempt at a wink. "If I craved the company of any other than yourself, I'd still be inside."

"Now, now, Mr. Milford, you know that our being alone together out here is not seemly," I said, endeavoring to sound playfully chiding rather than terrified, as I was now starting to feel. "We wouldn't want to give the others reason to gossip, would we?"

"Wouldn't we?" he countered, taking several steps closer to me, so that he closed the distance between us by half. He swigged what remained of the brandy in his glass and cast it aside in the grass. "Let's be frank, Miss Larkin. The others are already gossiping. There are no secrets here in the upper circles of society. Our impending union is already being widely discussed. Your family, my family, all of our acquaintances—every one of them is talking of nothing else. Why pretend otherwise? We both know what awaits us. There is really no need for such formality—such distance—is there?"

"If this is your idea of a proposal, Mr. Milford, I am sorry to say that you have been woefully misinformed about the practice," I said lightly, while silently cursing the distance between me and the house. Why had I walked so far into the garden?

138

"*Practice be damned,*" he scoffed, with what he must truly have thought to be a winning, roguish smile. "*What is the point of all this practice—all this etiquette? We are not strangers. We are soon to be joined. We are soon to know all there is to know about each other. What does it matter if we obtain some of that knowledge a bit early?*"

He took another step toward me, and there was a menace in that step, an intent that sent my heart into my throat and my brain into a panic.

"*Don't come any closer!*" I cried out without thinking.

He threw his head back and laughed, and it was a joyless, mean-spirited sound. "*My dear Eleanora, I do hope this isn't a glimpse into our future together as man and wife! I will be a very lonely man, indeed.*"

"*Please,*" I said, and I did my best to smile, but I cannot say what expression actually appeared upon my face. "*Please. It is late and you have had a good deal to drink. Let us walk in together arm in arm and rejoin the party. I do not want to begin our life together under the haze of gossip, and I am sure you do not want aspersions cast upon your new wife's character. Please. Please let's go inside.*" And little though I wanted to do it, I reached a hand out toward him.

And God help me, I thought it had worked. Harry's head sagged on his neck and he sighed. "*You are right,*" he said. "*Decorum above all else.*" And he stepped forward, offering me his arm.

I was so relieved at this show of acquiescence at last that I did not hesitate to traverse the last few steps between us and take his arm. Had I taken my time, had I moved more warily, I would surely have seen the gleam in his eye, the cruel smirk on his face. But I did not.

As soon as my arm was within the crook of his, Harry dropped his elbow, pinioning me to his side. Then with a rough gesture he grabbed the hair upon the back of my head and pulled me against him into a kiss. His breath reeked of brandy and his lips were greedy and forceful upon mine. I struggled. I pushed and shoved. I tried to cry out, but my cries were smothered against his lips. At last all I could do was cry inside my head, in desperation, a silent plea: Help me! Oh, dear God please, someone come and help me!

Nearly the instant the thought exploded in my head an icy blast of wind descended upon us, driving between Harry and me like a wall, knocking us apart. Then a second gust thrust us to the ground in opposite directions, so that we landed several feet from each other.

Harry sat up, shaking his head and staring wildly around for an explanation as to what had just happened. His eyes found me, and he seemed to conclude that I had somehow managed the feat on my own. Anger etched all over his features, his lips pulled back in a snarl, he began to crawl toward me. But I could barely concentrate upon him, for there was something standing between us that he could not see.

Lined up like a defending battalion, shoulder to shoulder, were seven spirits. Their faces were blank; as though each slept with his eyes open, and each was facing Harry as he came toward me again. They made no motion that they would stop him, no sign that they even knew he was there.

A strange, heady feeling came over me. I do not know how I knew it, but suddenly it was clear to me: these spirits were here to answer my cry for help. And they would do my bidding.

"Stop him," I whispered.

As one, they flew at him, and the force of their energy blasted him backward again, right off of the ground and into the air, twisting and flailing, until he landed with a thump and a shout in a flower bed twenty paces away.

He clambered to his feet, cursing and shrieking, staring at me as though I were an apparition myself. Then he turned and pelted for the house. I remained on the ground, motionless in abject terror, as the spirits floated back to me and waited, seemingly for me to give them further instruction.

"Go," I told them. "Just go."

And they went, vanishing on the spot, but lingering behind my eyelids like the imprint of a candle after you blow it out in the darkness.

Before I could think, before I could master my gasping breath, our Caomhnóir sprinted around the side of the house from where he had been waiting with our coach. Without a solitary word to me, without inquiring if I was hurt or what had happened, he took me by the arm and dragged me to our waiting carriage. He did not stop to find my mother or my sister, or to tell anyone where we were going. As soon as he had deposited me onto the seat, we took off at breakneck speed.

We are barreling through the night as I write this to you in the unsteady light of the wildly sputtering oil lamp. He will not answer any of my questions, nor explain where we are going, though my knowledge of the route has led me to the conclusion that we are headed for Fairhaven Hall.

Little Book, I am so frightened. What has happened to me? Why did those spirits attack? Did my cries for help summon them? Why did *they only act upon my spoken command? And how in the world can we possibly repair the damage they have caused to our secrecy and our reputation? I can only pray that the Council will be able to answer these questions that are burning inside me.*

Eleanora

12

―――――

THE LÉARSCÁIL

A DEAFENING SCRAPING of chair legs signaled the mass exodus from the room, but Hannah and I had barely risen to our feet when Celeste called our names over the commotion. I looked up to see her beckoning us forward. Milo followed us up the aisle to the edge of the platform.

"Thank you both for your input," Celeste said. "I know it was not easy for either of you to speak in such a hostile assembly."

"I didn't think we really had a choice," I said, shrugging. "This isn't the moment to think about that stuff."

"And yet few in this room chose to master their fear. I applaud you for it," Celeste said.

I didn't really know how to accept the compliment, so I said nothing.

"I would appreciate your help, both of you, as we continue to investigate this matter," Celeste said. "Jess, you are the only person to have witnessed both Habitations, and so I hope you will not mind making yourself available to answer questions."

"No, of course not," I said. "Anything I can do, just let me know."

Celeste reached out and squeezed my shoulder in a motherly gesture. "And Hannah, there is something in particular I may need you to help with, if you are willing."

"I'm happy to help, too," Hannah said warily. "Although you should know up front that I don't think I'll be able to Call the Shards. I wasn't able to Call the spirit fragments in Annabelle's apartment, either. I don't think an incomplete spirit is compelled to answer a Call."

"Yes, the Scribes have told us as much," Celeste said. "Did you understand what I said about the Naming?"

"Yes, I think so. Using the spirit's name gives us lots of power over it, right?" Hannah asked.

"Yes. And in the case of a Shattered spirit, knowing its name could be crucial. If we have the name, and most of the Shards have been contained, there is a possibility that we—that is to say, you—could Call the rest of the Shards into the circle even if they have not yet found Hosts."

Hannah looked surprised, but nodded eagerly. "If that's true, then I'll help in any way I can. Of course I will try to Call them, if you think it might work."

"Excellent," Celeste said. "We will likely ask you to try, when we discover the name. I will keep you posted. In the meantime, be sure to alert the Caomhnóir or a Council member if you sense any other Shards in the castle. Thank you both."

She turned back to the remaining Council members, which we took as the signal that we were dismissed. Finn was waiting by the doors for us, as were Savvy, Phoebe, and Bertie. Savvy was already in full rebellion mode about having to stay in the castle.

"I'd rather be a Host than have you staring at me like a bloody pervert all night while I sleep," she was shouting as we approached. "You can stay in the hallway or you can sod off."

Bertie stood there, spluttering something about "not a pervert..." as Savvy turned her back on him. "Food, yeah?" she said to me, and with a cock of her head, marched out the door, leaving Phoebe and Bertie with their mouths hanging open.

Food. Yeah.

§

It was a long night. I barely slept, every tiny sound setting my teeth on edge and my pulse thundering through my veins. Was I about to be invaded? Was Hannah still okay? I rolled over so many times to check on her that I made myself dizzy. After about the hundredth time, Milo's frustrated voice shot through the connection.

"I am watching her like a hawk, Jess. Calm yourself before you roll right out of that bed."

"Okay. Sorry. Thanks, Milo," I whispered.

"Just doing my job," he said.

I settled with my gaze on the wall, but I still did not sleep. Perhaps the worst part was that I was desperate to speak to Finn alone, and the new safety protocols had made it completely impossible. We had managed a tiny snatch of conversation when the new Caomhnóir, a hulking middle aged man named Patrick, arrived to relieve Finn for the evening shift. Hannah and Milo stayed in the room to explain his Spirit Guide status to Patrick, while Finn and I went out into the hallway to set up the cot.

"Are you alright?" he muttered so softly that I almost didn't hear him.

"I guess so. Scared," I murmured back.

"What did Marion—"

"Don't worry about Marion. I can handle her."

"But what did she want?"

"She wanted to dissuade us from running for the Council seat," I said.

Silence. I looked up. Finn was staring at me. "But you don't want the Council seat."

"I know that, but Marion doesn't."

"How did she even find out about the nomination?" Finn hissed.

"You know Marion. She's got ears everywhere."

"I don't like that she's here. I don't trust her any farther than I could throw her."

"I don't trust her any farther than Hannah could throw her," I countered. There was a pause as Finn unfolded an olive green wool blanket and spread it over the bed.

"I miss you," I whispered.

"I miss you, too," he whispered back. "A few more days and this will all be over, I'm sure of it."

"I hope so." And he let his hand brush gently over mine as he handed me a pillow. Then he straightened up, arranged his face into the most businesslike of expressions, and walked away.

I replayed this conversation over and over again in my head as I lay in the dark, not because of what I said, but because of what I didn't say. True, there had been no time, but I almost felt like I had lied to him by not mentioning it.

The truth was, my conversation with Marion had lit a spark inside me that I never could have predicted. The moment that she had advised me not to run for the Council seat, I had experienced a sudden, burning desire to do the exact opposite. I dismissed it at the time; after all, I wasn't exactly a pinnacle of rational responses when I lost my temper, and few people riled me quite like Marion could. But the feeling, though it had calmed considerably, had not gone away. I didn't think that Marion wanted to keep me from the Council just out of spite. I mean, I knew she was spiteful, but I also knew that she didn't let things like spite drive her decisions. Marion, first and foremost, was a strategist. She was nothing if not practical, and if she wanted me out of that Council seat, it had nothing to do with my personality, and everything to do with what I might do with that power. She feared me. She feared what my perspective would do to her precious system. She feared that I might shake things up, and start to influence the other members through regular conversation. Suddenly, that Council seat was looking less like a burden and more like an opportunity. It was almost exactly the same argument Hannah had already made in its favor, but it had taken Marion's opposition to help me to see it that way.

Taking the seat was not an option, I told myself, over and over again. I had a life in America. I had goals. I had a deeply-held disgust for Durupinen politics. And of course, there was my relationship with Finn. If we were back at Fairhaven for good, our relationship would be reduced to what it was now; an occasional stolen whisper and a permanent, aching sense of longing.

Just as I had spoken none of this to Finn, I had confided none of it to Hannah. What good would it do to express these feelings if I couldn't act on them? No, as usual, I could be counted on to make the mature choice for my own mental health: I stuffed the feelings down and buried them in other shit.

Yeah, that always worked, and definitely never backfired on me.

§

Thankfully, Hannah and I both woke still fully in control of our bodies and minds, and made our way to the dining room. We'd only just sat down with our plates when Mackie shuffled over, looking tired and disgruntled.

"Hey, Mackie," I said.

"Hey, yourself," she said. "Everyone coping alright?"

I shrugged. "I guess so. I mean, we're not currently housing any hostile spirits, so we can't really complain. You?"

Mackie groaned. "I've been on permanent damage control. Celeste has got me running interference for the Council, calming everyone down so they don't start a panic and break the quarantine.

People are losing their bloody minds, as I'm sure you saw from the meeting yesterday. Some of them honestly can't understand why they should have to stay. They think everyone *else* should stay, of course, but..." She trailed off with a disgusted shake of her head.

"They're scared," Hannah said. "I wish we could leave, too."

"Yeah, but you're not actually trying to do it," Mackie said. "That's the difference. We've had to post Caomhnóir at the doors to make sure no one is sneaking off."

"I have zero interest in becoming the next temporary resident of an unwanted spirit," I said. "But we'll sort it out soon, I'm sure. From what Celeste said, this isn't an unprecedented situation."

"Could you please share some of your common sense and rationality with the other, more skittish Durupinen among us? It would be much appreciated," Mackie sighed.

"Nah, we can't, Mack, sorry," I said. "We can't get a reputation for being calm and sensible. It will ruin our badass image."

"Well, never mind, then," Mackie said, with a shadow of a grin. "I wouldn't want you to compromise your badassery."

"Have there been any more Habitations overnight?" Hannah asked.

Mackie nodded, her expression deadly serious yet again. "Three."

Hannah dropped her toast in alarm. "Three?!"

"Yeah," Mackie said. "Two Durupinen from one of the Irish clans and Patricia Lightfoot."

"Patricia Lightfoot? Riley and Róisín's mom?" I asked, aghast.

Mackie nodded, and then hitched a thumb over her shoulder, indicating the far corner. Róisín and Riley were sitting at a table there, huddled together with Keira, who was holding Riley's hand. Instead of plates, piles of crumpled tissues lay on the table in front of them.

"Wow. So, they're all in the hospital wing now?" I asked.

"Yeah, inside the circle that the staff set up. Celeste said they're all behaving in identical manners—terrified of fire, confused, and anxious. They're talking occasionally, too, but it's all just vague nonsense. The staff is trying to figure out what it means, but they don't think they'll be able to make sense of it until all the Shards of the spirit are within the circle," Mackie said.

"This is terrible," Hannah whispered, looking down at her food as though the sight of it suddenly made her sick. "What if they can't find all the Shards? What if they can't cure the Hosts?"

"Oh, come off it, you can't think like that!" Mackie said. "They've had Shattered spirits at Fairhaven before, and it turned out alright. We just need to be patient and have faith. It'll be resolved in no time." She spoke with complete confidence and not, as many I had heard, with the false confidence that one puts on to convince oneself as well as others. Mackie believed in the system, bless her. I wasn't nearly as confident.

"So, seeing as all the sessions are canceled for the day, and you clearly aren't going anywhere anytime soon, I thought you might want to come see the Léarscáil with me," Mackie said. "I did promise to take you after all, and it would be a great way to hide from Celeste for a bit."

Hannah perked up at once. "Really? That would be so cool! I'm in! Jess?"

I gazed longingly at my waffle. "Can it wait until after I finish breakfast?"

Mackie shrugged with a smirk. "I suppose. Are you sure you want to be seen eating waffles? I'm not sure that's a breakfast choice that entirely lives up to your 'badass' image."

I shoved a huge forkful in my mouth. "I'll risk it."

Despite my sass, Mackie let me finish my breakfast before leading us up the South Tower. No one would ever have guessed how crowded the castle was; though all of the sleeping quarters in the building were occupied, the halls were nearly deserted. Those who did venture out did so in a constant hush, not unlike the quiet of hospital wards, or school corridors when classes were in session. Everyone seemed afraid of disturbing whatever malevolent force had nested in the castle, afraid to draw attention to themselves as possible targets. And so, when there was a sudden loud wailing sound, all three of us jumped.

We had nearly reached the base of the South Tower. Across from the spiral staircase that would lead up to the Léarscáil was the door to the hospital ward. It was from beyond this door that the wailing had begun.

Mackie threw us an anxious look, then cocked her head toward the door, beckoning us forward.

"No, Mackie, we can't go in there!" Hannah cried, her voice shrill and sharp in the deserted hallway.

"I don't want to go in. I'm not daft," Mackie said. "I just want to have a look."

148

We crept forward until we could all press our faces against the row of little glass-plated windows set along the top of the door.

All five of the plague's victims thus far were sitting on the ends of their beds in the same peculiar posture: legs tucked up in front of them, night dresses pulled taut across their kneecaps, and their right hands traveling rapidly back and forth, back and forth, across their knees.

"What in the world..." Mackie's voice trailed off in a kind of horrified wonder.

"What are they doing?" Hannah whispered.

"They're writing," I said. "Or at least, they think they are."

It was true. Each hand seemed to grip an imaginary writing utensil. Each set of eyes was watching a string of invisible, yet meticulously formed letters and words. It was hard to tell from this distance, but it appeared that they were all doing it in perfect unison.

"Blimey, I think you're right. That is... not normal," Mackie said weakly.

Mrs. Mistlemoore and several other Durupinen were circulating amongst the patients, tucking blankets around them and checking their temperatures. Each of them wore a heavy sweater or coat, as well as gloves and scarves. I was about to comment on this odd choice of wardrobe when one of them shifted away from the furthest bed, and I saw that the fire in the massive stone fireplace was not lit.

"The fire's gone out!" said Hannah, who had noticed it, too. "Are they insane, leaving the fire out like that? They'll all freeze in there! This place is way too drafty not to have the fires lit!"

"I bet it's because of the way Catriona reacted to the fire in the Tracker office," I said slowly. "She absolutely lost her mind when she spotted it. We thought at first she was going to throw herself into it or something, but then she ripped down the drapes and tried to smother the flames instead. And of course, Siobhán went mental when she saw that candelabra. Mrs. Mistlemoore can't risk a roomful of patients hurling themselves at the fireplace any time there's a spark. It's safer to keep the fire out."

"They've got space heaters, look," Mackie said, pointing into the nearest corner. Sure enough, a small rectangular box was plugged into the wall there. I scanned the room and counted at least half a dozen more.

"They'll need every one of them to keep that room above freezing," I said with a shiver. Just the thought of it made me want to crawl into my bed and never move. There was nothing as cold as a medieval castle in winter. The chill crept right into your bones and nested there.

"What about that writing, though?" I asked, shaking my thoughts away from the temperature for a moment. "Don't you think that's worth investigating?"

Mackie tore her eyes from the windows to frown at me. "How do you mean?"

"Well, they're trying to find out everything they can about that Shattered spirit, right? So why not give every one of those hosts a pencil and some paper? It might just be gibberish of course, but what if it's not?"

Mackie blinked. "That's a really good idea."

"No, it's not. It's a really obvious one," I said.

"Obvious to you," Hannah said. "You're a Muse. You know more about spirit-induced writing and drawing than almost anyone in the castle, aside from Fiona."

"I'm going to go tell them they should give them something to write with," I said, placing a hand on the doorknob. Mackie knocked my hand away.

"Mate, you can't go in there! You might get infected!" she cried.

"Mackie, those Shards already have Hosts! I doubt they're going to abandon the bodies they already Habitated in just because I showed up."

"Do you really want to risk it? I don't think you should tempt them by giving them the chance!" Mackie said.

"But how else are we supposed to—"

"We'll tell Celeste when we get back downstairs. The medical staff is giving regular reports on the Hosts to the Council. She'll pass it along, I promise." Mackie practically begged. "Come on, mate, don't give that thing a reason to attack you, okay? I can feel them through the door, and believe me, you do not want to have those feelings inside you, mate."

I blinked. I'd forgotten. Mackie was an Empath; it was her unique ability, similar to my gifts as a Muse. When spirits were trying to communicate with Mackie, she experienced their feelings on a level that none of the rest of us could comprehend. If the spirit was in pain, she felt every bit of that pain. If the spirit was grieving,

Mackie could not separate herself from that grief. The intensity of it all could be crippling for her. Anything I might experience when opening that door would be magnified a hundredfold for someone like Mackie. How could I see that look of sheer terror on her face and still turn that doorknob?

"Okay, fine, fine!" I grumbled. "I don't know why you think we're any safer out here than in there."

"We don't know if any spirit Shards are out here right now, but we know five of them are in that room," Mackie said. "I like my odds in the hallway, thanks. Come on, then."

We couldn't talk further on the matter because we had to use every ounce of our strength and breath to survive the climb to the top of the South Tower. It took several minutes after we finally staggered onto the top landing to sufficiently recover before we could knock on the door.

"State your name and your business," came a sharp, echoing voice.

"It's Mackie, Moira. I've brought two more Durupinen to see the Léarscáil," Mackie said, with exaggerated patience.

"Enter slowly and carefully, and be sure to close the door securely behind you," the voice snapped. It was both a tiny voice and a voice I wouldn't want to trifle with.

Mackie pushed the door open according to our instructions, very slowly and deliberately. I stepped confidently through it, but Mackie grabbed onto the back of my sweater and yanked me backward.

"You're going to want to tread carefully, mate. There's a steep drop through that door," she said.

"What?"

She eased the door the rest of the way open and I saw, with a start of surprise, what she meant. The floor of the room was about ten feet below us, reached by a narrow set of wooden steps that hugged the inner curve of the tower walls. Had I plowed ahead, I would surely have plummeted right past the narrow tread that was the only place to step upon entering the room.

"Wow, close one," I muttered. "Thanks, Mack."

"Anytime. Follow me, and mind you keep to a whisper," Mackie said, stepping past me and starting down the steps.

The room below us was perfectly circular, just like inside the other towers, but unlike the other tower rooms, there were no windows anywhere. In fact, there was nothing on any of the walls at all; no paintings, no tapestries, nothing. The unbroken stretch of bare stone reached up to the dark shadowy recesses of the rafters and disappeared. In the absence of windows, the only light in the room emanated from four large torches in tall bronze standing brackets set at what I knew instinctively, after creating countless Circles, to be the four points of the compass. These torches threw an orange, wavering light over the floor, which was painted with an enormous and incredibly detailed map of the world. I stared at it for a dumbstruck moment. Though it was clearly a map of the world as I knew it—I recognized the shapes of the continents—it was not the world as I knew it. The golden borders that snaked their way through the land masses were not of the familiar countries and cities I had learned in school as a kid, but instead divided the world up in Durupinen terms. This, I realized, was a clan map, carving out the strongholds and ancient seats of different clans through the ages. All of the words were in a form of Britannic so ancient that I was sure I wouldn't find a single familiar word upon it, even with all of my recent study of Gaelic and Britannic Castings.

But by far the most fascinating aspect of the room was the gargantuan gold pendulum that hung suspended over the map. It was easily the size of a small car, with a round, bulbous body and a pointed bottom, rather like a spinning top. Shining runes were engraved all around it, encircling its massive bulk like an equator. The gilded monstrosity hung on a great chain of golden links, which disappeared up into the rafters, and was swinging in a very steady rhythm, back and forth over the face of the map. Other than the swish of air, it made no sound, but the longer we watched it, I felt something like a hum—the steady, singing presence of powerful energy—ringing in my bones.

"Wow," Hannah breathed. Her face was alight with awe.

"Be careful not to step on the map itself," Mackie said. "Keep to the path."

When we reached the bottom of the stairs, Mackie stepped onto a wide gold stripe of paint that left a narrow pathway all the way around the outside of the room, and it was along this shining band we trod to meet the keeper of the Léarscáil.

The old woman was tiny, shriveled, and hunched, like an old crone in a fairy tale; I half expected her to offer me a poisoned apple. She wore a long, wool robe which fell to her ankles, revealing leathery old feet, the soles of which appeared to be tattooed with dozens of runes. She was seated on a rickety wooden stool at a long, narrow table that had been built into the curve of the wall. She was writing with a quill— I shit you not, an actual quill—on a long trailing piece of parchment covered in markings and words so tiny and cramped that they must surely be illegible unless you had your nose half an inch from the surface of the paper, as the woman now did. She did not acknowledge us right away, but finished whatever it was she was recording, and then slowly and carefully rolled the parchment up into a tight scroll with knobbly, gnarled fingers. Then, still without looking at us, she turned and tucked the scroll into one of hundreds of tiny cubbies built in rows above the table. Each was labeled with map coordinates, longitude and latitude recorded in degrees.

When the scroll was meticulously tucked away, the woman shuffled over to us and looked up. I actually stepped backward right on top of Hannah's foot, and she let out a sharp gasp, though it may have been as much a gasp of surprise as a gasp of pain. The woman was wearing a strange contraption on her face that was straight out of a steampunk fantasy. I guess for lack of a better word, you could call them glasses, but they were strapped onto her head with a leather thong, like aviator goggles. There were several sets of brass lenses, some of which she had pulled down in front of her eyes and others which stuck up at wacky angles around her face. But it was the fact that her eyes were magnified to such cartoonish proportions that had caused me such a shock.

"Moira, I would like to introduce you to Jessica and Hannah Ballard of Clan Sassanaigh," Mackie said, with a little tremble in her voice that made me certain she was repressing a laugh at my reaction.

Moira still said nothing, but twiddled several knobs on her goggles, so that the little gears began to turn and multiple lenses whirred up out of place. Her eyes, now visible behind only a single set of lenses, were much less shocking, though still nearly swallowed by the black of her wildly dilated pupils.

"Aye, I know who ye are. I knew ye were about. I felt the wee shifts in the balance," Moira said curtly by way of a greeting. She spoke with a thick Scottish brogue that left every third word almost unintelligible.

"N-nice to meet you," Hannah said, so softly that I don't think anyone but me heard her.

"You two gave Moira the most eventful few months of her life three years ago," Mackie said with a wink. "She's never had so much excitement before, have you?"

"Excitement in this room is not a desirable turn of events, lass," Moira snapped, frowning severely at Mackie. "But aye, I earned my keep that year, I did, and no mistake."

"Moira is the Mapkeeper here at Fairhaven," Mackie went on, for Moira had turned back to her table and broken into a string of muttered complaints. "She's been in charge of recording and interpreting the findings of the Léarscáil Spiorad for the last eighty years."

"Is that a Foucault pendulum?" I asked.

Mackie frowned. "A what, now?"

"A Foucault pendulum," I repeated. "I saw one once on a museum field trip in middle school. They used it to demonstrate the turning of the earth."

"Oh, I see," Mackie said. "Nah, this is different. This beauty moves according to the patterns of spirit energy in the world. When all Gateways are working properly and no major disruptive spirit events are underway, the pendulum swings in a perfect circle around the outside of the map. When there are disturbances, though, the pattern changes, and Moira can record and interpret those changes. For instance, look at what it's doing now."

We watched the pendulum swing, its curve slow and mesmerizing. But as it rounded the area of the map where the UK was located, it seemed to defy the laws of physics, breaking its pattern to create a small, looping motion over the spot before continuing its wider arc around the perimeter of the map.

"What was that?" Hannah asked, pointing excitedly. "Why did it do that?"

"Och, it's this lass what's upstairs, refusing to get on with it and open her Gateway," Moira said without looking up from her work. "What a numpty."

Hannah I looked at each other, and then at Mackie for a translation.

She grinned. "She's talking about Frankie. Her continued refusal to open her Gateway has caused a kink in the patterns, a concentration of spirit energy, sort of like a backup, and that's what's causing the pendulum to move like that."

"Oh, I get it," I said, and then a thought occurred to me. "So, when my mother Bound her Gateway, this pendulum could tell?"

"Aye," Moira said bluntly.

"And over time, the longer it was Bound, the larger an effect it had," Mackie said, then leaned in and added in a low voice, "Best not talk too much about that, mate. Moira likes her Léarscáil in perfect balance."

"Oh, right," I said, and I felt myself blushing.

"My ears are as good as ever they were, lass," Moira called. "And I dinnae care so much about that, not since the day of the Isherwood Prophecy, when the whole thing came to a stop."

"Came to a stop?" I asked. "You mean, the pendulum stopped moving?"

"Och, aye, lass." Moira whispered, and took off suddenly across the Léarscáil, tiny tattooed feet scuttling like an insect, until she crouched just to the left of where Fairhaven was marked on the map. Even as she came to a stop, the pendulum swooped down upon her. Hannah and I both cried out, sure she would be killed, but Moira did not even flinch. The great sphere came within less than an inch of her nose, before arching off again across the map.

"It stopped. Dead stopped. Quivering like an arrow. Right. Here," she hissed, jabbing a long, yellowed fingernail at the map. "Gobsmacked, I was."

I turned a stunned face from Moira to Mackie, who nodded grimly. "Only time I've ever seen her leave the tower. She came flying into the Council Room to warn everyone. It was the only reason we knew you were coming," Mackie said, glancing apologetically at Hannah.

Hannah dropped her eyes, and even as I watched, two tears splashed onto the gilded stones at her feet.

"Hey," I said to her, grasping her hand and squeezing it. "Don't forget who set that thing spinning again. Don't forget that in the end, we made it right."

Hannah looked up and found my eyes. I squeezed her hand again, and she obliged me with a tiny smile. Mackie punched her playfully on the shoulder. "Sorry, mate. I didn't mean to... we all know it wasn't your fault."

"Not all of you, no," Hannah said. "But thanks, Mack."

A strange whistling sound made us all look up. Moira was scuttling with unnerving speed across the map again toward the source of the sound, a small metal door set into the wall. As we watched, she pulled a skeleton key from the pocket of her robe and inserted it into the door, turned it, and yanked. The door creaked open and a pigeon fluttered in, coming to rest on her shoulder.

"What the—" I muttered.

Moira cooed at the bird, stroking its chest and offering it several kernels of corn that she pulled from another pocket. Then she untied a small leather pouch from the pigeon's leg and sat down with it at her table.

"Carrier pigeon?" Hannah whispered. "What does she use a carrier pigeon for?"

"Every clan stronghold has a Léarscáil and a Mapkeeper. This is how they communicate, to compare findings and interpretations," Mackie said. "It's not an exact science, and so they confer with each other to reach conclusions on what the patterns might mean."

"Is there, like... a legitimate reason not to just pick up the phone?" I asked.

Mackie grinned. "Moira doesn't trust technology. You know from working with your ghost hunting mates that spirits can mess with batteries and electricity and all of that. She knows it too, and so she won't have anything to do with it. She's been bringing up those pigeons for years. I think she's got about a hundred of them."

Moira was now unrolling a small scroll of parchment she had found tucked inside the pouch. She took a moment to read it, then snorted loudly and started muttering as she stood up. She pulled one of her own scrolls from its cubby, consulted it quickly, and then returned to the desk, where she scrawled a hasty response onto the scroll, rolled it up, and tucked it back into the pouch. She then tied it back onto the bird, kissed its head, and promptly released it back up into the shoot before slamming the door shut behind it.

"That Mapkeeper in the Nordic Clans is a real walloper," Moira grumbled as she returned to her work. "T'ain't a reading yet she's gotten right and that's the truth. Can't no one explain this spike of energy in the North Country, including me."

"The North Country?" Mackie asked, in a tone of polite interest.

"Aye, that's right. In the Inner Hebrides, round about the Isle of Skye. Can't make heads or tails of it," Moira said. She sat back and began fiddling with the knobs on her goggles again, leaning low over a stack of smaller maps. She continued her muttering, reaching into her pocket and pulling out a few errant kernels of corn to munch on.

"Skye," I murmured, frowning. "Why have I heard of that place before? Didn't someone just mention it to us?"

"It was Celeste," Hannah said, staring at the pendulum's progress around the map. "There's a *príosún* there. That's where Lucida is serving out her sentence, remember?"

I watched the pendulum as well as it made its funny little loop around the place where Lucida sat captive among many other Durupinen enemies. Then I imagined the pendulum crashing to the ground on top of the place and squashing it flat. It was a childish moment, but it was common knowledge that I was not above childishness.

"Well, we don't want to disrupt you too much, Moira," Mackie said. "So, we'll just be on our way."

"Get on with ye, then," Moira said without looking at us. She was now measuring angles with a protractor.

"Right, then. Good luck," Mackie said, and gestured that we should follow her up the steps again. We did so, leaving the tiny old woman scuttling around in the semi-darkness behind us, like a rodent in a lonely attic.

"I think the rule is one raving, tower-bound lunatic per castle, Mackie," I said, when we had closed the door behind us. "Between her and Fiona we've exceeded our limit here."

Mackie chuckled. "Yeah, she's an odd duck to be sure. But she's also the best Mapkeeper in the world, so we ignore the majority of her idiosyncrasies."

"Does she seriously never leave that room?" Hannah asked, pulling agitatedly at her own fingers. "Where does she eat? Where does she sleep?"

"Oh, don't worry, she's got her own sleeping quarters off of the map room," Mackie said. "And someone is tasked with bringing her meals and seeing that she's got everything she needs. Story is that she took over the Léarscáil when she was still an Apprentice, and she's tended to it every day since."

"That can't be healthy, though," Hannah insisted. "People need fresh air and sunlight. And besides, she looks much too old to be working like that."

Mackie smirked. "You go in there and tell her she's got to stop tending that map, and see what happens. They've been encouraging her toward retirement for years, but she just refuses. And it's hard to argue with her, because she is still the very best in the world at what she does. In fact, she's the one who discovered where you were, Hannah."

Hannah started. "What? What do you mean?"

"I mean the Trackers acted on a tip from her that a latent Durupinen might be active in the New York area, and that's how Lucida and Catriona first tracked you down. You started using your Calling abilities consciously and it caused a disturbance on the Léarscáil. So, in a way it's all down to Moira that you're here."

Hannah blinked. She looked over at me. "Did you know that?"

I shook my head. "I knew that the Trackers had located you, but Lucida never told us how."

Hannah was so lost in thought that she did not speak again all the way back down to the entryway, though Mackie kept prattling on about the Léarscáil and all of the fascinating types of spirit activity it could detect. I could not blame Hannah for continuing to ponder her first glimpse at the contraption that had been responsible for breaking her free from eighteen years of misery.

13

FINDING FRANKIE

THE MOMENT WE SET FOOT in the entrance hall we knew something else had happened. There was a heavy pall over the room, a silence as though at a funeral, and the whole chamber was thick with the smell of smoke.

"What is it? What's going on?" Mackie asked a young woman standing at the base of the stairs.

"Another Habitation," the woman replied, and her voice was full of tears. "Just now." She pointed a shaking finger toward the fireplace, from which puffs of deep grey smoke were billowing, though the fire itself seemed to have gone out. A glistening puddle of water was spreading across the floor in front of the hearth, and a small knot of people, including several Caomhnóir, were bent over, struggling with something just beyond it.

Then two of the Caomhnóir straightened up and turned, so that we had a clear view of the commotion. Patricia O'Toole lay pinned to the floor, whimpering and struggling. Finn rushed forward to help, but there was nothing for him to do. She was already being hauled to her feet and carried in the direction of the hospital wing.

I walked over to the fireplace and squatted down beside it. I hadn't knelt on this spot since a spirit had used me to cover the walls in a grotesque mural depicting the Prophecy. I woke from that trance with third degree burns from my elbows to my fingertips and no memory of having drawn the mural, which stretched all the way up to the ceiling two stories above.

I reached into the fireplace, careful to avoid the places where embers still glowed like rubies. I extracted several large fragments of porcelain—the remains of a large pitcher that Patricia had undoubtedly used to try to douse the flames.

"What is this about?" I said out loud, more to myself than to anyone else, but Finn answered me, having followed me over to the fireplace.

"The Shattered spirit must have died in a fire, or else had a terrible fear of it in life," Finn said quietly. "It seems to be one of the only characteristics strong enough that every Shard still remembers it and acts upon it. Celeste said that the Shards would be confused and disoriented, but they certainly show no confusion around fire."

"Yeah, I bet you're right, Finn. Spirits nearly always fixate on the major events of their lives, especially their deaths, and most especially if those deaths were traumatizing," I said, thinking through the many spirits I'd felt Cross through me. Hardly one had slipped through without a visceral flash of their own death.

Hannah and Milo had walked over to join us, their faces grim. "Since Catriona was the source of the Shattering, do you think Fairhaven was the source of the spirit itself?" Hannah asked.

"It's possible," Finn said, nodding his head. "I'd even say probable." Celeste and the Scribes are researching every clue that the Shards are giving them. They are trying to connect it to the spirits that they have records of here at Fairhaven."

"But the resident spirits here Crossed during the Prophecy," Hannah said, staring down at her twisting fingers. From where I sat on the floor, I could see guilty tears welling in her eyes again. "So, searching the history of the castle isn't going to do much good, is it? Any spirits from those recorded deaths will have gone."

"It's possible a few are still..." I began, but Hannah shook her head.

"I Called them myself, Jess. I didn't leave any behind," she said, a barely concealed sob in her voice.

As Milo leaned in to comfort Hannah, Finn went on. "There are many spirits here that have arrived since the Prophecy. Because of the Geatgrima and the high concentration of active Gateways, this place is a spirit magnet. The Scribes do their best to keep track of all spirits who take up residence here for any length of time, but even those will take a good long time to research."

"Who knows how long this could go on if the Council doesn't find the name themselves? If the spirit doesn't want to tell us its name voluntarily, how will we ever expel the damn thing?" I said, chucking the pieces of porcelain back into the soggy ashes in my frustration. "Hannah, remind me to kill Karen when we get home. I can't believe we are stuck here like this."

"There's really no chance the spirit came from somewhere other than these grounds?" Milo asked.

"Catriona had been on the grounds for a full day before the Shattering happened. I can't imagine she had a spirit Habitating in her for longer than that without noticing."

"Unless..." Milo started, and then stopped himself, looking embarrassed.

"Go on, Milo," Finn prompted. "Unless what?"

"Well, I was just thinking out loud," Milo said sheepishly. "But, what if the spirit didn't Habitate without permission? What if Catriona brought it here on purpose?"

Finn frowned, but not in skepticism. He seemed to be seriously considering the idea. Milo realized this, and he went on disgorging his theory.

"Look, obviously it sounds a little strange, but what if, while Catriona was off working for the Trackers, she came across this spirit? What if the spirit asked her to bring it here, or maybe she felt compelled to bring it here for some reason?"

"Why would Catriona need to do that?" I asked.

"There could be a million reasons," Milo said. "Most spirits get disoriented too far from the place where they died. I'm an exception, because I'm Bound to you, so anywhere you go, I can go too, without feeling those disorienting effects. But maybe this spirit needed to get here, and Catriona volunteered to bring it? Maybe it had unfinished business here that it needed to take care of before it Crossed."

Finn raised his eyebrows, looking impressed. "That's a very interesting theory, Milo."

Milo shrugged, trying to look modest. "I am one of the great minds of the deadside, we all know that."

Finn stood up. "I'm going to have a word with Seamus, and see if he will pass this theory on to Celeste and the Trackers." He walked a few steps and then turned sharply back to us. "Don't leave the entrance hall without me," he ordered.

I rolled my eyes. "You're like, the meanest babysitter ever."

As Finn marched past the staircase, Savvy came pounding down it, muttering angrily to herself. She spotted us and stalked over, her expression so fierce that I had to resist the urge to back away from her.

"That's it. I've had it. I quit. Someone give me the sack already."

"What's wrong, Sav?" Hannah asked, placing a consoling hand on her shoulder. Savvy did not shrug it off.

"It's Frankie. I'm done. She's not going to give in, no matter how many times I try to convince her. I just talked my bloody head off for an hour, and nothing. We've just got to close her Gateway and start over."

"I don't think you can do that," Hannah said gently.

"Well, the Council will have to figure it out without my help, because I'm bowing out," Savvy said, and her anger seemed to melt into exhaustion before our eyes. "I was so excited to help someone," she said, flopping into a chair by the fireplace. "I thought I could actually be of some real use to someone instead of always being the resident fuck up. I thought, if I could make this Durupinen mess easier for someone, then maybe it was worth it, everything I went through. Ha bloody ha. What a joke."

Hannah walked over and sat down next to Savvy, placing her curly brown head on Savvy's shoulder. Savvy lay her own ginger head on top with a defeated sigh. "What say you, wee one? Any pearls of wisdom for your ol' Savvy? I could use some, and that's the truth."

"You asked me before if I might be able to talk to Frankie for you," Hannah said. "Do you want me to go do it now?"

Savvy picked up her head and looked at Hannah with an expression of relief. "Would you? That would be brilliant!"

"I can't promise it will help," Hannah said. "But I can try. I can't stand you looking so gloomy. It's disrupting the natural order of the universe if you're not laughing."

And Savvy obliged, laughing heartily and pulling Hannah into something that was half-hug, half-headlock. "Ah, you are the best, Hannah, the absolute best. Shall we go up now, then?"

Hannah's voice was muffled, as she was still trapped in Savvy's armpit. "Why not? It's either that or sit around waiting for a Shard to infect us. I'd rather keep busy, wouldn't you?"

Savvy turned to Milo and me. "You two coming as well?" she asked.

We agreed, and then we all stood up and headed for the stairs. I flagged down Finn with a wave of my hand and told him where we were heading.

"I'll be right behind you," he told me, and turned back to Seamus to finish their conversation.

Frankie's room was on the third floor, surrounded by other Apprentice rooms. The hallway was empty, except for Caomhnóir standing guard in front of a few of the doors.

"This is her, here," Savvy said, hitching her thumb at the door. "Want me to come in with you? I've gotten pretty good at predicting when she's about to throw something."

Hannah stared thoughtfully at the door for a moment. "No," she said at last. "No, I think it's better if I go in there alone. She doesn't trust you, but she has no reason to mistrust me yet."

We turned at the sound of footsteps. Finn was rounding the corner into the corridor, followed by Bertie, who was panting and clutching at a stitch in his side.

"Been looking for you everywhere," Bertie panted, glaring at Savvy. "I'm supposed to be guarding you, remember?"

"Ah, piss off, you tosser," Savvy grumbled.

Hannah put her hand on the doorknob, and Finn stepped right up behind her.

"Finn, I want to go in there alone," Hannah said earnestly.

"I'm supposed to be protecting you," Finn said.

"But she's never going to trust me if I walk in there with a Caomhnóir. She already thinks everyone here is encouraging her delusions."

Finn bit his lip.

"What if," I said, "I let Milo Habitate and I use the connection so that I can see and hear everything that is going on in the room? That way, we can give Hannah the space she needs to talk to Frankie, but we'll be able to monitor the situation."

Finn nodded his approval. "Why didn't I think of that?" he said, with the merest suggestion of a smile.

"Please, Finn. We all know I'm the brains of this operation," I said breezily.

"What am I, then?" Finn asked.

"You're the brawn," I shot back.

"Exactly. Hannah's the talent, and I'm the style," Milo said, and then gasped dramatically. "We should get t-shirts made!"

Hannah laughed. "Okay, okay, it's decided. Now, can you two Habitate so I can go in there, please?"

I turned to Milo. "Come here, lovah," I said, waggling my eyebrows before closing my eyes.

"Ew," he said with a roll of his eyes, and stepped forward right into my body.

We took a moment to adjust to the bizarre sensation of it, the sense that my mental space was packed to the exploding point. Then, as quietly as I could, I thought, *Everyone here?*

Their replies rippled through my head as though I had thought them myself.

Ready, Milo thought.

All set, Hannah added. *I'm going in.* She turned the knob gently and eased the door open so that she could peek through the gap.

I kept my eyes closed and concentrated on picturing Hannah's surroundings. After a moment, a bedroom swam into view. It looked just like the bedroom Hannah and I slept in, except the draperies and bedclothes were lavender, and the fireplace was on the opposite side of the room. A girl sat in a chair by the fire staring at the flames with an empty, hollow expression. She was very petite and fair, with long sleek blonde hair and delicate features. As we watched, she raised a slender finger and brushed an errant strand of hair from her face.

Hannah took a deep breath and yanked the door open, leaping inside and slamming it shut behind her.

Frankie leapt up from her chair, startled.

"Who are—" she began, but Hannah shushed her harshly.

"Be quiet!" she hissed, her back still pressed to the door. "They're going to hear you!"

Frankie obeyed, too startled to argue, and continued to stare at Hannah.

What is she doing? I thought.

No idea, Milo replied. *But our girl obviously has something up her sleeve, so let's just watch and learn.*

Hannah pretended to listen at the door for a few moments, then turned back to Frankie, sighing with relief. "I'm supposed to be in my own room, but I slipped out. Celeste is going to be pissed, but I just couldn't take it anymore. Do you have a cigarette?"

"What?" Frankie asked, still in shock at Hannah's sudden appearance.

"A cigarette," Hannah repeated patiently, walking into the room. "Do you have one I could bum? I've been out for a week, and I just can't take it anymore."

What is she doing? She doesn't smoke. I wondered.

Yeah, but rich kids always do, Milo said, a laugh in his voice. *We used to get spoiled rich kids at New Beginnings all the time, and every one of them smoked like a chimney. It's like rich kid code for 'I'm a badass rebel.' There's no way she doesn't... see? What did I tell you?*

Frankie had recovered from her surprise and walked over to her nightstand, from which she extracted a package of cigarettes. While I watched Frankie take out two cigarettes and hand one to Hannah, I relayed the details to Savvy and Finn.

"Damn it," Savvy said through gritted teeth. "You mean to tell me Frankie and I could have been bonding over a fag this entire time?"

"Afraid so," I said, then tuned back in to Hannah, who was taking her first drag. For someone who didn't smoke, she certainly knew how to look like she was enjoying herself.

"Thanks," she told Frankie, who nodded a bit hesitantly while lighting up her own. She was looking at Hannah very warily, unsure whether she was supposed to acknowledge her existence or not.

"Relax," Hannah said, when she noticed Frankie staring at her. "I'm not a delusion. Although, I'm sure delusions have told you that before. You'll just have to take my word for it that delusions don't smoke cigarettes."

Frankie twitched the corner of her mouth into the barest suggestion of a smile and then went back to her cigarette, still watching Hannah closely.

"How long have they had you here?" Hannah asked. When Frankie didn't answer right away, Hannah added, "I've been here for six months."

Frankie raised her eyebrows in surprise. "Really? That long? I've been here four months. Why haven't I seen you before?"

Hannah laughed. "Because you never come out of this room."

Why is she doing this? Why is she lying about how long she's been here? What's the point? I asked Milo.

She's establishing trust. Every kid on the inside has trust issues. You've got to show some solidarity for them to open up to you, Milo explained. *There's a whole complicated social order for kids on the psych ward tour, and Hannah knows every inch of it. Trust me, she knows what she's doing, even if we don't.*

"My name's Hannah, by the way. Do you want to tell me yours?" Hannah asked.

Frankie hesitated, then said, "Frankie. Frankie York."

"Nice to meet you, Frankie York. You smoke really smooth cigarettes," Hannah said with a smile. Frankie did not return the smile. She was still examining Hannah closely. "You can poke me or something, if it will make you feel better," Hannah said, and she extended her arm slowly, offering it to Frankie. Frankie shook her head.

"I can pretty much tell the difference now," she said quietly. "Between the real ones and the delusions."

"Good for you. That usually takes a lot longer to figure out," Hannah said.

Frankie took a long drag on her cigarette. "You see them, too? The delusions?"

"Yeah, I do," Hannah said. "I have for practically my whole life."

"Really?"

"Oh, yeah. Imaginary friends were a great cover story for a while, until I outgrew them," Hannah said. "I'm guessing you haven't been seeing them for very long. When did it start?"

Frankie tipped a tiny shower of ash over the edge of her chair and nudged it with her toe to make sure it was out. "Not long. A few months."

"You probably won't believe me when I tell you this, but you'll get used to it," Hannah said.

"I don't want to get used to it," Frankie snapped, her face suddenly fierce.

"I don't blame you," Hannah said solemnly. "Neither did I."

Frankie stared at Hannah for a long moment, as though trying to decide if she could trust her. Then she blurted out, "Are they telling you the same thing they're telling me?"

Hannah smirked. "About what? You'll have to be a little more specific. So far, the only things I know about you are your name and that you smoke really expensive cigarettes."

Frankie actually smirked a little. "They're the same kind my mother smoked. I used to steal them out of her purse sometimes, when I was pissed at her."

Hannah grinned and took another drag.

Frankie settled back into her seat, a sign that she was relaxing around Hannah. "The people here are telling me that this isn't a psychiatric hospital. They're saying that the delusions aren't actually delusions: they're ghosts. And they've brought me here because I've been chosen to help them." She laughed a little hysterically. "Is that what they are telling you?"

"Yes," Hannah said. "They told me the exact same thing. You don't believe them?"

Frankie shook her head. "No! It's completely insane. I know what's happening to me."

Hannah raised her eyebrows. "You do? Enlighten me."

Frankie leaned in conspiratorially. "I had a psychotic break. I was under too much pressure at school, and I cracked."

"Really?" Hannah asked, sounding fascinated. "What makes you so sure?"

"I'm a pre-med student, okay? I didn't just Google this." Frankie stood up and jogged over to her nightstand. She opened the drawer and extracted a large file folder bulging with dog-eared packets of papers. She thrust it into Hannah's hands. "Take a look, if you like. I'm a textbook case of schizophrenia! I'm just the right age. The stress of starting college probably triggered the onset."

"Interesting," Hannah said, not even opening the folder. "Did they give you the blood tests and the brain scans to rule out tumors and hallucinogenic drugs?"

Frankie's eyes widened. "Yes," she said.

"Did they enroll you in psychotherapy?"

Frankie nodded.

"What kinds of anti-psychotic meds did they start you on? Usually they start with Thorazine, but Haldol is definitely getting more popular."

Frankie opened her mouth, then closed it again. "I... yeah, Thorazine."

"How is that working for you?" Hannah asked casually, as though she were asking about the weather.

Frankie shook her head a fraction of an inch back and forth, her eyes filling with tears. "Not good," she whispered. "It hasn't stopped anything."

"It didn't for me, either," Hannah said. She began ticking medications off her fingers. "I've been on Thorazine, Prolixin, Haldol, Loxitane, Trilafon, and Mellaril. When none of those worked, they tried some different combinations of Aripiprazole, Clozapine, Lurasidone, and Quetiapine. Every time, the delusions broke through."

Frankie's face was fixed in an expression of horror.

Hannah tapped a finger on the folder. "There's not a thing you could have highlighted in this folder that I haven't already had explained to me. There's not a single drug or treatment listed in here that I haven't tried. I have a gold medal in pointless consumption of anti-psychotic meds."

Still Frankie said nothing. Tears began to roll down her cheeks.

"Do you want to know why none of the drugs or therapies worked?" Hannah asked gently.

Frankie shook her head. "No. No, I don't want to know."

Hannah smiled sadly. "Neither did I. Because I didn't want to admit the truth about what was happening to me. And I can see that you don't either."

Frankie shook her head. "I'm not like you. My meds are going to work."

"Are they working right now?" Hannah asked softly. And I felt the tugging that meant she was Calling. Three spirits floated into the room almost at once and waited suspended just above the floor, waiting for further instruction.

Frankie could not stop her eyes from flicking quickly over to them, before staring straight ahead, refusing to acknowledge their existence. "They will work," she whispered through clenched teeth. "They will. I just have to find the right combination, and then I can go on with my life as though none of this ever happened."

"I get it, Frankie," Hannah said, and the empathy in her voice drew Frankie's eyes onto her. "I know why you want the medications to work. I used to want that, too. If the medications worked, then I could take control of my life again. I could move forward with all the plans I had for myself. I could not be what I was."

"What are you?" Frankie whispered.

"I'm the same as you. I'm a Durupinen," Hannah said.

"No," Frankie said. "No, I'm not."

"You are. And it doesn't have to mean the end of everything else," Hannah said, a little more forcefully.

Frankie's bottom lip trembled but she bit it fiercely to stop it.

"Stop. I'm not listening to that. I have plans. I'm going to accomplish them. I will not accept anything standing in my way."

She's pushing too hard, I thought.

She's pushing just right, Milo insisted.

"What's happening, then?" Savvy asked me.

I relayed the conversation to Savvy in whispered installments. She shook her head. "She's walking right into book-throwing territory now," Savvy said. "Best tell her to get ready to duck and cover."

"Do I need to get in there?" Finn asked sharply.

"Take it down a peg, Finn," I replied. "She's still in control of the situation. Now everyone shut up so Milo and I can concentrate."

I focused back in on Hannah, who was still sitting, calm as could be, in the chair opposite Frankie, cigarette dangling casually from her hand. I'm not sure if I'd ever appreciated just how much of a casual badass she really was. I would never be that cool.

Girl, neither will I, Milo agreed, picking up on the thought.

"What is your plan?" Hannah was asking Frankie. "Tell me your plan. What do you want more than anything?"

Frankie did not answer at first. It was as though she was trying to decide if sharing this information was going to cost her something. She seemed to decide that it wouldn't. "To be a cardiovascular surgeon." There was a defiant note in her voice, as though daring Hannah to scoff.

Hannah, of course, did not. "That's very admirable. Why do you want to do that?"

"Because it's hard. Because it takes skill. Because so few people can accomplish it," Frankie said, raising her chin.

"Is that all?" Hannah prompted.

Frankie shrugged. "I want to help people."

Hannah smiled. "That's really wonderful. How long have you worked toward that goal?"

"Practically my whole life," Frankie said. "I've wanted to be a doctor for as long as I can remember."

"So, why are you giving up on it?" Hannah asked.

Frankie glared at her. "Giving up? Who's giving up? Haven't you been listening? I'm fighting for it."

Hannah shook her head. "Every day you keep yourself locked up in this room, avoiding reality, that dream is going to slip further and further away from you."

Frankie's eyes grew bright, but her voice was still angry. "You don't know what you're talking about."

"I really do," Hannah said. She took one last drag on the cigarette before stubbing it out on the bottom of her shoe. "I'm going to tell you something right now, and you aren't going to like it at first, but hear me out. I spent years and years going back and forth. Some days I believed the spirits were real. Other days I took my meds and tried to ignore them, hoping against hope that they would go away if I just dulled my senses enough. Sometimes it almost worked, but never for long."

Frankie sagged in her seat, as though Hannah's words had deflated her.

"But not anymore," Hannah said, and she rose from her seat and sat herself beside Frankie on the settee. Frankie did not move away from her, which I took to be a very good sign. "I've accepted what I am, and I've learned everything I can about it. I do what I'm supposed to do; lunar Crossings and helping spirits out when they really need me. But it doesn't consume my life anymore. I can put protection up around any room I'm in, so that they can't bother me when I really need some time to myself. I've learned to feel them coming before I see them, so that they rarely surprise me anymore. And best of all, I'm helping people. They might not be alive anymore, but they are still human souls in desperate need of help, and I am one of the very few who can truly give them what they need."

Frankie began to sniffle. We were watching her resistance crumble as Hannah dismantled it, brick by stubborn brick.

Hannah pressed her advantage and continued. "I want to help people, too—kids who have been abused by the system, like I was. I'm doing it. I'm in school. I'm earning my master's degree in social work. I might even go to law school. But being a Durupinen is not preventing me from pursuing any of those goals. It does... complicate things, on occasion. But learning how to deal with those occasions? It is a skill. It is a craft. It's something that only a handful of people in the world can do. That's something I think you can appreciate."

Frankie's sniffles had dissolved into great, heaving sobs now. Very slowly and carefully, Hannah scooted herself across the settee and wrapped her arms around Frankie. Frankie fell into them, sobbing still harder.

"Just imagine," Hannah whispered. "Just imagine when you become that surgeon, because I know you will. And just imagine when you can save a patient's life, and how incredible that will feel. And then realize that you will be able to help them whether you can save their lives or not."

Frankie's voice, muffled with tears against the sleeve of Hannah's sweater, rose to answer her. "That w-would be p-pretty incredible," she stammered.

"The teachers here will guide you every step of the way," Hannah went on, planting a gentle kiss on the top of Frankie's head. "There are hundreds of Durupinen here from all over the UK and other countries, too, and nearly every one of them has a job, and a family, and a life apart from her role as a Durupinen. Right now, you've given the control of your life over to the spirits. But they aren't going away, so now it's time to take it back."

Frankie did not respond, though her crying quieted.

"Let me ask you this: are you a girl who things happen to, or are you a girl who makes things happen?" Hannah asked.

Frankie laughed—actually laughed—and looked up at Hannah with a red blotchy face. "I make things happen," she said. "I always have."

Hannah smiled down at her. "That's what I thought."

She is going to be the best social worker ever. Milo's pride came thrumming across the surface of my brain.

Yeah, she sure as hell is, I said, my own pride in my sister glowing brightly.

I turned to Savvy who had her ear pressed to the door, her long curtain of red hair draped across her face.

"You're in luck, Sav. She did it."

Savvy didn't answer. She seemed very intent on continuing to listen at the door.

"Sav, seriously, it's okay," I assured her. "Honestly, I don't think you need to worry anymore. The moment for throwing projectiles has passed."

Savvy still did not answer. Her hand, pressed against the wood of the door, was tensely white-knuckled.

"Savvy?" I asked again. Still, Savvy did not move, did not answer. I reached out and touched her shoulder. No response. My heart began to hammer.

"Finn?" I said, and I was surprised at how steady my voice

sounded even in my mounting panic. "Finn, something is wrong with Savvy."

"What are you on about?" Finn asked.

But at that moment, through the connection, I watched Hannah stop stroking Frankie's head. She looked up suddenly, staring around the room as though she had just heard a strange sound and wanted to find the source of it. Then she stood abruptly.

"Jess? There's one here!" she cried out. "A Shard! I just felt it! It's really close!"

"Hannah?" Frankie said tentatively, "Who are you talking to?"

But I didn't hear Hannah's reply. I was reaching a shaking hand out toward Savvy's mane of hair, pulling it back from her face.

Eyes stared back at me, deep and dark as caverns—eyes that had never before looked out of Savannah Todd's face.

"Savvy?" I breathed.

"Who's Savvy?" she whispered back.

14

TRYST AND TRUST

"**I** CAN'T BELIEVE IT. I can't believe that just happened," Milo whispered.

"She was right next to me. One moment she was Savvy, and the next..."

I shuddered. Milo, Frankie, Hannah, and I sat together in a half circle around Frankie's fireplace. A hollow, numb disbelief hung over us like a fog.

"We were focused on the connection," Milo said, sounding as though he'd like to take his own words and beat himself with them out of guilt. "Finn and Savvy both had all their attention on trying to hear what was happening through the door. Oh, sorry," Milo added, realizing what he had said and addressing Frankie. "We didn't want to spy on you or anything. We just wanted to make sure you weren't going to start throwing shit at Hannah."

"It's okay," Frankie said, more loudly than she needed to. "I've been known to do that lately." She was examining Milo with a half-fearful, half-fascinated expression. Now that she'd accepted what she was seeing, she'd been staring openly at Milo since he'd entered the room.

"You don't need to yell, sweetness. I'm dead, not deaf," Milo said, causing Frankie to flush pink.

"Sorry," she said softly, and then turned to Hannah. "So, what exactly happened to Savannah? I didn't really understand what that man was saying when he opened the door.

As Hannah patiently explained about the Shards to Frankie, I continued to dwell on what had just happened. The moment I'd seen that stranger staring back at me from Savvy's face, Finn had leapt into action. As he pulled Savvy tightly into a restraining hold, she hadn't even resisted him. Maybe it was because there was no fire visible in the hallway, or perhaps because the Shard itself hadn't yet acclimated to the new body it now possessed, but there was no struggle and no screaming, like we'd seen with the other Hosts. Savvy submitted quietly to the hands that grasped her. It wasn't until Finn and Bertie were rounding the corner with her at the end of the hallway that she began to moan and cry pitifully, like a wounded animal.

"But... I've kept my Gateway closed on purpose. Did... did I cause this? Did that spirit try to... to use me, but couldn't get through?" Frankie asked, eyes wide in alarm.

"No, no," Hannah said in a soothing voice. "The Shattering originated with Catriona's Gateway, which also happens to be sealed at the moment. You had nothing to do with it, although it's a good reason to keep the whole Gateway system open and working like it should."

"So, one of those things could infect any one of us, at any time?" Frankie asked. "Is this what it's going to be like now? I thought you said I'd be able to move on with my life!"

Hannah put a consoling hand on Frankie's shoulder. "No, this is not how life is going to be. This is a very rare phenomenon that's happening right now. Most of the Durupinen here have never even heard of a Shattered spirit before."

"Once you get your training, you can put this place in your rearview mirror and rarely look back," I told Frankie.

"You finished your training. Why are you back here?" Frankie asked.

"Glutton for punishment," I replied.

"I need another cigarette," Frankie muttered, and went to find herself one.

"I never would have imagined Savvy falling victim like that," I said, shaking my head sadly. "Honestly, I'd have thought any spirit who tried to get in there would have had one look around and think it wasn't worth the trouble."

Milo laughed, a sharp short bark immediately swallowed by a sob. "I feel like such shit for not realizing it was happening."

"Me too," I said.

"And me. Too little, too late," Hannah said.

We sat for a few more minutes in a numb sort of silence, until Frankie broke it with a polite little cough.

"Excuse me, Hannah? Do you think you could show me where I

could find Celeste? I need to talk to her about... about deciding that I'm ready to start learning."

Hannah looked up and managed a smile. "Of course. I can help you find her."

"I'll come, too," Milo said, rising from the chair. "I need some distraction. Jess?"

I stood up as well. "You guys go ahead. I'm going to the hospital ward to see how Savvy is. I'll check in with you both afterward."

"Do you think you should go by yourself?" Hannah asked anxiously.

"Hannah, do you really think it matters? Savvy was infected while two Caomhnóir stood within two feet of her," I said. "If I get infected on the way, I'm only two corridors from the hospital ward. I'll just show myself in."

"That's not funny," Hannah said, scowling.

"I know." I said. "For once, I wasn't trying to be cute."

§

When I arrived outside the hospital wing, I found I was not alone in waiting for news. Róisín and Riley Lightfoot were both occupying the bench outside the ward, faces pale and drawn.

"We saw them carry Savannah Todd past," Róisín said as I walked over to them. "Your Caomhnóir was with her."

"Yeah, we were all with her when... it happened," I said with a shiver. "I heard about your mom, too. I'm sorry."

Róisín nodded her appreciation. Riley kept her eyes locked on the floor.

"How long have you been here?" I asked, taking a seat on the opposite bench.

"Since breakfast. They told us there was no point, but..." Róisín shrugged helplessly.

"I saw Patricia O'Toole being brought up here as well. Do you know... has anyone else been infected today?" I asked.

Róisín shook her head. "No, not that I know of."

"Have... are Finn and Bertie still in there?" I asked.

"Yes," Róisín said. "I tried to follow them inside when they arrived, but the matron kicked me out." She bit her lip. "They won't tell us anything, but I can't convince myself to leave."

"Hey," I said, my voice gentle and thick with emotion. "You don't need to leave. Even if they tell you to go, you stay, if that's what makes you feel better. I'd be sitting right where you are, if that was my mom in there. Keep demanding answers. Be loud. Be persistent. You have every right to be here."

Róisín smiled at me. I'd like to think she was going to thank me, but she never got the chance. The ward door opened at that moment and Finn stepped out, followed by Bertie and Mrs. Mistlemoore.

"Hey," I said, standing up at once. "This might be a stupid question, but I'm going to ask it anyway. How is Savvy?"

"She's a Host," Mrs. Mistlemoore said. "So, for the moment, she is indistinguishable from the other Hosts in the ward." She sounded utterly exhausted, and perhaps she realized it was dulling her bedside manner, because she shook her head and added. "I apologize. It's been a very long couple of days."

"Don't apologize, it's okay," I said quickly. "We're just grateful you're here to help them."

"I don't know how much help I'm being, to be honest," Mrs. Mistlemoore said.

"I was just telling Mrs. Mistlemoore that you had a suggestion," Finn jumped in.

"I did?" I asked, confused.

"Yes," Finn said pointedly. "About the Hosts' tendency toward writing?"

"Oh, yeah!" I said. "We haven't even had a chance to tell anyone yet. When we came by here earlier today, we saw that the Hosts were writing—or at least, pretending to write. Is that still true?"

"Yes, it is," Mrs. Mistlemoore said, a bit wearily. I could tell she was already skeptical of whatever it was I had to say, and I couldn't really blame her. I'm sure she was getting all kinds of unsolicited advice.

"Look, I have some experience with spirit-induced drawing," I said. "As a Muse, it happens to me all the time. Sometimes it happens without warning, when I can't control it, like in a trance or when I'm sleeping. I always keep paper taped to the walls around my bed and a stack of pencils on my bedside table, so I'm ready when it happens."

"What's your point?" Mrs. Mistlemoore asked, pinching the bridge of her nose and rubbing her eyes. It was as though she was hardly listening. I took a deep breath and tried to swallow my frustration. It did not go down easy.

"I just thought I'd suggest giving the Hosts a piece of paper and something to write with," I said, and I was pleased to hear that my voice sounded calm. "It's a very real possibility that the Shards are trying to communicate through drawing or writing. If they have the tools they need, they might actually give you a clue about who they are, and what they want."

Mrs. Mistlemoore blinked. She stared at me for a moment like I was crazy, and I prepared a defensive reply, but then she nodded. "I'll consult the Scribes, to see if there is any precedent for this behavior amongst Shards, but that is an excellent suggestion, Miss Ballard. Thank you very much for sharing it with me."

I sighed with relief. "Sure. It might come to nothing, of course, but anything is worth a shot at this point, right?"

"Right, indeed," Mrs. Mistlemoore said. "I'm sorry if I've been short with you. It's not only the Hosts that I'm concerned about, though they would be enough to exhaust anyone's capacity for worry. The High Priestess has taken another turn for the worse."

"Oh, no," I said. "Really?"

Mrs. Mistlemoore shook her head, looking defeated. "I think she was holding on for the Airechtas. I think she wanted to oversee one last meeting, to ensure that all of the appropriate policies were in place and changes were made before she succumbed to this illness. But now that the Airechtas has been suspended indefinitely, her strength is fading fast. I'm just not sure how much longer she'll be able to hold on, and I know she does not want to leave Fairhaven and her clans in such a state."

"Everyone in the castle is on the alert," I said, trying to sound confident. "This Shattering might be scary, but it's also moving very quickly. I'm sure we'll be on the other side of it in a few days, and everything can proceed like it was supposed to."

"I do hope you're right, my dear. I do hope so," Mrs. Mistlemoore said, and she gave me a wan smile. "I'm going to consult with the Scribes and see if we can make some progress with your suggestion. Please excuse me." With a quick gesture to all of us, she backed into the ward again and the door swung shut behind her.

Finn nodded curtly at me. "Well done," he said. "That may very well make a difference."

"I hope so," I said.

"It sounded like a good idea to me," Róisín said. "We should be trying anything at this point, shouldn't we?"

Bertie, who was still standing just behind Finn, looked sadly deflated. "I don't know what to do for the best," he said. "Ought I to stay here? To find Miss Phoebe? The Caomhnóir handbook was not at all clear in its instructions for handling this type of situation."

"There's nothing you can do for Savannah here," Finn said, closing his eyes in an attempt to control his annoyance. "She is under the constant supervision of the staff. Phoebe is the vulnerable one right now. You should focus your attentions on her in case she is the next to fall to a Shard."

Bertie nodded thoughtfully. "Hmm... yes, you make a fair point. The statute about preferential protection could be interpreted as such, and yet I question—"

"Go. Phoebe. Now," Finn said through gritted teeth.

"Right-o," Bertie muttered, his face blazing red as he scurried off.

I took a breath that seemed to stagnate in my lungs. "I need to get out of here. Go for a walk. I feel like I'm suffocating in here."

Without saying goodbye to anyone, I turned and headed down the hallway, walking as quickly as I could.

"Jess. Jess!" Finn was following at a jog. He caught up with me easily with his annoyingly long strides. "Where do you think you're going?"

"I just told you. For a walk," I said without slowing down.

"It's December. It's freezing outside. The Caomhnóir are guarding all the exits," Finn reminded me.

"I'll be fine," I said. "I'll get my jacket. They aren't forcing people to stay inside the castle, just inside the grounds."

"Even so—" Finn began, but I held up a hand.

"Look, if you want to come with me, that's fine," I said. "But I'm going. I just... I can't be inside this castle right now."

My voice broke with the last word, and I gave myself away. Finn must have heard it, because he didn't argue with me again. He marched along silently beside me, waiting as I retrieved my coat from my room and then tailing me all the way down to the entrance hall. After a short, whispered exchange with one of the Caomhnóir guarding them, the great front doors swung reluctantly forward to release us into the night.

It was glorious, that fresh air. I drank it in, though it seared my lungs and made my eyes water. It felt clean, as though each breath of air in the castle was contaminated with fear, tainted with the possibility that, as you took it into your lungs, you were infecting yourself.

I set out across the barren stretch of lawn, frosted blades of grass snapping under my feet. I didn't know where I was going. I just wanted to put the castle behind me.

"Jess," Finn said, after a solid twenty minutes of walking. His voice sounded more like his real voice now, instead of the one he'd been using since we'd arrived here, the one that was layered over with indifference. I could have cried just hearing it, my name, spoken in that voice.

"What?" I asked. I had to unclench my teeth to answer him, and now they wouldn't stop chattering.

"Where are we going?"

"I don't know. I just... I can't be in there right now," I said.

"We can't stay out here, though," Finn said coaxingly. "We're both going to freeze."

I wanted to argue with him, but I could barely feel my face. "Don't make me go back in there," I said, though I was not sure he heard me. A needling wind seemed to suck the words right out of my mouth and carry them off into the air.

"I know a place where we can talk," Finn said. "Follow me."

He surged past me and struck out for the forest on the far side of the grounds. I followed him without asking where we were going, just so grateful that he wasn't insisting on dragging me back to the castle. We entered the cover of the trees and struck out along a path I knew.

"Finn? You do know where this path leads, don't you?" I asked him, slowing to a stop.

He turned and smiled reassuringly at me. "Don't worry. We're not following it to the end. There's a turn off. Come on."

I breathed a sigh of relief and followed. This winding path ended in the ruins of the Fairhaven *príosún*, an ancient prison that once housed those who committed crimes against the Durupinen. All of those prisoners were long gone, of course, but their pain and anger and fear lived on in a dangerous creature called the Elemental. It lurked among the ruins, feeding on the negative emotions of any person unlucky enough to cross its path. I had come face to face with it twice, and I had absolutely no desire to do so again.

As Finn had promised, a half-hidden fork in the path veered away from the *príosún*, and after a few more minutes of walking, a small stone hut loomed out of the darkness.

"What is this?" I asked warily.

"It used to be a sentinel checkpoint for Caomhnóir, back when Fairhaven was used as a battle ground," Finn said. "I hid in it three years ago, when I snuck back onto the grounds after..." After he abandoned us at the Traveler camp. He didn't want to say it, and I didn't want to remember it, so neither of us bothered to complete the sentence out loud. "Now it's just a ruin, like the *príosún*, left to rot. I found it while I was still a Novitiate. I used to come here to write, sometimes."

He pushed the door open and disappeared into the opening. After a few moments, a light flared, illuminating the interior. I walked forward and ducked inside.

The hut only had one small room, perfectly circular, with two windows set into the stone walls. The light came from an ancient oil lamp hung on a hook. It smoked and sputtered, filling the place with a rich, waxy sort of smell. The flickering light revealed several straw mattresses heaped with blankets, a small table with two stools set under it, and a cast iron, pot-bellied stove with a pipe that ran up past the wooden rafters and disappeared into the thatch of the roof. Finn was already kneeling beside the stove, shoving logs through the door on the front. Before long, a fire blazed in the grate and the tiny space was filled with warmth that sent an aching feeling back into my extremities.

"I'm just picturing you sitting out here in your abandoned cabin in the woods, brooding and writing in your journals," I said, rubbing at my fingers to help the blood flow. "It's just so... Thoreau."

Finn grinned. "Like that, do you?"

"Oh, yeah," I said. "Misanthropic writers are so sexy."

He stood up, brushed off his hands, and gestured grandly to the stove. "We'll be defrosted in no time."

"Does anyone else know about this place?" I asked, moving a few steps closer to the fire.

"No," Finn said. "Or if they do, they don't bother with it. Every time I've come back here, it's been just as I left it. I brought those blankets down from the barracks and chopped this wood. The key is always right where I've hidden it. No one has ever found me here, in all the years I've used it. So, let's talk."

He pulled the stools out from under the table and set them both in front of the fire. He sat down on one and patted the seat of the other. I sunk onto it, basking in the warmth from the flames.

"Talk to me," Finn said, after a few silent moments. "Why did you need to get out of there so badly?"

"It's just everything," I said sighing. "I know I should have been afraid of the Shards already, and I was. I watched Catriona and Siobhán both get infected. It should have been very real to me already. But..." I shook my head, swallowing back an urge to cry.

"I know," Finn said. "Savvy is one of your best mates. It's different."

I nodded. "And that damn castle already makes me feel claustrophobic to begin with. I hate being back here. I hate that every time I walk into the Grand Council Room, I feel like I'm on trial for my life. I hate the stares and the assumptions. I hate that I have to put everything in my life on hold to be here. And most of all I hate that you and I have to turn back into strangers to do it."

"We'll be out of here soon," Finn said soothingly.

"Not soon enough," I said.

I looked up. He was staring into my eyes with a look I knew, a look that sent my heart into my throat.

The look before a kiss.

He pulled me into him and kissed me like he hadn't been able to since we'd come here, a kiss without hesitation or fear. I melted into it.

"Oh God, I miss you so much," I said, my lips still pressed against his lips.

"I'm right here," he said.

"You are, but you're not. That's what makes it worse," I said.

Maybe it was to escape the fear of what was happening back at the castle. Maybe it was the fact that his lips burned every remnant of good sense from my brain. But whatever it was, I let it take me over. I stopped thinking. I pulled him down on top of me, right onto the pile of blankets and mattresses and God knew what else and let the delicious weight of him crush the last of my fear right out of me.

Every minute we'd been forced to act like indifferent strangers only served to fuel the hunger as we kissed each other, as he tugged at the buttons of my jacket, as I flung his cloak impatiently to the floor beside us. And in that moment, I didn't care what risk we might be taking, or who might come bursting in the door.

Let them find us, I thought. Let them try to pry us apart. I fucking dare them.

§

"So much for staying away from each other while at Fairhaven," I said.

Finn chuckled, a deep throaty sound. "Yes, there's that plan scuppered. I really do like this hair, you know." He was twirling a strand of it between his fingers.

I laughed. "I'll be sure to tell Milo."

Milo? Why Milo?"

"Any and all fashion decisions I make for the rest of my life are to be fully credited to him, apparently."

"Huh?"

"Never mind. Milo's just having an afterlife crisis, I think. If he wants credit for the vast collection of oversized black sweaters and scarves I bury myself in while we're here, he's welcome to it."

"You really don't even know how very beautiful you are," he added, running a finger along the curve of my jaw.

I snorted and jerked my head away, hoping he wouldn't notice the heat and color now flooding my cheeks. "Please. I know exactly how beautiful I am. I'm a freaking bombshell."

Finn smiled. "I'm serious, you know."

"So am I. You better be careful, Carey. I'm totally out of your league."

The smile faded a little as he found my eyes again. "You don't need to keep that armor on with me, you know. You'd feel a lot freer without it."

I dropped my eyes to my own hands, which were steadily shredding away at a frayed spot on the edge of the blanket we were lying on. "You seriously underestimate armor. It gets a bad rap, but actually it's very warm and comfy in here, thanks."

"Jess..."

"I fought for this armor, you know," I said, and my voice was angrier than I'd thought it would be when I opened my mouth. "I wasn't born with it. No one handed it to me. I earned the right to every single inch of it. Then I tested it, and I found every chink, and I filled them. This armor is a fucking masterpiece."

"It is impressive, yes," Finn said, with an air of surrender. "I suppose I was rather hoping you might make some room for me in there. It feels that since we've been here—and I don't think I'm wrong—that you've been pulling away from me. Do you deny it?"

Was there any point in lying to him? "No."

"What can I do to close the distance, Jess? How can I convince you to keep a space for me in there?"

The frayed spot on the blanket was starting to unravel nicely. I kept at it. "Here's the thing with that," I said. "I tried to do that a few years ago. I opened up to you. It didn't go so well, so I reinforced things. It gets harder and harder to get this thing off."

"I know. That's my fault. I'm here now, though. I'm right here," he said. "You believe that, don't you?"

"I believe it right now," I said. "But what about in a week? In a month? In a year? We're hiding, Finn, and it's only a matter of time before someone finds us. And then what?"

"I don't know," Finn said. "I can't predict the future, Jess."

"That's a bullshit answer and you know it," I said, dropping the blanket in frustration and sitting up. "This, right now—sneaking away to a remote place, looking over our shoulders—this is it. This is the most that we can ever be! Don't you want more than that?"

"You know I do."

"I just never envisioned love being like this. I mean, I'm not saying I want to marry you or anything," I said swiftly, feeling a strange panic welling in my chest. "I'm not trying to fly ahead to these crazy, huge commitments or anything. Maybe things will work out between us and maybe they won't. Maybe you'll always think I'm beautiful, and I'll always think you're adorably deluded about that fact. Or maybe we'll wake up one day and whatever this is between us will have cooled and solidified into something heavy that weighs us down, until one of us ends it. I don't know. You don't know. But one thing I know for sure is that we'll never get the chance to find out. We'll never walk out in the sunlight holding hands. We'll never..." I couldn't finish the sentence. A stream of images was flooding through my head, like flashes of memory from a Crossing spirit, images from another life, a happier one; walking along a beach hand in hand; moving boxes together into an apartment; running through the rain to his waiting car; even—insanely—him running a hand over my rounded belly. I didn't even know if I wanted these things. Some of them scared the shit out of me. I just knew that having the choices ripped out of my hands was as bad as having them forced upon me.

"I hate that this was our only time together in a week. I hate sneaking around like I'm your goddamned mistress. I hate watching you check to make sure you don't smell like my perfume," I said, as I watched him sniff surreptitiously at the collar of his shirt.

Finn looked affronted. "I don't think of you as my—"

"I know that, but it doesn't change how I feel," I said. "And if we're not going to try to get the rule changed, then I'm always going to feel this way."

"We've already discussed this," Finn said sharply. "You know why we can't do that."

"I could if Hannah and I took that Council seat," I said.

Finn laughed a sharp, short bark, then caught sight of my expression. "You're not serious, are you?"

I shrugged. "I don't know."

Finn turned to face me. "You hate it here. All you've said since we've arrived is how much you loathe this place and how you can't wait to get home."

"I do hate it here. But I'm starting to think I hate our permanent state of limbo more."

"And how exactly do you think taking a seat on the Council would fix that?" Finn asked.

"It might not," I said. "But it would give me a chance to do something about these stupid rules that are keeping us apart."

"And if you can't change them? If they refuse to lift the sanctions on Durupinen/Caomhnóir relationships?"

"We'll be no worse off than we are right now," I said. I could feel my temper breaking the barriers with which I was trying to keep it in check.

"Except if they find out about us. Which of course they will. We've been through this, Jess. Seamus already knows about us. Petitioning to change that rule will be tantamount to openly declaring our love for each other."

"He says as though that would be the worst thing in the world," I said through gritted teeth.

184

"It will be the worst thing in the world if it means they separate us, which they will undoubtedly do," Finn shot back.

"So, what if you just... quit?" I blurted out. I hadn't meant to say it. I barely realized I was thinking it, but the half-formed thought was out of my mouth before I could stop it.

Finn froze. "Quit."

"I didn't... I mean, I don't... well, yeah," I muttered.

"You think I should quit," he repeated.

"I don't know," I said, and I was angry at how small my voice was. I took a deep breath. "I didn't mean to say that, but... would you ever consider that?"

His face was a mask. His mouth was barely moving. "Would you consider it?"

I started. "Me?"

"Yes."

"I can't quit," I said.

"Why not?"

I laughed incredulously. "Finn, I am a Gateway. It's inside me. I can't turn it off, and I can't get away from it. If I quit, it would mean nothing; the Gateway would still be there. The spirits would still show up, demanding passage. There's no quitting this, or else I would have already done it already."

"I see. So, you think your calling is inherent and mine is a choice?"

I squirmed uncomfortably. "It's more of a choice than mine is," I said, hating the defensive note in my voice.

"I see. I see."

Finn started pacing. The silence between us spiraled and deepened; I shivered as though the temperature had actually dropped. Finally, he turned to face me, and I had rarely seen him look so angry.

"This is the world I grew up in. It is all I know. My calling is to be a Caomhnóir, and I have known it as long as I have known my own name. It is in my blood, just as much as being a Durupinen is in yours. This is not some job I can quit. It is who I am, and I resent the fact that you could ever think otherwise."

"Finn, I didn't..."

"I've never known you to be guilty of that Durupinen arrogance," he went on, speaking over me, "that inherent bias that puts the importance of the Durupinen far above that of their protectors. You are the queens, and we but lowly foot soldiers. It has always been that way, just never with you."

"That's not fair! I don't think that at all!" I cried.

"I would have said the same, until a moment ago," Finn said.

Angry tears flooded my eyes, blurring him from my sight. I brushed them fiercely away, silently cursing them for betraying me in a moment when I wanted that armor to be impenetrable. But when I focused on his face again, I couldn't find the words I needed.

He turned away from me, pulling his shirt from the back of the chair and over his head in one fluid motion.

"Are you leaving?"

"Yes. I need to get some air."

"You're not even going to let me—"

"No. I'm not." He stomped his feet into his waiting boots, and tucked his jacket up under his arm.

"Finn—"

"Make sure you put out that fire and lock the door behind you," he said, peeking out of the curtain to be sure the coast was clear before wrenching open the door. "I'll be waiting outside."

"Who's hiding behind their armor now?" I called after him as he pulled the door shut. He did not reply.

ELEANORA: 13 JULY 1864

13 July 1864

Dearest Little Book,

  When last I sat before you, I was full of questions. Now I put my pen to your pages with an answer, an answer so terrible that I wish I could unknow it.

  I was smuggled into Fairhaven Hall under cover of darkness in the moments before the sun rose. Like some kind of criminal or leper, I was brought not to my bedroom, where I could have found some much needed rest, but to a room off of the Grand Council Room. It was little more than a cell, with a single hard chair, a small table, a lamp, and a glass of water. There was no window, no fireplace, and worst of all, no person waiting there to tell me what was going on.

  On three separate occasions, Durupinen came in to question me, though none of my own questions, which had grown increasingly desperate, were deemed worthy of an answer. I was subjected to the most humiliating of physical examinations. The nurse seemed to be looking for evidence of Castings that had been placed upon me. I repeatedly denied that any such event had occurred, but she took as little notice of my protestations as if I had been incapable of coherent speech.

  After several hours of this treatment, I was escorted into the Grand Council Room, where the entire Council sat ensconced unsmilingly in their seats. Three spirits were also present, hovering near the High Priestess' seat. Without preamble or explanation, she demanded that I Call the spirits.

  "I'm sorry, I do not understand you," I said, barely able to answer through my frustrated tears.

  "Call them. Ask them to come to you," the High Priestess repeated.

  Bewildered, I turned to the spirits. "Would you be so kind as to come over here to me?" I asked them.

They all looked at each other as though conferring about something, then turned to the High Priestess, and shook their heads.

"No, do not make a request of them. Call them to you. Command them, as you did last night on the grounds of the Kentwood estate," the High Priestess said.

"Can you please tell me why I've been—"

"Do what is requested of you, Miss Larkin," the High Priestess said, raising a hand to silence me.

I fought back another wave of tears and tried again. "Come here to me," I said, though I felt foolish.

Again, the spirits did not respond. Again, they shook their heads.

Over and over the High Priestess demanded I do what I seemed incapable of doing. Over and over again, the spirits remained motionless. The Council members were all glaring suspiciously at me.

"Could it be, Miss Larkin, that you do not wish to comply with my request? Could it be that you are refusing to show me what you can do?"

"No, of course not!" I cried. "But what is it I'm meant to be able to do? What happened to me last night has never happened in my life! I was frightened and needed help! The spirits came to my aid!"

"And how did you summon them to you?" the High Priestess asked. "Did you shout? Did you scream?"

"No! That brute was upon me. I could barely breathe, much less make sound," I said.

"So, then what was it you did?"

"I... I just..." I closed my eyes and, in my fright and confusion and frustration, I shouted inside my own head, "Come here to me, spirits! Come to me now!"

At my words all three of the spirits' faces went still and blank. As though tied to me by strings that I could jerk and tug at will, the three spirits drifted toward me, stopping just in front of me. They simply hung there, empty, waiting for further instruction. They appeared to be completely at my command.

I stared at them in horror for a moment, but it was surely no match for the horror on every face staring back at me from the Council seats. The moment I had looked away from them, the spirits seemed to come to their senses. They seemed not to comprehend how they had come to be standing in front of me.

"Caomhnóir, remove her to the Warded chamber again. We must confer," the High Priestess called, and at once turned her back upon me. Then it was hours of desperate anxiety before anyone finally came to explain to me what was happening.

A Caller. That is what I am. I can exercise some measure of control over spirits, bring them to me and demand their compliance. No one can explain why I have this gift, nor where it came from. All they can tell me is that Callers—that I—am to be deeply feared.

I do not know what will happen to me now. They will not allow me to see my sister or my mother. They will not allow me to leave this room until they have determined where they can "safely" keep me. They will not accept my promises that I will not use the gift, that I will suppress it. And above all, they refuse—absolutely refuse—to explain to me what it is they fear I will do with my powers.

When did I become an enemy amongst my own sisterhood? What is to become of me?

Eleanora

15

ACCOMPLICE

FINN KEPT SEVERAL LONG STRIDES in front of me as we trudged back to the castle. Twice my feeling welled up into speech and I opened my mouth to shout at him, but both times the words died the instant they touched my lips. As we broke through the edge of the trees and onto the open lawn, Milo's urgent, terrified voice battered itself against the inside of my head.

"JESSICA! FOR FUCK'S SAKE, ANSWER ME!"

I cried out and staggered back, clutching at my head. Finn spun around and jogged back to me, looking alarmed.

"What is it? Jess? Is it a Shard?" he demanded.

"No, it's Milo!" I answered through gritted teeth. "Milo, stop shouting before my head explodes!"

"I wouldn't have to yell if you would just answer me!" Milo shot back, though much more quietly. "Where are you? Why couldn't I connect? Were you blocking me?"

"I'm fine, I'm fine. I just needed some air and some quiet. I closed up the connection for a few minutes, just so I could think," I said, looking up at Finn and nodding, as though to say, "That's the story and we're sticking to it." He nodded once, sharply.

"Well, you picked a great moment to go rogue," Milo said with mounting hysteria. "Come to the Grand Council Room right now. Something's going on. They've called Hannah in for questioning. They won't explain what's happening."

"Questioning? About what?" I asked, starting to jog toward the castle, Finn on my heels.

"They didn't say!" Milo cried, and he sounded close to tears. "Two Caomhnóir just cornered her in the hallway and told her she was being summoned immediately for questioning and marched off with her. They actually held on to her arms, like she was a criminal or something!"

"They did what?! Why the hell aren't you with her?"

Milo's indignation broke over me like a tidal wave in my head. "I have been, but she asked me to blink out and contact you! I'm right where I'm supposed to be! You're the one who vanished without letting us know where you were going!"

"Okay, okay, I'm sorry. I'm on my way. I'm almost to the front doors. Tell Hannah I'll be right there."

Milo snapped out of the connection forcefully, twanging it like a rubber band and leaving me dizzy.

"What is it? What's happened?" Finn asked, catching up to me.

"I'm not really sure yet," I said breathlessly, breaking into a run now. "He said that the Council wants to question Hannah about something. They're in the Grand Council Room."

"What the hell could they want to question her about?" Finn growled.

"I have no idea, but if I know Hannah, she is freaking out right now," I said. "Thank God she's got Milo with her or she might Call half the dead residents of England out of sheer panic."

"Is the whole Airechtas present, or is it just the Council?" Finn asked.

"I don't know. He said the Council wanted to question her, but that doesn't mean the rest of the clans might not be there." I wrenched open the front door and barreled past the Caomhnóir guarding it.

"Hey, what are you—" he began, starting after me.

I spun to face him. "If you prevent me for one more second from going to my sister, I will fucking end you," I spat at him. He was young, clearly a Novitiate, and probably a first year at that. Whatever he saw in my face made him take a hasty step back.

"We... we have orders to monitor traffic through these doors," he mumbled.

"Well, keep monitoring it, then," Finn said sharply. "To your post."

The boy—he really was just a boy—slunk back to his place by the door. Finn and I sprinted the length of the corridor and met a second set of Caomhnóir at the doors to the Grand Council Room.

"My sister is in there," I said, as calmly as I could. "I need to go in."

"Clan privilege," Finn added on the heels of my words. "You cannot deny her entry. She has the right to witness any official questioning of her fellow clan member, per the Charter of Clan Rights."

I probably should have known what the Charter of Clan Rights was, but I didn't, except for a vague memory of references to it in Celeste's Durupinen History class. But to my utter surprise and relief, the Caomhnóir were obviously quite familiar with it, because they did not question me or demand further explanation. They simply nodded at Finn and then stood aside.

The Grand Council Room was abuzz with conversation as I entered, but the sound quickly died out as the Council members realized who had walked in. The rest of the seats were empty except for a small group of spectators near the front. Marion was among them, along with several of her usual entourage. Hannah sat in a chair in the center of the room, a Caomhnóir standing at attention on either side of her, as though she were under arrest. Milo hovered just to the side of them, his expression twisted up with concern. The sound of my hurried footsteps made both he and Hannah turn.

"Jess!" Hannah cried, and her face was glazed with tears. She tried to stand up, but one of the Caomhnóir placed a restraining hand on her shoulder and she sank back down again, dropping her face into her shaking hands.

All of my fear and trepidation evaporated at the sight of Hannah's tiny, sobbing figure. "What the hell is going on here?" I shouted. "Get your hands off her!"

"Jessica, please calm down," said a sharp voice, and I looked up to see Celeste on her feet.

"I will not calm down!" I shot back. I skidded to a stop at Hannah's side, elbowing past the Caomhnóir in my haste to reach her.

The Caomhnóir started toward me, but Finn leapt between us. "Touch either one of them again, and I will make you very sorry, indeed," he growled.

Celeste stepped out from behind the podium and raised her hands, signaling for attention. "Everyone, please, there is no reason to—"

"Celeste, I swear to God, if you tell me to calm down one more time without an explanation as to what is happening here, I am going to lose my shit," I said.

"Jessica, please refrain from such language. I cannot answer you if you will not allow me to," Celeste said sternly. "We have convened a meeting of the Council in order to question your sister about the Shattering."

"Is there a reason that they're here," I pointed over at Marion and her cronies, "but you neglected to notify me?"

"They are here because Council meetings are open to any Durupinen who want to attend. We did attempt to notify you. We've been looking for you all over the castle for the last half an hour. I believe several of our Caomhnóir are still looking, in fact," Celeste said.

"I... wasn't in the castle," I said lamely, caught off guard by the response. I felt the color rising to my cheeks. Damn it Jess, if you blush now you could ruin everything.

"I had trouble tracking her down myself," Finn said brusquely, swooping in when it was clear that I wasn't going to whip up a brilliant cover story. "Despite my repeated reminders to her that I am to keep guard at all times because of the Shards, she still felt the need to slip off into the grounds to 'get some air.'" Finn put air quotes around the last three words, injecting them with liberal amounts of disdain. "Fresh air was more important than her safety, it would seem," he added.

Several Council members smiled indulgently, clearly appreciating Finn's apparent frustration with me. I threw him a dirty look, both because he deserved one, and because it would bolster his story.

"So, while I was committing the atrocity of daring to take a walk, what exactly has my sister been accused of?" I asked, looking to Celeste for my answer.

"She's not being accused of anything," Celeste said. She seemed to be willing me into calmness with the slow, soothing tone of her voice. "She is being questioned. That is all."

"They're saying she had something to do with the Shattered spirit," Milo said, "which sounds a hell of a lot like an accusation to me."

I nudged Hannah over on her seat and perched myself on the edge of it, wrapping my arms around her and glaring fiercely up at Celeste. "Explain. Now."

Several Council members were murmuring words like, "disrespect" and "insolent tone," but I ignored them, keeping my eyes on Celeste, who said, "I would be very happy to explain, if you would give me the chance to do so. We've just had a report from

Mrs. Mistlemoore. At your suggestion, the Hosts in the hospital ward have been provided with paper and writing utensils, in order to determine if their scribbling motions would produce any viable clues. It was an excellent suggestion, Jessica, and we thank you for it. Once provided with the necessary materials, every single one of the Hosts produced page after page of the same words."

She reached down and pulled a piece of paper from a stack in front of her and handed it to a Caomhnóir who was positioned beside the podium. He carried it down the steps and thrust it out toward me. I snatched the paper from his hand and looked down at it.

Over and over, line after line, the same five words:

The Caller has betrayed me.

I stared down at them, reading them again and again, as though by reading them I could will them to turn into other words—words that made sense.

"What is this?" I asked blankly. "What is this supposed to mean?"

"We do not know," Celeste said. "That is why we invited your sister to meet with us."

"Oh, an invitation, huh? Is that what we're calling it? Invitation implies a choice about whether or not to show up. That felt like an arrest to me," Milo said sharply.

Celeste furrowed her brow. "It was not meant to come across that way. I simply asked the Caomhnóir to find Hannah and escort her here to the Grand Council Room."

"Well then, maybe you should have a word with them about the meaning of the word 'escort,'" Milo suggested. The Caomhnóir standing closest to him bristled but did not speak.

I looked up at Celeste. "Celeste, you know what our experience with this Council has been. You know how our 'invitations' to this room have turned out."

Celeste grimaced. "Yes, I do, and I'm sorry. I would have come to fetch Hannah myself, but I was tied up in the hospital ward."

A Council member stood up, looking haughty. "It is not the duty of the Deputy Priestess to fetch people. This is a crisis. We need answers."

But Celeste put up a weary hand to silence the woman. "Thank you, Isla, but that is unnecessary and unproductive."

Isla, to whom I had never spoken in my life, but who I recognized as one of Marion's inner circle, nodded but continued to glare at me.

I glared right back at her before turning to Hannah. "Hannah, do you have any idea what this means?"

Hannah shook her head, still trying to control her crying. "I h-have no idea. I haven't C-Called anyone since I've been here. Oh wait, no, that's not true. I Called those ghosts into Frankie's room earlier today. But that can't have anything to do with the Shattering, because it had already happened."

Celeste's voice was kind and coaxing. "Think hard, Hannah. Is there any spirit at all that you've communicated with since you've arrived here?"

Hannah furrowed her brow. "I... I mean, of course I've said hello to them, in passing. No one has contacted me for help, though."

"There was a full moon the night before your arrival. Did anything unusual happen at your lunar Crossing?" Celeste pressed.

"I don't think so," Hannah said. "Jess, do you remember anything?"

I shook my head. "No. It was normal. Shorter than normal, actually. No spirits even made contact beforehand. It was a pretty quiet week all around, until we came here and all hell broke loose."

"You can understand our confusion, Hannah," Celeste said. "The Shattering happened here in the castle, and you are the only Caller at Fairhaven. There must be a connection somehow."

Hannah shrugged, looking bewildered. "I have no idea what it is. I'm sorry Celeste, but these words make no sense to me."

Keira leaned forward, clasping her hands in front of her. "No one blames you for mistrusting the Council, Hannah," she said, and it was clear she was endeavoring to keep her tone sympathetic. "We all know that our decisions toward you have not been fair in the past. Many of those decisions were motivated by fear and misunderstanding. But is it possible that your mistrust is preventing you from telling us the truth right now?"

Hannah's eyes widened. "No. No, of course not."

Keira looked at Celeste, who sighed before turning to Hannah.

"It is my duty at this point to remind you that lying to this Council is a crime under our by-laws," Celeste said quietly.

"I'm not lying!" Hannah cried, her eyes filling with tears again.

I stood up; every inch of me seemed to be vibrating with suppressed rage. "My sister is not a liar."

"No one is calling her a liar, Jessica," Celeste said, a warning in her voice. "But fear is a powerful motivator, and if Hannah is afraid to answer us truthfully—"

"If Hannah is afraid to answer you truthfully, it is your own damn fault!" I shouted. "She should never have to answer to anyone in this room ever again after what happened to her. You want to talk about fear being a powerful motivator; you should all look in the mirror! Every one of you sat there three years ago and let your fear drive us to the brink of destruction! Don't you dare talk to us about fear! Don't you dare talk to us about honesty within these walls!"

That was the line, and I'd crossed it. A general outcry rose from the Council benches as well as the knot of spectators. All around us, angry voices rose in response to my words. The Caomhnóir on either side of us shifted their postures as though awaiting an order to seize us. Finn, in turn, took a decisive step closer to Hannah and me, so that I could feel his physical presence directly behind me. The only person who appeared unconcerned was Fiona, who was shaking her head and laughing as she picked dried paint from underneath her fingernails.

"I request a call for order," Celeste shouted over the noise. She was looking all around for the gavel Siobhán had used in the first session of the Airechtas, but couldn't seem to locate it. "This behavior is out of keeping with Council guidelines."

The words, "Fuck your guidelines!" were halfway out of my mouth when Hannah laid her small, cool hand on top of mine and silenced them. I looked over at her. She had stopped crying. Her expression was determined.

"Permission to speak," Hannah called over the commotion, and I heard her master the tremor in her voice.

At that moment, Celeste found the gavel inside the podium and hammered it upon the wood several times, silencing everyone in the room. "Permission granted, Hannah, although this is not a formal session. It will quickly turn into a formal session, however," she called warningly over her shoulder to the benches, "if we cannot maintain order and civility." She turned back to us and let her eyes linger on me for a moment, a silent warning. I bit my tongue.

"I understand why you have all called me here. I am happy to help in any way that I can. I already offered my abilities to search for Shards within the castle, and I will continue to cooperate in whatever capacity you can use me. That said, I am telling you the truth. I do not know who the Shattered spirit is. I don't know what these words mean. I cannot force you to believe me. I can only promise you that I am not misleading you out of fear or mistrust—or any other motivation, for that matter."

"Not that I'm any kind of expert, but it's my understanding," Fiona said from the back row, "that these Shards are in a state of profound confusion. Is that correct, Mrs. Mistlemoore?"

"Yes, it is," replied Mrs. Mistlemoore, who had thus far been silent. She had deep purple rings under her eyes.

"And so, it would be reasonable to suppose," Fiona went on, still picking away at her fingers, "that the information and clues we gather from these Shards may be a load of tosh?"

Mrs. Mistlemoore cleared her throat. "The things they say will arise from their state of confusion, if that's what you mean."

"What I mean," Fiona said, looking up at last, "is that we have no idea what this spirit is referencing. Certainly, it *could* be talking about Hannah. But why do we assume this? True, she is the only Caller in this castle at the moment. But what spirit lives in the present? Most of them live in the past. This spirit could have lived a hundred, even a thousand years ago. Why do we assume then that this spirit is speaking of a Caller who is alive and in the castle right now?"

People were shifting in their seats and trading looks.

Fiona continued. "It's been my experience that spirits fixate on the circumstances surrounding their deaths. Maybe this spirit died at the hands of a Caller, or perhaps as the result of a Caller's actions. Hannah, have you murdered anyone since arriving here three days ago?"

Hannah looked startled, then cleared her throat. "Uh, no. No, I haven't."

Keira rolled her eyes. "Fiona, no one is suggesting that Hannah killed anyone."

"But you are accusing this poor girl of something devious, even though you've no clear reason for doing so!" Fiona shot back.

"We're not accusing—"

"Then what the bloody hell is she doing here? Why not just sit her down with Mrs. Mistlemoore in the hospital ward and hash it all out? Why do we have to make a show of power just to let the poor girl answer a few questions?" she asked. "Why are you dragging me down from my work to victimize her? And why the bloody hell did we let them in here, circling like vultures hoping for a fresh carcass?" She cocked her thumb over at Marion and her group of spectators, all of whom had gone stonily silent.

"It's how things are done," Isla said with dignity.

"Well, how things are done is rubbish," Fiona replied.

"What is your point, Fiona?" Celeste asked quietly.

"My point is, I'm done with the bloody witch hunts. I won't be dragged down here again for this kind of shite," Fiona said, and rose from her seat. She started walking down the rows of benches.

"Fiona, the Council has not been dismissed," Celeste called after her, the frustration clear in her voice.

"I'm dismissing myself," Fiona shouted back over her shoulder. "I look forward to the sanction or the written warning, or whatever bloody else you slap me with for walking out."

Celeste passed a hand over her face and took a long, deep breath. "Very well. If Hannah has nothing left to tell us, I would like to move that she be dismissed."

No one replied. Celeste looked around, confused. "Someone needs to second the motion," she said.

Again no one spoke. No one would look her in the face.

Finally, Isla stood up. "I am not satisfied that we have been given honest responses to our questions. I would like to move that Hannah be detained until conclusions can be reached regarding this matter."

"Seconded," Keira added. She was looking anywhere but at Hannah.

I stood to object, but Milo beat me to it. "What the hell does that mean, 'detained?' You just finished telling us that this was not an arrest. Are you walking that back already?" he asked. His anger was so intense that his form seemed to crackle with it.

"No, we are not," Celeste said, and she turned back to the other Council members, a warning look on her face. "Isla, you will kindly clarify and explain your motion."

Isla, who was still standing, raised her chin. I saw her eyes dart, for the briefest of moments, in Marion's direction just before she answered. "It is essential that all elements of this Shattering be entirely contained. It may very well be that Hannah is not the Caller that the Shards are referring to. But if she is, and if we need her to be a part of the process of expelling the Shattered spirit, we need to ensure that we have access to her."

"I'm not going anywhere!" Hannah said, her voice cracking with fear, though I could tell she was trying to hold it together. "I already told you I'll do whatever I can to help!"

"Fairhaven is under lockdown," I added, hiding my anger about as successfully as Hannah was hiding her fear. "She can't go anywhere anyway. None of us can."

"I agree," Celeste said. "This motion is redundant."

Isla widened her eyes innocently. "But you saw what happened even now. We invited Jessica to be here for this meeting, and she could not be located. Who knows how long it might have taken the Caomhnóir to find her if she had not returned of her own accord? We cannot risk the same thing happening if it turns out that Hannah is an integral part of the Shattering. We need to know where she is."

"We cannot detain a Durupinen in our dungeons without formal charges," Celeste said, and her own anger was rising now, bringing color to her wan complexion. "Some of us in this room ought to remember what happened the last time we tried to do such a thing." She shot a fierce look over at Marion. Her motion to remove Finvarra as High Priestess and lock her in the dungeons was the reason Marion no longer had a Council seat. Marion did not reply, though a suggestion of a smile played about her lips.

Isla, however, hoisted a look of horror onto her face. "I would never suggest that poor Hannah be relegated to our dungeons. I am merely suggesting she be confined to her room until we can clear up this situation."

"I repeat, I do not think such actions are warranted in this—" Celeste went on, but Keira cut her off.

"I agree it is a necessary precaution in this unpredictable situation," she said. "It would be in Hannah's best interest as well. If the Shattered spirit does believe it has been somehow betrayed by Hannah, we ought to detain her, for her own safety as much as anyone else's. The Shards might seek her out or look to attack her."

I laughed mirthlessly. This last point was a ridiculously transparent pretext, but the other Council members seized upon it gratefully, relieved to have a benevolent excuse for jumping on board with Isla's motion. There were concerned expressions and nods of approval all around the benches.

"I move that the Council vote to detain Hannah in her chambers until such time as we can determine that she is in no danger from the Shards, or that we determine she is not the Caller referred to in these documents," Isla said.

"Seconded," Keira said.

Celeste closed her eyes and flared her nostrils. She had no choice. "All in favor?"

Hands rose all around the benches. Every single hand, except for Celeste's.

"Very well. Motion carries," Celeste said in a tone of suppressed rage. She turned to us and spoke in a carefully measured voice. "Hannah, though it was merely my hope to ask you a few questions, it is the will of the Council that you remain confined to your room until further notice. We will assign a Caomhnóir to this post, so that Mr. Carey can continue his regular duties. Meals will be brought to you, and I will send regular updates to keep you informed on our progress."

"Celeste, this is insane and you know it," I said quietly.

"My hands are tied, Jessica," she said. "The Council has spoken."

"Oh, really? Well the Council are cowards," I said. "Every single one of you."

16

THE FAMILIAR STARE

"IT'S MARION. It has to be. This has her fingerprints all over it."

Though I could leave any time I wanted to, I was pacing our room like a caged animal. Hannah sat in the chair in front of the fire, watching me.

"Marion?" she asked, looking surprised. "How can she have anything to do with it?"

"Oh, come on, Hannah, I know you're not that naïve," I said. "She's had it in for us from the beginning."

"I know that, but what part of this do you think is her fault?" Hannah asked. "Do you think she Shattered a spirit and framed me for it? I mean, she's awful, but that's pretty far-fetched."

I shook my head. "No, I don't think she had anything to do with the Shattering. But you know her friends are still all over that Council. She knows everything that's going on, even if she doesn't have a seat anymore. She told Isla to have you locked up, I would bet my life on it."

"But why?" Hannah asked. "When they figure out that the spirit has nothing to do with me, everyone will realize it was a mistake. So, what would be the point?"

"It's Marion," Milo chimed in. "Does she need to have a point? I think she just likes destroying people."

"I think she saw an opportunity to get us out of the running for that Council seat, and took it. Even if it turns out that the spirit was referring to another Caller, the damage will be done. No one is going to waste a vote on someone who spent half of the Airechtas under house arrest," I said.

"I think it's a risky thing to do when you're trying to clean up your reputation," Hannah said thoughtfully. "Jess, for goodness sake, sit down! You're making me nervous prowling around like that!"

I flopped into a chair, pulling the elastic from my hair and letting it fall all around my face like a curtain I could hide behind. "It's my fault. I shouldn't have left the castle."

Hannah rolled her eyes. "Jess, they would have questioned me whether you were here or not."

"Yeah, but if I hadn't taken off into the grounds like that, they wouldn't have been able to use it as an excuse to keep you here," I said miserably. I shot a furtive look at Finn. I was selfishly glad that his face looked stricken as well. At least I wasn't alone in my guilt.

"Jess, it doesn't matter. They would have suggested it anyway. They're scared of me, just like they always have been. People don't think rationally when they're afraid," Hannah said, with a sigh. She looked so tiny, so forlorn curled up in her chair that the idea of anyone being afraid of her in that moment was laughable.

"Okay, so we need to be the rational ones," Milo said, floating to his feet. "If the Council is acting out of fear, then we need to be logical, and figure this out."

Hannah laughed a sad little laugh. "What can we possibly figure out that the entire Council, the hospital staff, and an army of Scribes haven't already discovered?"

Milo crossed his arms, looking truculent. "Maybe nothing. But you're Trackers now, and that means you have every right to investigate this situation. The Council is not handling this objectively. They are operating with a bias, and that means they are missing something."

"How do we know I'm not missing something?" Hannah asked. "I've encountered more spirits than I can possibly remember. How do we know one of them didn't feel betrayed and cause this whole mess?"

I shook my head. "No. No, this isn't about you. Something else is going on here. And I have no idea what it is."

I crossed over to my bed and flopped down on it, feeling defeated. I couldn't believe we were here again—at Fairhaven, at the mercy of the Council. Hadn't we been through enough? Wasn't there some kind of limit, some kind of quota of misery that a person could fill, and hadn't we filled it already? Wasn't this the point—after disastrous childhoods, after seventeen years of separation, after the catastrophe of the Prophecy—that we were allowed a free pass?

Surely it was someone else's turn to take the hits on behalf of the spirit world.

I rolled over onto my stomach, determined to bury my head in the pillows and not resurface, when I glanced past the edge of the bed and locked gazes with a deep, dark pair of eyes.

"Oh, my God."

"Jess? Are you okay?" Hannah asked.

"Oh, my God!" I repeated unable to look away from the eyes, which were staring up at me from the floor.

"Jess, what are you—"

But I had leapt from the bed and dropped to my knees on the rug. There, peeking out at me from under the bed where I had stashed her, was the occupant of the spirit drawing I'd created our very first day at Fairhaven.

"This is her," I whispered.

"This is who?" Milo asked, blinking into being right beside me.

"This is the Shattered spirit!" I told him.

"What?" Finn asked, dropping to the ground beside me.

"Jess, what are you talking about?" Hannah cried, jumping up from her chair and coming over to join us in the huddle around my sketches.

"I'm talking about this!" I said, smacking the paper with an impatient gesture. "I knew it! I knew when I looked into Catriona's face and saw those eyes looking back at me that I had seen them somewhere before. These were the eyes. This is the spirit that has been Shattered."

"Who is she?" Finn asked. "Have you met her somewhere before?"

I shook my head. "I have no idea. She came to me in my sleep. She didn't leave me any clues except these images." I pulled the second drawing out from under the first. The same haunted eyes gazed up at us from the second picture. "No name, no requests. Just these."

"We need to get them down to the Council," Finn said eagerly, standing up.

"No!" I shouted.

He stopped already halfway to the door, and scowled at me. "No?"

"I know that they're leading this investigation, but I don't trust them, not after today," I said.

"Jessica, this information might help them discover who the spirit is," Finn said.

"I'm with Jess on this one," Milo said. "I don't want to hand them any information until we know what it means."

"What do we do with it, then?" Hannah asked.

I thought for a long moment, and then the answer hit me. "Fiona. We take it to Fiona. No one knows more about spirit drawings than she does. We take them to her and see what she suggests."

"Fiona's still on the Council," Finn pointed out.

"You heard what she said before she stormed out of that meeting," I said. "She doesn't want anything to do with their witch hunts. She'll help us figure out what to do, and who we can trust."

Milo snapped his fingers. "I like it."

Hannah bit her lip, but nodded.

I stood up, rolling the pictures together into a tight scroll.

"You're going now?" Finn asked blankly.

"Yes, of course I am!" I cried. "What the hell would I be waiting for?"

"I can't come with you until the next Caomhnóir arrives to start his shift here with Hannah," Finn said. He threw a guilty half-glance at Hannah as he said it.

"So, stay here," I said impatiently. "Milo can come with me, right Milo?"

"But I need to protect—"

"Oh, for God's sake, Finn, just back off!" I cried. "Milo will be with me. Everything will be fine. I'm not waiting around for another Caomhnóir to show up. We are losing time here, and the sooner we find out who this spirit is, the sooner we can end this nightmare. When the new Caomhnóir shows up, meet us up in Fiona's studio."

I pushed past Finn, refusing even to stop to hear his protestations. When I turned back at the door, I avoided looking at him, and addressed Hannah instead. "We'll use the connection to let you know what Fiona has to say. Don't tell anyone that's where we've gone. It's probably better if no one knows about these drawings until we have a better idea of what we're dealing with."

"Good luck!" Hannah called after us as I pulled the door shut.

Milo and I set off down the hallway. There was a new edge to my awareness now; before, I had been on constant alert for the presence of a Shard, but I had been fearful of it. Now I was silently begging a Shard to make itself known. Perhaps if I confronted it with its own identity it could be controlled, mesmerized by its own image.

Come and find me, I thought. *I know what you look like and soon, I'll know your name.*

"Jess, are you okay?" Milo's voice broke through my silent challenge. I turned to find him looking intently at me.

"Yeah. Yeah, I'm fine," I said shortly. "I just... I kind of lose it, when people come for Hannah. I lose what little ability I have to stay rational."

Milo laughed grimly. "Girl, you are preaching to the choir over here. I just thought there was something else... with Finn?"

"I don't want to talk about that right now," I said. The words were thick in my throat. I'm not sure what I let show on my face, but Milo didn't press me. I couldn't have answered him even if he had. We had just reached the base of Fiona's tower and I was going to need every molecule of oxygen for the climb.

I didn't stop to catch my breath at the top of the stairs, but stumbled straight over to the door and started pounding on it. The Caomhnóir stationed outside of it didn't even blink. Evidently, he didn't care who we were or what we were doing there as long as we weren't Shards.

"If you want me back in that meeting, you'll have to break that door down and drag me out by my ankles. And I warn you, I'm a biter," Fiona shouted in reply.

"Fiona, it's Jess! Can you let me in? I need to show you something. It's important!" I called back.

There was a pause. "Are you alone?"

"I'm with Milo, but that's it."

Milo snorted. "That's it. You should BE so lucky."

I ignored him. Then I heard some banging, a few crashes, and a stream of cursing before the door finally swung open.

"Come in, then. Mind your step," Fiona said, waving us in.

Milo and I followed Fiona into the studio. She slammed the door behind her. The place was usually in a state of organized chaos, but today it was utter pandemonium. Papers and tarps were thrown over nearly every surface, and paint cans, brushes, pastels, pencils, and charcoal were scattered everywhere. The sight of the bedlam froze me for a moment.

"Fiona, what's... what are you working on in here?"

"The same thing everyone else in this bloody castle is working on; I'm trying to identify those Shards. I'm having tremendous success, as you can see." She flung her arm out to embrace the mess, then grabbed an open wine bottle off her desk.

"Fancy a nip? You look like you could use it," she said, offering it to me.

"Uh, no that's okay. I'm good," I said.

"It's coffee," she said, shaking it at me so that it sloshed.

"Huh? Oh, okay," I said, and grabbed it, taking a large gulp before sputtering and coughing.

"And whiskey," Fiona added, taking the bottle back from me.

"Thanks for the warning," I choked.

"Coffee and whiskey in a wine bottle," Milo said, shaking his head and smirking. "Girl, you have elevated vice to an art form."

"Cheers," Fiona said, and took another swig before plunking the bottle back onto her desk and settling her piercing, beady stare on me. "How are you holding up?" she asked.

I laughed. "I'm too blinded by rage to accurately address that question."

"And your sister?"

"She's scared. And feeling betrayed," I said. "Everyone keeps telling us we are welcome here, and every time, they prove themselves wrong. Thank you for sticking up for us in there, by the way."

Fiona clicked her tongue. "I've had it with the whole lot of them. If I wasn't worried about what would happen without my voice, I'd quit the bloody Council right now. Shouldn't have walked out when I did, but I can't stand that kind of backstabbing. Celeste means well, but she needs to grow a backbone or the whole lot of them will just keep walking right over her."

"Did you say you were trying to figure out who the Shattered spirit is?" I asked.

Fiona nodded. "I've been trying to connect with my gift. I'm opening myself up to communication, surrounding myself with media that might tempt a Shard to use me, but so far I've got nothing."

"You were trying to become a Host?" Milo asked in an awed voice.

Fiona shrugged unconcernedly. "Why not? We can't get rid of it until every Shard finds a Host. Might as well speed up the process, especially if I can produce some clues in the process. Fecking waste of time, as you can see."

"Well, speaking of clues, I need your help. I think I know who the Shattered spirit is. Or, at least, I know what she looks like," I said, handing Fiona the scroll.

She took it from me, eyes wide. "What's this, then?" she asked as she unrolled it. Her eyes widened as she looked it over. "You drew these? Just now?"

"No. That top one I drew three days ago, on the day we arrived for the Airechtas. I'd barely been here an hour. I woke up to the second one the next day."

"Do you have any idea who she is?" Fiona asked, fishing a pair of bifocals out of her overalls and pushing them up onto her nose.

"Not a clue. She hasn't come back since, but I think that's because she can't. If she's been Shattered, she might be too confused to reestablish contact."

"What makes you think this is the Shattered spirit?" Fiona asked.

"It's the eyes," I said, and even as I spoke the words, a shiver ran down my spine as I recalled their gaze on me. "I saw those exact same eyes staring at me, first from Catriona's face, and then from Siobhán's. They are the same ones, I'm sure of it."

Fiona did not question my statement. She knew too much about the Muse process to doubt my surety. Instead, she swept an arm across her desk, sending everything on it crashing to the ground. She lay the sketches on the newly cleared surface and bent so low over them that the tip of her nose nearly touched the paper.

"And did she indicate to you what the words 'little book' mean?" Fiona asked, not looking up.

"Did she... what?" I asked.

"These words, 'little book.' Any idea what they mean?" Fiona repeated.

"What words? What are you talking about?" I asked, utterly perplexed.

Fiona flung out a hand, grabbed me by the arm, and hauled me roughly around to her side of the desk. "Did you even bother to glance at this sketch after you drew it? These words here, around her neck!"

I bent low over the paper, and even then, it took a few seconds for me to realize that what I had taken to be a necklace around the girl's neck was actually the same two words, over and over again, forming a delicate chain: "little book."

"I never noticed that before," I whispered, staring down at the tiny script in wonder. "I've never produced anything like that in a psychic drawing before."

"That you've noticed," Fiona said.

"Hey, you've looked at almost every psychic drawing I've ever done," I said defensively. "You've never noticed anything like this before either, have you?"

Fiona ignored the question. She was busy poring over the sketch again. "The clothing and hairstyle are classic Victorian aristocracy. 1850's I'd say, maybe slightly later. And that brooch can only mean one thing." She tapped the young woman's bust with her finger, indicating a decorative pin she wore there, peeking out from a delicate trim of lace. It was a tiny Triskele.

"She was a Durupinen," I whispered.

"Too, right she was," Fiona said. "Well, this narrows things down quite a bit, doesn't it?"

"Is there some kind of… roster? A list we can check?" Milo asked.

"That huge book in the Council room, the one that Bertie was recording all the names in!" I cried. "She's got to be in there!"

"Somewhere, yes, but there's no way to verify which one she is," Fiona said. "There will be hundreds of names that could fit this time period, even just among the Durupinen."

"What about clan portraits?" Milo asked, slightly desperately. "Is that a thing? Rich people loved getting their portraits painted back in the day, right?"

Fiona shook her head. "High Priestesses had official portraits starting during the Renaissance, but not regular clan members. I am the official historian for those portraits. I've cleaned and restored every single one. I know them backward and forward, and I've never seen this girl's face before."

"Okay, so what do we do?" I asked, slightly desperately. "Where do we go from here?"

Fiona tapped her finger rapidly on the sketch, her eyes unfocused as she thought. Finally, she banged her fist on the desk, making Milo and me jump.

"We've got to get into the hospital ward. We've got to try to use the Shards there to communicate," Fiona said. She started digging around in the piles of paper and art supplies around her desk, shoving fistfuls of seemingly random objects into her pockets.

"But I thought they couldn't communicate clearly," I said, as I watched her toss three paint trays and a canvas over her shoulder.

"Isn't that the whole problem? That they're too confused to tell us who they are?"

"Shards are like pieces of a puzzle. The more of them you've got, the more complete the picture," Fiona said, chucking a palette across the room. "That's why it's so important to keep them together. If we can get into the hospital wing and encourage them to communicate with you, they might just give us enough to complete the picture. Dogs! Where are my bloody shoes?"

I looked down at her feet; sure enough they were bare, speckled liberally to the ankle with paint, plaster, and clay. Finally, she unearthed two filthy penny loafers from beneath a tarp and slid her feet into them with a look of disgust, as though the societal norm of footwear was actively oppressing her. Then she snatched up the two sketches and marched toward the door.

"What's happening? Are we going there now?" I asked her, jogging in her wake.

"Yes, of course," Fiona said. "Why the hell would we wait?"

"The hospital ward is closed. Quarantined. There's no way they're going to let us through the doors, is there?" I asked.

"Desperate times, and all that," Fiona said with an impatient wave of her hand. "They need to keep the Shards in, but there's no reason to keep us out. I'm a Council member."

"You maybe, but what about me? You don't think they'll be suspicious? Now that they think Hannah has something to do with it, they aren't going to want me in with the Shards," I said.

Fiona halted mid-stride. "Good point, that," she said testily. "Right, then. You're going to have to think this one out a bit."

"Me? Don't you mean 'we?'" I asked.

Fiona cocked her head to the side, glaring at me. "Have we met? I don't think things through. I'm a 'barrel-ahead-and-damn-the-consequences' kind of lass. You want proper planning? Plan it yourself!"

Milo and I looked at each other, a mirror of each other's panic.

"Got any brilliant ideas?" he asked me.

"Not one," I said confidently.

Milo nodded at me, then turned to Fiona. "Barrel-ahead-and-damn-the-consequences it is," he said, and we all marched out the door.

Finn met us on the staircase as we descended.

"How's Hannah?" I asked him before he could even open his mouth.

"She's fine," he said, and when I raised a skeptical eyebrow, he elaborated, "She was calm when I left her. She was going to call Karen and fill her in on what's been going on."

"Oh, my God, Karen," I said with a groan. "She is going to go through the roof. We barely talked her out of jumping on a plane just because Marion showed up to the Airechtas."

"I agree," Finn said, "which was why I suggested that she wait to call her. However, Hannah made the excellent point that if you two don't call her, Celeste or another Council member will. It will be easier to control the fallout this way."

"You're right," I said. "I'm just glad I'm not the one doing it." I turned to Milo. "Since we've got Finn here now, can you go check on Hannah?"

"Sweetness, you know you don't need to ask. Keep that connection open, and call me if you need me," Milo said, giving me a look that was almost a reprimand before blinking out of existence before my eyes.

The hallway outside the hospital ward was so jammed with people that no one even noticed that we had joined the crowd. A cursory glance at the group was enough to confirm that nearly all of the Council members were there.

"Wait back here, and don't let anyone from the Council see you," Fiona said, shoving me back around the corner. "I'll see what's happening."

While Finn and I hovered uncertainly just out of sight, Fiona elbowed her way roughly through the crowd toward the door. I could see Riley and Róisín still huddled on the bench, keeping their vigil for their mother. Both looked as though they'd been crying, and a tall, stony-faced Caomhnóir had been stationed beside them.

Fiona shoved her way back to us, looking grimmer than usual. All she said was, "Celeste," but a shrieking cry from within the ward made her meaning clear.

"She's a Host?" I whispered in horror.

"Yes," Fiona said. "Just a few minutes ago, right in the middle of the meeting."

"Now what? Without her to stand up for Hannah..." I choked on the end of the thought. With Celeste gone, what was to stop the rest of the Council from chucking Hannah into the dungeon, or interrogating her for more answers she didn't have? First Savvy, now Celeste—our only allies in the castle were dwindling down to nothing.

A strange puffing, shuffling sound from behind made me turn. Moira, the keeper of the Léarscáil, was chugging up the hallway in as close to a run as her bent little frame could muster, her bare tattooed feet slapping against the stones. She had a scroll clutched so tightly in her hand that she had crushed it flat.

Fiona followed my gaze and frowned curiously. "Moira? What the blazes are you doing away from the Léarscáil?"

"I cannae find Celeste anywhere!" the shrunken old woman grumbled, sucking on the air as she stumbled to a halt. She thrust out a hand and clutched my shoulder to keep her balance, then shoved me away as though I had been the one to grab her.

"What do you need with Celeste?" Fiona asked impatiently.

"Dinnae be an eejit, lass, I've readings to deliver o' course!" Moira spat at her. "There's strange patterns aboot, and I have to show them to Celeste! She's been takin' all my reports since Finvarra's fallen ill!"

"Well, she won't be taking anything today, Moira. She's a Host now," Fiona said tersely.

"Och aye! I knew somethin' was amiss!" Moira said, shaking her head violently. "Someone's got to take these! Somethin' strange is afoot, make no mistake. The energy pull from Skye is—"

"You always think something strange is afoot, you old loon. Give them here," Fiona said impatiently, and snatched the scroll out of Moira's hand.

"Make sure you show them to—" Moira began, but Fiona waved her off.

"I haven't got time for your ravings, woman! There's an emergency here! Go back to your tower!" Fiona snapped.

Moira scuttled off back down the hallway, muttering something that sounded like, "Away and boil yer head!"

"What's your problem with her?" I asked.

Fiona rolled her eyes. "She's a complete nutter, that's what. Locked away in her tower all day, raving to herself."

"You do realize that's exactly what most of the people in this castle think of you, right?" I asked, smirking.

"Yes, I do, thank you. But there's only room for one eccentric tower hermit in this bloody castle, and that's me." Fiona said, shoving the scroll into the pocket of her overalls.

At that moment, Mrs. Mistlemoore pushed the door open and the muttering knot of Council members fell silent.

"Celeste is resting comfortably now," she said wearily. "We gathered the Hosts into the circle, but they did not respond to the Casting, which means there are still more Shards out there. There is still nothing we can do to expel them until each one has been contained within the confines of the Casting circle at the same time."

"And there's no way to know how many Shards are still out there?" Keira asked.

"No," Mrs. Mistlemoore said with a resigned sigh. She had clearly answered the same question a dozen times already.

"And there's no way to lure them here?" another voice called in desperate tones.

"No," Mrs. Mistlemoore said again.

"So, what the hell are we supposed to do?" a third voice cried.

"We wait," Mrs. Mistlemoore said, and there was a steely note in her voice now. "We do not panic. We do not lose focus. We wait."

"Council members, let us return to the Grand Council Room. We must reorganize and elect an interim Council chairwoman and discuss our next steps moving forward," Keira called over the murmuring. "Mrs. Mistlemoore is right, we must not lose sight of our goal. We shall overcome this challenge as we have overcome so many others."

The crowd followed Keira down the hallway, leaving Fiona, Riley, and Róisín behind.

"Oughtn't you to go with them, Fiona?" Mrs. Mistlemoore asked upon seeing Fiona still standing there. "Selecting an interim chairwoman is an important vote."

"They'll do just fine without me," Fiona told her. "I need to speak with you, and I don't want the Council involved." She turned and jerked her head, signaling Finn and me to join her.

Mrs. Mistlemoore looked wary at the very sight of me. "I'm not interested in being dragged into your political intrigues, Fiona, so don't ask me."

"I'm not asking you to," Fiona snapped. "Just hear me out. Jessica here drew these psychic drawings a couple of days ago. We believe it's the Shattered spirit."

Mrs. Mistlemoore held a hand out for the sketches. "What makes you so sure?"

"Just look at the eyes," Fiona said. "They speak for themselves."

Mrs. Mistlemoore's own eyes grew wide as she examined the ones on the page. "My God," she whispered. "My God, you're right!"

"You can tell?" I asked excitedly.

"Oh yes," said Mrs. Mistlemoore, and she shuddered as she looked away. "I've been staring into those very eyes over and over again for days now. I don't think I will ever forget them. Who is she?"

"We don't know yet," Fiona said. "But if you can let us in the ward, we might just be able to find out."

"Let you in?" Mrs. Mistlemoore frowned. "To do what, exactly?"

"That spirit, whoever she is, connected with Jessica before. I think she might be quite eager to do it again, even if she is in pieces."

Mrs. Mistlemoore looked unconvinced. "The Shards are very disorientated. Their level of self-awareness is patchy at best."

"Patchy may be just enough to get what we need," Fiona said with a wry grin. "If Jessica can connect, even a partial message could complete the puzzle. Isn't it worth a try?"

"And why are you coming to me with this?" Mrs. Mistlemoore asked, a single eyebrow arched as though she already knew the answer.

I jumped in. "You already know the Council thinks my sister Hannah has something to do with this. I want to prove that that isn't the case, but I don't think the Council is inclined to give me that chance. We thought you might let us in without telling them."

Mrs. Mistlemoore looked up at the ceiling as though praying for patience. "I do not have the time or the desire for intrigues and subterfuge."

"Nor do we, but we're running out of options here," Fiona said through gritted teeth. "We want to discover what we can without red tape or interference. If we thought the Council would make this easy, we'd have gone through them, but you heard them back in the Council Room. They're terrified of Clan Sassanaigh. Any attempts by Jessica to reveal the identity of this spirit will be met with suspicion and obstruction. It needs to be like this."

"And if you discover the identity of the spirit? What then? You can't keep that information from the Council," Mrs. Mistlemoore said, crossing her arms.

"We don't want to keep it from the Council!" I cried. "Like Fiona said, we would have gone to them with those drawings, but we thought they might just stand in the way! If I get any information from those Shards, you can give it to the Council. You can tell every member of the Airechtas, if you want to. I just want the chance to help."

Mrs. Mistlemoore considered me for a long moment. "You must understand that I can't predict what will happen in there, Jessica. No one has tried to connect with the Shards in this manner. There is no way to know how or if they will respond."

I felt Finn shift anxiously beside me, but I ignored him. "I understand that."

"Let me be clear. They may attack. They may abandon their Hosts and converge upon you. They may not even acknowledge your presence. There is simply no way to know. This is uncharted territory. Not even the Scribes, with all their research, could predict how the spirit might respond."

"Jessica," Finn said, and there was dire warning in his voice.

I turned to him and found that his careful façade was cracking. His face was fighting for composure.

"Finn, I understand that you are bound to protect me, but we can't let fear make our decisions for us, or we are no better than the Council," I said quietly.

He pressed his mouth into a thin line, sealing in whatever else he wanted to say. And for the first time ever, I was grateful for the front of indifference we had to maintain at Fairhaven, because I knew he had the words to dissuade me, but he could not use any of them without giving us away. Assuming, I thought with a pang of guilt, that he still felt the same way after what had happened between us that afternoon.

Mrs. Mistlemoore's expression seemed to soften at my show of bravery. Fiona saw this and pounced on it. "Come on now, Máire," she said, and her voice was much less combative, much gentler than I'd heard it yet as she called Mrs. Mistlemoore by her given name. "You know better than anyone how the Council's interference does

216

more harm than good. How many times have they prevented you from doing your job? How many times have they second guessed your healing capabilities, and how many of our sisters were the worse off for it? Don't let the Hosts in there suffer a moment longer than they have to."

"Very well," Mrs. Mistlemoore said, dropping her arms and with them, her resistance. "I won't pretend the situation isn't desperate. But I am going to oversee your attempts, and I will summon the Council at my discretion, is that clear?"

"Yes, of course," Fiona said at once.

"And, if asked, I will say you told me that this was all being done on the Council's orders," Mrs. Mistlemoore said sharply. "And you will corroborate that story. I will help you, but I will not shoulder any blame for it."

"Agreed," Fiona said. "And let's be honest, the Council will be more than ready to believe that I lied to you. They're itching to slap me with some kind of a sanction, so they'll be grateful for the excuse."

"Fiona, I don't want you to get in trouble over this," I told her, but she snorted loudly.

"Trouble? Me? Jessica, I thought you knew me better than that, but you seem to have mistaken me for someone who gives a damn."

I grinned. "I won't make that mistake again."

"Too right you won't," Fiona said. "Let's go then."

17

THE GIRL IN PIECES

THE HOSPITAL WARD WAS UTTERLY STILL. In a long row along both walls, the Hosts lay on their backs, hands folded on their chests, staring unblinkingly up at the dark ceiling above them. There were ten in all now, more than I'd even realized. In the bed closest to the door, Savvy was barely recognizable as the boisterous friend I had grown so fond of; her usually ruddy cheeks were wan and chalky, her thick red hair limp and damp around an expressionless face.

"I'll wait by the door," Finn said in a stiff voice. "I will alert you if any Council members approach from the hallway."

"Thank you," I said, looking away from him. I was scared enough. I didn't need his disapproval to make this even harder.

"Right, then. Jessica, over here in the circle," Fiona said, pointing to the large chalk drawing in the very center of the room. "I know circles aren't meant to keep out Shards, but there's no harm in taking advantage of any modicum of safety this might provide you."

"Okay," I said weakly, and took my place at the heart of the circle. I felt the hum of energy as I entered within its boundaries. The familiar sensation calmed my pounding heart just a bit.

Fiona followed me into the circle and knelt down beside me, placing the rolled-up sketches on the floor beside me. "I think we should treat this like a Summoning," she said. "Have you got your Casting bag?"

"Yes," I said, pulling it from the pocket of my jeans. "Never leave home without it, right?"

"Cast a Summoning, and invite the Shards in. I know Castings aren't meant to work on Shards, but if this spirit really was a Durupinen, then she will recognize a Summoning, and the familiarity of the invitation might put her at ease," Fiona instructed. She reached into her own pocket and lay several items on the ground within reach of my hand: a gold dip pen with a pot of ink, a charcoal pencil, a paintbrush, and a tiny pot of oil paint. "These will give the spirit some options, if she's particular about her method of communication. Many of them are."

"You just happened to have a Victorian-era dip pen sitting in the cup on your desk?" I asked incredulously, picking it up to examine it.

"Yes, of course," Fiona said, scowling at me.

"Right," I said, putting it back down again. "Sorry. Please, continue."

"Just talk to her, whoever she is. Try to get her to connect again. She may respond, or she may not. We won't know until you try," Fiona said.

"Okay. Well, we're wasting precious time here, so let's do it," I said, with as much confidence as I could muster.

"I can call in my staff to help if the Hosts need to be subdued," Mrs. Mistlemoore assured me.

"Good to know," I said. I took a long, deep breath but the air seemed to meet a barrier in my lungs. "Let's just do this before I lose my nerve."

Finn made a strangled sort of sound, like he had started to speak and then cut himself off. I swallowed hard, pretending I hadn't heard it.

Fiona backed out of the circle and squatted down just on the outside of the border, like an animal tensed to spring. She nodded at me. "I'll feed you instructions. Give a go, now."

I spoke the words of the Summoning as I retraced the circle with my own chalk. My voice echoed softly in the cavernous room, but faded quickly. As I finished, I held my breath, waiting for a sign of life or response from the Hosts around me. Nothing happened.

"Talk to her," Fiona whispered. "Remind her what she looks like, who she is."

I nodded and cleared my throat. I unrolled the sketches in front of me and smoothed them so that they lay flat against the floor. "I'm speaking to the spirit who is residing here in these Hosts," I said tremulously. "I know that I have connected to you before."

Still no one moved. Nothing stirred. I felt no pulses, no thrums of energy. All was still.

"I don't know your name," I said, imagining that the girl in the sketch was sitting across from me, that we were merely friends having a chat over coffee. "But I know what you look like. When we connected, I drew you. Do you remember? Do you remember who you are?" I picked up one of the sketches and held it up, turning on the spot with it like a teacher making sure each of her students could see the illustration in a picture book.

As I displayed the sketch to the very last of the beds, there was a sudden rustling sound. The figure in the bed sat up with alarming swiftness, staring intently at the sketch I held out before her.

It was Catriona.

"Breathe, Jessica," Fiona whispered to me, and I drew in a ragged gasp of air I didn't realize I was holding. "Keep talking."

"I know this is you," I said, holding the picture out further, closer to Catriona. "Do you recognize yourself?"

Very slowly, Catriona raised a shaking hand to her own face and caressed it, tilting her head to one side, her expression bewildered. All around the room nine other figures sat bolt upright in perfect unison. As I looked around me in terror, each made the very same motion, running her hand gently over her face and cocking her head to the side. Every set of eyes, fixed on the sketch in my hands, was identical—deep, dark, nearly swallowed by the black of the irises.

"Christ on a bike," Fiona muttered. Over by the door, I could hear Finn quietly cursing under his breath.

It took several attempts to find my voice again as I fought my own panic. She's just a girl, I told myself. A girl like me. She's just lost—in pieces. She needs help. "That's it," I said, trying to sound warm and encouraging. "That's you, isn't it?"

Ten heads nodded slowly at me.

"Good. That's very good," I said, attempting a friendly smile. "I want to help you. I want to help discover who you are, so that we can put you back together again. You've been... broken. Broken apart. But I can help you. Do you want me to help you? Isn't that why you reached out to me in the first place?"

Again, ten heads nodded at me. Ten hands dropped from ten cheeks into ten laps.

"Do you want me to draw for you again? If there is something you want to say, something you want to show me, use me again," I said, and I pointed to the supplies Fiona had placed in the circle.

As one, all ten Hosts bent over their laps and began to mime the act of writing, just as I had seen them doing the day before.

"The pen," Fiona hissed. "Use the pen."

But I was already unscrewing the lid from the ink pot and flipping the sketch over to reveal an expanse of blank surface on which I could write. Then I took the pen in my hand, dipped it carefully in the ink, and set it to the paper.

I closed my eyes, feeling out into the mental space around me, trying to find a presence to latch onto. What I found instead was disturbing. The points of light that would have guided me when dealing with whole spirits were absent. What I found instead were flickering sparks that sputtered and died before I could connect with them. They darted around, dull and fluttering. They did not pull upon my senses, as a whole spirit would, but instead they left me feeling disoriented and confused, like a traveler trying to follow ten different sets of directions at once. The pen did not move. I felt no intervening consciousness, no drive to create taking control of me.

"She's not connecting, Fiona," I murmured. "I'm not sure if she just can't or won't. I'm not getting anything at all."

"That's not surprising," Fiona answered. "There's a good chance this will all be for naught, Jessica, but we've got to keep trying. Start asking her some questions."

I returned my concentration to the energy in the room, reaching my mental feelers out as far as they would stretch, looking for something to latch on to.

"Can you help me write your name?" I asked. "Or maybe a place that you remember?"

The sparks wandered aimlessly, helplessly, exerting no pull upon me.

I tried again. "You wrote before that 'The Caller betrayed' you. Can you tell me what that means?"

I was so intent on the sensation in my hand—on trying to encourage the artistic connection—that Fiona's tense whisper startled me.

"Jessica, don't move. She's right beside you."

"What?!"

My eyes refused to open; they were glued shut with abject terror. Suddenly, I heard a slight shifting—a gentle rubbing sound of fabric against fabric—from just beside me. Then a ragged, labored breath caressed my ear. Every hair on my arms stood up as I battled my instinct to jump up and out of that circle as fast as I could. My own breathing sped up.

I heard a quick scuffling step, and then Fiona hissed, "No, Finn! Stay in position!"

Slowly, I forced my eyes open. Catriona crouched next to me like a skittish animal, her face inches from my own, staring at me with those haunted, borrowed eyes. I tore my gaze from her and looked around the circle. Every Host was crouched in an identical position all along the edges of the circle, their breaths coming in perfect unison.

She's just a girl, I repeated to myself. She's just a girl in pieces and she needs my help.

I forced myself to look back into those eyes. "Do you know your name?" I asked softly.

Catriona just stared. I couldn't even tell if she recognized that I was speaking words.

"Can you tell me who the Caller is? How did she betray you?" I asked, trying again.

Catriona leaned in incredibly close and whispered, with terrifying intimacy. "Promises. Shattered. Agony."

All around me, the Hosts echoed her words, and each whisper of a voice throbbed with pain. If Mackie had been here, she would surely never have been able to bear it. Even my heart ached with it, and I was not an Empath.

"Ask her something else, Jessica," said Fiona, a warning in her voice. "If she gets too upset, too worked up, you won't get anything useful out of her. Go back to the sketch. That's what got her to listen in the first place. Bring it back to the sketch."

I wasn't at all eager to give up on that line of questioning, but Fiona was right; we didn't want to push our luck. I reached down slowly to pick the sketch up off the floor and held it up so that Catriona could look at it.

"You were beautiful," I said softly.

The borrowed eyes filled with tears that spilled over and ran down Catriona's cheeks. She reached a tremulous hand out and touched the picture gently with one finger. All around us, all the Hosts mimicked her movement.

"Look here, at your neck," I told her, pointing to the place. "This necklace, here. This isn't a real necklace. It's words, see? These are words you wanted me to know. It says, "little book." Do you know what that means?"

Catriona's head snapped up and her mouth began to move in a

rapid, silent mantra. I leaned in, so close to her lips that I might have kissed them. I watched as they formed the same words over and over again, heard the breath rushing in and out, carrying them just far enough to reach my ears.

"Little book. Little book. Little book."

"Yes, that's right. Little book," I told her. "What is the little book? What does it mean?"

"Little book, little book!" Catriona cried imploringly, but her voice was suddenly ten voices. Every Host was repeating it now, and every face was alight with desperation.

"What is the little book?" I repeated.

Every Host immediately dropped into a sitting position and began to mimic the act of writing.

"Give her the pen!" Fiona whispered to me. "Give her the paper!"

I slid the piece of paper across to Catriona and very carefully slipped the pen into her moving hand. At once, words began to appear in a messy trail behind her hand. "Dear Little Book, Dear Little Book, Dear Little Book."

"She's writing, "Dear Little Book," I told the others excitedly, before addressing Catriona again. "Was the little book yours? Was it some kind of... journal, or diary?"

Catriona dropped her pen abruptly and placed her hand upon her chest. "Little book!" she answered, nodding vigorously.

"Where is it? Is it here? Does it still exist? Can you show it to me?" I asked her, my heart beginning to pound with anticipation.

With alarming speed and agility, Catriona leapt to her feet and dashed to the window overlooking the grounds. The rest of the Hosts followed like so many puppets controlled by a single set of strings. I watched in fascination as each of them raised a violently shuddering hand and pointed off down the path into the darkened grounds beyond.

I stood up and joined them at the window, squinting into the gathering darkness. I turned to the Host right beside me and realized with a start that it was Celeste.

"Is it close?" I asked her. "Here on the grounds?"

She nodded solemnly.

"Can you show me?"

Every head nodded before turning again to stare off into the night. Every mouth began working in the silent mantra again. "Little book, little book, little book."

I turned back to Fiona, Finn, and Mrs. Mistlemoore, all of whom were standing and watching with their mouths agape.

"We need to go where they lead us," I said. "We can end this tonight."

"I'm going to alert the Council," Mrs. Mistlemoore said at once, turning and hurrying toward the door.

"No, you can't do that yet!" I cried, running after her.

She turned around to stare at me. "Why ever not?"

"They'll just hold us up!" I said. "Let's just go, let's just find this book and see what it says!"

"Jessica, I have indulged your whim, despite my reservations, and I do not doubt that it has paid off. But I will not proceed any further with this new information until I alert the Council and they give us their instructions."

"I'm on the Council," Fiona said, crossing her arms. "Can't you just take my instructions?"

"You know very well that I cannot," Mrs. Mistlemoore said impatiently. "Letting you in here is one thing, but letting any of them out," and she pointed over to the Hosts still crowded around the window, "is another matter entirely. It would mean breaking the quarantine. It would also risk one of the Hosts escaping, and we cannot possibly risk that without authorization. If one of the Hosts escapes, we won't be able to reassemble the Shards or expel them from the rest of the Hosts."

I let out a deep sigh of frustration. "They will find a way to screw this up, I know it."

"That is a chance I am willing to take," Mrs. Mistlemoore said. She had nearly reached the door when Carrick came shooting through it.

"Mrs. Mistlemoore, we need..." Carrick began, but stopped abruptly when he caught sight of me. His face went blank. "Jessica? What are you doing here? Where's Hannah? You're not... she's not a Host?"

"No, no, we're fine," I assured him. "But are you? Is everything okay?"

"It's Finvarra." Carrick said shortly. His face spoke volumes.

"Is she..." I couldn't finish the sentence, as my heart had risen into my throat.

"No. But she is failing quickly," Carrick said. "Mrs. Mistlemoore, we need you in the High Priestess' chambers."

"Oh, Carrick, I'm so sorry," I said. I took several steps toward him, my hand reaching out, but then I abruptly stopped myself. What exactly did I want to do? Hold his hand? Hug him? I didn't really know, and I certainly didn't have the emotional capital to invest in figuring it out. So, like any mature adult, I pretended it hadn't happened. Luckily, Mrs. Mistlemoore burst through the awkward moment, popping it like a bubble.

"Of course, I'm coming now," she said, snatching a large, black leather bag from a nearby table before turning back to me. "I must go tend to the High Priestess. Stay here. I'll speak with the Council and return as soon as I can."

She gave a stern, lingering look at Fiona before turning and heading for the door.

"I must go with her," Carrick said, and there was something of an apology in his voice. "Are you... you're alright here, are you?" He asked the question with a quiet sort of desperation, a tone that indicated that he could only bear to hear one answer.

And so, I gave it to him. "I'm fine. Don't worry about me."

He nodded in grateful acknowledgment of the lie, and shimmered out of view just as Mrs. Mistlemoore pushed the door open and Frankie stumbled in, looking startled.

"Frankie! What are you doing here?" I asked, momentarily distracted.

Frankie answered nervously, her eyes darting around and taking in the bizarre scene. "I went with your sister to find Celeste, so that I could tell her I wanted to start my training, but we never found her, and then a couple of those big burly guys came and took Hannah away."

"They wanted to ask her some questions about the Shattering," I said, attempting to keep the anger out of my voice.

"Yes, that's what they said, but... she seemed kind of freaked out," Frankie said. "I went to Celeste's office, but the Caomhnóir there told me she was down in the Grand Council Room, and that she would be back later. I waited for a while, but she never showed up. So, I decided to come down here and see if I could find out how Savannah was doing."

"She's... well..." I gestured helplessly into the back corner of the room, where all of the Hosts, including Savannah, were still gathered around the window, murmuring and pointing like they were all having the same sleepwalking nightmare.

Frankie's eyes went wide as she watched them. "What are they doing?"

"They're trying to lead us to a clue somewhere out on the grounds," I said, "but we can't let them out of the ward without Council permission."

Frankie looked utterly horrified. I wanted to tell her something comforting—it would all be okay, or some other cliché like that—but I just didn't have it in me to lie to the poor girl. I turned back to Fiona. "Now what? We just wait here, doing nothing?"

Fiona pursed her lips, running a paint-spattered finger over them as she thought. Then she walked over to the crowd of Hosts and elbowed her way through them to the window.

"Fiona, what are you—" I began, but the rest of my question was swallowed in a gasp as I watched her lift the catch and push the window wide open.

"We tried to stop her, but she overpowered us and escaped through the window," Fiona said, shaking her head in mock regret. "We had no choice but to go after her."

I laughed nervously, and then stopped. "Are you serious?"

"Have you ever known me to joke?" Fiona shot back. "Just Catriona, though. We can't risk letting them all out. We'll never be able to keep track of them all, and if we lose one, we are well and truly fucked."

I turned to Finn. "Alright, let's have all of your objections."

He stepped away from the door and crossed his arms. "I have none. As long as we can make sure the other Hosts are safely contained, I think it's a brilliant idea."

I gaped at him. "I'd ask if you were serious, but you joke about as often as Fiona does, so I won't waste my time."

"We must be careful, though. Someone has to stay here with the other Hosts," Finn said. "And someone needs to alert the Council that Catriona has escaped once we are safely out of the building."

"I'll stay with them," Frankie said in a voice cracked with fear.

"Are you sure?" I asked her. "Don't be a hero if you don't think you can handle it, Frankie, honestly."

Frankie's face was set. "No. I can handle it. I can do it. I want to help Savannah."

"If she says she can do it, then let her," Fiona said impatiently.

"Who do we send to the Council for help?" I asked, but it was Frankie again who answered.

"There are two girls sitting on the bench out there," she said, pointing to the door out to the hallway. "I could wait until you've gone and then run out there and ask one of them to go for help. Maybe the other one can stay and help me, if I need another set of hands."

Finn looked surprised, but nodded. "Brilliant. Do you think they would do it?"

"Róisín and Riley have been sitting out there for hours. I think they'd do anything we asked if they thought it would help their mother," I said.

"Right then, what the hell are we waiting for?" Fiona barked. She turned to Catriona and gestured toward the open window. "After you, then."

18

———

GRAVE ROBBING

ONE BY ONE, we led the rest of the Hosts back to their beds, leaving Catriona at the window, where she kept vigil like a seaman's wife keeps watch on the horizon after a storm. When we were quite sure every Host was calm and resting again, I turned to Frankie.

"Give us maybe a five minute head start," I said. "Then send one of the Lightfoot girls for help. The most important thing is to keep all of the Hosts in this room. Fire completely freaks them out, so if you've still got that lighter, keep it hidden. Remember the cover story?"

Frankie nodded obediently and repeated it back to me. "Catriona broke free and climbed out the window. You all followed her so that she wouldn't escape. You are going to bring her right back. I saw you head in the direction of the river."

"Perfect. Thank you, Frankie. I really appreciate this, and I know Savvy would, too."

Frankie nodded again, and then went to sit on the edge of the bed where Savvy lay, unnaturally still and quiet.

I joined Finn, Fiona, and Catriona where they stood waiting for me by the window. I placed myself between Catriona and the glass, so that she was forced to look at me.

"The little book. Can you take me to the little book?" I asked her slowly and clearly.

Catriona picked up the familiar refrain, "little book, little book, little book," and in one swift movement, pushed herself up onto the window ledge and disappeared through it.

"Blimey!" Finn cried, leaping after her. The hospital ward was on the first floor, thank God, but it was still a sizable drop to the ground. Luckily, the December wind had swept the snow up into a pillowy drift against the wall of the castle, and both Finn and

229

Catriona landed softly. I helped boost Fiona through the opening and then followed her, dropping like a stone into the snowbank.

Catriona moved with the blind purpose of a sleepwalker. It was difficult to tell who had control of her body at this moment. Either the spirit was having a hard time maneuvering the body or some part of Catriona was fighting against the spirit's impulses, but every motion seemed to take an enormous effort, as though Catriona was trying to move and not move at the same time. Nevertheless, she trudged forward across the grounds, plunging through the buried flowerbeds, taking no heed of the paths, and making no effort to avoid impediments. Several times Finn had to rush forward and guide her around a potentially dangerous obstacle. She seemed unable to follow anything but the most direct path between herself and her destination. He pulled a flashlight from the waistband of his jeans and clicked it on, so that a wide golden beam of light could illuminate some of the potential obstacles in our way.

"Do we have any inkling as to where she might be headed?" Fiona asked breathlessly after a few minutes. She was struggling the hardest of all of us to keep up because she kept losing her ratty loafers in the snow.

"That way," I said unhelpfully, pointing ahead of us. "There's no way to know, Fiona. We just have to keep following her and hope she isn't heading for the open countryside. This was your brilliant plan, remember?"

Fiona swore under her breath but kept plowing forward, teeth chattering.

A few minutes later, though, our destination became clear. We were headed straight to the southeast corner of the grounds, where stood the ancient Fairhaven cemetery, nestled in a grove of towering pine trees. Closer and closer we drew, falling in line with a path at last, as it became the shortest possible route leading straight to the wrought iron gates.

No one spoke as the realization set in. I repressed a shiver that had nothing to do with the frigid temperatures and everything to do with the prospect of entering a graveyard in the dead of night. It may seem ridiculous that the place would have any sort of effect on a person who was permanently haunted, but I had to admit I was not thrilled that this was where Catriona had led us. As far as I was concerned, there was a big difference between a spirit and the rotting corpse they left behind. I'd take the spirit any day.

Catriona walked right up to the gates, which were secured with a massive length of chain, and began trying to squeeze herself between the bars. Finn rushed forward and firmly, but gently, closed his arms around her and prised her fingers from the metal.

"Now what?" I asked, clutching at a cramp in my side that had me nearly doubled over. I looked up, trying to judge the height of the fence. "Do you think we could just climb it?" I placed a hand on the nearest bar; it was slick with frost.

But Fiona was already pushing past us. "No need, no need. I know the combination," she said.

"Why the hell would you know the combination?" I asked her.

"From all the late night grave dancing," Fiona said baldly, then rolled her eyes. "There are statues and carvings in the graveyard. Their upkeep falls under my purview." She slid the sleeve of her shirt down over her hand so that she could hold the bitterly cold metal against her skin as she whirled the dial on the lock. For a few moments, there was no sound but for Catriona's ragged breathing as she strained against Finn's hold.

With a heavy clunk, the lock fell open. I jumped forward and helped Fiona heave the heavy loops of chain off the bars, pulling it link by link until it lay curled on the ground like a sleeping serpent.

The moment the chains were gone, Catriona pulled free and heaved herself against the gate, which swung forward with a deafening screeching sound. Finn lunged forward to catch her before she plunged headfirst into the snow. The silence inside the graveyard was oppressive, intensified by the muffling blanket of snow and the towering canopy of pine trees. The golden beam of Finn's flashlight did not seem to penetrate nearly as far now, as though the darkness itself was deeper here. The snow was scanter on the ground; the trees had caught most of it, and were now bent nearly double with the weight of it. Graves stuck up out of the ground at strange angles, as though they had sprung up naturally, nourished like plants by the death and decay nestled beneath them. The stones were clearly all very old, the corners and carvings worn to soft curves and vague impressions. Even if anyone ever did come to visit this graveyard, how would they even know who lay beneath the ground? The graves were nearly indistinguishable. And despite the vast number of spirits in and around Fairhaven Hall, the place seemed to be completely devoid of ghosts.

"So strange," I breathed through my now chattering teeth. "I would have expected this place to be packed with spirits."

But Fiona shook her head. "No Fairhaven spirit would ever hang around here. Everyone here, living and dead, understands too much about the reality of death. They know the bodies we leave behind are just shells. There's nothing here for them."

There was no time to digest this nugget of wisdom, for Catriona had struggled her way up off the ground and was now stumbling forward down the path. We hurried after her, huddled together partly for warmth, and partly to keep to the narrow strip of visibility provided by the flashlight beam.

Without warning, Catriona came to a sudden stop, and we all plowed into her, knocking her to her knees. She did not seem to notice. Her eyes, her attention, indeed every fiber of her being was fixed upon the low stone structure looming out of the darkness in front of us. The sight of it seemed to freeze her in her tracks.

"What is it?" I asked, although I wasn't sure I wanted the answer.

"A mausoleum," Finn replied. He raised the flashlight to examine it. The beam illuminated the greenish copper roof, the gracefully curved stone sides, and the arched wooden door before finally revealing the name carved above the lintel: Larkin.

Larkin. I'd never seen or heard the name in my life, but it rang through my body like a current, shooting down to the tips of my fingers, and making them twitch with a desire to draw a now familiar face that had been haunting my sleep for days.

"This is it," I murmured. "Larkin. This is right, I know it is."

Catriona had recovered from her shock or whatever it was that had kept her momentarily still. She stumbled forward until both of her violently shaking hands were pressed up against the mausoleum door. Her whispered mantra rose to a shrill, keening cry that raised the hairs on my arms and made me feel, somehow, even colder than I'd already felt.

"Little book! Little book! LITTLE BOOK!" she shrieked to the night. She raised her hands above her head, clenched them into fists, and then began to pound, with alarming force, on the heavy wooden door.

"Stop her!" Fiona cried out. "Stop her before she hurts herself!"

Finn wrestled Catriona back from the door, deftly catching both fists and pinning them securely behind her back. Catriona fought against him like a feral animal; despite her diminutive frame, Finn grunted with the effort of keeping her restrained.

"She's not going to stop this until we get in there and see what it is she's trying to show us," Finn said. "So, what's the game plan here?"

"What?" I asked, and my voice shot up an octave in my horror. "Get in there? What do you mean, get in there? It's like... a giant coffin! You can't just break into it!"

"Well, we shouldn't, obviously, but we're going to anyway," Finn said through clenched teeth. "Fiona, do the Durupinen put any Castings on these things?"

"I can't be absolutely sure, but I highly doubt it," Fiona said. "We don't give a terrible amount of thought to death beyond the spiritual part. In fact, it's rare for any of us to be buried anymore. That's why the graves are in such disrepair and the gates are locked; no one visits it anymore, except for me, to repair an occasional statue. We're usually cremated and scattered nowadays. Still, let me check, just to be safe."

Fiona began a slow circling of the mausoleum, closely examining the stones. As she worked, I knelt down and clamped my arms around Catriona's waist, trying to take just a little bit of the strain off of Finn, who was panting heavily now with the effort of restraining her.

After a minute or two he called through gritted teeth, "You about done there, Fiona?"

"Yes, yes," she said, coming around the far side of the mausoleum. "I don't think there are any Castings to contend with. Nothing active, anyway."

"So, how do we get in then?" I asked.

"We just have to force our way through, don't we?" Finn said.

Fiona nodded. "There's a window on the back side, near the roof. If you break it, you should be able to get in that way."

"Okay, then," I said, steeling myself against the creeping horror that was rising in me like flood waters. "Let's get it over with."

"Should we let go of her?" Finn grunted, as Catriona continued to struggle.

"Why not?" I said. "She's not going anywhere except into this tomb, so the sooner we open it, the sooner she can stop this."

"I'll stay right here with her," Fiona said, her face set in a determined grimace. "She won't go anywhere, you can be certain of that."

Finn released his hold on Catriona, and she immediately flung herself once more at the mausoleum door. Fiona rolled her sleeves up and pulled Catriona into a kind of bear hug, preventing her from injuring herself too badly as she clawed at the stones. I followed Finn around to the back of the mausoleum, where we found a very narrow window shaped like an egg that was set into the wall just below the point of the roof.

"Blimey, that's small," Finn said. He turned to me and looked me over appraisingly. "You're probably the only one who can fit through there," he said.

I stared at him. "Me?"

"I'll boost you up, and you squeeze through, if you can. Then go to the door and let us in," Finn said.

For a moment, my brain refused to comprehend a single word he'd said. Then I blinked, shook my head, and drew a long, shaky breath. "Sure. Pitch black room full of dead people. Sounds fun."

"Well done," Finn said. He positioned himself beneath the window and pulled the flashlight from his pocket. With one big, grunting leap he sprang into the air and smashed the glass of the window with the blunt end of the flashlight. We covered our heads with our arms as the shards of glass rained down on us. Finn handed me his flashlight, which I tucked as securely as I could into the back of my pants. Then Finn interlocked his fingers and boosted me up to the window. I pushed my head through the hole and then immediately pulled it out again, gagging.

"Oh God," I cried. "Oh God, it smells like dead things. And there's dust. It's dead body dust, and it's just hanging in the air!"

"Well, just hold your breath, then, and be quick about it," Finn said impatiently. "And mind the glass along the edges."

"Get a move on, you two, Cat's going mad over here!" Fiona shouted.

I made another involuntary whimpering sound and then hoisted myself through the window, pulling each of my legs after me with a grunt. With a deep breath that I instantly regretted, because it tasted like death, I dropped to the ground inside the chamber. I attempted to pull the flashlight from my waistband with violently shaking hands, and immediately dropped it on the ground.

"Shit. Oh, shit," I cried.

"What, what is it?" Finn shouted.

"I dropped the damn flashlight and now I have to touch things to find it!" I answered shrilly. I squatted down and began feeling around on the ground in the impenetrable darkness for the flashlight, silently praying that I wouldn't accidentally touch anything other than bare floor. Luckily, my scrabbling fingers closed around the flashlight within seconds. My eyes filled with tears of relief as I turned it on, still uttering a constant stream of gasps and curses over which I had no control. Large shapes loomed up at me on both sides in the darkness, and I knew they must be coffins, but I did not stop to examine them. The only thing I wanted to see, the only sight that could keep me from passing out, was the way out. I trained the flashlight beam—and my gaze—on the door directly across from me. Fighting back a recurring, heaving urge to vomit, I forced my feet forward, one in front of the other, until I reached the door.

I could hear Finn's pounding footsteps outside as he ran around to meet me at the door. I reached down and found the latch, an ancient rusted thing that hadn't even been locked properly—the only thing keeping this door closed was age and decay.

"Fiona, pull Catriona back from the door. I'm going to try to open it now!" I shouted.

I waited until I heard Fiona's groans of effort as she muscled Catriona away from the door, and then I pressed a palm against the wood, which was cold and slimy. I pushed hard, but it did not budge. I leaned in with my shoulder and heaved my body weight against it. The door gave a loud creak, and a low grinding noise. A narrow crack of moonlight appeared.

"It's really heavy! You have to help me open it!" I called. My voice sounded hysterical, even to me.

Finn rushed forward, dug his hands into the gap, and began to pull. The ancient hinges shrieked with protest at being forced to move, and did not give easily, even with both of us tugging with all our strength.

Despite my best efforts to control it, my breathing was becoming rapid, shallow, and panicked. "It's not opening! It's not going to open! How am I going to get out of here?!" I shouted.

"Jess, it's moving, I promise!" Finn called. "Take a deep breath and try to remain calm. Listen. Listen to the scraping sound. It's moving!"

Finn grunted with effort as we forced hundreds of years' worth of rust to give way. At last we had created a gap large enough for me to squeeze through. I forced myself through the opening with a guttural cry of relief and collapsed to my knees in the grass, where I began to heave and retch.

Finn dropped to the ground beside me and pulled my hair up out of my face, which was shining with cold sweat.

"It's okay, Jess. You're okay," he said, over and over again, until the vomiting subsided.

"I... I'm sorry. I... I don't know why I went to pieces like that," I said between gasping sobs. "It... it was just so dark, and there was all this dust, and the dust smelled like dead things and the air... it's like there's no air in there, like someone already breathed it all. And there are these coffins everywhere. I just... I felt like I was being crushed. I've never reacted to anything like that before, ever. Do you think it was some kind of Casting?"

I looked up at Finn, who was wiping sweat from his face with filthy hands. He shook his head. "No. I think you just had a good old case of claustrophobia. The proximity of the corpses probably didn't help."

Even in the few moments I took to calm myself down, Catriona had pulled free of Fiona and was now shoving her body through the crack of the doorway without any kind of regard for her well-being. Cuts and scrapes were already visible up and down her arms as she forced her body through the opening. I had no doubt the spirit controlling her would break her limbs if it meant reaching its goal. Little though I wanted to, I grabbed the flashlight off the ground where I had dropped it, jumped up, and reached the mausoleum just in time to watch Catriona's mane of golden hair disappear into the darkness.

"Whoa, whoa, what do you think you're doing?" Finn asked. "You actually want to go back in there?"

"No, of course I don't. But this spirit reached out to me, and I'm not going to let a little vomit stop me from finding this book. I think I'll be okay now that the door is open and I'll be able to see better."

Finn was eyeing me skeptically.

"If I can't handle it, I'll just come back outside," I said. "Look, I won't puke on you, I promise."

Finn rolled his eyes at me, but didn't argue any more. With one last, almighty thrust, he wrenched the door right off its hinges; it toppled over and onto the ground in a plume of dust, rust flakes, and displaced snow. The mausoleum interior lay beyond, a yawning black hole, the renewed sight of which made my skin crawl.

Finn gestured as though to say, "After you." I opened my mouth to tell him that chivalry was officially dead, and that he could bloody well march in there first, but then I remembered that I was the one holding the flashlight. Holding it out in front of me like a weapon, I took a cautious step into the dim interior, then another, then another. The flashlight flickered as though tired from the strain of having to cut through a darkness deepened with the immovable finality of death.

I inched forward along the path the flashlight had created for us. I felt Finn's breath on my neck and it made me feel calmer, more sure of my steps. I finally found the courage to look around properly at what was inside the chamber.

Stone coffins lined the walls of the mausoleum, but they did not look as I would have expected. The top of each had been carved into the likeness of the corpse it contained, each a perfectly preserved granite effigy of the former owner of the rotting bones beneath it.

"What the hell..." I breathed, approaching the nearest of these with a hammering heart. Beneath the reposing likeness of a long dead woman with a hawkish profile was the name, "Virginia Larkin."

"It's like a pyramid in here!" I hissed. "Please tell me it wasn't a custom to wrap the bodies of Durupinen like mummies, because I might lose it."

"I don't think so," Finn said. "Did you see where Catriona went?"

"She's got to be in here somewhere," I said, tearing my gaze from the stone effigy. "Wait, I hear something."

A dull, thumping, scraping sound was coming from the far corner of the room. We followed the sound, shuffling forward and searching with the flashlight beam until, at last, it fell upon Catriona. She was crouched beside one of the stone coffins, pounding her fists against it and gouging at the edges of the seam that ran all the way around it. Her fingernails were already broken and bleeding with the desperation of her efforts.

"Little book!" she was positively sobbing now. "Little book! Little book! Little book!"

I knelt down beside her and took her face in my hands. "Little book?" I said, tentatively.

She froze in her efforts and her eyes locked onto mine. "Little book," she answered, nodding solemnly.

"Inside this coffin?" I asked with a convulsive swallow. My mouth had gone completely dry.

"Little book. Inside," she whispered, and she pointed emphatically at the coffin. Then, her eyes rolled back in her head and she slumped against the stone, motionless.

Finn reached past me to press two fingers to Catriona's neck. "Pulse is quick, but strong," he said. "I think she's alright, for the moment, but it will be best to find this book quickly and get her back up to the castle where Mrs. Mistlemoore can keep an eye on her."

We dragged Catriona away and lay her on her side, to give us room to work, and then returned to examine the coffin she had been so frantically trying to pry apart. The stone likeness on the top of it was of a young woman with high cheekbones and a gentle smile on her lips. Her hands were folded demurely over her white marble chest. The name carved along the edge of the coffin's lid was "Harriet Larkin."

The name did not bring the jolt of recognition, the instant clarity I thought it would. I felt no tingle in my fingertips. I turned to Finn. "Do you really think this is right?"

He stared incredulously at me. "Catriona damn near tore her own fingers off to get into it, so it bloody well better be right. Why are you asking me that?"

"I just... I thought the name would ring some sort of Muse bell for me, but it doesn't. I don't think this is the spirit that's possessing her."

"Look, maybe it's her and maybe it isn't, but there's clearly something here she needs us to find, so let's open the bloody thing and find out what it is!" Finn cried.

"What's going on in there?" Fiona called from outside. Her anxious face appeared around the doorway, bathed in pale moonlight. "Have you found anything?"

"Catriona... or rather, the spirit possessing Catriona, wants us to open this coffin," Finn told her, pointing to it. "Do we have the Council's permission to do that?"

Fiona rolled her eyes. "The Council's highest priority is containing this Shattering. I hereby give you my permission to crack the bloody thing open. Now get on with it, it's fecking freezing out here and the Council is bound to send someone looking for us soon, if they haven't already."

"Awesome," I said, with a slightly hysterical laugh. "Officially adding grave robbing to my resume. Let's file that under 'sentences I never thought I'd say.' So, now what?" I turned to Finn, but he wasn't paying attention to me. He was wandering the room, scanning the walls and floor.

"What are you looking for?" I asked him.

"Something we can use to pry that cover off. It's much too heavy to move without proper leverage," he said, and then clapped his hands suddenly together, making me jump. "Ah-ha! This will do nicely." He pulled a long metal bar from under a pile of ragged, tattered fabric on the floor in the corner, the remains of a velvet privacy curtain. He strode over and held it out to me.

"I'm going to try to lift that cover. As soon as you see a gap, shove this pole in there as quickly as you can, alright?" he said.

"What? Oh. Yeah, okay, I'll try," I said.

Finn squatted on the ground beside the coffin and placed his shoulder beneath the lip of the lid. Then he grasped it with both hands and poised himself, ready to lift.

"Ready?" he asked.

"Ready," I said, my eyes focused unblinkingly on the seam.

With a guttural cry, Finn shoved with all his might against the lid of the coffin, pushing off the ground with his legs, the muscles in his arms trembling with the effort. A narrow gap appeared between the lid and the coffin, barely a couple of inches wide. As soon as I saw it, I thrust the stick forward, wedging it between the slabs of stone with a horrible squealing, grating sound.

Finn collapsed to the ground, panting. "Well done," he gasped.

"Me? Well done, you!" I said. "I can't believe you actually lifted that."

"Won't mean much of we can't pry it off," he said dismissively, standing up and dusting himself off. "We've got to push down on it, like a lever, and it should slide off. Help me, will you?"

"Of course," I said. We both placed our hands on the pole, preparing to push. A foul, musty odor was beginning to permeate the room, and my stomach roiled at the thought of what we might be about to see when the lid was removed.

"On three, then," Finn said through gritted teeth. "One, two, three."

We shoved downward with all our might, lying nearly flat along the length of the bar as we put every ounce of weight into our efforts. The cover lifted, tipped precariously, and then, with a floor-shaking crash, it toppled off the coffin and landed on the ground in a choking cloud of dust.

As we coughed and spluttered, Fiona's face appeared around the doorway again. "What in blazes was that?"

"We're fine. We've got it open," Finn said between coughs.

As the dust finally began to settle, we walked very slowly forward. For all his heroics, I could tell from his very grim expression that Finn did not want to look over the edge of that coffin any more than I did. I took in a deep breath and held it.

I'm not sure exactly what I expected to see; a pile of bones, or something rotted and maggot-eaten, I guess, like out of a horror movie. But the body within the casket, whether by Casting or by a strange combination of natural elements, was almost perfectly preserved beneath its translucent white shroud. The face, which I could only assume belonged to Harriet Larkin, was waxy, and the eyes, still closed, were somewhat sunken, but long black eyelashes still rested on her cheeks, and her lips were still closed demurely over her teeth. She lay just as the figure above her had done, with her hands folded over her chest. Except...

"Little book," I whispered, my heart pounding.

"What's that?" Finn asked.

I pointed to Harriet Larkin's chest. There, tucked between her hands and her dusty ivory silk gown, was a small, black, leather-bound book.

Finn stepped forward, hand outstretched, but I grabbed onto his sleeve.

"What?" he asked.

"We can't just... I mean, are you going to just... take it?" I asked.

"Jess," he said impatiently. "We just shattered the window of the mausoleum and broke into her coffin. I think we've said 'sod it' to any modicum of respect we had here. So, let's just do what we need to do to end this, shall we?"

I blinked. "Right. Yes. Good point. By all means, defile the corpse."

Finn reached his hand forward, but then stopped suddenly.

"I can't."

"What?"

"I can't defile the corpse."

"You picked a really weird moment to have a crisis of conscience, Finn," I said.

"No, I mean I literally can't. Look." He thrust his hand forward as hard as he could but it seemed to meet with some kind of invisible resistance. "My hand won't go any closer than this. It must be some kind of Casting."

I threw my hands up in the air. "Well, now what the hell are we supposed to do?"

Finn withdrew his hand, brow furrowed with concentration. Finally, he said. "You try it."

I stared at him. "Me?"

"Yes, you. Who else would I be talking to!"

"But why would I be able to do it, if you can't?" I asked, fighting back an urge to be sick. I did not want to stick my hand in that coffin. I did not want to touch that body.

"I have no idea. I have no idea what this Casting is. But whoever put this book here obviously wanted to protect it. They may have wanted to keep in out of certain hands."

"I would think burying it in someone's cold dead hands would be a pretty effective way of doing that," I hissed.

"Yes, but it apparently wasn't enough. Perhaps this Casting ensures that only a Durupinen can remove it? We won't know unless you try!" Finn growled.

"Okay, okay!" I cried. I tried to take a deep breath to steady my nerves, but the air didn't make it past my throat. I shuffled forward on legs that were protesting the responsibility of keeping me upright until I was leaning right up against the edge of the coffin. I took what little breath I could in through my mouth, in a desperate attempt to avoid the smell of death that was permeating the room. Very slowly, I stretched out a violently shaking hand, careful to keep my eyes just on the book and nothing else. My hand moved closer and closer without meeting any resistance until, finally, I was able to brush the fabric of the shroud with my forefinger.

"I can touch it!" I cried, snatching my hand back out of the coffin as though it had been burned, and barely repressing the impulse to turn and run right out of the mausoleum.

"Brilliant!" Finn said. "So, go on, then. Take it."

I looked at him, and I knew there was a plea in my face, but he

241

ignored it, as we both knew he had to. And so, I swallowed back the horror rising in my throat and extended my hand once more into the coffin. I pinched the gossamer fabric of the shroud and peeled it gently back from Harriet's form, until the little book lay exposed in her hands, ready for the taking. Then I closed my fingers around the book, which was shockingly cold, and pulled experimentally. It didn't budge. I tugged a little harder. Still nothing.

"Oh God, the corpse doesn't want to let go of it!" I cried. My voice was shrill with blind horror.

"Just yank it out of there!" Finn cried, his voice sharp with the same taint of hysteria I was drowning in. He didn't like this any more than I did.

I grabbed onto the book with both hands and, with a thrill of absolute dread, pulled with all my might. There was a dull cracking sound, and the book came free in my hands. I stumbled into Finn and we both fell backward onto the floor, where we lay utterly still for one long, horrified moment.

"Finn."

"Yeah."

"Look down at the book I'm holding and please tell me there aren't corpse fingers still attached to it," I whispered in a strangled voice.

Finn actually laughed, easing the deep tension of what we had just done. "No. Corpse finger free, I promise you."

I sat up and opened my eyes, looking down at last upon the "little book," and wondering what I would find within its pages.

As though he read my mind, Finn said, "Now, just what do you suppose we're going to find in there?"

"Only one way to find out," I replied.

And by the quivering beam of the flashlight, we peeled open the damp, moldy pages and began to read.

ELEANORA: 21 JULY 1864

21 July 1864

Dearest Little Book,

I must write quickly, for fear they will discover that I have you. I have kept you hidden in a crack between the stones, and that alone, I believe, has kept you safe from being burned.

I am alone now. My mother has refused to see me. She has sent me a letter, in which she begs me to understand why I must be imprisoned "for the greater good of the Durupinen." She has chosen her position and her power here over her own daughter. She has bent to the will of the Council as easily as a blade of grass to the wind. And poor Hattie was so overcome at my imprisonment, that she fell terribly ill. She lingered for days while I begged to see her, to show her that I was alright. But even as her life hung in the balance, the Council never relented. They could not risk me being reunited with the other half of my Gateway, could not fathom that I could refrain from wreaking ultimate destruction upon them, when all I wanted was to see my sister. Now it is too late. She is gone.

Tomorrow, my sister's funeral will commence without me. It will be lavish, a black silk-draped confection of an affair. The mourners will have been hired by the dozens, and the coach will be a bower of blooms in which to bear my sister home from London to our mausoleum at Fairhaven. I wonder how my family will account for my absence. Perhaps they will instruct one of the mourners to take my place in the family pew, draped in a thick black veil and too devastated to speak to anyone. After that, they will explain me away with some elaborate tale: I am so overcome with grief that I have gone mad and must be confined to my room. Or else, eager to find a fresh start away from the sorrowful memory of my sister's death, I have been sent abroad to further my studies in music, or else to wed a foreign nobleman. Yes, mother would love to spin out that story. I can just see her now, waving around a stack of forged letters detailing my lavish European lifestyle, trips to exotic locations, and a manor house too large and full of visiting dignitaries to spare me for even a short visit back home. She may even start to believe the stories herself, as she weaves them into her own reality. Perhaps that is how she will be able to live with herself, and to forget the hand she played in the demise of her own daughter. I shall be erased from the world with a lie, my truth lost forever to all that knew me.

I have been allowed this single moment only: to stare down upon the mortal shell of my beloved sister before it is taken away. I am expected to say goodbye to a soul that has already fled this world. How cruel, knowing what they know of spirits. I am ashamed to say that I have shed no tears for Hattie. My heart aches with a pain beyond description, but I have no tears left in me. I have had no tears for a long time.

I do not know for sure what will become of me. For the foreseeable future, I am to be imprisoned at the *príosún* on the Isle of Skye under a multitude of Castings, kept under the watchful eye of the *Caomhnóir* so that they can be sure I will not bloom into the terrible threat the Council fears I shall become. If they decide that even those walls cannot contain my danger... no, I dare not speak the words, let alone record them upon these pages. It would make the possibility too real—and therefore too dreadful—to fathom. But one thing is for certain; the Durupinen will never allow me, in body or spirit, to tell my story.

But you can. You are my truth. You are the last recorded testament of what has become of me. My true thoughts, my hopes, my dreams: they all live in you. I hide you in the coffin of my beloved sister in the hope that, someday, when the irrational fear of the present has subsided, I can lead someone to you, and all shall be revealed. It will surely be too late for me, but perhaps my story can save another Caller from the strangling clutches of this fear.

Tell them, Little Book. Tell them I was Eleanora Larkin. Tell them I did no harm to anyone. I had so much to give of myself to the world.

And the Durupinen destroyed me.

Eleanora

19

NAMING ELEANORA

I FINISHED READING BEFORE FINN DID, and so I had a full minute to let the horror of what I'd just read wash over me like a tide.

"So, this is it. This is her. The Shattered spirit," Finn said, somewhat breathlessly.

I nodded.

"But this is brilliant!" he said, and leapt up, book in hand. "We can end this!"

Fiona appeared in the doorway. "What is it? Did you find something in there?" she asked. Her teeth were chattering.

"We've got it. A name. Eleanora Larkin."

And even as he said it aloud, the name rang a bell in my mind, a bell that struck just the right note, just the right frequency, to send a shivering sensation down into my fingers, which twitched with the truth of it all.

The terrible, terrible truth.

"Oh, at bloody last!" Fiona said, and she looked absolutely weak with relief. She reached out a hand for the book, and Finn gave it to her.

"Let's get this up to the castle. The sooner the Council see this, the sooner the Shards can be expelled."

"And what about Hannah? What does this mean for her?" I asked, standing up.

Fiona shook her head. "I don't know yet. We won't know, until we get this spirit patched back together. She should be able to communicate better then, and we will finally get to the bottom of what she's after."

Eleanora.

This was the name of the ghost, the spirit who had turned Fairhaven upside down for the last few days. She wasn't just a

245

spate of Shattered fragments—a scourge of which we needed to be cleansed. She was a person. A girl with a heart and a mind and a will to live and love and make her mark in the world.

And the Durupinen had destroyed her. They sacrificed this poor girl on the altar of their own terror—terror of a Prophecy they could not escape, no matter who they flung into its waiting jaws to satiate it. Just as they sacrificed The Silent Child. Just like they sacrificed my mother.

Just like they had nearly sacrificed Hannah and me.

When would this damn Prophecy release its hold on us? When would we be finished cleaning up its messes and sidestepping its horrific consequences? Wasn't fulfilling it enough to be free of it? Would it seriously follow us forever, dogging our footsteps, forcing us to wade through the shadows of the travesties it left behind?

"Well," Finn said, and I knew he was swallowing back many things he wanted to say, "We've got a name, here, haven't we?"

"Yeah," I said. "Yes, we have."

"That's it, then. If we've got a name, we can begin the expulsion," he said quietly.

"Yes, I suppose we can."

"You don't sound very happy about it."

I looked at him. His expression was set. "Are you happy about it?"

"I understand what you mean. This," and he tapped a finger on the book, "is terrible, and no mistake. But what can we do? She's got to be expelled."

"I know. I just... what happened to her..."

"I know."

Every heavy, anxious, desperate feeling I had welled up inside of me at once. "Finn, I'm sorry about what I—"

But Finn shook his head. "Don't. We don't need to do this right now. There will be time for that later. Use your connection to let Hannah and Milo know what we've found, and then help me get Catriona back up to the castle, will you? The Council will be going spare if she's missing too long."

I swallowed all of those feelings, pushing them right back down where they belonged. "Yeah, okay. Let's go."

§

We struggled back toward the castle with Catriona draped

between us, barely conscious. Fiona marched several yards ahead of us, leading the charge. We'd made it about halfway across the open stretch of lawn leading to the front doors when a shout stopped us in our tracks.

"There they are! They have her!"

We turned to see Seamus and Braxton jogging up the path that led to the barracks. "What's happened?" Seamus called as they reached us. "What's happened to her?"

"She's fine," Finn said. "Just weak."

In one deft movement, Seamus hefted Catriona over his back in a fireman's carry. "Where did you find her?" he asked.

"She led us down into the graveyard," I said. "She wanted us to open one of the mausoleums so we could find that." I pointed to the book in Fiona's hands.

"A book?" Seamus asked, incredulous. "She leapt out the window and braved these temperatures just for a book?"

"It's a very important book," Fiona said testily. "It's given us the spirit's name. We can expel her now. That is, if we don't all freeze to death while we stand out here and explain it to you."

Seamus narrowed his eyes at Fiona, but stopped asking questions. He turned to Braxton. "Alert the Council and tell them to meet us at the hospital ward. Make sure that Mrs. Mistlemoore accompanies them."

Braxton saluted and ran for the castle doors. We all followed him in shivering silence.

§

Waiting outside the hospital ward doors while the Council examined the diary was excruciating. I paced in the same tight circle so many times that I was surprised not to see a hole in the floor beneath my feet.

"Jess, you've got to calm down," Finn said at last.

"Finn, never in the history of the world have the words 'calm down' ever made anyone feel calmer," I snapped.

He almost smiled. "Fair enough."

"I just don't understand why they couldn't let us in there!" I said for at least the fifth time. "We are the ones who found the diary! I'm the one who drew the pictures! I'm the one the spirit tried to communicate with!"

"The Council values its privilege," Finn said, shaking his head.

"The only thing they value about their privilege is abusing it," I grumbled. "I should be in there, I could help. I mean, did you see the way they looked at me when they walked in there? They were all glaring at me like I'd done something wrong—well, besides lying, breaking Catriona out, and robbing a sacred Durupinen burial ground."

"Imagine them not inviting you in there, after all that," Finn said with a chuckle. "I'm surprised they even allowed Fiona in, quite frankly."

"What do you think it meant?" I asked. "Eleanora's message about the Caller betraying her?"

Finn shrugged. "I can't say. She was a Caller, after all. Maybe she meant that being a Caller is what led to her betrayal?"

I considered this. "That's possible. She didn't mention any other Callers in that diary."

"Don't fret about that now," Finn said. "When the Council unites the Shards, they'll be able to ask Eleanora what she meant, and then they'll know at last that Hannah had nothing to do with it."

I shook my head. "They still blame her. Hannah was the victim, not the enemy, but they still blame her for everything to do with the Prophecy. They were just salivating for a reason to punish her for something."

"Fear is a powerful thing. People think hatred fuels the great wars and feuds of the world, but it's simply not true. It's fear at the root of that hatred. It's always been fear first," Finn said. "The men who wreak their destruction upon the world have always been utter cowards at heart."

I took a moment to digest this. "Speaking of fear, I didn't see anything that would have explained the fear she seems to have of fire. Did you?"

"No," Finn said, "although that diary ended just as she was being arrested. Whatever happened with the fire may have happened after she stashed that book with her sister."

Unbidden, I imagined staring down at Hannah's body, and desperately hiding the only honest evidence of my existence in her cold, dead hands. I choked back a sob. Emotion flooded over me so quickly that, for a moment, I thought I must be having an Empathic episode.

"Are you quite alright?" Finn asked.

I shook my head. "I'm trying to separate myself, but it's just too awful. Hannah and I came very close to a fate like that. I just hate that these echoes of the Prophecy are still reverberating through the spirit world. It's like the damage will never be finished, even though it's over."

The door to the hospital ward burst open and Fiona marched out, followed by Braxton. Fiona made a beeline right for me, but Braxton marched past as though I did not exist and disappeared around the corner.

"What? What is it? What's going on?" I asked swiftly.

"They're setting up the Circle now," she said, and she looked relieved. "I don't know whether they believe our story about Catriona escaping on her own, but it doesn't matter at this point; they can't prove otherwise, and we've handed them exactly what they needed to name the spirit and end this fecking nightmare."

I let out a sigh of relief I didn't even realize I was holding. "So, this is it, then. They're going to expel her?"

"Seems like it. But they want you and your sister in there," Fiona said.

"Us? Why?" I asked.

"Well, you were the first one the spirit made contact with, through those sketches. They feel that Eleanora might be more likely to talk if she sees you, because she reached out to you before. As for Hannah... well, the Council wants to clarify that Caller comment, so they think she should be present as well."

I shook my head. "This is ridiculous. Okay, should we go get Hannah?"

"No, that's what Braxton's just gone to do," Fiona said, pointing up the hallway after his retreating form. "The Council isn't trusting you to go fetch anyone after our little jaunt into the Larkin mausoleum."

"That wasn't my idea," I said indignantly. "They can blame you and Eleanora for that. I'd better warn Hannah that Braxton's coming for her, though."

I sailed through the connection easily probably because Hannah and Milo had the mental door wide open, desperate for news. "Hannah? Milo?"

Their words tumbled over each other in a cacophonous jumble, so that I winced with the force of it.

"Jess!"

"What happened?"

"What is it?"

"Did they read the diary? What did they say?"

"Braxton is on his way up to get you. The Council wants us both here for when they start communicating with Eleanora."

"Did... did they say why they wanted me there?" Hannah asked, her fear thrumming through the connection like an electric current.

"For the same reason they've got you trapped in our room; they want to make sure you aren't the Caller Eleanora was referring to," I told her, trying to combat her fear with calm, soothing energy. "They are just being thorough. I'm glad they want us there; it will be even more satisfying to witness their realization that they were wrong in person. Bring some popcorn."

"Ha, ha, ha," Hannah scoffed, utterly unimpressed with my attempt at humor, although Milo gave an appreciative chuckle. "We'll see you in a few minutes."

Finn, Fiona and I waited in tense silence for Hannah, Braxton, and Milo to appear. From inside the hospital ward, a series of moans and screams signaled that the Hosts were being disturbed in some way—perhaps from being herded into the Circle in preparation for the Casting. The sound made my skin crawl. How horrific for this spirit to find herself back in the same castle where she was so demonized and vilified, all for a gift she had no control over. I half wanted to charge into the hospital ward, throw open the window and set all the Hosts free, just so Eleanora wouldn't have to spend another minute here. But of course, I knew that wouldn't actually solve anything.

Hannah, Milo, and Braxton appeared. Braxton at least had the good sense not to use his authority to intimidate Hannah physically; he walked alongside her rather than escorted her, and kept a respectful distance. Hannah, though obviously nervous, at least had her head held high as she reached us.

"Ready?" I asked her, holding out a hand.

"Ready," she said, and took it.

The Hosts were all sitting in the center of the Circle, back to back in a tight little knot. They seemed to find some comfort in the physical proximity of their fellows; the moaning and shrieking had dulled into a soft sort of collective whimper. The Council stood around the perimeter of the Circle, tense with anticipation. Off in the corner, Mrs. Mistlemoore stood tensely next to a desk, where two Scribes had piled all of the Fairhaven resources on Shatterings.

"Jessica. Hannah," Keira called, motioning us forward. "We would like you on hand for this Casting. It is possible the spirit will want to communicate with one or both of you." Her tone was friendly enough, but I still felt Hannah tense beside me at the sound of her own name.

Neither Hannah or I answered, but stepped forward, still clasping hands. I squeezed Hannah's fingers and caught her eye, winking at her. She gave a tiny smile in reply. Through our connection, Milo's support broke over us like a warm, loving tide.

Keira began the words of the Casting, reading them from a book so ancient that she handled the crumbling pages with a pair of gloves on. The moment she began, all of the Hosts went suddenly rigid.

"We Summon thee, Shattered one, to the Circle hence. We gather your Shards together to resume your true form. We name thee, Eleanora Larkin, and with the speaking of your name, our Summons cannot be resisted."

For a long, loaded moment, absolutely nothing happened. The very air in the room seemed to have frozen, each molecule suspended in place.

Hannah's hand tightened in mine. "Something's wrong," she whispered.

"What?"

"The energy. Something's not right," Hannah hissed.

As though to confirm her feeling, the Hosts all opened their mouths at the same time and unleashed piercing screams. A phantom wind, borne of their collective energy, swept through the room, ripping the sheets from the beds and the curtains from the windows, and extinguishing every candle. Then the Hosts' heads drooped onto their chests and their screams faded and died.

Keira dropped the page of the book and stepped back from it in alarm. "What was that about?" she asked the room at large.

Blank stares met her question. Mrs. Mistlemoore shook her head, her mouth hanging open. The Scribes were feverishly flipping through their books, clearly at a loss. But after a moment, it was Hannah who answered.

"They're not all here," Hannah said. "The Shards. There's still at least one missing."

Keira frowned. "That doesn't make sense. The Naming is meant to draw all of the Shards back together. Any others left in the castle should have been drawn here at once."

Hannah shrugged defensively. "I don't know why it isn't working," she said. "I'm just telling you what I sense. I don't sense a complete spirit here. The pieces don't make a whole."

"Well then, we must have the wrong spirit," Isla said, throwing a hostile look at me. "If the Naming has not worked, then we must not have the right name."

"You've got the right name," I snapped at her. "That's Eleanora Larkin in there, I'm sure of it."

"You must be wrong," Isla said with a dismissive shrug. "You've simply misinterpreted your drawings, and led us on a wild goose chase."

"She hasn't mistaken shite," Fiona shouted. "You might be a Council member, Isla, but when it comes to the gifts of a Muse, you don't know your arse from your elbow."

"That's quite enough of that, thank you," Keira said sharply before turning back to Hannah. "So, what does this mean, then?" she asked in a muffled voice. "Where is the missing Shard?"

Hannah gripped my hand for support. "I don't know."

"That Casting should have gathered them," Mrs. Mistlemoore said. "Once the naming has been performed, the Shards can be pieced back together and then expelled. That's how it's meant to work."

Keira looked frantically from Hannah to Mrs. Mistlemoore, and then around at the circle of waiting Council members. "What should we do? Should we try again?"

They all looked around at each other, at a loss for what to do. But something else had caught my eye. Over the window behind Keira, the curtain hung off to one side, its tassel swinging back and forth, back and forth, like a pendulum.

Like a giant, ancient pendulum. I gasped.

Frantically, I clawed at my own jacket until I found the folded piece of parchment that Moira had given me and tore it open. I scanned it and then let out a sharp bark of excited laughter.

"It's Lucida!" I cried.

Every face in the room turned to stare at me, startled, including Hannah's.

"What about Lucida?" she asked, eyes wide.

"It's Lucida! That's how all of this started! She's the Caller Eleanora was talking about, and she's the reason we can't piece Eleanora's spirit back together!"

Keira narrowed her eyes at me. "I don't follow. How can Lucida have anything to do with this?"

"Okay," I said, beginning to pace as I talked through all the dots, connecting them as much for myself as for everyone else because though the light bulb had gone on, the details were still dim. "None of us could understand why or how Catriona could have brought a hostile spirit into the castle. We couldn't understand how it Habitated in her without her noticing, or how it did so in a Warded room. But it didn't, don't you see? It wasn't Catriona at all! It was Lucida!"

They did not see. Everyone was just staring blankly at me.

I went on, "You all read the diary. Eleanora was a Caller. She was targeted by the Durupinen leadership because they feared that she might be the Caller of the Prophecy. She was arrested and locked away in a *príosún*. Does anyone remember where that *príosún* was?"

I looked around expectantly, but everyone was still just goggling at me like I had sprouted an extra head that was now expounding on all of this.

"It was on the Isle of Skye! It was one of the last things she mentioned—how terrified she was of being sent away to the Isle of Skye. And it wouldn't be a great leap to guess that she died there as well, since Callers were so feared. Well, just a few hours ago, Moira, the keeper of the Léarscáil, came to the hospital ward to find Celeste. She wanted to inform her of a strange pattern of spirit energy linking Fairhaven to the Isle of Skye. Look. Look at it!"

I shook the paper in Fiona's direction and she took it from me, still looking somewhat frightened of my outburst. But I couldn't calm myself. With every word I spoke, every thought I articulated, I grew more and more convinced that I was absolutely right.

"Hannah and I saw it! Mackie took us to see the Léarscáil for the first time a couple of days ago, and Moira was already recording some sort of spiritual disturbance connecting Fairhaven to Skye. We actually watched the pendulum link the locations together in a weird little loop, remember?" I turned eagerly to Hannah, who was nodding in confirmation, though she still looked confused. I went on, "So, Eleanora lived out her sentence on Skye and her spirit lingered there, for over 150 years until, at last, she encountered another Caller. Are you following me yet?"

Fiona gasped as the realization finally hit her. "Lucida is serving her sentence at Skye!"

I pointed to her like a mad professor proving a hypothesis. "Yes! I'm willing to bet she may be the first Caller ever to set foot there since Eleanora was alive. Maybe they talked to each other. Maybe they formed some kind of bond through their mutual suffering at the hands of this Council. But whatever happened, Eleanora tried to force her way through Lucida's sealed Gateway."

Hannah clapped her hand over her mouth. Several of the Council members gasped.

"Catriona wasn't the source of the Shattering," I said. "The Shattering didn't even happen here. It happened hundreds of miles away in Skye. But somehow, when Eleanora Shattered, she Shattered right through Lucida's and Catriona's connection and the Shards wound up here! It's the only explanation that makes sense!"

Keira rounded on Mrs. Mistlemoore, her expression incredulous. "Can that happen?"

Mrs. Mistlemoore shrugged her shoulders helplessly. "I don't know. It... certainly seems to fit the evidence."

Keira turned to one of the Scribes. "Is this possible?" she demanded.

The Scribe, a shrunken old woman, nodded slowly, looking very thoughtful. "I don't know if it has happened before," she said. "But it is possible, I believe, due to the nature of the connection between Passage and Key."

"Just think about it!" I cried eagerly. "We can't put Eleanora back together again because we don't have the source of the Shattering here! The original Host isn't in this room; she's sitting locked up in a cell hundreds of miles from here. That's why the Léarscáil is connecting Fairhaven and Skye together!"

"So, then what did Eleanora mean when she said, 'The Caller betrayed me?'" Hannah asked. "Betrayed her how?"

"No idea," I said, shrugging. "But at least now we know how to find out!"

The Council members began conferring and muttering to each other. Mrs. Mistlemoore had hurried over to the corner where the Scribes had set up a small desk and was whispering excitedly with them.

The other Scribe, a mousy young woman with horn-rimmed glasses, raised her hand tentatively, as though she were in class.

"Um, I have made a fairly intensive study of our *príosún* system," she said in a squeak of a voice that matched her appearance. "The *príosún* at Skye was struck by lightning in 1907 and burned to the ground. It was rebuilt and reopened in 1910. Dozens of prisoners were among those killed in the blaze."

I turned to the Hosts, who all still sat as though sleeping with their chins on their chests. "My God," I whispered. "She must have burned alive in that place. That's why the Shards fear fire so much."

Keira spun around and gestured to Braxton, who stood sentinel at the door. "Call over to the head of Caomhnóir security at the Skye *Príosún*. Explain the situation and tell them to examine Lucida and report back immediately. If what Jessica says is true, we will have to transport Lucida here in order to reverse this Shattering."

Braxton nodded briskly and marched from the room. Keira turned back to Mrs. Mistlemoore. "Let's settle the Hosts back down to rest. If we do indeed have to wait for Lucida to be transported from Skye, it will be many hours before this Casting can be performed."

"Yes, of course," Mrs. Mistlemoore said, and immediately hurried toward the Circle to begin the process. Several other Council members hastened to assist her.

Keira skirted the Circle and approached Hannah and me. I felt Hannah pulling back on my hand, like she was fighting the urge to retreat, but Keira smiled at us.

"Thank you both. You may return to your room, for now. We will keep you informed of what we discover."

§

"You may return to your room," Milo said, imitating Keira's lofty voice and proper English accent. "Like you're a pair of brats being excused from the dinner table. I could have bitch-slapped her."

"Bitch-slapping requires physical form, Milo," I said. "But we appreciate the sentiment."

"I don't think she was trying to be rude," Hannah said, her voice a bit slurred. She'd been nodding off in her chair, barely able to hold her eyes open.

"Being rude doesn't require effort, especially when it comes to the Council," Milo retorted.

More than six hours had passed since the failed attempt at reassembling Eleanora's Shattered spirit, and still no word had reached us. Milo had even taken to popping out of the room and haunting the corridor outside the Council office, but since he couldn't get in due to the Wards, he was reduced to listening at the door like a thief. A rosy glow had begun to illuminate the tops of the trees outside our window. I was mind-numbingly tired, but I couldn't sleep. A tiny part of me was still feeling anxious and jumpy, and that part seemed to shake me mentally any time I drifted too near the beginnings of sleep.

"I just wish I knew what they were doing," I yawned. "The longer we're stuck here, the wilder my theories get. At this point I wouldn't be surprised if they were holding a full criminal trial without us."

Hannah sat up in her chair looking alarmed.

"I'm kidding, I'm kidding!" I said quickly.

"I am too tired and tense for kidding, Jess!" she admonished.

"I know. I'll shut up now."

I slid out of my chair and walked over to the window, watching the bright pink on the horizon bleeding up into the gradually lightening sky. What I really wanted was to talk to Finn, but yet again, societal Durupinen norms kept us separated. I knew he stood only feet away in the corridor, guarding the door to my room, and yet it was impossible for me to just open the door and confide in him. I was afraid. I was frustrated. I was torn about what the future could or should hold for us. The longer those feelings were bottled up, the less sure I was that I could even articulate them clearly.

Ugh, this was why I should just withdraw from romantic life and fulfill my inevitable destiny as a haunted old cat lady. I was clearly too emotionally stunted to handle anything else. Maybe Hannah and I could find a creepy house somewhere and become the second coming of the Lafayette twins, frightening the neighbors with our reclusive, Grey Gardens-esque antics.

As I pondered the possible benefits of spinsterhood, a vehicle appeared at the far end of the Fairhaven entrance road. As it zoomed closer, I determined that it was a black SUV, identical to those driven by the resident Caomhnóir staff.

"There's a car approaching the castle," I said over my shoulder.

Hannah sprang from her chair like a startled cat and ran to my side to stare down at the road below. Milo blinked into form on my other side. His eyes, following the vehicle, were already narrowed in suspicion, as though he had a bad feeling about whatever or whoever might be in it.

The great wrought iron gates swung open to admit the SUV, which did not slow as it whipped through them, but zoomed around the circular drive before skidding to an abrupt halt right in front of the main doors, spewing gravel everywhere.

Although we couldn't see the front doors from our window, we knew they were thrown open at once by the flood of golden light that spilled out across the drive, illuminating the car and the stoic, black-suited men now jumping out of it.

"Caomhnóir?" Hannah asked.

"Yeah, but I don't recognize them. You?" I asked.

Hannah shook her head.

The Caomhnóir who had exited from the driver's seat now threw open the back door. Both men leaned into the back seat, seeming to struggle with something, and then they stepped away from the car, now carrying a flailing figure between them. I did not need Milo's gasp, nor Hannah's soft cry of horror to help me recognize who it was.

Lucida had returned to Fairhaven Hall.

20

ELEANORA RISING

S OMEONE HAMMERED ON THE BEDROOM DOOR, making all three of us yelp. Before I could gather myself to cross the room and open it, the door flew open and Finn's face appeared around it, his jaw set with anxiety.

"Seamus is here. The Council wants you both back in the hospital ward. They want to warn you that—"

"Lucida's here," I said. "We know. We just watched her pull up."

One of the muscles near Finn's temple was twitching. "You don't need to do this."

I frowned. "Don't need to do what?"

He stepped fully into the room. "You don't need to go down there. You can refuse. You are under no obligation to subject yourself to that woman again. The Council has no right to ask it of you, and not one among them would have the nerve to require it."

I looked at Hannah. She was visibly trembling, and her hands were clenching and unclenching at her sides. I could feel my own palms sweating. The very sight of Lucida had sent my heart leaping into my throat. It now felt like it had lodged itself there, restricting my airway with every frantic beat.

And yet, within that fear was something else. Something made of fire. If I were to find myself in the same room as that woman, I may very well beat the ever-loving crap out of her.

In a weird way, the violent thoughts calmed me. I knew I wouldn't fall to pieces at the sight of Lucida. The fact that I could summon anger in the face of fear and traumatic memories made me feel stronger, somehow. Then again, I wasn't really the one I was worried about.

"I'm leaving this entirely up to you," I said to Hannah, taking both of her hands in mine and forcing her to look me in the eyes.

"We won't go if you don't want to. The Council can kiss my ass. Or yours."

"Or mine!" Milo piped up.

I winked at him. "Someone's ass will be kissed. But seriously, Hannah. What do you want to do? Don't be brave. Be honest."

As I spoke, some of the blind animal panic faded from Hannah's eyes. When she answered me, her voice was surprisingly steady. "I'll go, because the Council might need a Caller. But I won't speak to Lucida. Not even while Eleanora is using her, I will not speak to her. I will not compromise on that."

I squeezed her hands, swelling with pride. "Good for you. And don't worry about talking. If anything needs to be said, my mouth is big enough for the both of us."

"I know," Hannah said, and actually smiled.

"You don't have to agree with everything I say," I said, pretending to pout.

Hannah shrugged.

I laughed at her, and then turned to Finn. "Hannah and my big mouth agree to come to the hospital wing," I told him.

If he appreciated my attempts at humor, he didn't let on, although Seamus was standing right in the doorway, so I couldn't blame him for keeping a determinedly straight face.

"Very well," he said. "It is your decision. After you, then," he said, gesturing out into the hallway.

§

One fact was abundantly obvious upon entering the hospital ward: there was nothing to be feared from Lucida in her current state. She sat propped like a child's doll, back to back with the other Hosts, utterly incapable of independent thought or movement. She was much thinner and frailer than the last time we'd seen her; her tightly curled hair was now shot through with gray and her face looked pinched and haggard. The sight of her so vulnerable was comforting; in fact, Hannah very nearly smiled when she laid eyes upon Lucida in such a state. Her hand certainly relaxed in mine for the first time since I'd taken it, and I finally felt safe to release it from my protective grasp. Milo continued to send calming soothing energy washing over us, but I could see from his expression that he, too, felt that Hannah was in control of herself.

Fiona came and stood next to us. She said nothing at all, but I knew exactly what she was doing; she was determined to support us in some way, even if all she could manage was her physical presence side by side with ours. If Celeste and Savvy hadn't been trapped in the Circle before us, I knew that they would have stood firmly by our sides as well, and even that knowledge bolstered me.

Keira began speaking the words of the Casting immediately upon our return to the room. Maybe she was afraid we would change our minds when we saw Lucida up close, or else perhaps she simply wanted to end this catastrophe as soon as humanly possible. Either way, she launched into the Casting before the door had properly shut behind us, and a relieved sort of murmur rippled through the rest of the Council as she started.

The energy in the room was already roiling and churning like a stormy sea; the motion of it actually made me feel dizzy. I turned to Hannah, the question on my face, and she answered it without a word. Lucida really had been the last missing piece. All of the Shards were now present, and aching to be reunited. Even as I watched her nod her head, my own head began to nod in unison. I could feel it: the familiar, if damaged, energy of a whole disembodied soul.

Seamus stood beside Keira, ready and waiting to expel the Shards at the precise moment of the Naming. The moment Eleanora's name fell from Keira's lips, Seamus muttered his Casting and thrust his arms forward as though physically pushing the Shards from the Hosts' bodies. In response to his gesture, the Hosts threw their heads back and opened their mouths. But instead of the piercing screams of pain they'd issued during the first attempt at the Casting, they all gave a long, deep sigh. And on the tide of that collective expulsion of breath, the Shards were borne up into the air above the Hosts.

I wish I had looked away, for there was nothing I had experienced yet in the spirit world that could match the heartbreaking sight of a Shard. Each one was made of the same ephemeral, gently luminescent substance that all spirits are made of, but they appeared unstable. Their energy pulsed and swirled with constant attempts to mold themselves into a recognizable mental and physical shape, but they simply morphed from one twisted, partially-formed shape to the next, all the while exuding an oppressive sense of confusion and despair.

I knew I was not the only person in the room to feel the overwhelming sadness of it. All around the Circle, Durupinen faces were rapt with anguish, eyes glistening with tears. We watched, transfixed, as the Shards writhed and contorted themselves, sometimes achieving an almost human physicality before shivering back down into serpentine forms. All the while, a sound halfway between moaning and music rose from them, a chorus of anguish, that vibrated inside my bones and tore at my heart. Hannah gave a shuddering sob beside me. Across the Circle, Fiona had dropped her eyes to the floor, her shoulders shaking.

"Keira. The rest of the Casting. Finish it," Seamus said gently. Keira shook her head and dragged her sleeve across her face, stifling a sob.

"The Casting. Yes. I..." she fumbled with the book in her hand, swiping at her eyes again when the tears obscured her view of the page. She could barely keep her voice steady as she spoke the rest of the words in a mixture of Gaelic and old Britannic. I recognized just a single word of it: "ceangail," the Irish Gaelic word for "bind," which I had come across in my reading about the Binding my mother had used to block spirit contact when I was growing up.

The word seemed to act as a trigger, for as soon as Keira uttered it, the Shards began to spin very fast over the heads of the Hosts like a luminous halo. They spun so fast, that it became impossible to distinguish one from the other; they were simply a blur. Then, with a force like an explosion, they merged.

The force of the event blew out across the room, knocking everyone off their feet. The energy that blasted past us felt like a tidal wave, and my breath caught in my throat as it rushed over me like a powerful ocean current, threatening to drown me in a sea of negative emotion.

And then it was gone. And only Eleanora remained.

She hovered in the space above the Hosts, blinking down at them in surprise and then concern, as though she could not possibly comprehend what any of them were doing there. She appeared just as she had in my sketches; her thick dark hair was swept up into an elegant mass of curls, delicate tendrils framing her face. An elaborate formal dress fanned out beneath her, swaying slightly, so that she might have been dancing on a breeze. She looked beyond the Hosts to the Circle, and then at the space around her, trying to understand where she was.

I scrambled to my feet and walked forward to the edge of the Circle just as the others in the room were beginning to stir. I did not wait for instructions. I did not care.

"Eleanora?" I asked softly.

Eleanora looked around and spotted me. Recognition broke across her bewildered expression.

"You," she said. "You are the Muse." Her voice was an echo, a distant song that I struggled to recognize the tune of.

I nodded. "Don't be afraid. Do you know where you are?"

Eleanora looked around the room again. "I know this place. My sister died in this room."

"That's right. You're at Fairhaven Hall."

The other Durupinen were assembling around the Circle again, but no one made any movements to stop me from speaking with Eleanora. In the corner, I heard the Scribe's pen scribbling across paper, recording the content of our conversation.

"You don't need to be afraid," I told her, for at the mention of the name "Fairhaven," terror had spasmed across Eleanora's face. "No one here wants to harm you. The Prophecy they once feared has come to pass. You were not to blame for it. They have no reason to fear you anymore."

Eleanora covered her face with her hands, trying to compose herself. "Oh, thank God. Thank you dear, sweet God," she whispered. Then she looked up at me. "How do you know about that?"

"I found your little book," I said. "I read it. I know all about what happened to you."

"How? How did you find it?" Eleanora asked.

"You led me to it," I said. "Don't you remember?"

Eleanora shook her head. "No... I... I don't think I... what happened to me? How did I get here?"

I looked over at Mrs. Mistlemoore for guidance. "The Shattering was very disorienting. She likely remembers or understands very little of it," she whispered.

"Take me back to the last things you do remember," I prompted. "You were in the *príosún* on the Isle of Skye, right?"

Eleanora nodded. "I have been trapped there for well over a century now. I was first brought there to await examination as a Caller, an examination that never came. They locked me away under every Casting they could conjure up that would prevent me from Calling. It seemed I would languish there forever, and then a new High Priestess came into power. She was more sympathetic to my plight, less prone to allow fear to guide her decisions. My clan petitioned her on my behalf, and I was hopeful that I might soon be free. But then, three days before my petition was to be heard, a great fire came."

Her face contracted as she said it, and she nearly flickered out of sight, as though the trauma of the memory sapped her energy.

"It swept through the *príosún* in the dead of night. I cannot believe it was an accident. A strong smell of oil was the first thing to wake me up. The guard that was usually posted at the end of my corridor was inexplicably absent. I screamed and screamed from my cell for help, but no one... no one ever came." She shuddered and wrapped her arms around herself, as though the gesture could prevent her from falling to actual pieces. "Dozens of us perished, but though the *príosún* crumbled, the Castings that held us there remained intact. We could not make ourselves heard. We could not flee the ruins, even as spirits, could not roam in search of help or even for a Gateway to Cross us. We were forgotten."

I couldn't help but glare at the Council members, even though they had not been alive when Eleanora's sentence had been handed down, and obviously weren't responsible for it. Every one of them looked utterly horrified, which gave me a modicum of satisfaction.

"When the *príosún* was rebuilt, it was simply built over us. No one searched for us, or made any attempt to strip old Castings away. I cannot say for sure if this was purposeful, but if not, it was an inexcusable oversight. And so, I continued to languish there, until the other Caller arrived."

At that, every Council member perked up, looking from Eleanora, to Hannah, and to Lucida, now slumped unconscious on the floor. But I would not allow their suspicions to persist a moment longer.

"Who was the Caller that you met?" I prompted, knowing, of course, what her answer would be.

Eleanora looked below her and pointed to Lucida's motionless form. "There."

I wanted to be very, very sure. "And she is the only other Caller you've ever met?"

Eleanora nodded again. "I would have given anything to meet

others, to know that I was not alone in my gift that was far more curse than blessing. Alas, I never had that chance."

I looked back at Hannah, who smiled gratefully at me. It was what I wanted to know above all else, but there were other questions still to be answered, and although I was growing more and more positive that my theory was correct, I knew we all must have concrete answers to them.

"What happened when you met Lucida?" I prompted.

Eleanora shook her head ruefully. "We sensed each other by our gifts. She was so sympathetic, so understanding of all I had been through. She pressed me for every detail, and told me in depth of her own mistreatment by the Durupinen. I thought I had found an ally at last. She promised to find a way to undo the Castings upon me, so that I could finally seek rest."

"Did she keep her promise?" I asked.

"She did," Eleanora confirmed. "I do not know how she did it. Perhaps she found someone to help her. I cannot say. But at last, she kept her word. I was free."

"And what did you want to do with that freedom?" I asked.

"All I wished for was to Cross. I was so very weary, so ready to see my sister and my family again. Most spirits are left behind because they want to stay, but imagine the unendurable agony of wanting to go and being forced to remain behind. It was torture of the cruelest kind for more than a century."

I swallowed an urge to cry, and pressed on. "What did Lucida think of that?"

Eleanora looked down upon Lucida, examining her face with a long, sad look. "She wanted me to seek revenge. She kept trying to convince me, over and over again, that I must come to Fairhaven and make the Council pay for what they had done to me, and to all the Callers who had the audacity to simply exist since the Isherwood Prophecy had been foretold. I admit I was tempted. I argued with myself. Surely, I owed it to the many victims of injustice to seek an explanation? But in the end, I knew that my desire for peace was far greater than my desire for revenge."

"So, you refused?"

"Yes. I refused. She was clearly angry with me. I thought perhaps she might then refuse in turn to set me free, but she surprised me. After a few moments of silence, she apologized to me. She said she applauded my integrity, and she would not deny me the rest and peace I so deserved. She promised to free me anyway. And at last, she did."

"How?" I asked. "How did she do it?" I asked in a whisper.

"I do not know how she broke through the Castings," Eleanora said. "She had no Casting bag, nor any accomplices that I could discover. Suddenly, one night, I felt them lift. It was like great chains had been removed from my form. I could leave my cell. For a brief moment, I could have gone anywhere, done anything; but then she Called me."

Hannah stifled a sob behind me. I knew how painful it must be for her, hearing another of Lucida's victims tell her story.

Eleanora went on, "Her Call was so powerful. I never knew what it felt like for a spirit to be Called, only what it felt like to do the Calling. It was intense, hypnotic. It was as though she opened me up and thrust purpose into me, a purpose that I could not ignore. I could only think of one thing: to Cross through the Caller as soon as possible.

"I threw caution and knowledge to the wind; they held no sway over me. I only knew that I could feel the pull of the Gateway, and that I must answer it. 'Come to me,' she was saying, drawing me ever nearer. 'Come to me, and find your rest. Cross here, right now.'" Eleanora wrung her hands, her eyes filling with spectral tears. "I ought to have known that I could not, but her Call and my desperate desire overwhelmed me. I saw the glimmer of it ahead, nestled in the Caller, and I could not stop myself. And then..." She raised her hands in a helpless gesture, then crumpled in on herself.

"You Shattered," I said.

She nodded, shaking with sobs. "I remember little after that, but scattered, blurred moments I can barely piece together. These faces..." she gestured to the slumping mass of Hosts below her. "I was searching. I was lost and scattered. I remember you," she said, pointing a shaking finger at me. "I remember recognizing myself, and... and wandering in the snow to find Hattie..." She dissolved into sobs again.

"So, Lucida knew," Hannah said, realization dawning in her tone. "She knew that there was a chance that Eleanora would Shatter, and that the Shattering could break right through to her connection with Catriona."

I looked down at Lucida, crumpled on the floor, and nodded. "She tried to use Eleanora for revenge on the Council, but when Eleanora refused to go, Lucida decided to Shatter her instead. She knew there was a chance that the Shattering would disrupt the Airechtas and wreak havoc on Fairhaven."

"My God," Fiona said from the far side of the Circle. "This wasn't an accident? This was an attack?"

I nodded, repressing an urge to walk right over to Lucida's motionless body and kick it. "A calculated attack. One betrayed Caller used another to wage her revenge. And it worked."

"She couldn't have really thought it would work!" Keira said incredulously. "Shatterings are incredibly rare. There was no way to predict if the Shards would break through to the other half of the Gateway!"

"She didn't need to predict it," I said. "It was a desperate last attempt. She had nothing to lose if it failed, but if it succeeded, she could wreak havoc on the Airechtas from afar. How would anyone ever have known it was her that caused all of this?"

No one answered. They didn't need to. We all knew the damage that could have been caused if we hadn't been able to trace the Shattering to its source. Savvy, Celeste, Catriona, and every other Host, trapped forever in bodies they couldn't control.

"It's okay now, Eleanora," I said softly. "Everything will be okay now." I turned to Keira and the other Council members. "Haven't we had enough of this? She's suffered terribly. She's told you what she can. Please. Please let her go now."

I expected resistance. I expected a lecture about procedure and votes and the proper way in which things must be done. I expected the kind of compassionless "justice" Catriona had shown to Irina just a couple of months prior.

Instead, Keira stepped forward, placed a hand on my shoulder, her eyes glassy with emotion, and said, "Yes. Our sister has earned the peace of the Aether." She turned to address the room at large. "We will close out this Casting and return the Hosts to their beds. Then we will allow this soul to Cross at last. Jessica and Hannah, would you please do the honors?"

Hannah stepped forward eagerly to stand beside me. If any of the other Council members had objections, they did not voice them. As soon as Keira muttered a quick incantation, they all came forward into the center of the Circle to assist in moving the Hosts back to their beds. Mrs. Mistlemoore called out instructions, hovering like a bee at a blossom over each bed in turn, ensuring that the occupant was okay. Under cover of the general commotion, Hannah and I knelt down beside Eleanora, who was still trying to control her crying.

"We are so very sorry for everything you went through," I whispered to her.

"I was such a fool," Eleanora gasped. "I oughtn't to have allowed myself to be taken in like that. But I was so lonely and so desperate and Lucida said so many of the things I needed to hear."

Hannah knelt down beside me. "I know exactly what you mean," Hannah said. "It wasn't your fault. Lucida is a master manipulator. She is to blame, not you. Please let that go. Don't carry it with you to the other side. It's not your burden, and you shouldn't have to bear it."

I nudged Hannah with my elbow so that she turned to look at me. "I think I know someone else who would be a lot happier if she took that same advice."

Hannah blushed and dropped her eyes, a tiny smile appearing on her face. "Yeah, I think I do, too."

I squeezed her shoulder before turning back to Eleanora. "Hannah's right. And anyway, it's much more my fault than yours. You tried to reach out to me, but I didn't know what it meant. I only wish I could have discovered who you were before the Shattering happened. I could have prevented all of this."

Eleanora looked up at me, her face glazed with tears. "Reached out to you? What do you mean?"

I frowned. "The sketches. The psychic drawings I did of you—the ones that I showed you to help you remember who you were."

Eleanora looked blank. "What about the drawings? I didn't have anything to do with them."

"Of course you did," I said, half-laughing. "You had to have reached out to me those nights while I was sleeping. How else could I have drawn them?"

"I haven't the faintest idea," Eleanora said. "I never saw the drawings, or you, until the moment you showed them to me. How could I have? I was still trapped in the *príosún*, unable to communicate."

I simply stared at her. Her words made no sense. "But how did I—"

"Eleanora? Are you ready now?" Keira came to stand beside us.

I looked up, startled. The Hosts lay in their beds, and the Council members were all standing around expectantly.

"Oh, yes," Eleanora breathed, rising and smoothing her dress in one of those endearing human habits that sometimes carried over into spirit form. "I have been ready for a very long time."

"The Council promises a full investigation into the injustices perpetrated against you," Keira said. "You have my word on that."

"Thank you," Eleanora said, bowing her head.

Keira turned to look at Hannah and me. "Clan Sassanaigh, whenever you are ready."

Hannah and I took hands, the power of our gift—our destiny—coursing between us like the blood we shared.

§

"So obviously, you lot are never allowed at another Airechtas," Savvy announced, slapping me on the back.

Hannah, Milo, and I were all sitting around her bed in the hospital ward, waiting for her to finish lacing up her boots. Three days had passed since Eleanora had Crossed, and the Hosts were finally being cleared for release by Mrs. Mistlemoore.

"Oh, come on," I cried. "Even Marion can't pretend we were responsible for this one."

"It's got nothing to do with responsibility, mate. You're just bad bloody luck. You attract it, just like I attract blokes who like to mess me about," Savvy said matter-of-factly. "The sooner you accept it, the easier life will be."

I just laughed. I was so happy to have Savvy back that I didn't even bother crafting a scathing reply.

"What's the matter then, Hannah? You don't agree?" Savvy asked, nudging her on the arm.

But Hannah hadn't been paying attention. She was staring at something across the hospital ward. "Huh? What? Oh, sorry. What did you say?"

"She ain't awake yet," Savvy said gently, cocking her head in the direction that Hannah had been gazing. "Mrs. Mistlemoore said the effects were harsher for Lucida, what with her being the point of entry for the spirit and all. They don't know how long it'll take for her to recover."

We all looked over at the bed in the far corner. A privacy curtain blocked Lucida from view, but the four Caomhnóir standing guard around her were clearly visible.

"And when she's well enough they are transferring her straight back to the *príosún* at Skye," I said firmly. "She'll be gone again before any of us even have to look at her."

"I personally still haven't ruled out a long, dramatic telling-off," Milo said, his eyes narrowed in Lucida's direction as though he could shoot laser beams of sass right through her privacy curtain.

"Have they decided when the sessions will start up again?" Savvy asked, swinging her legs down off of the bed and getting to her feet. She was still moving a bit gingerly, like she had spent too long at the gym or something.

"Day after tomorrow," I told her, extending a hand in case she needed it, but she waved it aside with a snorting sound. "There's a lot for them to sort out, and all of the clans need to make new travel arrangements so that they can stay longer. If Lucida was looking to cause a logistical nightmare, she definitely succeeded."

We walked out of the hospital ward, moving a bit slower than usual to accommodate Savvy, and found Frankie waiting on the other side of the door. She was holding a notebook and looking sheepish.

"Oh, hi," she said, twisting the end of her braid around her finger nervously. "I... some of the other girls at breakfast said that a few of the Hosts had been released today, so I came to see if... how are you feeling?" she asked Savvy.

"Right as rain," Savvy replied with a cautious smile. "Or I will be, when the muscle pain subsides. Nice of you to come and look in on me. Cheers."

"No problem," Frankie said, looking tremendously relieved at Savvy's friendly tone. "I just wanted to apologize for before... it wasn't really you, I just couldn't handle all of this." She gestured vaguely around her, but Savvy nodded knowingly.

"I could tell you a story or two about how I rebelled when I first came here, if you like," she said, grinning. "I had my teachers in a right state, I can tell you. Fancy a walk?"

Frankie returned the grin, nodding. "That would be great. I started doing that log thing you told me to do—keeping track of the Visitations." She held up the notebook.

Savvy held her hand out for it, and Frankie gave it to her. "We'll catch up with you all later, then?" Savvy said, turning to me.

"Absolutely. Go be all responsible and stuff," I said.

Savvy winked and headed off down the hallway with Frankie, already beginning to thumb through the notebook.

"Jess!"

I turned to see Celeste walking toward us, a warm smile on her face. Carrick was hovering just behind her, following like a shadow.

"Celeste, hi! We saw you'd already been released. How are you feeling?"

"I'm well, thank you," she said. "Although every time I think about how much work there is to do salvaging this Airechtas, I have a strong urge to climb right back into one of those hospital beds and refuse to come out."

"Don't try to do too much at once," I told her, noting the lingering pallor in her complexion. "Take it easy, or you might land yourself right back in there."

Celeste reached out and squeezed my shoulder. Then she turned to Hannah. "Hannah, I owe you an apology. I would give it to you before the entire Council, but I think you've probably had enough of being called in there, haven't you?"

Hannah smiled. "Probably."

"I didn't mean for you to feel attacked. I only wanted to be able to ask you some questions, so that we could ascertain the meaning of Eleanora's message. We were all rushed and panicked and, I don't mind admitting it, scared that we would be next. It was never my intention to—"

Hannah raised a hand to silence Celeste. "It's okay, Celeste. I understand. I know you trust us. I just wish the other Durupinen would do the same."

Celeste sighed. "They will, in time. As we learned from the tragic tale of Eleanora Larkin, our fear of Callers and Prophecies has been ruining lives for a very long time. It is going to take quite a while to repair it all. But repair it we will, I promise you that."

I managed a small smile, but didn't reply. I didn't feel that was a promise that Celeste could keep—at least not on her own.

"Anyway, that's not why I came to find you," Celeste said. "I am under strict instructions to deliver this message to you." And she handed a folded piece of paper to Hannah.

Hannah took it, looking both puzzled and wary, but her expression cleared as soon as she read the words on the page. "It's from Karen! She won her case!"

"That's excellent!" I cried. "I mean, of course she was always going to crush it, but now it's official!"

"And she's going to be on the next plane out. She'll be here tomorrow," Hannah went on. "So, she says we can head home and she can represent the clan for the rest of the Airechtas."

"Oh," I said blankly. "I... can she do that? Can a clan switch representatives once the Airechtas has already started?"

"Yes, they can," Celeste said. "It will mean a bit more paperwork for Bertie, but it is allowed. Several other clans will likely have to do the same, now that we are so far off from our original schedule."

Hannah handed the note to me. "That's good news, isn't it?" she asked.

"Yeah. Yeah, really good news," I replied automatically, looking down at the note.

"Well, if you all will excuse me, I've got a frightening amount of work to do," Celeste said with a little bow. "I've got a meeting with Finvarra upstairs that I mustn't be late for."

"How is she?" I asked, looking straight past Celeste to Carrick, whose stony expression faltered.

"She is... much the same. Failing," he said brusquely, keeping his eyes trained on a spot somewhere over my shoulder. "But she is determined to see this Airechtas out to its conclusion, and I have never known her to falter in any task to which she sets her mind. She has stabilized in the last day or two. Gathering her strength, I assume, for the days ahead."

"Please send her our best," Hannah said, when it became obvious that I didn't know how to respond.

Carrick jerked his head in acknowledgment. "I shall do so. Thank you." And with one last gesture, somewhere between a wave and a salute, he followed Celeste down the hallway.

Milo sighed. "Wow, you'd think that over time that relationship would get less awkward, but it just doesn't, does it?"

"Yeah, estranged ghost dad isn't really a role that deepens with time," I said, rolling my eyes.

"At least he's... trying? Kind of?" Hannah half-asked.

"Trying is generous," I said. "But he's got a lot going on right now."

Hannah and Milo nodded. We all knew what the real implications of that sentence meant, but no one wanted to say it out loud. Suffice it to say, if we were ever going to have a chance to salvage any sort of real relationship with our father, we were quickly running out of time to do so.

"Jess. There you are," Finn's voice rang across the entrance hall as we descended the stairs. The place was empty, except for the Caomhnóir guarding the front doors.

Speaking of salvaging relationships...

"Hey, Finn. Sorry, were you looking for us?" I asked, sounding as casual as I could manage. Hannah and Milo muttered cursory greetings to Finn, but immediately slunk away toward the couches near the fireplace. I glared at them. They had the subtlety of a jackhammer, those two.

"Yes, I... I've just been informed that your Aunt Karen will be arriving on—"

"Yeah, we know. Celeste just caught us upstairs and told us."

"Oh. Very good, then," Finn said, looking almost disappointed.

"We've hardly seen you," I mumbled. "Seamus has had you all very busy over the past few days, huh?"

Finn nodded, squaring his shoulders in a characteristic show of pride in his duty. It was kind of adorable, actually—like a little kid throwing out his chest to have a merit badge pinned on. "Security has been stepped up with Lucida here. We've been in shifts in the hospital ward and around the perimeter of the grounds. We don't want to take the chance that the Necromancers might get wind of her whereabouts."

"What interest could they have in her now?" I asked, my eyebrows contracting in confusion.

"She is a powerful Durupinen with a grudge and an unusual gift," Finn said. "She could still be very useful to them, if they were ever able to break her out. As long as she lives, she is a threat to the Northern Clans."

I shivered involuntarily. "Well, she'll be locked back up in the *príosún* soon, and hopefully none of us will ever have to hear her name again."

"Indeed," Finn agreed. "And when she's gone we will all return to our regular duties. We... that is to say, we will have a chance to—" he cut himself off, throwing a nervous glance over his shoulder at a knot of Caomhnóir gathered near the front doors. His eyes full of things he couldn't say, he clicked his heels together, and marched away to join them.

I turned back to see Hannah and Milo both looking at me with sympathetic frowns on their faces. I joined them on the sofa and pointedly avoided looking at either of them, choosing instead to watch the flames dancing in the grate.

"It'll be okay," Hannah said quietly. "We'll be heading home as soon as Karen arrives. You'll have plenty of time to talk then."

"I know it will be fine," I lied. "But Finn and I will have to wait a little longer than that for a heart-to-heart."

"Why?" Milo asked.

"Because we can't leave when Karen gets here. We need to stay," I said, still looking at the fire.

"What for?" Hannah asked. "You heard Celeste: Karen can take over on the voting. There's no reason to stay."

"Actually, there's a very good reason. Finvarra is still going to offer us that Council seat."

Hannah laughed bitterly. "Jess, forget about it. I know I said we should consider it, but that was naïve. Just look at how the Council treated me this week. It was ridiculous to think we should run for that seat. No one wants us here."

"You're right. But that's exactly why we should run for it," I said.

Hannah's mouth fell open. "Jess, you have got to be kidding me."

"Nope, not kidding. Completely serious."

Hannah laughed incredulously. "Jess, you're not making any sense! You hate it here! Everyone turns on us at every possible opportunity. I just spent two days being interrogated and placed under house arrest. I think they would have thrown me into the dungeons if they thought they could get away with it. And now you want to stay here?"

"I know it sounds crazy—" I began.

"Because it *is* crazy," Hannah pointed out.

"But I realized something this week. Everything you've said is true. The Council hates me and is scared to death of you. I can't imagine anyone voting for us even if we do decide to run. But I think we need to do it anyway. Well, actually, I think you need to do it anyway. I think you should be the one to run for the seat."

"Me?" Hannah asked weakly. "Jess, come on. You're not making sense."

"Look, just hear me out, okay?" I said, taking both of Hannah's hands in mine. Our connection zinged beneath my skin, invigorating me and filling me with a sense of rightness in the words I was speaking. "We both know it can't be me. I've got a big

274

attitude and an even bigger mouth. I don't argue things rationally. I let my emotions run away with me, and it clouds my judgment. They would be sanctioning me or kicking me out of every other meeting."

"No lie there," Milo said. I grinned at him.

"But you! You're incredible! You find a way to be rational and level-headed, even when you're scared to death. You never let them get the better of you. You could be a real voice of reason in there!"

"But Jess, it doesn't matter how much sense I make if no one will listen to me! No one trusts me!" Hannah said.

"But that's why you need to do it! No listen!" I cried, because she showed every indication of interrupting me again. "The Council mistrusts you because they fear Callers. They've been fearing Callers for centuries. In fact, most of the major crises they've faced have sprung from their own fear. The Silent Child, Lucida, and now Eleanora—and who knows how many others? The Council has been letting their fear call the shots for far too long, and it's caused nothing but catastrophe."

Hannah didn't reply, although she was still looking at me like I'd started speaking in tongues. Milo nodded encouragingly. I pressed my advantage and went on.

"You already made the rest of this argument yourself, when Finvarra first told us that she was planning to nominate us. We could make a quantifiable difference. We could change the perception of who we are and what we mean to the Northern Clans. We could propose new rules instead of just getting constantly screwed by the old ones. The Shattering might have changed your mind about all of that, but it's changed mine, too. I'm sick of having to pick up the pieces for people like Eleanora, people whose only crime was existing. It's time to start shaping things so that what happened to Eleanora—to us—never happens to anyone else ever again."

Hannah's face became very serious. Then she leaned forward, put a hand on each of my shoulders and shook me violently.

"Ouch! Hannah, what are you—stop!" I cried, pulling myself out of her grip.

She sat back and smiled at me. "Sorry, but I had to check."

"Check what?"

"That you weren't a Host. The only way my sister would start talking like that was if an invading spirit took over her body."

"Very funny," I said sarcastically as Milo rolled over in the air in a fit of cackling.

Hannah's grin faded quickly. She turned to Milo and waited for his laughter to subside. "What do you think, Mr. Spirit Guide?"

Milo sobered up at once. "In a stunning plot twist, I agree with Jess. You would kick ass on that Council. Obviously, it would cause an uproar, but sometimes you have to shake things up to make a real difference."

"There will be pitchforks," Hannah said with a wry laugh.

"We stared into the jaws of the afterlife itself and won. I think we can handle a few pitchforks," I said.

"I hear pitchforks are the hottest new winter accessory," Milo added brightly. "They're basically the new oversized sunglasses."

Hannah looked from me to Milo and then shrugged helplessly. "Okay. I don't know why I ever listen to either of you, but I'll do it." Then she pulled us into an awkward, three-way hug that I quickly had to squirm out of, because hugging Milo was like hugging an ice sculpture.

"Okay, then," I said. "That's decided. Let's throw this place into chaos again. It's what we do best."

§

As we sat in silence by the fire, I stared out the windows at the whirling snowstorm outside, my eyes fixed on the horizon for the sight of the car that would bring Karen to the castle. And as I waited, I cradled Eleanora's little book in the crook of my arm, running my finger backward and forward over its spine like I could bring it—and her—some comfort from my touch. I had carried it with me ever since her Crossing, as though the weight of it was something that I ought to bear—like I owed it to her. It was she, more than anyone else, that had helped me reach the decision to stay at Fairhaven. And there was still a mystery to solve here, one that I hoped Fiona could help me with. I did not know how I had come to create the sketches of Eleanora. If she had not reached out to me, where had the images come from? It felt crucial to my understanding of my own gift as a Muse that I figure it out.

Hannah had told me once that she thought I liked trouble. It was becoming clearer by the day that she was right. Though I felt we were making the right decision, there was no doubt that it was going to be a difficult road, with no guarantee that we would succeed. Karen and the other Council members would likely try to dissuade us from our course. Marion would certainly try to thwart us at every step. And Finn... there was no doubt that staying at Fairhaven would force us to a crossroads in our relationship. But wasn't it better to make the choice to fight for us, to proudly stand together in the sunlight, hand in hand, rather than always hiding in the shadows?

In my heart, I thought I knew the answer to that question, and so I'd chosen my path. Now all I could do was hope that Finn would choose to walk beside me.

E.E. Holmes is a writer, teacher, and actor living in central Massachusetts with her husband, two children, and a small, but surprisingly loud dog. When not writing, she enjoys performing, watching unhealthy amounts of British television, and reading with her children. Please visit www.eeholmes.com to learn more about E.E. Holmes and *The World of The Gateway*.

Made in United States
Orlando, FL
22 November 2021

10647735R00174